ANDERSON VERSUS DEATH

2000 AD FICTION

Judge Anderson: Year One
Judge Anderson: Year Two
Anderson versus Death

Judge Dredd: Year One
Judge Dredd: Year Two
Judge Dredd: Year Three

Judges Volume One
Judges Volume Two
Judges Volume Three

The Fall of Deadworld Omnibus
Apocalypse War Dossier
Rico Dredd: The Titan Years

ANDERSON VERSUS DEATH

ANNA SMITH SPARK

REBELLION

First published in 2025 by Rebellion
an imprint of Rebellion Publishing Ltd,
Riverside House, Osney Mead,
Oxford, OX2 0ES, UK

www.rebellionpublishing.com

ISBN: 978-1-83786-591-8

Judge Anderson created by
John Wagner and Brian Bolland

10 9 8 7 6 5 4 3 2 1

A CIP catalogue record for this book is available from the British Library.

Designed & typeset by Rebellion Publishing
Cover image by Tula Lotay

Printed in Denmark

MIX
Paper | Supporting responsible forestry
FSC® C104608

To my son,
who loves 2000 AD now
as much as I did as a child,
and to Jamie,
who first introduced him to it.

PSI

CASS

1.

THE PERP FLED into the tower block, and the Psi-Judge followed him.

CASS IS HALF out of breath. Steps up to the doorway, slippery with rain. She takes them two at a time, leaping, raindrops shoving in her face. Kicks the door open, pushes through, stops. Panting, waiting.

Searching. Her mind more than her eyes.

Dark hallway, closed in with the piss-smell of every stairway everywhere, even the lux-blocks. Empty, the floor heavy tiles and grime, so no trace even of wet footprints. Whirr of aircon, babble of TV/music/shouting/laughing/children masking anyone's panted breath.

Wide scan. Like tasting the air.

Her mind catches it.

Him. Her?

Already up the stairs, one flight.

Oh, come on. Grud's sake. How quick could a perp run? Hadn't looked like some kind of speed-freak superman. Just an ordinary small-time perp and she's only chasing him at all because he started running like murder when she walked past him, and now he's running like murder through a smart-side hab-block up multiple flights of stairs. And Psi-Judge Cass Anderson is… following a small-time perp up multiple flights of stairs.

Call for backup.

Or: shouldn't she have her partner beside her?

Or: she's a Psi-Judge, not a Street Judge grunt; why is she doing this again? Any of this?

His mind's screaming panic. White noise static fear. He runs, she runs.

On the first floor, one apartment has music blaring out of the closed door at nose-bleed volumes. That great late-twentieth-century occult masterwork 'Last Chris Mast,' so popular the people of the time believed a curse came down on you if you heard it played without adequate protection. The guy playing it certainly isn't cursed, is in his little personal happy safe world broadcasting his thoughts loud as the music as he presses repeat—repeat—repeat. The guy's next-door neighbour's trying to watch TV nice and quiet, he's gone beyond anger to fury to almost enjoyment at the noise wafting through his door like cooked meat. Been sat staring at the shared wall for the last hour.

So she could probably make an arrest for crimes against music, taste and tenancy agreements, and make the neighbour's day, month and year. But the perp is still running up the stairs with his brain screaming, and the Psi-Judge still needs to follow him. Everything else will have to wait. The music starts up again in all its dangerous glory (organ legging's illegal, remember, you crazy kids!); Cass hears clear as day the neighbour contemplating giving away not only his heart but his eardrums.

That's organ legging *and* illegal body modification, don't even gruddamn think it, Cass flashes at the door as she sprints past. Up. Up. Up.

The second floor.

The third floor.

The fourth floor. Up. Up. Up.

This guy is more than a small-time perp, Cass decides, when she reaches the fifth floor and he's still going, pulling further ahead of her every floor they go up. By the time she gets to the sixth floor, she's concluded she's chasing a multiple-murderer and gang boss and Grud knows what else at the very least. *The death sentence in twelve sectors* or something.

Finally, on the seventh floor, *finally* the perp stops running.

Cass stops. Panting. Winded. Sweat moustache on her upper lip.

Silence: no TV, no music, no one yelling/thinking panic. Empty hallway stretching before her. The first apartment feels empty.

The second apartment's door has been kicked in.

Cass stops outside. Draws three long breaths. Grips her hand tighter round the trigger of her Lawgiver. Stretches her mind out deep.

He's in there. She can feel him. Crouching. Hot and angry and coiled.

"Justice Department! Drop your weapon! On the ground now! I'm coming in."

Silence.

"I'm coming in now! I want to see you down on the floor with your arms out."

Silence. Cool pale light and cool scented air drifting through the smashed front door.

She stops on the threshold. Sounds crazy, but she feels… scared. The door off its hinges, expensive carpet in the hallway, walls magnolia bright. A welcome mat, an occasional table with the usual clutter, a print of the ever-popular painting 'The Singing Judge' (this block! She could arrest this lot for crimes against art). Mum's, dad's and kids' shoes lined by the door, but Cass has no sense that the family is home. Only the perp, sat in her head somewhere. She can just feel him. Itching there in her skull.

"Justice Department! I'm coming in!"

Her hand itching too, on the Lawgiver's trigger. Grud's sake, Cass. Grud's sweet sake. Over the threshold (over? threshold?—

it's a gruddamned line in the floor where the carpet changes from cheap and grotty to expensive and clean). Feels like stepping over maybe a chasm. Like she's on a highwalk and just stepped off. Strong desire to go in shooting blind. Maybe a couple of rounds of gas grenades.

High explosives.

Incendiaries.

Space lasers and nukes.

So she gets both feet over the threshold thinking that.

Well done, Cass!

In the apartment the air is almost flowery, air freshener and new paint. Clean. All the doors are closed, and the perp is behind one of them. He's a migraine in her head now. Almost see him behind one of the doors.

Never mind the mutie psi-powers, she thinks then: she should be able to smell his BO. Can certainly smell her own, in this nice clean calm place. Hear his breathing. If her heart pounding wasn't loud enough to drown everything.

She stops. Wait. What?

Gruddamnit. She's lost him. His traces, her sense of him, her sense of following, running, needing to run after him because…

Gone.

Like he's jumped out of a window. Or died. Or never been there with her chasing after him. The apartment is clean and neat and empty. No one here. Not even the memory traces of any inhabitants. Like no one has ever lived here.

Shivers, the hair on the back of her neck standing up. Scared by the silence, the cleanness, the feeling she has of no life.

She spins round, he must have somehow got past her, back out of the door and off. She'd been wrong, he'd gone on up the stairs, eighth floor, nineth, tenth, the kicked-in door has misled her somehow. I mean, in my defence, she thinks, a kicked-in door might be a tad misleading, if you're chasing a perp through a luxury housing block. Like a sign saying HE'S IN HERE, really, if you want to be charitable to yourself, Anderson, you spug. You made the obvious call.

So she turns in relief to leave.

So now a scream rings through the apartment.

Oh for grud's sake, Cass, she thinks.

The first door. A bathroom. Clear.

The second door. A bedroom. Bed, wardrobe, dresser. Seems clear.

The third door. A bedroom. Bed, wardrobe, dresser, built-in cupboards. Nice-looking place.

A man with a gun.

"Justice Department! Drop it! Now!" She knows before she's halfway through saying it that he'll shoot. Hands on the trigger, her hand and his hand, and she's a Psi-Judge and one of the best, and he's too fast.

Stings her. Painful. Reels back—pushed back—her shoulder smashing against the door. All this blood soaking into the lovely thick creamy-pale carpet. The perp staring back at her with big eyes. Frightened?

"I didn't… I mean… didn't mean… to do that…"

His fear rolls off him. His eyes on her face. His eyes on the wound he's made in her. His eyes on the gun he's holding, and he looks at it baffled. Like: what's this? How? Why?

He's going to shoot again. She can feel it. She can see it, not quite a pre-cog, more like… like she's a second behind him, she can see the delay like watching something on television and in real-life. He's going to shoot her and hit her in the chest, in the heart, unless she—

Where's her partner? Where's her backup? Some shoot-first-ask-questions-never Street Judge coming steaming in big and burly, Lawgiver spitting fire, Grud, he's biked up seven flights of stairs down those nice cool residential corridors tires tearing up the rubber floor tiles, comes in all guns and cannons and shouts blazing to take this place gruddamn apart.

Confusion rolls off the perp worse than fear. Hairy fingers squeezing the trigger right at her heart.

Cass shoots with everything in her. Kind of howl and whimper from the perp's mouth. He goes back shredded. Slumps crashes on the king-size-max silk duvet. Cass's arm hurts where he shot her, then suddenly like a magic trick it doesn't hurt.

She goes to check he's dead. She knows he's dead because she can feel he's dead, obviously, and also because it's highly unlikely even in this weird world of hers that anyone could survive what she just did to him. There are bits of him on the far wall staining the magnolia paintwork crimson, and bits of him on the mirror above the bed, brainstuff grey-white and a bit of skull bone that's cracked the mirror from side to side. But she goes to check.

He still looks confused, from what little she can see of him.

Assures herself: he's dead, yes.

Cass goes out into the hallway. The apartment's so empty of everything, no traces, no memories it's ever been lived in, like trying to get something out a lump of plastic. No sense a man literally just died in here. The next door opens onto the living area. Nice place, expensive furnishings, windows and a balcony looking out over a light well. Lots of plants, on shelves and tables and on the balcony, deep green feathery curling leaves. Makes her think of tongues, like snakes' tongues maybe. No flowers on any of the plants. Just rolls and rolls of unfurling reaching leaves.

She walks over to the window. The drapes are new, and expensive; they work automatically using a remote. View out of nothing—neighbours windows going up and up and down seven stories, aircon units staining the rockcrete, dank courtyard, slime and puddles, birdshit, birdshit covered anti-bird spikes. A couple of scrawny pigeons stare back at her from the opposite window ledge. If she cranes her neck, she can maybe see a patch of grey sky up and up and up.

A noise from behind her. She spins round. Almost as confused as the perp was as she shot him—this place is empty, she'd swear it. No one here now, or for years.

There's a child sitting on one of the big overfilled armchairs. The chair's creamy pale, like everything in the apartment. The child's got candy-pink hair, she's wearing a yellow dress. She's maybe six. Seven? Four? A child, anyway, definitely. She scrabbles back into the armchair, trying to disappear into the cushions, when she sees Cass has seen her there.

A stink. The child's shat herself. Snot leaks down the child's face; eyes fixed huge on Cass, the child licks it off.

But still no… no sense of anything. Cass reaches out for a scan.

A kind of whiteness, like the snot. Pushes back, like the girl's tongue. Cass winces. Painful. And frightening. And wrong.

The child whimpers. She looks—seems—terrified, whatever else she is. Wriggles back in the chair.

Cass holds out her hand.

"It's alright. I'm a Psi-Judge. Judge Anderson. Are your… your parents at home?"

She thinks suddenly and horribly of the perp in the bedroom. Gets a horrible sudden idea what the child's going to say.

"There was a perp—a man, in your house," she says carefully. "I followed him. He was dangerous. Are your parents at home?" Like if she says it again and again…

"Mummy and Cae have gone out," the child whispers. Cass feels a million years younger. Could dance round the room.

"Daddy's at home," the child says. Her voice is louder when she says it. She's not a young young child, definitely old enough to know what *Justice Department! Drop it! Now!* then about six million bullets firing means. "Daddy's in the bedroom," the child says. "Putting some clean washing away." Her voice is so loud she's shouting. Cass wants to put her hands over her ears. She stands looking at the child. The child looks back.

Tries to image a fellow Judge's voice: *We all make mistakes, Anderson. Show me a Judge who hasn't made a mistake.*

Yeah, she thinks. Sometimes we let a perp go rather than shoot someone who might be innocent.

I think?

She'll be sent to Titan for the rest of gruddamn eternity.

Which will be a happy ending compared to what's happened to this kid.

She thinks: he tried to shoot me. She flexes her right shoulder. He did shoot me. It just… healed again. Super quick.

Maybe the child means another bedroom, she thinks. Her dad's crouching in terror in another hint of magnolia luxury bedroom behind another closed door. He'll come out and thank me for saving his kid's life.

She holds out her hand to the child to do something. The child coils back into the armchair. Doesn't, funnily enough, seem to like Cass.

He tried to shoot me first, Cass thinks. He was standing there pointing a gun at point-blank range.

And it still feels so clear to her—she was walking along doing nothing, this guy saw her, began to run—and she could feel his guilt and the crimes committed, she knew absolutely that she had to chase him down and bring him in.

Or shoot him.

"Daddy's in the bedroom," the child says again, keeping her eyes fixed on Cass. "He went in there to put some clean washing away so the place would be tidy when Mummy and my brother came back."

Oh, come on, Cass thinks. This is laying it on a bit thick.

"They went out to get some dinner," the child says. "Because it's my birthday today."

Oh come *on!* Cass thinks. This is too much. So much too much. She finds herself frightened she might vomit on the nice clean creamy carpet.

This vague sense in her head: shouldn't her partner be here? And backup?

Her comm should be roaring with her partner's voice and her backup. *Where in Grud's name are you, Anderson? We've got some guy here crying there's a perp in his apartment with a gun, and he's worried about his daughter.*

She finds she's looking at the child, kind of waiting for the child to say something even more emotively OTT. *I just recovered from life-saving surgery last week,* or something. The child just stares back at her with big sad eyes kind-of-knowing-not-knowing everything that's happened.

Maybe the child's decided herself she's been laying it on too thick.

"Stay here. Don't move, okay?"

The child begins to nod. Realises that counts as moving. Stops. Just stares and stares at Cass.

"Good girl," Cass says weakly.

Cass goes back into the bedroom. The perp's lying sprawled on the bed where she left him. Blood… everywhere. His hand on the gun.

He looks like anyone could look. His hair's brown and greying where he's got a bit of his head left. If he had pink hair, that might be more useful.

Actually, in some places, where the blood…

She thinks: shut up, Cass! Presses her hands to her eyes. I'm going to be sick, I'm going to be sick. She imagines someone back at headquarters, Judge Winstanley maybe, saying, *How did this happen, Anderson?* trying to make it better by helping her understand any of it. There was this guy, he seemed… I felt I should chase him, he was running… I was running… I shot him. I really thought I needed to… He felt… like he was a really bad guy.

I am the Law, she tries to think.

Look at this place, guy *must* be guilty of something, she tries to think. Judges' iron law: everyone's guilty of something if you look.

She opens the doors of the wardrobe at random. In the wardrobe there are—as promised—plenty of clean clothes. The perp liked jumpers and chinos in navy, charcoal, beige. His wife likes pastel slacks and blouses. Dad clothes. Mum clothes. Matches their dad and mum life.

Wait.

Cass feels something like elation. Like she could dance round the room and sing. Perp was guilty all right. Saw a Judge coming his way, freaked, ran for it; must have come in here hoping to destroy the evidence.

A bag of sugar.

Neatly stacked beside a pair of Mrs Perp's kitten-heeled leopard-print shoes.

I knew this place was too good for an innocent guy to live in, Cass thinks. I knew it.

She thinks, somewhere between laughter and sorrow: Chances of someone in the Big Meg *not* turning out to be a criminal? Close to zero percent.

"Honey? Why's the door open?" a voice calls from the hall.

Cass's heart sinks again.

"Honey? We brought the dinner. We—"

"Mummy?" the child wails from the living room. "Muuummmyyy?"

A woman's voice says something no one should say in a child's hearing. Rage and grief hammer into Cass's mind like an alarm clock sounding. Builds and builds, a woman's fury and two kids' terror and panic. Cass reels.

There's a sound from the hall that Cass knows very well.

Mr Sugar-Dealer-Teeth-Rotting-Scum saw a Judge, freaked, ran seven flights of stairs to get away and hide. Would have gotten away with it, too, except the pesky Psi-Judge followed him.

Mrs Sugar-Dealer-Teeth-Rotting-Scum doesn't need to see a Judge to know what's going on here. The muscle behind the operation, obviously (the kitten-heeled leopard-print slingbacks and pussybow blouse should have been a big give-away there,

Anderson). Comes into the bedroom packing a gun the size of the White Cliffs of Dover. Shrieks, "Murderer!" Fires.

Cass hits the floor as the bullets hit the walls, the bed, the wardrobe. Synthi-feathers and glass and shreds of navy jumpers flying. Grud Grud Grud Grud *Grud*.

The pink-haired child stands in the doorway clutching her mother's legs. A boy a couple of years older stands next to her. They both watch in silence.

Oh, come on, Cass thinks. You're only sugar-dealers. Not big league.

Aren't you?

They're gruddamn guilty of child cruelty, she thinks, watching the two children watch her. And that thought makes her shiver somehow she can't understand. She tries to shoot back, get the Lawgiver up pointing in the right direction at least. But: the children… But: she's moving so slooowww. Everything's got really slooowww. The Lawgiver's so heavy. Trying to lift it, trying to squeeze the trigger, it's like moving through drying cement.

When she gets a round off she can see the bullets travelling, they're going so slow.

She can't see the bullets coming towards her. They're coming at normal speed. As in: too fast to see.

She feels them hit, though.

2.

Blackout.

Nothing.

If this was a comic, it would be a blank page.

3.

She can't move.

She can't hear.

She can't see.

4.

Her hand jerks. Her fingers.

Nothing. Trying to move them. Feel the muscles. Feel the joints click. They don't move. Can't move.

Her whole body screams, trying to move. She gasps, gulps for air, she can't feel even the air on her face. Can't feel hot or cold.

Breathe.

She imagines she can breathe, at least. Pretending she can breathe.

She can hear what could be her heart beating, but that must be a dream, like her breathing. She can't push her chest out to breathe deep.

"…Help… me…"

Her voice halts in her throat. She can't speak.

Wrenches her eyes open. So… her eyes were closed? The effort is terrible. Outside her eyelids there's still nothing. Still can't see. Not darkness, the pressing black weight of waking in the night in a shuttered room. Just… nothing. Nonsense.

She can't feel any pain. She registers this slowly. Not sure if she's lying down, or sitting up, or standing. She gropes around her, tries to feel any awareness of her body. Focusses her mind on her skin, her limbs.

She can feel… Her stomach muscles knot and flex. Absurdly, she tries to cross her eyes to see her nose. Pushes up her upper lip. Two pink half-visible blobs, if she squints and squints.

No. She can't move her lip, can't see her own nose. She blows out hard, lets out a breath she didn't realise she was holding, and she can't feel it on her face.

Her mind is utterly silent. She realises this slowly, also. Then, like rain, or the sun rising, gradual, then fast, and everything's changed, she realises it almost as a punch to her face. She's alone without any awareness of other people around her.

Other minds. Memories. Feelings. Vague, constant sense of… just a sense, always, of people living. Of… life.

All gone.

She feels the scream rise up in her, uncontrollable, uncontrolled, breaking out of her through her mouth, her nose, her eyes, the pores of her skin. Can't hear herself screaming, no sound, her mouth still unmoving, her body unmoving, the horror rips through her but she can feel the horror, at least, feel herself shaking in her insides, sickness, her bowels, her mind hurting, howling.

Sometimes she goes somewhere silent, distant, the top of a high empty building, a locked room down empty corridors, sealed away, and she enjoys being alone, the silence, the novelty of it, a strange feeling of isolation, of emptiness, because only then can she be truly alone. But it's… she's tried to put it into words, it's like… like… "Like when you go to the dentist and he gives you a deep clean, you know, the way your teeth feel afterwards, you can't stop running your tongue over them, they feel so different and clean and not like your teeth. It's like that, in my head," she says at last, and Neirn or whoever looks at her baffled and says after some thought, "No. I don't get that after I've been to the dentist," but that's the only way she can describe it. Like… it's a good feeling, but not a normal feeling you'd want every day.

And getting away up on the roof is a feeling she's chosen. An experience she wants, for a while, then she can make it stop. And lying still and calm without moving, eyes closed to let herself float: then she can open her eyes again, wiggle her fingers, feel it all, that's the whole point…

This…

She reaches out desperately, strains her mind, she can almost hear her mind creak. She can't see. Can't hear. Can't feel. Can't move. Can't sense.

WHITEOUT.

NOTHING.

NOTHING.

5.

Your first time *dying. Quick, this time. I thought I would be kind to you. Though you were not kind to me.*

I can feel it. I watch you with children's eyes. Your confusion. Your guilt. Because… [laughter] [drum-roll, please] *you're guilt* [sic]. *You shot this child's father. Murdered him. 'Oh, but he was guilty of a crime.' 'Oh, but you didn't know that then.' Guilty, guilty, guilty. And the child watching you with her big sad puppy-dog eyes, she's—what, seven? Loves her daddy, doesn't know he's a criminal and a law-breaker, he's just her nice kind tucks-her-up-at-night-and-tells-her-stories dad. You killed her father, she knows—killed a bit of her, too, murdered her deep inside, and what had* she *ever done?*

Lots, obviously.

Let's start at the beginning, shall we? She's alive. Been born. She's guilty, deserved everything you did to her. And you deserve it too, for doing it. You're guilt and her guilt [sic sic sic].

Guilt never stops somewhere. Folds itself in layers like skin over fat over flesh over bone. Like the way a brain's folded over and over itself, if you take a man's brain, start opening it up the way you can unfurl a flower, uncrease it, reach into its folds… Layers and layers, deep and deeper and… not deepest. You can always go deeper in and back. In the beginning there was God, or a word, or a single-celled organism spawned from a primordial soup of amino acids, and it was guilty of something.

And guilt has to be punished.

And the only sure and certain punishment is death.

So it's quick this time, the first time, because I want you to understand what life is and what death is.

A simple lesson.

There's life, then there's death.

Life is short and ends.

Death does not.

The line between the two is nothing. Far too easy.

The difference between the two is everything.

6.

The voice hisses in her skull. "*Did you enjoy that?*" crawls its way through her senses. She thinks of old TV screenings, an insect burrowing down a person's ear canal into their brain. The voice makes her mouth taste sour, like eating garbage. Stinks. Chafes her skin. "*Wasss it good, Cassss? Dying?*" She wants to gag at the sound, it spreads across her body like ripples on dirty water, laps at her, leaving a tide mark. She could scrub and scrub herself with soap and water until her skin's rubbed off, she'll never get rid of the stain the voice makes. "*Wasss it good? Tell me. Casssss.*" In her ears and her eyes, prising at them. "*You died. Cassss. Wasss it good? Tell me.*"

She's sitting in the Grand Hall of Justice cafeteria. A round formica table, a spindly-legged chair. Caff stains in rings that make her think of the rings of Saturn. A pile of napkins, a bottle of sauce with a brown crust on it. Her cup has an old chip in the rim.

Beyond this table, everything's blurred. People eating, sipping caff, sitting down, getting up. Clatter of trays, a strong vile fart whiff of beanz as someone walks past with a meal. If she tries to look at them, she won't be able to see them.

Someone pulls out a chair with a screech that sets her teeth on edge.

She toys with the cup. Turns the handle round to point towards her. The chip is almost opposite the handle. Compass needle pointing south. Clock hands reading six o'clock. She turns the cup so the handle is pointing away from her, at the figure sitting at the table opposite. Caff sloshes over the side, runs down to make a new stain on the tabletop.

She thinks, slowly: It's all true. Real. Really truly happened.

She thinks: I wish I had been shot.

She wants and doesn't want to look up.

The voice croons at her. "*Casssss... I want you to feel dying. Casssss. Tell me, Casssss. Pain and death. Death, Casssss.*"

She keeps her eyes fixed on the cup in front of her. Ripples on the drink's surface when the figure opposite her speaks. She imagines drops of its spittle leaking into the caff.

"*Tell me. Casssss. Tell me about dying. About death.*"

Hisses back and back and back, echoing. *Casss Casssss Casssssss Cassssssss.*

"*I ssshowed you what it feels like to die, Casss. I gave you a gift. The bessst gift. The only true gift.*

"*Cassss.*"

She counts: one, two, three.

Looks up.

Her eyes close. Open. Close. Open.

Can't close. Won't. She can't bear to look, but she can't bear not to look.

The shock is worse almost than the first time she saw it.

It's all real. True.

There was a craze in the long distant past before the Atomic Wars, before the Big Meg was the Big Meg. A craze for stuffed dead animals. As ornaments. On walls, on shelves; people even *wore* them. Dead hair, dead skin, dead teeth. Dead, dried body fluids, flaking.

A tiny, desperate part of her mind tries to see something like that, when she looks up.

TEETH. OLD BONES scavenged from a garbage pile and gnawed yellow grinning teeth. And they are grinning, at her, at everything. Skin around them strained, on the edge of ripping. The skin of something pulled back for surgery. The skin of an old man's hands, dry and cracked, too thin, too old, fumbling at the zip of his piss-soaked flies. Green and putrid, too taut, too dry, yes, but also there's a sense, if she… touched it, shoved her hand into its face, it would be soft, waxy, cheesy, yield, let her crunch and squeeze it, running fluids, because of course it's dead, dead, dead. Gangrenous. Collapsing. Dead.

There's a mercy that it doesn't realise—its helmet covers its eyes. She's never seen Dredd's eyes, rarely sees even friends' like Neirn's and Winstanley's. But. Its helmet closes with a visor like a barred gate, and what it doesn't know is that it's a kindness—that it's stopping her from seeing into where its eyes should be.

It grins at her. Stretching the skin around its mouth tighter. Its gums are grey and red. She imagines its teeth opening. Biting.

It has too many teeth. It's in her skull, and she thinks of teeth chewing their way out of her. Its claws following where the teeth bite. Ripping.

Its fingers are very long, and its hands are too big. Its fingernails are yellow and filthy as its teeth. Nicotine stains. The ceiling of a Smokatorium. Its fingers twitch and waggle like insects. She can feel them running across her skin, peeling her face back. Probing at her brains, her lungs. They're too long and awkward for living hands, couldn't touch, hug, eat, drink. Barriers again, from being or doing anything living.

It's dressed in a parody of her own uniform.

She looks… pretty drokking hot, actually, in her uniform. She's not stupid, she has eyes and everything, she knows perfectly well she looks hot. [Also the thoughts broadcast loud as a Lawmaster revving its engines full throttle pretty much everywhere she goes.] "*Practical, these skintight uniforms with the easy-open zipper front.*" Dredd looks gruddamn terrifying in his uniform, like he's made of solid rockcrete. Hard to think there's an actual body with bellyflab under there. Winstanley looks so smart and neat you really would trust him to help your granny cross the road or your kids find a lost kitten.

This thing, this sick twisted parody of her and Dredd and all of them, it manages to make the uniform look...

the only word for it is...

...obscene.

It's dead. Vile. Dead and dried up and crusted and rotten. If it ever was alive, it can't remember that life. Like a dead stuffed animal from the olden days, as she said, sickly-unreal like that. But it lolls in its chair, its too-long fingers, too-big awkward hands it can't use to touch or hold or live with, its dead smile, its dead face, its red gleaming gums, and the way it moves its body, the thrust of its limbs... Its body is obscene.

It reeks and runs with its desire for death.

SHE—ANDERSON, JUDGE Cassandra Anderson of Psi-Division—stares at the visor hiding the dry holes it must have instead of eyes. Its fingers curl, opening and closing. It lounges in its chair. *Judge Death*, it calls itself.

She'd laughed so hard she blew a snot bubble when she first heard it called itself that. *Judge Death!* And these words it keeps repeating, like they're so gruddamn profound: it grins at her now, knows what she's thinking, says them now in its stupid hissing evil voice: "*The crime iss life. The sssentence iss death.*" Its empty hidden eyes wink as it speaks. When she first spoke to it, heard it say that—part of her had wanted to laugh until she wet herself.

"I WON, REMEMBER?" she says. Tries to sound forceful. Tries to convince herself. It steeples its fingers, wiggles them at her. She forces herself not to recoil from them, as if they'll dig into her mouth.

"*If this is you winning, I wouldn't want to sssee what you call losssing.*"

She glares at it. It smiles back its blank hungry wanting grin.

"Winning means stopping you killing anyone else. Winning means judging you and finding you guilty and bringing the law down on you to lock you up. Which I did."

"*Stopping me killing?*" It shrugs again, obscenely, its smile opens wide to crack its skin. "*Everything that lives diesss, Judge Andersson. You just shot a little girl'sss father in the head. You're Judged and found wanting.*"

"That wasn't real."

Its fingers wiggle. An insect on its back, legs scrabbling. "*Wasn't it? You tell me you've never ssshot a little girl'sss father, Judge Andersssson? Never ssshot a father'sss daughter or ssson? You're alive. So you're guilty of crimesss.*"

"I'm alive," Anderson says fiercely. "You got that bit right." She thinks of herself strolling across a broad-way on a nice sunny morning. Gunning her Lawmaster into the sunset with the light on her face.

"*But you're trapped now,*" it says. Its grin spreads vast. Clouds mounting on horizon, piling up and building and growing until you can't see the sunset she was just thinking about. "*You're trapped in here. With me.*"

It's like the grin is swallowing her up. Those horrible dead yellow teeth. And the visor with the dead dry holes behind it, it comes down over her like a blade. "*Trapped. For ever. Andersson.*"

It's right, of course. She is trapped. Sacrificed herself. She's alive in that her mind is still working. Can imagine a world around her. But she's trapped, yes. In some ways—in all the ways—she might as well be dead.

She'll never ride through Mega-City One on her Lawmaster with the warm wind in her hair. Never look up at the moon and the stars, dreaming of the ships up there and the colonies and the aliens she can't see (okay, so that one's a bit far fetched anyway, what with the air pollution and the light pollution and the massive City Blocks blocking most of the sky out).

She'll never eat again, or drink, or sleep.

Never hear or see or touch anything.

SHE CLOSES HER eyes. Dizzy in the dark she's floating in, and when she closes her eyes it's easier to breathe. She thinks of herself shooting until the man's head was meat-paste, the child on the armchair terrified of her, knowing what she'd done. All the lives she's taken in the last few years as a Judge. Every one of them a person. Gone. Hail of bullets, flash of laser fire: doesn't even notice people dying.

They're still dying, she thinks. All over Mega-City One, killing and dying in pointless ways. Gang violence and gang warfare and dumb-as-drokk accidents because the people she's supposed to protect are useless, stupid, walking, talking bags of human waste. Whole huge blocks of them, and if they all died no one would notice because they were so pointless when they were alive. And she sacrificed everything, might as well be dead—for them.

"*You see?*" it says. "*Dear Cass.*" Its voice is all around her, ringing inside her, she feels it probing at her heart and her lungs, peeling her layers away. She's swallowed up inside it. Consumed. She thinks: this is what dying is.

"*Oh, no,*" it says. "*Dying isss much better than thisss. You can't even die, Casss. Just ssstay here. Trapped. With me.*"

She sees herself, tiny, a light flickering out. The horror of what she's done chokes her.

"*You* wisssh *you were dead, Cassss.*"

SHE OPENS HER eyes. The darkness lurches around her. Inside it. Lost.

Lost. Lost.

"Judge Anderson," she says. "Not Cass. The best Judge in Psi-Division," she says.

She touches the cup on the table. Traces the chip in the rim. Turns the handle to point away from her. She can't see it. The cup or the table. Just darkness. Not darkness, even, she realises then. Just nothing.

Dead.

But she can *feel* the cup and the tabletop. Sticky formica. Not been cleaned for weeks. Not been cleaned cleaned for... "Probably before the Atomic Wars," she hears Winstanley saying. She can almost see the look on his face when he rubs his (clean, short, neat) fingernails on the tabletop and examines the grime he drags up. "Yeauk," he says. She can feel the sudsy, over-washed cup.

She raises the cup, takes a sip.

Lukewarm. Disgusting.

Oddly beefy taste.

That's proper cafeteria caff.

She puts the cup down with a click.

Never get wounded and slow and grouchy, she thinks. Never muck up in the line of duty, or embarrass myself, or get bawled out by the Chief Judge or—Grud knows, fart on parade or something. I mean, let's try to look at the positives, Anderson.

She looks right at the thing opposite her and it's small and shrunken, and it's almost just a man. If it was a man, she realises, she'd be taller and stronger than it.

"Your Reign of Terror over the Big Meg lasted... one day," she says. "During that time, you served judgement on a petty hoodlum called—and I quote—'Tiny the Tap,' followed by a button jock and a rabble of badly dressed kids at a nightclub called—again I quote—'The Rabbit Hutch,' and, finally in this terrifying catalogue of vast and depraved supervillainy, a second-rate Judge called Geller Ross. After which Judge Dredd flame-grilled you. I've arrested *children* with more impressive rap sheets than that."

She finishes the caff. Sets the cup down with the handle pointing towards her.

"And you can drop the stupid spooky voice and all. You're a disembodied voice in my gruddamn head. You can talk however I gruddamn want you to talk."

She says, "You don't have to look like that, either. You *don't* look like that, in fact. You don't look like anything. That body's shredded and burned and shredded again. That body's crispy fried lettuce.

"I won, yes. Beat you. Stopped you.

"Easily. Barely broke a sweat.

"I'm not trapped in here with you, creep," she says. "You're trapped in here with me."

7.

Flashback: Anderson

To explain What The Actual Drokk

Cassandra Anderson. Year Three out of the Academy. Rookie-ish up-and-coming young Psi-Judge. She's in the Grand Hall of Justice cafeteria talking to Judge Winstanley. They're both on a break, ran into each other in the doorway. She's having a cup of caff, Winstanley's shovelling down his dinner. A plate of fried meat. Winstanley's an old friend from the Academy. A desk Judge. But a good friend. She doesn't get to see him too often.

"Perp was a fatty," she says. "Well, an ex-fatty. His skin—Grud, you should have seen it—actually, you really wouldn't have wanted to see it, it"—a thought strikes her, wicked, as Winstanley raises a forkful of food to his mouth—"it looked just like that bit of sausage casing you're about to eat. Sort of empty and sad like that."

She tries not to laugh too hard at Winstanley's expression. The way he puts his fork down very carefully.

"I'm sorry," she says. "Kidding."

He picks the fork up again, looks at the thing on the end of it, pushes the plate away.

"I'll get you another caff," she says. "Anyway, this ex-fatty... And I went gunning in, angry, maybe a bit over-confident..."

"Judge Cassandra Anderson, over-confident?" Winstanley clutches his chest like he's having a heart attack. "I'm shocked. Shocked, I say."

Walked into that one. Opportunity for Winstanley to get one back on her—so maybe she set it up for him?

"Oh, ha-ha. I said *maybe*. A bit. Anyway, then he..."

There's a chewed-up lump of the mystery fried sausage stuff Winstanley's eating stuck on his upper lip. It bobs around when he talks [now, watching her flashback, she has to hang on to human things like that]. Although mostly he just nods at her stories rather than talking. His stories mostly begin "*There was this massive budget form eyeballing me to fill it in... Bravely I did battle with the procurement team, and once, indeed, verily I almost won.*"

"You said you'd get me a cup of caff?" Winstanley says.

There's a general disturbance in the cafeteria. Buzzing on various Judges' comms, someone gets up, hurries out. Something big going down, Anderson can feel it and Winstanley can... not feel it but *feel* it. They watch with interest. Anderson's itching, wishing she could get drawn in.

"Actually, hold the caff, Anderson," Winstanley says. "I've got to get back to my desk. Spreadsheets to grapple with."

Later the rumour goes round the Justice Department: some Judges out on patrol got so panicked by something, they called in Judge Dredd. General snorting laughter at that: I mean, come on, there *are* other Judges in the Meg.

Later again, the rumour goes round that the tech guys are saying the perp in the case Dredd was called to is several hundred years dead. "I swear to Grud. I know a Judge who knows a Judge who saw the skin fragments." Anderson laughs at that, too, but she knows she's partly laughing out of nervousness. Fear. Dread, even, natch. The air in the Grand Hall feels strange and wrong. Psi-Division try not to catch each other's eyes, find excuses not to leave the Department. Find excuses not to go for a *pee* unless someone else is headed for the bathroom. Anderson keeps her guard up, her mind closed.

Then the message comes in: something big has gone down, and badly. Can hear the fear over the comms. Fear, and a lot of confusion. A Judge is dead; the perp's, um… no one can quite make sense of this bit, but Dredd's at the morgue with the perp's corpse, wants a psi operative.

Not *a* psi operative. The best operative Psi-Div have got.

They send her. Judge Anderson.

SHE WALKS DOWN the hallways to the sound of her heels clicking like a bitch. Cassandra Anderson: the best of the best! The closer she gets to the morgue, the worse the fear builds. She can taste it, vomit-rank in the back of her throat. She walks hard with her heels clicking like all the times she dreamed of this in the Academy; never stops sounding good. Her helmet tucked jauntily under her arm. Ignores the fear. Cracks a smile when she enters the morgue.

Dredd's waiting with the tech guys. She recognises him, of course, but this is the first time they've properly met. She's kind of nervous. Who wouldn't be? Plays it cool and snarky and cracks a joke. Funny thing is, he kind of means it, when she says a telepath knows everyone's guilty secrets and he says he hasn't got any secrets he's guilty about. His mind hits her like a punch. Clear as crystal. Solid as granite. Clean as her kitchen sink.

He wants her to probe a dead perp. A skeleton. Charred bones. Not an everyday job, but not that unusual. Creep's killed a Judge and a load of kids in a nightclub, she's keen to make him talk. The full weight of the Law—even death's no excuse.

"I want—" he begins.

"Yeah, yeah. On it."

The skull grins up at her. She grins down at it. Right, then…

Pulls off her gloves, puts her hands over its eye sockets, makes contact.

Oh, *Gruuuddd*...

The power of it runs through her like...

...like...

It's a blur, what happens then. She knows it's talking through her. She can feel her mouth moving. She can just about hear the words. "*The crime iss life!*"—and there's so much pain, her mind's screaming, fighting, but at the same time she's crying inside with laughter at the absurdity. "*Life itssself was made illegal!*" Umm, yeah, uh, you can see there's a massive gaping logical flaw in that, right? And its stupid weird creaky hissy voice. When it pulls out of her head she rocks backwards, physically sore from it, but at the same time it's so unreal she can't register what's happened. Feels like any other scan-job. Some creep. Some weirdo. Some nut job off his tits on sugar and XXX-rated comix. So nothing that out of the ordinary for a Judge in the Big Meg after sunset. Dredd looks grim about it, but then Dredd always looks grim. She says, "Am I done?" because she's tired and it's been a long day and her head feels kind of icky, and they nod, yes, yes, she's done, not much more they can do right now but wait. She stamps her heels extra hard on the walk out, enjoys the click. They wanted the best and they sent for her, Judge Anderson!

It's hard to remember what happened in the morgue, but she has to stop three times on the way home to vomit, and once to scream.

She's at home, in her bedroom, stripping her armour off, pooped, when it happens. Just kicked her boots off. What happens then

isn't a blur.

* * *

A VOICE. CALLING. Not in her head, outside the window. She turns and she can see it. Its face and its hand, the grin it gives her, so welcoming, so happy to see her. Its long fingers beckon her. "*It's me. Let me in at your window, Anderssson.*" It's neither real nor unreal. A cloud of reeking smoke, such as might rise from a mass grave when the pestilence has hit. The skies of the old world must have run with such smoke when the Atomic Wars were at their height. A cloud of gas like a chemical weapon plume. Or if you could see a really nasty fart. Even with the window between her and it, the stench is so strong she gags. But it calls to her, croons, sings, "*Let me in at your window,*" and she finds she's pushing at the catch. A crack, merely, not enough for a human finger to get through; the smoke wriggles inside her bedroom, gathers itself. She can't step away. It's drawing closer. She can't— She feels it forcing the muscles of her jaws open. Clenches her teeth, but it presses her jaws apart. The taste of it, as it forces itself into her mouth, down her throat. She gags, gasps. It fills her head so she can't think or see. The taste of it in her mouth is rancid. The pain is blinding white.

It enters her. Takes her and fills her mind. She pushes it away, psi-blasts it. Two sets of thought-waves, wrestling.

Nothing. Pushing at a mountainside and thinking it will roll away. Trying to push *herself* out of her head.

She belongs to it. Her body, its mind. Her body twitches, her skin crawls like there's insects all over her; she staggers on her feet, and she's dizzy, she can't keep standing upright, she can't feel her legs.

The room moves. Slides sideways. She was facing the window. Now she's facing the door.

It's not the room that's moving. It's her.

She can see it making her limbs move. Making her walk. She can see what she's—it's—doing—making her body do. Watches her own arms lift and fall, her legs bend. She can feel it nestling itself more comfortably into her. Horrified/flattered that it seems to *like* her mind. *We can do great things together, Anderssson,* it whispers. *You're a Judge. We can bring true Judgement.* Crooning. Singing.

She can see it. Oh, yes. The things she and it, it and she, could do. It's going deeper inside her, not just talking *through* but *inside* her, burrowing down to her core, and so she can understand something of what it is. The enormity of what it is, what it's done.

What it will do here in Mega-City One.

It laughs.

Yessss.

But not just thisss city, Anderssson. Too sssmall.

Think big.

You ssssee?

Images appear in her mind. Blood and fire. Fire and blood. The Cursed Earth, Mega-City Two, Brit-Cit [why bother?], the Sov-Block. The world, with that vile smoke rising, and above the ruins that terrible dead grin and those closing devouring teeth.

Luna. Titan.

And on.

The stars. The sun.

Everything.

Partners in death, you and I, Anderssson. Ssso. Much. Death.

The universe is in need of Judgement. We are the appointed Judges.

She thinks: one gruddamn City Block's too much loss of life. One gruddamn apartment. One drokking poxy ungrateful certainly-guilty-of something low-life human.

She hears herself say, "Yes."

She watches her body moving under its control. Jerking, awkward as it works her arms and legs. She pounds at her own mind, screams at herself to stop, to fight, and she is fighting, in her mind her fists punch down and out and up. In her body, she can just about grit her teeth.

It giggles. "*Oh, ssstop that, Andersssson. It ticklesss.*"

She can see and feel like walking inside a hazmat suit. Like there's layers and layers between herself and the world. Hammers at it in her mind. Only hurting herself. Like she's bound and gagged and biting the inside of her cheek.

It fumbles to get her boots back on. There's a strange fascination in seeing her feet and feeling-but-not-feeling her feet. She staggers as it pulls her up to standing.

"*High-heeled bootssss, Andersssson? Really? Ssshocking fall off in Judgesss' uniformsss on thisss world. Ssshocking. We'll need to do sssomething about that ssstraight off.*"

She and it leave her apartment, the bed she was about to flop into to sleep. In the doorway she strains to throw out her hand, clutch the doorframe, hold on. One finger flexes to touch. Her little finger… the first joint on her ring finger moving. It snatches her hand away, makes her smash her own hand on the wall. The pain is far worse than it should be. Stuns her. She tastes blood on her teeth. Her mind pulls back into itself.

She feels it lick up the blood.

She passes one of her neighbours in the lift lobby, it croons with the desire to kill, she wants to scream, weep as she watches her right hand, knuckles red and bloody, rise towards the man's plump throat. She—it—could crush the guy's windpipe as easily as picking her nose. A horrified thrill and fascination. She's never killed like that. Her hand is flexed and held out. Then the lift pings as the doors open. It smiles in her head. "*Asss you wissssssh, Andersssson. I do admit, I crave to kill. But firssst thingsss firsssst. Be patient. We have all the time in the world, now, you and I. So much time to kill.*"

The lift has a mirrored back wall; it inspects her body as they go down to the ground floor. She stares out of her own eyes like a mask now, like she's watching television as it marches her down pedways and crossways, she can't move her eyes to look apart from where it wants to look. She feels the air on her skin as it moves her body but that, too, feels artificial, like she's imagining it. The crowds surge around her then creep back from her Judge's uniform, she fights to call out for help. Dribbles of sound stick at the edges of her lips.

Its excitement is building. It doesn't know where it's going, but it uses her mind to know. Not that she can't easily guess. They're there so quick, too quick.

She feels herself open the Grand Hall of Justice doors.

Feels the button she presses in the Hall of Justice lift. Feels the lift run up. So quick. So quick.

In the morgue she stands in front of its ruined body. Charred, stripped-down skeleton. Through her eyes it regards itself with some interest.

"*Fasssscinating, don't you think, Andersson? Sssso few have had the privilege of ssseeing how beautiful they look in death. The living body is ssso ugly. Cadaversss are ssso much more... noble, I always think.*"

She wants to vomit as she watches herself gather the skeleton in her arms, cradled lovingly as a mother carrying a child.

A morgue attendant appears from an inner doorway. "What are you doing? Judge Anderson! This is a restricted area! That's body snatching! Do you have permission to do that?"

It growls. "*Even I might baulk at judging the reclamation of one'sss own ssskeleton as theft.*"

She watches her leg fly up, kick the man out of a window. Watches the look on his face, betrayed, horrified, as he falls away. She's horrified at her own strength. Tries to croak out something. Tell him she's sorry. Tell him it's not her.

It snickers inside her: "*Are you sssure about that?*"

She calls the lift again. The doors open, she steps in. A dangling skeletal hand brushes against the closing doors.

"*Careful with that, Anderssson! I almossst lossst a finger bone.*"

Grud, you seen the state you're in, creep? she thinks. You think a finger here or there's going to make a difference?

"*Andersssson. I warn you. There are a lot of people in this city I could make you kill... We could take a little detour to a nursery ssschool, for inssstance. Lots of plump throatssss...*"

The lift doors open and she's in a vehicle bay. Lawmasters, riot trucks, ambulances. It looks with hunger at the biggest armoured vehicles and she can see—beauty, wonder, buildings exploding. It sighs. "*Patience.*"

Its bones clink like bottles as she seats it carefully beside her in the passenger seat of an ambulance. Revs the engine, drives without knowing where she's going, sudden jerks that make her arms turn the steering wheel.

"You might want to hurry up and get that guy to the hospital, lady," someone shouts through the open window. "Whatever's wrong with him, it looks pretty serious." The willpower she feels it exercising, to keep itself from making her steer into pedestrians.

It's excited now, distracted by its body beside her and its plans. If she strains hard enough, she can just about force herself to beg people to stay away. She sends out her location on psi-waves, broadcasts it desperately, loud as a satellite. Someone must hear it. Another Psi-Judge. Anyone. If the Judges find her, they can stop this. And they will find her. They must. She can see what it will do if they don't make it stop. She begins to hear names whispering in her head: *Judge Fire, Judge Fear, Judge Mortis.* Flash images of pain, of darkness, of hunger. White bones and burned bones and a sea of blood. And the word, repeated eagerly, hungrily, echoing inside her head ugly and crude:

Death.

"Stop this!" With all her power, she is able to crash the ambulance into a traffic light. Whiplash wrenches at her neck.

The thing in her head hisses in fury. "*Ssstupid.*" She finds herself clambering out of the ambulance. Carefully cradling the bones in her arms again. Walking fast. Now with shaking legs and a crick in her neck.

Yes, stupid, she thinks. Cars and trucks speed past her. She could try... to throw the bones into the traffic's path. She thinks of the morgue attendant falling backwards out of the window. The thrill that went through the thing squatting in her mind as it fell. And the sense of... completeness. Satisfaction.

Righteousness. Coursing through its mind and thus through *her* mind. How good it felt to kill. She thinks: if the Judges find her, they can shoot her. Kill her, if they have to, to stop this monster from killing.

It laughs. "*I like your mind, yesss, but I can easily find another hossst. Once my own body isss repaired, nothing can stop me. And even if you destroy that body again—again—again—I can find endless, endless hostsss. Until everyone on thisss world isss dead.*

"*You can't ssstop people dying.*

"*You can't kill Death, Anderssson.*"

She realises that's the truth. She can see it happening: they shoot her, it seizes control of another Psi-Judge's body—she visualises Judge Judy—they shoot Judge Judy, it seizes control of Psi-Judge Jools... On and on, until they've done half its work for it. Brought Judgement. If she dies—it wins. If she pushes it out of her head—it wins. Whatever she does—

it wins.

It lets her let out a cry of pain, then, because her horror amuses it so much.

Trapped, she thinks. No way out.

It sniggers in agreement, "*Yesss, indeed. No way out. Nothing can escape Death.*"

SHE KNOWS, THEN, what she has to do.

SHE RELAXES, LETS it move her arms and legs, take her along without fighting it. It likes that. On the edge of her mind she's screaming out to her fellow telepaths. It tries to block her, obviously, but she pushes back. At first, she'll admit, she's not quite willing. Hesitant and frightened. Trembles even as her mind blares it out. If her fellow Psi-Judges hear with understanding, she might just save the city, but at the cost of her own life. The visions build in its mind and hers, the living herded into pens for slaughter, human bones piled higher than mountains, human skin stretched for bloody miles across the earth, a kingdom, a universe of empty death. Her conviction builds. Her plan must succeed. Her city's life is worth her destruction. She focusses all her power. The best psi operative in the Big Meg. Broadcasts one word, repeated over and over. Whispers. Hollers. Sings it joyfully and mournfully. Shouts it out to the assembled Psi-Judges. Pleading, begging that they hear, that someone hears and understands this one word. One word, desperate, on which her life and the life of every single person in Mega-City One must now depend. One word of power and hope and pain and her own ruin. One word to vanquish Death.

One. Final. World-saving. Life-saving. Life-ending. Word.

AND WHAT IS this great word, this word that will save all the world, if only someone, man woman or child, has the wit to understand its terrible meaning and message? This word that means the difference between a universe of life and one of death? This word that will doom Judge Anderson? This word that Anderson is pounding out to her fellows, pleading with them to understand? This word of life's salvation? This terrible, ineffable, deep and inscrutable, singular word? What in all creation is this mighty gruddamn word?

Why, this word is…

Boing®.

Which is an even more ridiculous word than 'Death.'

HER LEG KICKS open the doors into a hab block called the Conapt Building. Low rise, nice place. She tramps upstairs and into an empty apartment, into an empty room. Watches herself carefully lay Death's skeleton down on a table. Spreading it, treasuring it, like a proud homemaker spreading an expensive tablecloth.

Watches her hands caress the bones to adjust their position. It spends a long time ensuring its left big toe is correctly lined up.

"*Wouldn't want to get a bunion*," it says. It sniffs, dusts down its ribcage, makes her make a clicking noise, tongue against teeth. "*Honessstly, Andersson, your uniform isss a disssgrace. Look at thisss fluff. One of your hairsss is on my sssternum.*" Finally it seems satisfied. Steps her back a pace. She feels its smile.

"*Now... let the death fluidsss... FLOW.*"

Magic words. They summon a rain of liquid, black and stinking. The putrid ooze at the bottom of a garbage bin. Drips down on the thing's skeleton and she can only think of... of rain on green plants making them unfurl and grow. The body begins to repair itself. Corrupted grey flesh growing back bloodless over dry bones. A parody of healing. Healing itself not alive but long dead.

She keeps shrieking out the word. She can't sense anyone coming. She can't move her eyes to watch the door. The thing's body blossoms, dead rot, desiccated flesh, travesty of growth from embryo to newborn. If anyone comes now, it'll almost be too late. And she feels deep down a mixture of horror and... relief. It will leave her. It *is* leaving her. Any moment now, she will be free.

It'll kill her, obviously. But she'll be briefly free.

She can feel its grip on her mind loosening. It thrusts and dribbles its way out through her mouth and she gags and it's vile and painful like vomiting up broken glass, like her body being invaded even as it leaves her body, and she should try to keep it inside her because... It sings its delight. She feels the relief that comes with vomiting yourself empty. She sees the city fall, dying.

If you're coming, Dredd, she thinks, it had better be now. Oh, Grud.

Now...

Now...

* * *

NOW. THE DOOR crashes open. Dredd crashes in, weapons first, weapons blazing. His weapons being his famed Lawgiver—and a small metal tin.

THE THING FINDS it frankly funny: Judge Dredd thinking he can save the day by shooting up the corpse that he's already shot and burned. Finds it frankly hilarious to make Judge Anderson punch Judge Dredd in the face. To make Judge Anderson grip her hands around Judge Dredd's neck. Bring Judgement. Anderson presses herself close, her hands squeezing. Get close enough to Dredd.

All her strength, mind and body, to make herself speak to Dredd. Sweating, staring, she whispers it.

"Do it—the Boing® tin."

She hopes those are the last words she'll ever speak.

She thinks: of all the last words a person could speak.

Her mind fails her. Collapses.

Dredd lets rip like a true lawman. Weapon blazing, blazing, blazing.

Sprays Anderson with novelty plastic.

BOING®, THE WONDER toy! Boing®, the 22nd-century marvel that turns people into human pinballs! Just spray on and stand back! Boing®—new miracle formula lets you breathe while you bounce!

LITERALLY THIS. THOUSANDS—millions—have enjoyed a bout in the Palais de Boing®. The can sprays out a liquid that expands and sets, enveloping the, uh, Boing®er in a sphere of clear, solid plastic. A huge, person-sized bouncy ball. The Boing®er in the middle of the ball.

Instantaneous.

Unbreakable.

In her face, her mouth, her eyes, her ears.

Setting.

Set.

And she's trapped.

She tries to keep her breath steady. To remember she can still breathe. Still see, albeit with clouded vision through the layers of plastic. As through a glass darkly and that. And sounds, distant, faint, odd, like she's far away underwater, before the Boing® fully sets. She can see Dredd staring back at her. His grim dark face—he looks almost humbled. Awed, perhaps, at what she's done. She can't move. Can't speak. She gulps air through the plastic. Tries again and again to remember that she can breathe. Breathe. Breathe. Breathe.

Panic. She wants to tear herself out of this. Scream for help. The plastic wraps tight around her. She can just about blink. Just swallow the spit that's filling her mouth.

Breathe. Breathe. Breathe.

She thinks: I chose… Scrub that, I didn't choose but I… I *had* to do this. From outside she can hear Dredd saying the same thing as more Judges pile into the room, stop, gasp, what—? "There was only one way," she can hear Dredd say. Slowly, solemnly, almost awed. "He's trapped in Anderson's head."

Then the plastic gets into her ears and she can't hear anything more. Dredd's words summing up her end.

THE THING DOESN'T understand at first. Strangely enough, it's not encountered Boing® before. It tries to make her arms move, to throw her back into combat with Dredd. Eager, hungry, to kill the Judges still filing into the room. So many lives to take! Big, bulky, lives! Judges who refuse to grasp the final logic of what it is to be Judged. *So good* to take. Her arms shake, trapped in plastic. Muscles bulge, sinews strain, bones creak… and nothing. It can't move so much as her little finger.

Can just about make her blink. Roll her eyes aggressively at her fellow Judges.

It screams. Its voice can't get out through her sealed lips. She chokes on the words pressing against her mouth. Swallows hard. Feels the words burn her throat.

"*Mussst kill! They are alive. Guilty. The sentence isss death*."

It screams, "*What have you done, Andersssson?*"

She says through her pain, "I've won."

It tries again to leave her body. Drag itself out through her mouth the same way it came in. Pain shatters through her. She clenches her teeth and her lips tight. Stops herself breathing, every muscle in her body rigid, makes herself swallow, as if she could hold it in with gripped arms and legs. Screws her eyes shut. Tries to close her earholes. She thinks, somewhere in the part of her mind that's gone past anything and everything now into some absurd unreality: like being on parade trying to hold in a fart.

It rips against her mind. Pushes her lips apart, tears at the plastic pressing against her mouth. Drums at the plastic. Scrabbles at it.

And the plastic holds.

It screams. Screams. Howls. Tears at her, at itself.

The plastic holds.

It's trapped inside her. Can't escape, now or (she hopes, hopes, hopes) after her death.

She forces herself to relax slightly. Breathe.

Fart.

It's trapped.

Welcome to eternity, creep, she thinks. You wanted a body. Seemed to like mine. Lucky for you: it's yours for the rest of gruddamn time. No more killing. Just you and me.

It shrieks and shrieks and shrieks and shrieks and—

She closes her eyes. Tries to think of something good.

The plastic presses on her eyes. A single tear squeezes down her cheek.

8.

Flashback: Judge Death

[Question: can Judge Death have time? Is 'time' not inherently a construction of living beings? Can there be a chronology, 'before' and 'after,' for that which does not live?]

Trapped.

Trapped.

Trapped.

He batters at her. Tears into her mind. His rage should shake the stars from the sky, rip the very foundations of the earth to bloody bits. His rage should make a charnel house of her mind and body, every last atom of her being should be ground to dust beneath his hate. He claws at her, hammers at her mind, bends himself to gnaw at the deepest roots of her self. She holds back, impassive. Only stares at him, then stares away into herself somewhere so deep inside that he can't follow. He screams.

Anderssson. What have you done? What have you done?

Fury, and—

Humiliation.

Not something he's used to.

HE DESTROYED HIS own world. Killed everyone who lived there. Waded, wallowed, gorged himself on blood.

Life is a crime. Death is the sentence. And he is a good Judge. A skilled Judge. Every report card he's had has said it: dedicated; committed; hardworking; tireless in his pursuit of Justice (naturally—perhaps, indeed, he should not now see that last as any particular quality he can boast of, no achievement or ability on his part, what with him not being overly bothered by tiredness/fatigue/the need for downtime/mealtime/bathtime, what with being long years dead). It's not quick work, granted. Detailed. Frustrating. At times it can be lonely, seem futile, even verging on the tedious, the craftsman's recognition that the labour necessary to produce true art can, must, at times be ponderous, crawling forward by inches slow. But if you put in the effort, grit your teeth for the long haul, commit yourself, believe—anyone can achieve great things. Actually, thinking about it, make that—if you put in the effort, grit your teeth for the long haul, commit yourself, believe—a being of *his* calibre, talent and ability can achieve great things.

And no one can say of him that he has not achieved great things.

All these years, and the revelation still delights him, the scope of it, so vast, all-encompassing in its implications, and yet so clear and simple, so easy (like life itself) to boil down to its bare bones.

All crimes are committed by the living. Therefore the living are all guilty of crimes.

Therefore again, following the logic—only on a world where there is no life is there no possibility of a crime being committed.

Therefore again-again, following the logic—since crime is universally recognised to be undesirable and something to be stopped and abolished and avoided, it is a moral imperative to make a living world into a dead world.

Thus, the conclusion is reached—life must be eradicated. As quickly as possible.

So simple. So true. Groundbreaking in its implications for the Justice Department and his role as a Judge. He'd even say it was breathtaking, if he still had breath to take. The billions governments have spent trying to tackle crime! The reams of reports, plans, initiatives they've drafted! Morons. All of them. Unable to follow any logic to its conclusion. 'Early intervention,' 'preventative measures'—they don't know the meaning of the words. The only certain way to ensure the law is upheld is to kill everyone in the world before they have a chance to offend. Only the dead cannot sin.

He reaches out eagerly to share this realisation. How delighted people will be, he thinks, when they see their new-made crime-free world. To his astonishment, his confusion, only three men in all that world truly understand what his revelation means. (Only three! Now, years later, it still shocks him to the core—only three!) But they are good men, dedicated, hardworking; more importantly, they are Judges like him. Together they walk in blood and fire, bring righteous Judgement to those who can only be guilty. Together they enact punishment. Work to make their world a better place.

The four Dark Judges: Judge Fear, Judge Fire, Judge Mortis. Judge Death. And the greatest of these is Judge Death.

JUDGE FIRE KILLS by burning. Where he walks, human bodies run as liquid flame, cool and set like glass. Other bodies entombed there, staring. Faces. Broken limbs. Drowned and boiled in human liquid. In places the earth is shiny, slippery, where human fat has been rendered. In places the earth still burns where human fat has sunk deep.

Judge Fear kills by showing a person their… can you guess? Massed ranks of screaming faces, the terror so great some have tried to tear their eyes out to stop from seeing. But the horror is inside. Then they rot and their expressions are lost. Skulls flash their rictus grins into eternity, eye sockets staring at nothing and everything. The dead see the truth.

Judge Mortis kills by touch. Places his hands upon the living and their flesh crumbles away. As the cliché has it (come on, it has to be said): dust to dust. Mortis cherishes the beauty of human bodies in their opened ruin. Flesh like flowers. The silken gleam of rotting skin.

Judge Death kills by sinking his claws into a person's heart. Tears their life away.

THEY USE GUNS and bombs and plagues and so forth if they have to, obviously. It being a lot of work to judge and punish a world. Eight billion people one by one would be stretching it, even for him. The best deaths are those delivered personally, but one can't indulge oneself too much, sometimes one has to accept the good in place of the best. Sometimes one has to look at the bigger picture, find a work-around, make do. There's no real craft in dropping a bomb that wipes out half a city at once, but it's an imperfect world and needs must. Think of being the one having to explain to some poor innocent victim of a crime that said crime could have been prevented, only he was too slow. Their pain and his guilt! And even with guns and bombs and a zombie army [He didn't mention the zombie army? Never mind, they weren't particularly important] it takes a while. But he gives the job his all, really puts his backbone into it, wears himself down to skin and bones, works his ass off. And he does it. Achieves it. With nothing but fire and fear and rot and tearing, rending claws and a massive arsenal of high-spec weaponry and a zombie army, he makes his personal dream… real.

He

Kills

Every

Single

Living

Thing

On

His

Planet.

There

Is

Nothing

Left

Living.

Not.

Even.

A.

Cockroach.

* * *

IMAGINE IT—A whole world, cleansed of the sin of life!

A LONG STRUGGLE, and a hard one, and there were times even Judge Death himself might have felt almost despondent at the weight of the task. He was promising a better world! A world without sin, crime, guilt! What else was the justice system created for? When all else fails, every politician reaches for that old chestnut, law 'n' order, tough on crime. Unfailingly, the people love it. But really, you try to give the people what they want, and are they grateful? Are they hell! [lit.] The way people acted, you'd think he was being unreasonable. Even unfair. But come on! He was entirely and absolutely impartial, as the law should be. If a person could prove they weren't guilty of anything, he didn't kill them. If you were innocent, you had nothing to worry about.

To be candid, the ingratitude he experienced shocked him.

Shocked him!

Anyway. He digresses. Not like he's bitter about it or anything. He worked himself to the bone, day in, day out, bringing Judgement until his own world was cleansed of sin. Literally. Honestly. Killed. Every. Single. Living. Thing. In. The. World. [Has he mentioned that recently? Yes? Oh.] And were they grateful? Did they thank him for giving them an end to crime? What they wanted, nay, demanded?

What do you think?

He even gave up his own life as an example to people! No hypocrite, he. He died so that they might die too. Showed them the way, that life is short and quickly over, then you die and that goes on and on and on. Nothing to be feared, dying. It is a far better thing I do today, etc. etc. and all that jazz. Fear, Fire and Mortis did it too—died, that is—and they thoroughly enjoyed it. Yet when he rose up to render Judgement, so, so often, almost always, the wretches tried to resist. Fought back.

Raised a ruckus. Acted like he, Death, was the one who was in the wrong.

Okay, yes, confession: dying and being brought back to unlife again by a pair of beautiful scantily-clad nymphomaniac demonic witchqueen twin-sisters, as he was, is—going to go out on a limb here—is possibly—to be very pedantic here, —is possibly, just maybe, a slightly different experience to just, you know, being killed and being dead.

Okay, yes, confession: being dead and brought back to unlife again such that bullets can neither harm nor hurt you, your body being torched to burned bones by a flamethrower can't strictly speaking harm or hurt you, not needing to eat or drink or sleep or breathe, does maybe make the whole Killing Everyone In The Whole World thing easier to manage. Would have been exhausting trying to wipe out Every Living Thing On His Planet in eight hours a day minus a lunch break while worrying about little things like some ungrateful drokk with a gun/knife/half a brick in a sock fighting back and killing him.

But look, you: he sacrificed everything to give his planet what people kept saying they wanted. Not many people out there have that kind of dedication to their job. As another visionary once said: some people dream of success, while others wake up and work hard at it.

He… may have enjoyed it more than strictly necessary. But that's the 21st-century dream. Finding your authentic, fulfilled self through work.

Anyway. He digresses. What he felt and how the people he judged felt is neither here nor there. What matters is that crime is wrong and Judgement must be given. What matters is that he succeeded in his task.

In fire and fear and rot and ruin, the four Dark Judges brought a world to its end.

A DEAD WORLD. Verily, a Deadworld. Death is Judge and Jury and Executioner and King. Fear and Fire and Mortis are most delighted and admiring. "*Well done, that man!*" "*Well, but I couldn't have done it without you, lads. It seemed like a lot of work at the beginning, sometimes I even asked myself if it was truly worth the effort. But when the going was hard, you always supported me. Believed in me. So thank you.*"

Impossible to describe the beauty that they have created. A perfect world without a single crime to blight it. Law and order rules supreme and all is pure and good. Drifting clouds of ashes. Piles of corpses a mile deep. Rivers of blood, and the blood dries and clots, congeals, and there are islands, mountains, *continents* of scabs. Death and Fear and Fire and Mortis stand wondering. Awed. Delighted. There is no sound but the wind in the bone trees and the bone towers and the forests and plains and canyons of bones; the sun beats blinding on the bones. Red meat and white fat lie in glistening piles, Judge Death sinks his arms into them as a living man might once have sunk himself into cleansing waters, and for the same reason. Feels the warm pleasure of softly rotting flesh wash over him.

A dream fulfilled.

A hope realised.

A task complete.

Behold a righteous world without sin!

BUT… A DEAD world is… the Deadworld is…

For a lawman, a Judge, for one dedicated to the upholding of law and the investigation of crime, the Deadworld is… whisper it… boring. He lived and died and unlived for his work. Judge Death: his work literally defined him. So what is he now, with no one left to Judge and kill? And we all know the positive impact work can have, not just on our finances but our health and wellbeing—a good work ethic is right up there with calls for law 'n' order crackdowns and a reduced crime rate as something he's long taken to, um, heart. Finances and health aren't that much of a concern for him, granted, but wellbeing is about a holistic mind-body balance, so the basic point still stands. Alive or undead, work is good for you. Gives you purpose. Drive. A reason to get up in the morning.

And it nags at him as a lawman—he looks at the sky above, out into the universe, and he knows: there are more lives to judge, more crimes to punish—somewhere—out there. It itches at him, both pain and desire—somewhere, life still thrives, crimes are still committed.

He is a Judge. Judgement must be given. The Law must be upheld. He can almost taste that somewhere out there the law is being broken.

He needs to find more people to kill.

FORTUNATELY, JUDGE DEATH is nothing if not resourceful. The crimes of this world having been exhausted…

…he crosses into a parallel universe to a planet bursting full of life.

Travels across the dimensions. Blazing like a baleful star. Long he falls, darkness takes him, he strays out of thought and time. Hurled headlong. Crossing oceans of time.

Time and space fold before him. Without movement, without conscious thought.

Seeking. Searching. Hoping. Fearing. Yearning.

Begging. Hungering.

To find—

To find—

Mega-City One, 2102 AD.

The Big Meg.

A vast city. Glittering. Positively *blinging*, indeed, if you'll forgive the vulgar expression. Full of life. The hated, hateful sounds of laughter, lives and living. The sounds that stir hatred in his heart. The sounds that, strangely, give his dead hard heart—hope. For the sounds mean more lives in need of Judgement. Again, he can take up his mighty burden. Again, he sets himself to his appointed task.

He can taste it. Had almost forgotten, in the perfect world he had created, the thrill of the chase.

Alone now, without even the support of his Dark Judge lieutenants. They would enjoy this world, he thinks, and yet it is pleasing to him to be alone here at first, the purity of Judge Death alone killing. This world is perhaps for him alone to kill. Back to basics: no army, no vast stockpile of weaponry and poisons. Nothing but the weight of the Law to aid him.

Claws unsheathed, he steps out into a world of echoes and shadows, prowls catlike through this 'Mega-City One.' A few steps are enough to tell him that crime runs through this city like sugar through a junkie's veins. Its inhabitants are human sores, foetid with lust, misery, rage. Swollen with violence. Rank with sin.

Ah, brave new world that has such people in it! And thus, and thus, onwards and upwards forever, once more into the breach and such great works await! A long time since last he killed. The taste of his first Judgement on this world is sweet.

And—

Then—

How did she describe it?

He crossed into a different universe, travelled through space and time, mere dimensions could not contain him. He, who has consumed and destroyed a world. So vital his mission. So inexorable his Judgement. To find—

How did she describe it?

To find:

I. a petty hoodlum called 'Tiny the Tap';
II. a bug-eyed 'button jock' with no taste in music and a rabble of badly dressed, badly dancing kids at a nightclub called 'The Rabbit Hutch';
III. a second-rate Street Judge called Geller Ross;
IV. Judges Anderson and Dredd; and
V. a spray can of novelty plastic.

I mean… Wow! Amazing!

The Deadworld cowered before him. Fell. He waded glutted through streams—rivers—seas—oceans, yes, vast oceans of blood. His work is glorious. His task a noble one. And this flippant woman Anderson, and a can of Boing®, defeated him.

Wrapped in plastic. Stuck in this woman's head.

An illegal Boing® defeated Death.

DEATH

9.

Can't move. Can't move, can't stretch, can't speak.

Both of them together. Anderson. Death.

Can't move. Can't speak.

Fight it, fight it, fight it, fight it, fight it, scream and rage and smash my hands against a plastic wall that holds me and I can't—I'm not—

Who am I?

What am I?

* * *

Two minds in one mind. Can't move. Can't speak. I can't—I—I'm—

Shadow in my mind fighting me, holding me. Someone in my head and I can't move to tear them out and I'm trapped. Can't move. Can't speak. This thing in my mind with me, part of me, and I can't get it out and it's wrong, not like me, it hates me, it wants to destroy me and I can't escape it, trapped here, it and me, me and it and I don't know what's it and what's me and I can't find myself, I can't move, I can't speak, I can't see, I can't—can't—

Hands batter against plastic. Nothing. Trapped. Ended. But I am… I was… I can't end like this. It can't end… like this… I was… I did… I wanted… This thing in here with me. This other mind. Hates me. Like poison. I can't make it stop hating me. I can't escape.

I can't escape.

10.

Hold on, Anderson. Hold on. Hold on. Breathe. Hold on. You can do this.

11.

The Grand Hall of Justice cafeteria. Or, rather, the Grand Hall of Justice cafeteria as Judge Cassandra Anderson visualises it. It might be cleaner and prettier in real life. Or worse.

Anderson pushes her chair back, making the legs squeak horribly on the flooring. She notices Judge Death wince at the noise. It occurs to her that it's not a sound it can have heard much recently. Vast suppurating mounds of flesh, deserts of bones, dust clouds of human ruin—tend to be silent. At most, the occasional dry sad rattle of bleached bone falling.

She'd like to burp or fart for the same reason. The joys of the human body in all its living, breathing, beautiful ugliness. Only a shame she can't wave a tampon at it or something.

Well, she thinks then, as they're both in my head, I suppose I could.

"I said you don't have to look like that," she snaps. "We're in my head, creep. None of this is real. You can look like anything you want."

The thing opposite her steeples its fingers, peers at her over them. The blank gate of its helmet visor is almost worse than the dead face beneath. Funny, she thinks, no one's ever seen Dredd's face beneath his visor either, and that's fine. Sort of. (There's a rumour some of the Street Judges have a pot going, fifty credits an entry, the first one to see Dredd without his helmet on wins.)

"*What would you rather I looked like, Andersssson?*"

"I said you don't have to speak in that stupid fake scary voice, either, creep."

It flickers. Widens its dead mouth into a smile. She sees raw-head and bloody bones. Children with their skin melting off them red and liquid. The child in the sugar-dealer's apartment when Anderson shot her dad in the head.

"*Isss that better, Andersssson?*"

"Just lay off. You're not scaring me."

"*I'm not trying to ssscare you.*"

She glares at it. Truth is, of course, she's terrified of this thing. Impossible not to be. But the anger at everything she's finally having to accept she's lost, because of this thing—it's stronger even than the fear.

"Trying to charm me, then, are you? Dazzle me with your sweet voice and good looks? Gentlemen prefer blondes, but all the nice girls like a desiccated corpse?"

"*I'm dead,*" it snaps. "*How elssse do you expect me to look?*"

"I can give you some hints."

It hisses at her. The way its mouth twists, the curl of its fingers—she's made it angry. For all it claims it's dead, she thinks, it has strong feelings.

"*Oh… All right. If you insssissst. To humour you.*"

She'd almost say it was… pouting.

The skull face shivers. Flickers. Nothingness, darkness, formless as a bloodclot, and then it rearranges itself into a living man's face.

Blond hair, cut in regulation short back and sides. Pronounced eyebrows, darker than the hair (she thinks: it's *bottle blond?*). An unpleasantly upturned nose. Petulant expression, sneering, angry and weak.

She recognises him instantly. The kind of nasty little shit who peeps under toilet doors at school.

"Is that better?" he says in a normal human voice.

His voice is quite nice, actually. Soft, not too deep. She can imagine he'd make a good singer. Telesalesman.

"It was a long time ago, but I think this was how I *usssed*—sorry, I mean used—to look."

Relief at not having that dead blank void staring into her. Such relief! She shrugs. "I guess."

"You're not my idea of beauty either," he says sweetly. "Think of me, can't you, having to look at all that disgustingly shiny hair, those rosy, healthy cheeks. But no matter. I'll contain my revulsion. That's—I'd say 'life,' but I fear that would be too on the nose."

He's got big, almost puppy-dog eyes. Sort of winks at her, again—trying to remember all this stuff like 'eyelids' and 'eye contact'—he looks so… yeah, the creepy little boy, the man who definitely hasn't been getting any lately, but he looks so normal now, boring, unmemorable, even a bit like if she'd met him as a new recruit to the Department she might feel sorry for him. "Poor guy," she can imagine herself saying. "Do you think he knows how much of a dweeb he is?"

She really, really, really wants to smash his gruddamn face in.

Maybe looking at the corpse and the gated helmet was better, she thinks. Harder to bear, but easier to bear too. He—

The cafeteria jolts.

Shakes.

Her cup of caff goes flying across the tabletop.

She grabs the table. Grabs at the cup. It slides away from her, she knows it's not real but she watches it shatter on the cafeteria floor tiles, a pale puddle of caff running towards her boots.

No, wait, the cup was empty. She'd forgotten she drank it all. The building shakes again, harder, and the spilled caff pools around her chair leg.

"Are you doing this?" Mind storm, she thinks in a panic. Psychic shock. Her mind can't hold itself together with this monster inside it. Or: he's going to take over her head completely. Kill her, squat inside her dead body. Not that killing her will do him any good, he'll still be trapped inside the plastic. But he's an insane psychopath. It's—kind of what they do.

But Judge Death's human face looks almost surprised himself. Confused, alarmed by whatever's happening. The shaking gets worse and worse, and there's a sound, distant, she's not sure if she's imagining it, a grinding, rumbling noise, like the shingle on a beach churned up by a winter sea.

She's not imagining it. Judge Death can hear it too, turns his head, trying to find the source of the noise. Looks at her as if he's frightened *she's* doing something to *him*. Some trick. The cafeteria shifts, the walls shaking and the tables and chairs are vibrating, jumping, now. She has to grip on to the tabletop. He has to grip on. Two sets of teeth chattering. The noise whines, pounds in her head, makes her wince, it's almost loud enough to be painful.

Fades a little. The shaking slackens off a little. Then redoubles. Anderson's head vibrates and her teeth knock together and she almost bites her own tongue.

What is this? What's the monster done? Yet it—he—looks as confused as she feels. Doesn't like the feeling or the sound.

In desperation, Anderson opens her real eyes. Stares out through the layers of Boing®. Blurred figures that must be Judges are moving around the plastic. She can see helmets and armour. Shapes cast in black and blue and the bright glimmer of the gold eagles on their shoulder pads, surfacing as they turn and move around her like fish in a tank.

And something else.

Panic. She wants to scream. A tiny part of her leaps in joyous relief. The noise and the shaking is a power saw cutting into the Boing®.

They're cutting her out.

* * *

"WHAT ARE YOU doing? What are you fools doing?"

She screams it for real, tries to, the words jam in her mouth, clog it, she fights and sobs to open her lips, move the muscles in her throat. *Stop it!* She'd thought Dredd had understood. And now she's felt something of what Judge Death claims he's done to his own world, any doubt about what's she's done is—almost—banished. If one millionth of what he claims he's done is true, he has to stay in her head, trapped in here. Whatever happens to her.

She thought Dredd understood.

A tiny, tiny part of her wants to cry, she's so happy. She imagines the plastic splitting open, light and air washing over her. Vomiting Death out of her head. She wants to shout *Quick! Quick! Faster with the saw!* An overwhelming, desperate need to wiggle her fingers and toes.

They must have taken pity on her. Decided they couldn't bear to leave her sealed away like this.

The saw gets louder again. A technician looms over her, holding the sawblade aloft. She closes her eyes in panic, finds herself trying to throw her arms up over her face. The blade cuts down above her. The plastic shudders.

Judge Death croons in delight. Her eyes closed, back in her head, she can see the hunger in him, his face half death mask half human. He's licking his lips. And she can't help seeing what he's imagining—the saw cutting down, slicing her skull open, the blood exploding over shards of plastic, his ghostly hands wallowing in her death. The first beautiful sight of death before he gets to his work.

The saw moves away a little. Up over her head, then down towards her feet.

He gloats like a cat. "I knew it. The Judges in your world are so weak. So stupid."

"They value my life," she spits back at him. Tries to believe that what they're doing in saving her is neither stupid nor weak. If I was outside and Dredd or someone was in here with Judge Death, she thinks, what would I do?

More figures loom close over them. Blocking the light, so close up it's like she's looking down into deep water. But she can tell from the build and the set of the shoulders that one of them is Dredd. He puts his hand on the plastic right over her face. She shuts her eyes as if he's touching her.

She's screaming in fear and rage and hope. Any minute. Any moment. They'll get me out of this coffin. Save me.

The saw cuts off.

Dredd lifts his hand away.

Steps away.

They'll open it up any moment. Grud. Grud.

Any moment.

Any moment.

Any moment.

Any moment.

Any moment.

The need to move her hands and feet and legs and arms and head and every single muscle in her body is overwhelming. Just shout, run. Just stretch her arms out.

She's so tense. Breathe, she thinks. Breathe, Anderson.

Just to see something…

"*Come onnnnn*," Judge Death croons. "*Come onnnnnnnn. Do it.*" She can feel lust oozing out of him.

What have you done, you gruddamn fools? He'll kill us all. I've seen it, fragments of what he's done and will do.

Save me from this, please, she thinks. Please. I don't care what comes after. I can't do this.

She thinks: no, please, you can't do this. You have to leave me here. Stop. Please.

Any moment.

Any moment.

Any
Moment.

Any

Moment.

DREDD AND THE other figure walk away. The plastic encasing her is still inviolable and intact.

Judge Death makes what can only be described as a keening sound. As though his whole being is shattering apart, as though he's watching the only person he loves die.

THEY'RE NOT TRYING to save her. Or, rather, they are trying to save her and everyone else.

"They've stopped. They've stopped!" She wants to dance and sing even as she wants to weep.

"*But I have to be free*," Judge Death screams. Her mind reels at the fury crashing out of him. "*I am the Law. I have to bring Judgement. I have to punissssh.*"

A noise. Very distant, muted through the layers of plastic. Metal, clattering. An engine revs. She thinks: a bike? The cafeteria rocks again. Anderson feels herself rising into the air. Flying.

She peers out through the plastic, straining to see. The wall of a building swings past her. Then bright light. She's staring straight up into the sun.

They're lifting the ball of Boing® out of the room in the Conapt Building, she realises. They've... she thinks of the saw... they've cut the ball down to something smaller, easier to manoeuvre, now they're taking it out by crane. Her stomach lurches as she's swung sideways. Sunlight on her face, brilliant; she closes her eyes and everything's warm and red. It's wonderful to feel the sun. Then she's swung away into shadows, she opens her eyes to see a building looming above her. Drops suddenly, she panics and tries to clench her hands, clutch at something. Hold on.

Another jolt as the Boing® makes contact with the ground. More technicians loom over her. She wonders if they know she can see them. Maybe if she blinked at them? She tries to work out what the drok they're doing. Seem to be wrapping something around the Boing®... she's going to have to think of it as a 'coffin.' They vanish, but she can't see clearly now, whatever they put over her is over her eyes, obscuring her vision. There's a pause, then she can feel the vibrations of what might be an engine. Not the ground, she realises. She's on a truck, being transported somewhere. Flickers of light and shade as they drive down flyovers and boomways.

"*What are they doing?*" Judge Death hisses. "*Why?*" He seems frightened.

For a dead man, she thinks, he really is full of emotions.

"I don't know. They're taking me somewhere." They can hardly leave her in the room in the Conapt, she thinks then. What would they do, lock the door, put crime scene tape across it? *Warning, biohazard. Do not enter (on pain of death, natch).*

She thinks with sudden horror: they'll have to bury her deep underground. Sealed away like nuclear waste. The Boing®, and then layers of lead and rockcrete, earth, a hole a mile deep. Or seal her in a crate, drop her into the sea. No one can know where she's buried.

Judge Death makes a croaking sound, like a toad. He's realised it too.

"Looking forward to eternity, creep?" she says, trying to keep the pain out of her voice. "Going to be fun, isn't it, just you and me?" She's already choking on the weight of earth over her, miles and miles deep, pressing down on the plastic; she can almost taste soil, feel it filling her nose and her mouth. She stares at the light, the grey sky unreal through the plastic. Never see the light again. They'll take her right out of the city, maybe. Bury her someplace far off in the Cursed Earth, where no one can live.

Bit like taking the Long Walk, she tries to think.

You wanted a dead world, creep, and you're going to get one, she tries to think. Be happy.

"What are they doing?" Judge Death says again. He sounds frantic now. The human face he's wearing in her head looks like it's aged ten years. His teeth worry at his lower lip. "Why? Why?" It strikes her that he's disturbed by the Judges' determination. Their strength in leaving a colleague to suffer like this for the greater good. The sacrifice they are all making by leaving her like this is so far beyond him.

Oh, he'd leave a colleague to suffer and die, all right. She can see that in his mind, huge as a planet. Enjoy doing it. But doing something that he didn't *want* to do... something that *hurt* him...

"Someone else dying will never hurt me, Anderson," he hisses. "Never has and never will. Watching a colleague suffer and die is a celebration." His voice is so petulant. Tetchy as a kid when you confiscate his football. Despite everything, she snorts with laughter when he says, "And I died myself. Let myself be killed. What was that, if not an act of sacrifice?"

The truck or whatever she's being carried on stops. The technicians are back, fussing around the... the coffin. Dredd appears again, again he puts his hands over her face. She blinks, and maybe he can see her blink, or sense it, because he nods his head. Other Judges appear; she can't see clearly, but she thinks one of them's the Judge she's been working with the last few weeks, Neirn. She'd liked working with him.

The coffin lurches violently. She realises the Judges are carrying her on their shoulders, four on her left, four on her right. She shudders: pallbearers. Just like carrying a coffin. Oh, Grud, she thinks. Drokk drokk drokk. Oh, Grud, here we go...

They bring her inside. As they pass through the doorway she takes a gulp of air like she's about to dive underwater. This is it. The end. Even Judge Death is silent; she closes her eyes one second to look at him in her head, and his face is white. The ceiling above her is very high, a grand Big Important Place. For a moment she thinks they've decided to actually bury her, sort of pretend she's really dead. I mean… that would be appropriate, I guess, she thinks. Fluorescent tube lights flicker above her. A brightly lit area, then what might be a corridor where half the lights have blown and need replacing, then another wide, well-lit space.

The ceilings above her look familiar. Air vents and cheap white paint. Oh. She can sense Judge Death make the same connection she has. She feels him start to twitch. *Oh. Oh, yesss.*

They're carrying her through the Grand Hall of Justice.

Absently, she thinks: the cafeteria's just down there. The real one. The—I bet the Judges carrying me can smell the beanz from here.

Again, she thinks with panic: they're going to try to get me out. They think they can control things in the Grand Hall, put some kind of shielding up, get Judge Death out of her head and trap him.

Judge Death's excitement pounds inside her skull. In her head she sees him almost dancing. His human face grins worse than his dead face. All the Psi-Judges. All the Street Judges with bulging muscles and personalised heavy guns. All the hi-tech ways of killing.

"All for me? How thoughtful of someone." He smiles. "Oh, but, Anderson, you really thought…?"

His voice grows stronger, she can hear the eagerness in it. Positively chatty, now he thinks he's about to get free. "I must admit to finding your body… pleasing. Oh, purely in the sense of being strong and agile and well trained to kill, of course. I wouldn't want you to think anything so base as that I might be… *attracted* to you. But you do have a fine body and fine mind for my purposes. I mean that quite sincerely. We could have done wonderful things together, you and I. My own body is perfectly serviceable, of course, but speaking candidly as one who was once briefly a red-blooded young man: I admit, I was looking forward to using yours for a while.

"But I'm afraid to say I've changed my mind. As soon as

we get out of this, I'll kill you. Judge you. The charge..." She hears his bared teeth as he licks his lips. "False imprisonment? Flippancy towards a representative of the Law? I'm sure I can find something."

They stop. A pause, then she's being lowered. A jolt as they set her down. Eight Judges stare down at her. Sleeping Beauty in her drokking coffin. She can see Judge Dredd, Judge Neirn, Judge Alexander, Judge Winstanley. It's hard to see clearly through the plastic but she thinks Neirn, Alexander and Winstanley are all crying.

She waits now while they set up whatever they think will save the day. Any desire to be set free... Grud, she'd be lying even now if she said every cell in her body wasn't screaming for them to let her out. The desire to scratch her nose is overwhelming. She feels a sudden agonising need to break wind.

Now that would be a dramatic ending. They cut the Boing® open, Judge Death leaps out of her head with a shriek like murder, Anderson sits up, Judge Death lets rip at her throat and at the same moment she lets rip a massive fart.

It must take him a few seconds to get out of me, she thinks. I might have time to warn them. In her head she can see what he's planning to do to them. Cheap white paint and tube lighting soaked in Judges' blood. His promise to kill her first is almost a comfort. In her head she can see a tide of blood sweeping over Mega-City One.

Dredd reaches out. Again, he puts his hand on the plastic. Just over where her Judge's badge is. He steps back, Neirn steps forward, does the same thing. Then Winstanley. Then Judge Yakob. Judge Ho. Chief Judge Griffin himself. More and more of them. Each puts their hand over her badge then backs away, head bent. Some of them are crying. Some move their lips, saying words she can't hear. One or two of them put their hand over her badge, then their own badges.

She blinks at them, tries uselessly to roll her eyes so that they realise she can see them. Wishes she could lip read. So many Judges. Like... every Judge in the Meg.

Tears in her eyes. Trapped: they can't roll away down her cheeks. She blinks madly, because she can't see through the tears and this is something so beautiful she has to see.

Like taking the Long Walk, indeed. They're saluting her. Honouring her. And now she knows where she is.

The Grand Hall of Justice Hall of Heroes.

An exhibit.

That's… an achievement of sorts, she thinks.

Every Judge dreams of having their picture or their old uniform displayed here, in that unreal way you might dream of saving the world or being made Chief Judge. If you're really, *really* lucky, do something amazing, they might put up a small and badly made statue. If you're unbelievably, *insanely* lucky, they might file the sprue off the statue. Now here she is and here she'll rest. The actual living Judge Anderson.

She went on a school trip to the Hall of Heroes when she was maybe eight. Got an eraser in the shape of Chief Judge Fargo at the giftshop.

Judge Death has fallen silent again. Huddled himself into the edge of her mind. His hopes—if that's the right word, which it really isn't—crushed, crushed, crushed. Now that's an achievement: Dredd couldn't have planned a way to torture this monster better if he'd tried. Death hates this. The grief and pride her fellow Judges have for her is so strong she can feel it, very faintly, through the plastic. She imagines it must actually be painful for him. Like acid on an open wound. Massed ranks of living faces all so full of life and feeling, all that's best in people and in human life and even in the Judge system, so close to him, so much life, so close up, thrust into his face—and he can't touch them. All these hands that deal out real justice, skin worn and calloused, scarred by long hours' working to protect the people they serve, they touch her coffin over and over and over and over—almost literally rubbing in the fact of his defeat.

Then finally the last Judge pays her respects and exits.

Silence.

Then the lights snap off.

Anderson stares up into the dark. Strains to find patterns, interest, in the Hall of Heroes ceiling. Until the light fades completely and she can't see even that.

Her nose still itches. Muscles she didn't know she had in her stomach, her back, her gruddamn ears, are shrieking to move. Her throat's dry. She really needs a piss.

"You lost, Judge Death. You're judged and found guilty and the sentence is eternal imprisonment. I won." She says it loud and confident and when she reaches the last words her voice cracks. "I gruddamn won."

The realisation of what that means hits her again. Again. Again. Again.

She repeats it desperately. I won. I won. In the dark, trying to hang on.

12.

Trying to keep her sanity intact: day 1

Going to a safe good place with a good story to tell

THE PERP FLED into the tower block, and the Psi-Judge followed him.

SHE'S NOT OUT of breath this time. Her story, told her way. Also she's still working hard on remembering to keep breathing.

The perp's driving, jumps a red light and damned near causes an RTA; Anderson's on her way to the local section house when she sees it happen. Poor guy's brain all but pops out of his skull when he realises there's a Judge on a Lawmaster cruising in the right-turn lane who's seen everything. He panics. She kicks off after him. It's at the point he's doing seventy miles an hour the wrong way down a flyover, other drivers literally diving to avoid him, that she decides she should probably call for backup.

Judge Neirn's voice crackles over her comm: "Anderson? I'm in the area. What's the problem?"

"Some spugwit who thinks he's immortal. On the boomway

between Taylor and Bey, heading east-north-east towards the Ora. You're on your bike, I'm guessing?"

"Yeah."

The perp takes a corner too narrow for any comfort. Howl of brakes, stink of rubber, a truck crashes out of the way. Anderson grits her teeth, kicks down on the Lawmaster. "Unless you've got a jetpack handy?"

They take a boomway so fast the traffic's a blur around them. So fast Anderson can barely sense the cursing, screaming and occasional excited cheer. Ora Block looms up too sudden, they're headed straight for the filter lane down to the block's parking zone still doing seventy, then at the last possible moment he swings a hard left, tears towards Lupa at least one-hundredsixty kph. Anderson slaloms round a jack-knifed lorry, teeters on the brink of crashing, pulls herself out of a skid to see Neirn's Lawmaster closing. Neirn's grinning ear to ear. Spins his bike around; lifts the front wheel off the road. His blast of psychic joy almost makes Anderson lose control of her bike.

"We can head him off outside Lizzo," Neirn shouts over the comm.

"Yeah. Great." If I survive that far, Anderson thinks. The perp's in a Judges' lane now—she mentally adds another fifty years in the cubes, taking the perp's tally to a conservative three hundred-plus. Neirn's following. Close.

"Got him!" Neirn shouts over the comm.

Pride, fall, etc. Neirn overcooks a corner, shoots across the boomway at right angles to the oncoming traffic. Gets it together enough to vault his bike over the central partition.

She can still feel him whooping.

Boys, she thinks.

So... it's up to her now. Anderson grits her teeth, pushes on. Lizzo Block appears and disappears in a glitter of lights; they're going so fast there are neon trails on Anderson's vision.

More voices over the comm, but it's hard to concentrate to hear. To think. The perp swings left-right-left-right, accelerating, decelerating. Someone's yelling she should just shoot and get it done. She's honestly not sure, even with all her targeting gadgetry, she'd hit him.

And Neirn's back swinging to meet her, half a synthi-hedge caught in his shoulder pads.

"Ummm...?"

"Never came off," he says. Like that's the Judges' Achievement of the Week.

The perp pulls a three-sixty. How his car's not exploded by now, Anderson's not sure. Neirn and Anderson split, one left, one right, draw a heart shape in burned rubber across the boomway.

"...lost him...?"

"Lost him. Grud!"

"No... Wait... Over there!" She points with her mind, hoping Neirn gets it.

Neirn shouts over the comm, "His car can drokking *fly?*"

He's in the Amadeus Block parkarama. Grudd knows indeed how he got there. The two Lawmasters cut through another synthi-hedge, roar across a walkway sending pedestrians running. Anderson catches Neirn's inner shout of *Stampeeede!* They hit the parkarama just as the perp's finally decided to abandon his vehicle. Taken pity on it, maybe. It might be an inanimate object, but Anderson would swear it's crying. *No more. No more. Please.*

The perp very carefully locks the car door before he runs towards Amadeus Block. Which is thoughtful of him, car theft involves a lot of paperwork.

Unfortunately this commendable act of proactive personal responsibility and citizenship is rendered irrelevant approximately ten seconds later, when Neirn's Lawmaster hits a puddle and slides.

Neirn eats tarmac.

The bike slices into the perp's car.

Weapon systems locked and loaded.

KABOOOM!

[If this was a comic, this page would be up in flames].

* * *

"Oh, for Grudd's sweet sake!" Anderson takes the time to brake and steer and park and generally not cause any more vehicles to explode. Dismounts without falling off. She can still see light-trails in waves across her vision. Long gleaming tresses of neon. All the glitter of a summer night in the Meg. The air smells of burning oil and car tires. Warm, dirty wind against her skin. She can sense Neirn getting himself together off the ground like a cat, *Nothing happened and anyway I meant to do that.* She can sense what must be the perp, kind of keening about the car's untimely end. She can sense a general gawping from ten thousand people in Amadeus Block all staring out of the windows, disappointment and happiness in equal amounts as a good third of them settle their bets on the chase's outcome.

Oh, I'm so sorry I cost you fifty credits, chap in Apartment 22011B. How inconsiderate I am. Obviously I'd have crashed first, if I'd only known. She thinks: can I cube an entire block for illegal gambling?

She growls at Neirn. "Get it together. Get moving. We got him."

The perp flees into the tower block, and the Psi-Judge follows him.

Neirn, limping, follows them both.

Running upstairs, and it's a real memory now, not some game of Judge Death's, and she's not breathless or sweating. Although she is cursing the broken lifts. She's close enough to see the perp on the stairs above her, hear the clatter of him running; the rhythm's broken and he curses when he nearly slips. On the second floor he turns into a corridor, barges a woman out of his way, as careless as he was about cutting up traffic. Anderson hears it as a gasp and a clatter, comes down the corridor herself to find a woman in a blue raincoat standing staring, two bags of groceries like a flood around her feet. The woman points, croaks, "He went that way."

"Thanks."

"What about my shopping?" the woman shouts at Anderson's backside. "A week's groceries. You come back here and help me pick it up."

"Take it up with Citi-Def," Anderson shouts back. Shots ring out in the corridor ahead of them. "Grud—look, just get under cover, never mind your drokking veg."

"Never mind my veg?"

More shots. Multiple weapons. An apartment door gapes open; dark inside, a faint dry stale smell. On the threshold a blast of psi-pain punches into Anderson. Someone's injured in there.

"Justice Department. I'm coming in." Her Lawgiver's ready, itching.

A whimper: ghostly, lonely, hurting. A smell of dirt. Dark in the hallway. A closed door, its outline drawn in white light. Pain is flowing out from beneath the door. She can sense fresh blood.

Neirn is behind her now. He smells of smoke. Pain is beating off him, as well. Deafening.

"Grud, keep it down," Anderson snaps at him before realising it's hardly his fault. He nods; in the dark she sees him bite his lip.

"Ready?"

He nods again.

Anderson kicks the door, they go in guns first, Neirn yells, "Justice Department! Hands in the air!" White light bursts over them. Like cold water poured over Anderson's head. And the pain, and fear, and… hope.

A young woman is sitting tied to a chair, a gag in her mouth. Huge terrified eyes fix on Anderson. Blurred and red with tears. The perp is lying sprawled, his arms thrown out. His blood is soaking into the carpet. Blood trails seem to reach towards the woman. Yearning towards her.

His murderers are poised and armed and ready. Waiting. Eager to get them some Judge's blood.

Anderson feels them fire.

Crackle of bullets.

Neirn lets rip with his Lawgiver. Grud, Anderson pleads, don't hit that woman. Please. Her finger hesitates on the trigger. Neirn hits—but Neirn's hit. He yells, fires again. Terror in the woman's eyes. She makes a horrible grunting noise through the gag. One of the two gunmen's down like Neirn's bullets have eaten him. The other's wounded but still going. Dives to use the woman as a human shield.

Neirn throws up his arm to check his fire. "Drokk!" Pop of bullets. Blood on the woman's face, sudden and deep. Two more Judges closing from the corridor. Angry. Both about to shoot. Drokk, drokk, drokk.

Anderson throws out a mind blast.

THE GUNMAN GOES down hard. She feels the impact in her own head, the jolt as a consciousness is switched off. Almost physical, as if her fingers have dug into the man's brain. A moment of nausea. Her and him. She wavers, steadies herself, bends to cuff him. He blinks to as she's getting the cuffs on, opens his mouth to cuss her, she kicks him in the face. He blinks off again.

So. That's kind of that.

Neirn's wounded: a bloody hole in his left sleeve. Anderson realises she's wounded too. They both ignore it, sort of shrug at each other, all their attention needs to be on the two... um, she guesses they must be victims? Neirn takes the perp on the floor dying. Anderson pulls the gag out of the woman's mouth.

"George!" the woman screams. "George! They've killed him!"

"No, no, calm down." Anderson puts her hand awkwardly on the woman's shoulder. "I'm going to untie you. I'm a Judge, my colleagues are calling for help, we'll get you and... George to hospital." She shouts into her comm, "You got that? This is Anderson calling for medical support."

"He's dead!" the woman screams.

"He's not dead." Neirn is kneeling beside the perp, hands

clamped over a gunshot wound to the guy's chest. "He's going to be okay, I hope." Two Judges coming in with a stretcher even as he speaks. "See?" Neirn says.

"What's your name?" Anderson asks.

"Katherine." Eyes fixed on Judge Cheng securing George for transport to the block hospital. "George's my husband. But he's going to die, isn't he?"

"He is not going to die," Neirn says firmly. He and Anderson share a glance. He's not going to die, true, but he's looking at several decades minimum in an isocube. The parking violations alone... Anderson can distinctly remember his car was encroaching on two bays in the parkarama before it exploded. And then of course there's the damage the car did to Neirn's bike.

Katherine might not strictly be a widow any time soon, but...

The look between the two Judges isn't lost on Katherine. An image of the couple on their wedding day flashes into Anderson's mind, quickly followed by an image of Katherine dressed in mourning black.

A wave of exhaustion crashes over Anderson. Her shoulder aches where a bullet hit her through her armour, her head's hurting, she feels so gruddamn tired. The apartment reeks of pain, physical and mental. Whatever happened here was hard.

Neirn mouths what Anderson thinks is "Can we find a way to let this chap off?" Anderson stares at him unblinking. We're Judges. We can't get emotional. The Law is the Law.

She looks back at Katherine's tear-stained face.

"I need you to tell us what happened here," she says firmly but gently. "I'm a Psi-Judge. As you can see. So it's probably a good idea if you tell me the truth. You and your husband live here, I can see that. Those men were holding you prisoner?"

Katherine's face lights up. She nods frantically. Doesn't need to speak, the story's playing out in her mind so loud Anderson's surprised half the Meg isn't watching it. George getting in with the wrong crowd as a juvie. George trying to straighten himself out and inevitably mucking up. George getting in with very much the right crowd when he meets Katherine. George and Katherine crazy in love.

George's past catching up with him.

"They wanted George to store drugs and weapons in your apartment?"

Nod.

"But he refused."

Nod. More tears.

"So they came here looking for him, found you alone?"

Katherine goes rigid. Screws her eyes and her whole face shut. Tries to screw her mind shut.

Oh, Grud. Anderson has to stop herself from vomiting.

Neirn stares at Anderson. Anderson stares back. We're the Law, gruddamnit. Upholding the Law is what we are and what we do.

Anderson says hopelessly, "So they called him, told him what they'd done, what they'd do if he didn't get back here now to talk to them." She presses her hands over her eyes. All she can see is Katherine's memory. The gunmen's faces. Katherine screaming in pain. No wonder he drove like a madman. She'd have driven anything off the road to get home, if it'd been someone she loved. Except she wouldn't, because the law on traffic violations doesn't allow any excuse.

Neirn says suddenly, "No. That's not what happened. Your husband was here all the time with you. One of the perps burst in with a gun, threatened you both, tied you up. The other one stole your husband's car to get here and join his friend. Yes?" He says it fast, hesitant, an uncertain desperate rush of words. "Yes?"

Katherine shakes her head in confusion. "Why would…?"

Neirn repeats it slowly, firmly. "They tied you up. They stole your car. Isn't that right, Judge Anderson?"

He says very firmly, "That's what happened. And you can help Katherine remember it, can't you, Psi-Judge?"

"I…" That's totally, vastly, absolutely, unarguably, I can even say *indubitably* unethical and illegal and immoral and in breach of about nineteen different psi-resolutions and, and,

and, gruddamnit, thank you, Neirn, you kind, good, beautiful human being, you.

Anderson takes a deep breath. Then another. Clears her mind of Katherine's screams. "That's exactly what happened, isn't it, Katherine? I can see that, you don't need to tell me. You were tied up, George was threatened at gunpoint by one of the perps, the other one took your car for a joyride.

"In a few minutes, some more of my colleagues are going to come through that door to join us. You don't need to worry or do anything when that happens; Judge Neirn and I will tell them everything important, get it all straight."

She fixes her eyes on Katherine's skull. As if by staring hard enough at the woman's head she can convince herself it's at all true.

"Got that, Katherine?"

Katherine's eyes finally meet Anderson's with a look of hope somewhere deep within them, faint and small and weak. Already, an image of one of the perps taking George's car keys is drawing itself into Katherine's memory. Like a tiny seed putting out shoots. It is true, it is true, Anderson thinks. It could be true, so it might as well be.

"Good.

It's going to be okay," Anderson says. "Trust me, Katherine."

Katherine nods.

13.

THERE SHOULD BE a punchline to that memory. George recovers from his injuries, comes round from surgery to tell Katherine he's leaving her for his true love, his dentist. It turns out George hired the perps to juice Katherine. It turns out Katherine hired the perps to juice George, only the commission got subcontracted and catastrophically miscommunicated. It turns out Katherine's mum, dad, granny, kid brother and childhood pet dog died in one of the RTAs George caused. The cost of a new car plus the increase on their car insurance premium leaves George and Katherine behind with the rent, on the edge of divorce and ultimately homeless.

Nope.

The surviving perp was already wanted for a similar hit job, is serving a deserved life sentence in the cubes. Neirn and Anderson strike up a friendship. George and Katherine have a bouncing baby boy. Nobody finds out what Neirn and Anderson did.

Sometimes, very occasionally, things have a genuinely honest-to-Grud happy ending.

14.

Really.

Well.

Let's go back to those multiple RTAs that began it all, if we may? A few people might have died or been injured and the very least had to spend a lot of credits on a new car and been ruined by the massively increased insurance premiums, possibly, do you think? If you want to go very deep down and dirty, one of the perps might as well be dead, since he's looking at life in an isocube and he also has a wife who might as well be a widow now, and the other perp is literally dead, leaving a wife who's a literal widow now and five already born and they love him and he loves them kids. Or do they not count? Just not part of the story we're telling here? In Anderson and Neirn's story, there was a genuine honest-to-Grud happy ending and that's where this story is leaving it? A good, warm, happy place for Anderson. The End, and ignore the rest.

15.

"OH, HOW CHARMING. *How delightful. What a cosy memory, Andersssson. You mussst be ssso proud of that one. Thank you for ssssharing it. I'm ssssure the memory will keep me warm on cold nightssss. And a little baby! Don't tell me: they named it Casssss?*"

SHE'S SITTING IN the Grand Hall of Justice cafeteria. A round formica table, a spindly-legged chair. Caff stains in rings that make her think of the rings of Saturn. A pile of napkins, a bottle of sauce with a brown crust on it. Her cup has an old chip in the rim.

So it's been... She's been trying to make sense of time. It was dark, then it got lighter, more people came into the Hall of Heroes to pay their respects, a few last Judges and some tech guys, then it got dark again. So she'd guess she's been here twenty-four hours or so. Time seems to pass as slowly as Boing® flows. Judge Neirn came to visit her, stood looking at her a long time. (She thinks bitterly: two minutes? Three? Long enough for her to feel he should have got old and grey in front of her, so maybe as much as four minutes.) She tried to make him notice that she could see him. He didn't. Notice, that is. Realise she could see him. Judges Ho and Yakob came for a while too, shortly before the lights went off. Shuffled awkwardly around her coffin, then fled.

She was hoping going into a good memory would pass some time, give her… hope? Turns out memories don't last as long as the reality. Like those dreams where you've lived a whole alternate life then wake up to find it all took place in the time it takes to hit snooze. She knew that, obviously, but… hope?

"Shut the drokk up, creep. That memory was private."

She can hear his grin. "*Nothing issss private in here, Andersssson. I can ssssee… everything.*"

Cue image of Judge Death handcuffed to a lamppost with a traffic cone on his head.

"*Oh, very witty, Andersssson.*"

Judge Death is sitting opposite her, also playing with a cup of caff she assumes he has no intention of 'drinking.' Or is he enjoying pretending he can eat and drink like a normal living person in this world in her head? He looks like Death again.

"*I enjoyed coffee while I wasss alive, I'm perfectly entitled to enjoy it now I'm dead. I don't hate the requirementsss of life, Anderssson. Only the crime of living.*"

"What the drokk does that mean? Never mind. And I thought I made myself clear about that stupid voice."

"*Oh, Anderssson.*"

"Look, you gruddamn creep, you can look like that if you insist on it. Grud knows it's not much worse than you looked when you were alive. But we're in my head and that voice stops. Got it?"

He says nothing. Waggles his fingers at her. That's worse than the drokking voice.

The voice is merely creepy-crawly. The fingers, the grin, the way he moves—it's… obscene. Almost… suggestive, Grud help her. She wants to rinse her eyes out with hot water and soap.

"*A cup of coffee isssn't a crime, Anderssson. Blamelesssss. Unlesss one thinksss of the little darlingssss who harvesssted the coffee beansss for ssslave wages. In which cassse, a cup of coffee isss positively rank with children'sss blood.*" He raises the cup. "*And therefore a pleasssure to drink.*"

"It's synth-caff. It's made in a factory by machines."

"*And thussss the little kiddiesss had no income and their whole familiesss ssstarved?*"

"Grud! Just shut up."

"*But I wassss enjoying thisss debate.*" He flashes that grin. She can taste the rot between his teeth. "*Fire, Fear and Mortissss are fine fellowsss. But not perhapsss given to deep thoughtsss about mattersss of life.*"

She opens her eyes. Tries to stare at the patterns of darkness on the Hall ceiling.

"*You can't deny it'sss an interessting quessstion, Anderssson. Issss it better to sssuffer and live or to ssstarve with dignity?*"

She closes her eyes, snaps back to the table at the cafeteria. "You want to debate moral issues with me?"

"*We have eternity, Anderssson. What elssse isss there for usss to do?*"

Drokk, drokk, drokk. He's just as bored as she is. And this is his way of trying to make time pass *marginally* more quickly.

"Almost anything. Your voice is getting worse."

"*Iiisssss iiiiittt?*"

She drinks her caff.

"*Iiiiiiissssss iiiiitttt, Aaannnndersssonnnnnn?*"

She drinks her caff.

"*Aaaaaannnddddderrrrsssssonnnnn?*"

Don't rise to it. Don't. Just ignore him. It. Sit here. Lie here. Think about, um, kittens. Daisies. Needing a pee. That's it! Concentrate very hard on how much she needs to scratch her nose and have a pee. Puddles of deeper darkness on the Hall of Heroes ceiling, texture of the dark, there's a million shades, a million details and worlds up there in the dark if she looks long enough and hard enough. Faint currents and eddies of darkness. Layers of darkness.

"I'll kill that child, Anderssson. Little Cassss, or whatever its name isss. Sssteeped in sssin before he wasss yet conceived. You'll sssssee."

The shifting sense of her own body. A click in her left ear when she swallows, her tongue on each of her teeth in turn, a new complex awareness of the tides in the muscles of the shoulders. She can imagine she's aware of her fingernails growing. Every strand of her hair. She thinks hard of the sense she has of her body as something alive.

"One of my firssst victims, I think. Asss you were ssso kind asss to sssuggessst him to me."

Her toenails, the gnarly one on her big toe in need of clipping. An itch on her nose. Period cramps. Will her roots grow out?

"I mussst confesss, Anderssson, when I stepped through from the charnel house of my Deadworld into this Mega-City One of yours, I felt briefly... What's the right word? Perturbed?

"After the beauty of my Deadworld, it seemed so unutterably depressing, its inhabitantsss ssso caught up in trivia, I wasn't entirely ssssure it wasss worth the effort. I wasss sssorely tempted to turn around, go ssstraight home.

"My fellow Dark Judgesss argued I was making a mistake coming here. Mortisss wasss posssitively upssset, poor chap. 'We've got it all sssso nice here finally. All that work, and it'sss paid off in the end. Why would we want to leave now it'sss done?'

"I remember my mother asssking my father the sssame thing about moving houssse when I wasss a child, I wasss inclined to agree with her, for once.

"It turned out we had to move becaussse he'd filled the garden up. Run out of ssspace for his vegetables. But we didn't know that at the time, of courssse. If the poor man had only sssaid...

"But I digressss. That was in another world, and besssidesss my mother and father are dead. It's been a while sssince I had a fresh pair of earsss to talk to.

"I travelled through time and ssspace to reach your world. The marvelsss, the wondersss, of modern technology! And there I

wasss, on the ssstairsss of sssome decaying old tower block. I'd had no ssstrong preference for what I'd find when I ssstepped out of my world into yoursss, yet the place I found myself in wasss rather more depresssssing than I'd hoped. I will admit to sssome disssappointment.

"And then, behind me, on the ssstairsss... sssomething I hadn't heard in a long time. Breath! Breathing! A music I'd long longed for and long missssed. Alasss, asss you found, it wasss over far too quickly. A man that sssteeped in sssin—I ssshould have known he'd be a failure in death as well asss life.

"But the nightclub, the lovely young thingsss, the boysss and girlsss I met there—briefly—that wasss when I realisssed how right I wasss to come to your Mega-City One.

"I'd got into a ssslump, I think, after I'd finissshed crafting my Deadworld. A very beautiful place but... the more I think of my Deadworld, the more I begin to think it'sss the journey that mattersss more than the dessstination. I realissse that I wasss... anxiousss about coming here. It wasssn't until I killed that pretty girl I realisssed how much tensssion I'd been holding. I hadn't killed anyone for yearsss, I realisssed, and I'd been beginning to worry I'd—

"Don't laugh, but I was beginning to worry I might have lost the knack of it.

"So many millions I'd killed—and I'd been nurturing a fear, difficult ass it isss to admit it, that I might be out of practissse.

"It sssoundsss absssurd now, but imagine how embarrassing it could have been. You travel through time and ssspace, acrossss dimensionsss, make landfall on a new world crying out for Judgement, and disssscover you've got russsty. Forgotten the movesss. Out of practissse. I would have died of ssshame if that had happened. Figuratively ssspeaking. I had hoped that killing was more like riding a bicycle than learning a foreign language, but you can never be sssure until you're sssure. Sssuch a relief, when it turned out my concern wasss unfounded. If anything, I really think I might have improved my technique. Benefitsss of a good ressst.

"*What a little worry head! as my poor mother usssed to sssay.*"

"*I am looking forward to exploring all the opportunitiesss your world offersss, Andersssson. Ssso many crimesss calling out for Judgement. A proper tessst.*"

He finally falls silent. Thank Grud. Before he can start up chuntering on about death again, Anderson says flatly, "Your 'improved technique' didn't exactly get you far, did it?" She makes an attempt to wiggle her left foot. Her manky big toe can just about flex inside her boot. "Yeah, together we can butcher the whole drokking city, creep. Talk about a reign of terror."

"*I'll get out of here sssoon enough…*"

Silence.

She says after a while, "And I've been thinking. You said we have eternity, yes?

"*You've* got eternity in here, creep. I've got, what, three days? Four days? Then I die of thirst. And you're stuck in my corpse."

A flicker of pleasure runs through him. "*Ssssuch sweet thingsss you sssay, Anderssson.*"

"I'm serious. I'll die. I can't drink or eat. Grud knows, I'll die of *toe-cramp* pretty soon, if that's a thing. When that happens, you'll be here in my head. Completely alone. My eyes won't work, my mind won't work. You won't have anything."

Silence.

"*Good.*" She can feel—taste—the hesitation. The fear. The horror. In Death's voice.

"You'll be dead in every way that counts. Far more than you pretend to be dead now. I mean, you can walk, talk, kill, make bad jokes, you can obviously feel emotions. That's not strictly how I'd define 'death,' and I've seen quite a few people die in my time as a Judge. I've been there at the moment of a person dying—and, believe me, it *ends*. It's horrible. Actually, scrub that, it's not horrible, because that suggests there's something there. But there isn't. Death's just… nothing. Just emptiness. A void, where there was joy or pain or horror or happiness. Like the world's been demeaned.

"You're not dead, Judge Death. You're not a void, you're full to bursting with feelings and enjoyment. This whole thing is an… an act. A game. You're no more dead than I am. A stupid little man making an absurd pose he can't possibly understand. Have you ever felt someone's mind as they die? Seen through their eyes? The grief when all that… that *being*… that possibility to *be*, to *do*… Grud, I don't know the words for it… but when it ends and there's just… nothing. I've felt that. I know what that means.

"You don't have a drokkin' clue what death means.

"But in a few days… you'll have a better idea what it means to be dead. You'll be able to think and feel still, I grant you. But that's it. You'll have nothing but boredom. Your entire universe will be my dead brain. Forever. For all eternity.

"In a few days, Death.

"A few days."

16.

A LONG SILENCE from Judge Death.

"*...I...*

"*...That isss...*

"*...I mean...*"

The human voice, little Sidney who's scared of the world: "That's... I mean... I mean..."

She says, "Are you frightened by that thought, creep?"

She says, "You should be. You're not nearly frightened enough."

She says, "I'm glad you're frightened."

Little Sidney, so scared of the big wide world full of life and light and living, so scared of everything. So insecure about himself. He sits at the table opposite Anderson, old enough to be in a Judge's uniform but still a kid inside, struggling and failing at this thing called 'being grown up.' You take responsibility for stuff, Anderson thinks. Like I did with George and Katherine. That wasn't easy—if anyone had found out it wouldn't just have been me and Neirn with our necks on the line, they'd have come down on Katherine maybe worse for going along with us. I broke the Law to uphold it, I lied, I mucked around in someone's head and I do feel guilty about it, and that's what being a human being is. Mess. Shame. Guilt. Hope.

And you...

Nobody will come and fix it for you, Sidney. You killed everyone in your world to stop you having anyone to be scared of, and now there's no one to make it all better. No one you can feel superior to. And this is all you'll ever have now. Being stuck in my dead braincase. Alone with yourself for all eternity. No distractions, nothing to see or hear or touch, just yourself, your thoughts going round and round in circles, forever and forever and forever and forever and forever and forever and forever and forever and forever and forever and forever and forever and forever and forever and forever just you, your memories of yourself.

How much that thought terrifies you.

THE CAFETERIA VANISHES. Eternity stretches out brilliant around them. Anderson is enormous. A giant, towering over Sidney; the moon and the stars and the sun are caught in her hair, for she is taller than the moon and the stars and the sun. She shines, a light like the sun indeed surrounds her; a perfume; radiance like the storm wind. In her eyes such power and knowledge. She is as the tempest, the holy fire burns from her eyes, she is as the world destroyed and remade awakening in golden brilliance, the world renewed, filled with wonder. She is as a god.

Sidney is... nothing.

He knows. He's always known. Sad-sack Sidney. Mr Scared-and-Weak.

She sees him as a child, snotty nosed and afraid. Sees him kill his father, his sister, his mother. He knows he despises his father almost as much as he knows his father despises him. Mutual loathing: why couldn't you be better than this? He knows his mother and his sister love him. He knows how sad he makes them feel.

She sees him with his two lovers, the sisters who call themselves Nausea and Phobia. Sees how afraid he is of them, that they'll break his heart, that he loves them but they don't love him back and they'll abandon him. How desperate he is to impress them. The things he does, the humiliations he endures, the horror of what he's trapped in, attempting to impress them.

How disgusted he is by them.

But who else, he thinks—fears, dreads—who else would ever want him?

He goes along with what they do, because he's scared to say anything.

Pathetic. He doesn't want to hurt them.

Anderson is whole universes, she towers over him to fill up all the sky. Stars and suns and moons are atoms of her being, she is life without beginning or end. Sidney cowers, huddled, the light in her strips him away. He begins to cry. As if she could return him to his past. Make a world for him where he could just be an ordinary, bored, dull little man called Sidney De'Ath, with an ordinary, sometimes-good-sometimes-frankly-rubbish life. Bicker with his partner. Moan about the neighbours. Scrub the mildew off the toilet window. Put the bins out.

Drokking *live*.

She reaches out her hands that are themselves vast, teeming worlds. Animals, plants, forests, oceans. Lush drifts of stinking rotting summer green.

Perhaps in this world in her head she could give him a chance at a new rubbish, dull, ordinary life.

She thinks, in her omnipotence over him, that she might even pity him. Want to help him. His father hurt him. His world hurt him. She can understand that. Hears him so clearly in her head, a child, crying out in pain, frightened, wounded so deep.

She—

She—

That pity for him is where it all goes wrong.

* * *

"YOU'RE JUDGING *ME* now?" Little Sidney, shaking scaredy voice, whining, trying to sound cocky and failing so bad it's painful, don't hurt me, please, Mummy, Daddy, please don't.

And timid: it's unnerving, talking to a lady. She's got, like, ladybits and everything. Under her uniform.

"No. Not judging…"

"But you, you see something… You…" Like a dog that's been whipped its whole life. "You see something… something worth helping… worth caring about?"

Astonished, almost: "In me?"

Wheedling. Desperate now. Too scared to believe it. But there's a note of… hope? Someone might care. What a difference it would have made if someone, one person, had cared about him.

She says, "I suppose I—"

She says, "I suppose—"

She says, "I… yes?

She says, "Yes."

"Really? You mean it?" Grud, he sounds like a kid when you've said they can have an ice cream.

"I—"

Pity's too easy though, she thinks.

"Not… care… I—Well—"

"You care? You pity me?"

"I—"

"*You pity me, Andersssssson?*"

Blank page.

Nothing.

Darkness like a disease.

THE SHADOWS COME to meet her. Darkness roaring painful beating fury, crashing over, over, over and she can't think or see or hear or be and all she is is drowning in his pain and her pain and darkness, endless nothing, all is shadows, nothing, the darkness of the void. Phantoms, sickness—that's all she is. Her own words thrown back at her. Her horror and fear of death.

And his, which is far worse.

"*I destroyed a world, Judge Anderssson. You ssstill can't comprehend that, can you? The enormity of what I did. What I am.*"

His teeth close as a gate shuts to block the light and can never be reopened. Grim, remorseless death. His voice rings out to her.

"*What I will do.*"

She's on the floor at his feet. He's like the night sky when she stares up and she can't sense the life there because there's nothing there indeed, only the crushing emptiness that will outlast all life. Beyond death, now, even. Beyond living and dying. Merely the absence of life.

His weight comes crushing down on her. She throws her hands up to try to shield herself from breaking. As when the storm waves crash over a single figure swimming, sweep it effortlessly thoughtlessly away. As when a bomb falls to bring down a tower block, and a child thinks it can ward off ruin by holding its arms over its face. Everything is shattered. All is ashes. All is dust. Curled into a ball, arms and legs pressed, head buried, trying, failing, to keep the sense of her mind, herself, her flesh and her skin. She is only dust. Never lived.

"*Oh, yesss. Yesss, Anderssson. That'sss how it isss, yesss. You do sssee.*" But the voice smiles so sweetly, so happy: "*But not for you, I think. For you, Anderssson, I will make an exception. You want to die to trap me. And you're quite right, of courssse: waiting out eternity in your dead body would indeed be… boring. Not quite the kind of living death I ever envisaged for myssself. Oh, yesss, I admit, I may be sssomething of a hypocrite there, death—as in* being *dead—isss not sssomething I am essspecially keen to experience.*

"*You don't ssssee not far enough. Sssuch a lack of visssion.*

"I am Death, Anderssson.

"I won't let you die."

THE VOID THAT was briefly Anderson thinks: I was never alive to die. All I am is ashes. All I ever was. Sin and filth—rightfully wiped out. But her eyes open, she stares up at the ceiling of the Hall of Heroes, a new day's dawning pollution-sky rose-petal pink and lovely, her eyes track a flicker of movement. An old Judge with grey hair has come in to draw back the curtains. Neon lights blink on off on off on. Her lungs heave to suck in air through the plastic. She can hear her heart beating. Feel her blood rush like the rosy dawn in her fingers.

Her stomach rumbles.

"*You'll ssstay alive, Anderssson.*

"*Asss you ssso rudely pointed out, I am Death, but I am not dead. The bessst of both worldsss.*

"*You, on the other hand…*

"*You will be alive in all the waysss that matter. You'll feel hunger, thirst, ssorrow, boredom, dissscomfort.*

"*But asss far asss the world outssside your head is aware, you'll be dead.*"

The grey-haired Judge is wiping the dust off the exhibits. Stands deep in thought in front of Judge Hurst's uniform, very carefully adjusts the left shoulder pad. Puts his head on one side, readjusts the left shoulder pad, then the right shoulder pad, then the left shoulder pad. Nods in a way that suggests deep satisfaction. A bike convoy must be heading out down the road outside the Justice Department; headlights dance across the ceiling in stripes of light and shade that make Anderson think of long, loose hair. Something in the look of the headlight beams and in the colour of the light from the windows, something makes her think it might be raining. The grey-haired Judge cocks his head, listening to a roar of engines that Anderson can't hear.

Something big's going down, she thinks. A few days ago it was Judge Death. Now that's done and forgotten, something else has hit the Meg. She's aware suddenly of movement coming towards her: Winstanley, a styrofoam cup of caff in his hand; he approaches her coffin, stops. His fingers dig into the cup. Grud, she's always hated that sound of styrofoam breaking, makes her teeth stand on edge. He looks down surprised to discover he's sprayed caff onto his uniform sleeve. He too seems to listen to something, turns and hurries out of the room. A beam of light from the window illuminates the dust motes swirling in his wake. She can almost taste the caff and the lumps of styrofoam. That smell of crumbling styrofoam when it gets in your teeth.

She tries to close her eyes, but she can't close her eyes. Her mouth is so dry, her nose itches, she needs to pee so bad it hurts. An odd sweaty feeling in her frozen body that's kind of but not quite like—maybe worse than—the sweat you feel when you've been in bed a long time ill. She stares up and she stares up and stares up and stares up and stares up at the Hall of Heroes ceiling, light beams and headlights and dust motes move and sometimes a shadow, and once someone she doesn't recognise comes in and goes away. She gets a strange mad need to crack the top joint in her right thumb. A million years seems to pass. So… ten minutes? Fifteen? Dear Grud, she's hungry. She's totally unable to move, but somehow her uniform seems to have got crumpled, a ridge of cloth pressing into the back of her left knee, her belt rubbing—she can't *move*, how in Grud's name can it be *rubbing?*—against a knot of bone she never knew she had but is suddenly aware of as about twice the size of Texas in the middle of her lower back. Fifteen minutes? Twenty?

Twenty-five? That's almost half an hour more out of the rest of eternity. Twenty-five minutes must have passed by now?

Please?

17.

THEN SHE'S BACK in the cafeteria, Death opposite her, smiling with steepled fingers, and it's worse. He's set her up at the table with a cup of caff and a water jug and a plate of food. Pours her a glass of water. Splashing sound like a knife in the bladder as he pours. It's not real water, or caff, or food. She can chomp it down all day and it won't assuage her thirst and her hunger.

"*But that's life, Anderssson. You eat and drink and sssoon you feel hungry and thirsssty again. You sssleep and wake and sssoon you're tired again and might as well not have ssslept.*"

Don't speak to it. Don't take the bait.

Now she can't open her eyes.

"*You pissss and pissss again until you've pissssed your life out.*" He raises his own glass like he's making a toast to her. "*I thought you liked life, Anderssson?*"

Or she *won't* open her eyes. Can't bear to see the real world, the cobwebs on the Hall of Heroes ceiling, the play of light. Tears leaking down her face.

I saved the world, I won, really truly, think of children, flowers, friends, normal people not being dead, going on living, it was worth this worththisworththisworththisIsavedtheworldIwonIwonIwon.

Judge Death smiles.

"*Oh, I do enjoy hearing these lovely ssstories you tell yourssself, Anderssson. So... cheering. Brings a new warmth to my poor weary old bones. Almossst remindsss me of the ssstories I used to tell myssself when I wasss a boy. Sssometimes, you know, you almossst remind me of my younger ssself.*

"*I do mean it, Anderssson. You underssstand, don't you?*

"*I will keep you alive. You and me, trapped together, forever. I assume it will start to get rather boring, yesss. For you, anyway. You'll be almossst like I am. Not quite alive, but not quite dead.*

"*Except that every day, every minute, for all eternity—you'll missss your life.*"

He breaks off. Smiles. Behind her closed eyes, Anderson feels the light change as a shadow falls over her coffin. Death almost cackles at her. "*Isss that another one of your friendsss come to say hello? How popular you are, I had no idea you were ssso... loved.*" She tries not to open her eyes. Not looking, not looking, not looking, I can't bear it, not to see someone else, that sorrow in their eyes, that reminder of my life. Her eyes snap open as she thinks it, she's staring up at Psi-Judge Saleemi, caught in the act of placing a bouquet of plastic flowers over Anderson's chest.

Anderson screams with her mind, "Judge Saleemi! Henna! I can see you! Can you hear me? Listen! Henna! Hennaaaa!"

Saleemi cocks her head. Her eyes widen. For a moment it seems as if Saleemi hears her. Realises Anderson is alive and able to communicate. A ghost voice, and Anderson is so certain it's Henna's not her own imagination: "Cass? Is that you?" Then Henna Saleemi shakes her head like she thinks she's deluding herself. Like she'd hoped so hard she could break through the Boing® to reach Anderson that now she's managed it she refuses to believe it's true. Reaches out her left hand, almost touches Anderson's coffin. Shoulders sag, whole body seems to bend with a weight of grief on it, walks away.

"Come back. Henna. Judge Saleemi. Please!"

At the edge of Anderson's vision Henna does stop, cocks her head again, again Anderson's so sure Henna can hear her and is almost about to say something back. Then the Psi-Judge is gone. Anderson's body slumps against the plastic. Her hands hurt like she's been pounding them against a wall.

Saleemi never thinks enough of her abilities. So kind and unassuming. "Oh, no, you can't mean me."

That's the reason Anderson likes her so much.

Maybe she'll come back tomorrow. Or tomorrow or tomorrow or tomorrow after that. Then she'll hear me. But Anderson knows in her heart that Henna came to fix her memories, pay her respects, say goodbye. Won't come back. Henna's not the sort of person to linger over the dead.

Her stomach rumbles.

She lets out a fart she can't hear or smell.

Will it be better or worse, she thinks, when they all stop coming?

Cobwebs on the Hall of Heroes ceiling. Dapples of light—or damp in the ceiling tiles?

She imagines dust and cobwebs over her coffin. Burying her deep.

"*You'll alwaysss have me, Anderssson,*" Death says. "*Don't worry.*"

Grud. Just shut up.

He sniggers.

"Really, honestly, you don't think winding me up is going to get at all dull?"

He shrugs in that horrible obscene way again. Spreads his teeth so the cafeteria lights gleam on them. "*I'm sssure given time it will become more tediousss than either of usss can imagine.*"

"So stop doing it, creep." She thinks about kittens, puppies, pastel colours. Got the distinct impression pastel rainbow glitter kittens really bother Judge Death.

Which is logical but… not in any way logical as well. I mean, they're just animals. No more 'alive' than… than beetles or rats or something.

Anyway. She grits her own teeth, thinks of frolicking kittens and puppies.

"*You don't think that will quickly become equally tediousss?*" Judge Death snaps.

"You can end it, creep." False bravado.

Sort of. Partly.

She thinks bleakly then: if I give in to a desire to die… he's won.

It has won, she thinks. Stop thinking of it as human.

Death raises his glass again and again he's back to looking like any Street Judge she might walk past in the Justice Department corridors without noticing to give him the time of day.

It, she thinks. It.

"Mr De'Ath," it says politely. "Sidney."

"You really think this is going to keep you entertained for the rest of human existence? Civilizations rise and fall, continents collide, the sun burns itself out, and we go on, verily until the very heat death of the universe you'll keep me alive—so you can pass the time winding me up?"

A long silence. Sidney flashes her a boyish smile. Rumples his hair, fiddles with the collar of his uniform.

"Maybe… maybe you're right. Cass. Cassandra. Maybe we've… got off on the wrong foot. It's been a long time since I've been around the living. I fear I may be forgetting my manners. You've told me such a nice story about your life as a Judge, and I'm sure you have many more stories you can tell me. I'll listen. Promise not to make any further rude remarks. Behave like the nice respectful young man my mother raised me to be. I'm sure we can be friends in time. I might even learn something from you. Mend my ways."

Pain closes over Anderson.

Blankness.

White.

Nothing.

She can't feel to scream.

"*But I think first it's my turn to tell you a story.*"

The picture fades to black.

Now she screams.

PSI

ANDERSEN

18.

Something to hold on to and help while away the days: day 2

A LONG TIME ago in a dimension far, far away, there was a Judge called… well, it's not strictly speaking his *name*, but for the sake of this story and the profound, symbolic lesson it's intended to impart, we'll cut to chase and call him Andersen. And he was a very nice, very ordinary man, and his world, while indeed far off in another dimension, was a very ordinary place very much like this one. And this is his story.

A story from the Deadworld. Don't tell me we haven't all been not-so secretly waiting for this.

Are you sitting comfortably? Good. Then I'll begin.

OUT OF THE darkness: light. Out of the light: pain. Out of the pain: the supreme wonder that is death.

That is how his world, at least, is remade.

* * *

On the edge of living. There. Look at it. Taste it. Red. Many of them are already wounded. He can smell it, feel it. The blood hangs in their veins slowly. Makes him quiver with need. Their bodies are pain are blood; their skin is weeping. Rot-hope-death feel. Eager. So close now, coming to him, and he will take them. Show them.

I am the Death-Bringer. I am the decay of weak, mortal flesh. I am your Judgement. I am your Redemption. Ah, I will show you what it is to be blessed.

Curl his teeth around the words. Caress them. He is killing and he is dying and he is long dead and fallen to dust and ruin and it is so very sweet.

Ready. Death licking at his enemies. Rot spores blooming down the blade of a knife. Where his body touches living flesh, the two melt together, gripping each other, embracing, flesh metal, flesh corroding, making new wounds, his victim crumbling, falling. His enemies are encased in armour, encased in meat, rotting, their hands curl around gun triggers, knives, nails out to rip. Flies swarm over them, crawl across their armour, one of them pushes back his head, lets them come down on his face soft as rain. Breed in him! The living face is black with fly swarm. Then the flies and the maggots themselves die around him. Like ashes as a building burns, the flies bloom and fall and die as the loving man dies.

He did this. All he touches must wither and die. There is nothing he cannot corrupt.

He would so much like simply to wander, embracing, touching, killing. He knows they yearn for him to bless them, touch them. But a crash and the air is crackling with gunfire. The ground beneath him is shaking. He can taste and smell fire and heat.

There. Oh, sweet wonders! Oh, sweet world that has such things as killing in it, only waiting for him! The enemies come!

A company of them, all red-faced from cleanness. On the edge between life and death. Their blood is too thin, too hot. Their skin and their armour is harsh raw-clean. Unpleasant. He once might remember that... locked-in feeling of clean smooth skin. The flies buzz in his ears. They will know, soon. He recites it, pants out the words: *I am the Death-Bringer, I am decay and ruin, I am the blight. I am your Judgement, I am your Redemption, I will show you what it is to be blessed.*

Life's Last Stand: Third battle

The Dark Judges will triumph and the world will be cleansed

"We got a gang-bang going on at the intersection of Cromwell and Moore. Calling all Judges: assemble at Thomas Squared Square."

"Meth-heads." Andersen sighs into his comm link. Thought of what's coming makes him want to puke.

He kicks his bike into action. Gloom. Yet more juiced-up wastrel kids. They tear each other's throats open, sometimes drokking *eat* each other, they're so strung out. The Judges are sent in en masse to deal with it before an innocent bystander gets involved and eaten, but usually the perps are so wacked on meth they can't see what's coming at them. Die in a hail of bullets with a vaguely surprised expression, like: *I've got this crazy idea like a stonking great big hole's just opened up in my head...*

"Newsflash: it has, kiddo. Two-inch armour-piercing titanium bullets tend to do that to a chap." Weeks, he's been rehearsing that line. Woah, it sounds as good as he'd hoped! (Perp presents as female, but still...)

Even in her death throes, the perp's whingeing: "...I wasn't... wearing armour..."

"No? What do you call this baseball cap?"

"But..."

Grudsake. How long does it take for someone's synapses to shut it? Kid can't have had more than two or three brain cells left in her head before the Lawgiver took the top of her skull off like unwrapping a birthday gift. He kicks the kid in the head, hard, then shoots her again at point-blank range because on top of gang-membership, possession of illegal substances and cannibalism, she's now guilty of damage to a Judge's boot.

Calls it on the comm. "Judge Andersen to Control: I'm at Thomas Squared Square, you can hold off those Judges. Got it all dealt with and clean."

"Copy that, Judge Andersen. Well done."

"It was nothing. Only ten of them. Frankly, a child could have handled it."

Frankly, he thinks, they *should* have sent a child. Waste of his abilities, dealing with stuff like this.

He heads back to his apartment. Evening coming; looks at the sky, dark and ragged, cloud-torn, there's a storm coming over the horizon, he thinks. The rain falls on the just and the unjust alike, or something, as a wise man once said. He presses the bike hard to get inside before the storm breaks. Hates getting rained on. The roadway stretches before him slick with oil and garbage, grinds beneath his bike's wheels. Smoke in the litter fields out towards the west where the sun is dying, some of the fires there are years old. Burning underground. Erupting. A burst of flames even now; he slows his bike to watch the fire thrust upward through layers of human life's detritus. Rush of white flames. Dancing columns of black smoke. Poisonous, searing heat even at this safe distance. Moans, cries of panic, as the people who live there flee. Garbage homes, whole garbage villages, go up like this sometimes when the old fires spread. Charred earth, yet more pollution. The filth erupts, burns, smoulders down again, and the inhabitants, those that survived, come picking their way back. What else can they do? he thinks as he watches them: What else could *anyone* do? Look to windward. Blink back the tears. Carry on. He hums to himself to the rhythm of the engine. *Smoke gets in your eyes/ And your lungs/ And that woman's/ unborn baby's/ lungs.* She's starving, big eyes follow his bike's passage, pinched face of someone who's never had a good life, for even one day. He presses the bike to go faster. Get away. Thinks again: what else can anyone do? As the sun sets, he's almost home in safer, richer pastures, white tower blocks with the last of the sun and the streetlights flashing on their roofs silver, like the towers are great bells ringing. His apartment's in their shadow. Aspiration, perhaps, to one day live high up in one of the white tower blocks that look like silvered bones. When the clouds come down, the very tallest are cut off from the world. Faces turned to see only the sky and the sun. He thinks often what a fine thing that would be. Not to have to look at it. The rain starts in earnest just as gets to the parking lot. Washes the filth of the litter-fields off his bike and his helmet. Which is a cliché, but a thing he cannot help but delight in. He stands fixed, watching in fascination as the last globs of meth-head brains fight the running water, cling on to his boot leather, resist, give in, are washed off. Cold hard rain, a rumble of winter thunder. Forecast said it would set in for days once the storm broke. He thinks of the pregnant woman at the roadside, caught between the fire and the flood. If she stays in the ruins of her garbage-village home, she'll burn, her flesh and bones charred and curled and blackening and melting away consumed to ashes, floating away like autumn leaves on a hot wind. Her smoke eating itself into other lungs. If she leaves, she could so easily die of cold out in the rain without shelter. Die begging blue-lipped for the all-consuming heat.

Beautiful paradox there, he thinks. There must be some way to resolve it. But if there is, he's not found it yet.

He gets himself some food, tries to relax a while before he goes to bed. Runs through tomorrow's to-do list. Do his laundry. Buy a birthday card for his sister. Buy biscuits for the office. Clean the fridge?

Andersen's young, but he's already one of the best Judges in the metropolis. Firm, but fair. Hardworking. His kill rate's coming on for ninety percent.

He's not one of those who dreamed of being a Judge since forever—a tad embarrassingly, his earliest career aspirations were gold-medal winning trampolinist (inexplicable, don't ask, he was, like, four), morgue attendant or, like every little boy ever, H-bomber pilot. That last dream died harder and slower, inevitably; there was a glorious two-year period when he was maybe eleven when it really seemed he and indeed the rest of his class would be able to go out in a blaze of glory, hopes and dreams very briefly fulfilled. Went as far as to mention it to his careers teacher, who to her great credit didn't quite laugh in his face. "Competition's very fierce, Andersen. You have to have triple A scores across the board for that. I'm afraid, looking at your predicted grades… Here: have a look at these leaflets I've got here. Might be a bit more realistic for you.

"More suited to your skillset, I mean."

English teacher.

Copy editor.

Social worker.

Street Judge.

Everyone gets the social worker and the Street Judge ones.

Nothing about running a funeral parlour, and there's something in the way she's looking at him, kind of… *scathing*… that makes him think there's not much point mentioning it. A childhood dream up there with the whole 'trampolinist' fantasy—being a trampolinist is probably more realistic, he thinks. What are the chances that someone like him would be able to do a job like that? He can hear the teacher's voice in his head already: "*With* your *predicted grades, Andersen?*"

He spends a long time diligently researching the different options, entry requirements, opportunities. Discusses it carefully with his mum. Copy editor looks promising. But in the end Street Judge offers a better career progression. So now, five years later, here he is.

* * *

HE'D CERTAINLY NEVER say he doesn't find the job satisfying. It may not be his life's passion, but he worked hard at the Academy and now as a Judge he takes the responsibilities he's been entrusted with very seriously indeed. If you do a job, you do it well and properly, as his mum always says. It's more just… Things are hard, seem to be only getting harder. He gives so much of himself and he cares so much to do what's right by the people he's working to help, but it never seems to end. So much of the society around him seems worse than it did when he was child. Darker, more violent, less caring. People are more selfish and less friendly. The world seems far more dangerous and complicated than it did when he was young.

He tries to raise this with his superiors in the Justice Department. They shrug. "You're a Street Judge, Andersen. You see the worst of our society. The violence, the chaos, the drugs. You don't tend to see the nice bits of the world in our job."

He tries to raise it with his sister. She's a hairdresser. When he describes his fears about the world to her, she looks astonished. "Ummm… no? The world's really not like that? You don't believe that? Do you?" Her eyes fill with tears. Real concern in her voice: "I had no idea you felt this way… I'm so sorry. That you feel like this."

He looks at his feet. She's *sorry?* The silence stretches away between them like it always does.

He's about to walk off when his sister says suddenly, "We had a really good childhood, you know? Really good. And I guess… maybe… the adult world's going to seem darker and bleaker and more violent, when you stop being a kid. Do you think that might be it?"

To keep her happy, he mumbles something non-committal like, "I guess."

These idiots, he thinks. Can't they see anything?

"I'm doing the brides' hair for a wedding on Saturday," his sister says. "Really nice couple. You can come as my plus-one, if you like. Might cheer you up?"

He agrees to go. Just to keep his sister happy: she looks worried about him and he doesn't want her to worry.

The brides are indeed a lovely couple, everyone's friendly and kind and nice. But he looks around him at the wedding and he can't… They don't understand! he thinks. They all seem happy, laughing, jokes about the patter of tiny feet… but…

You could be robbed and murdered, he thinks. Any one of you. Be the victim of some terrible crime that you'll never recover from. Any. One. Of. You. You, mother of the bride, crying as your daughter and her new wife cut the cake—a year from now your daughter could be killed by a meth head, I could be leading you in to identify her maimed body, anything could happen—how can you be happy, knowing that? You, the bride's twin brother, cradling your little son in his pageboy outfit—he could grow up to be a meth-head, a rapist, a drug-dealer, you don't know that he won't come to a bad end. I see it all the time. Every day, I'm looking at the dead and the dying and the criminals and the victims—and they're all ordinary people just like all of you. You must know this. It's on the TV every night. How can you… go on, knowing this? Block it out? I arrested a perfectly respectable-looking woman for speeding yesterday—how many people could she have killed if I hadn't stopped her? Look at your children and your friends; tomorrow or tomorrow or tomorrow, any one of you could commit a crime or suffer one, leaving you prostrate, grieving, broken—but you laugh and raise a toast to the happy couple like that doesn't matter to you.

Your lives are chaos. Horror. Corruption. How can you ignore it?

How stupid are you?

THERE'S SO MUCH crime, he thinks. Every night, every day, it goes round in his head, makes it ache. So much violence. I try my hardest to keep it back, keep you all safe. Can't you see, any of you, how hopeless it is? The more he looks at the world he lives in, festering, foetid, bloated with crime, the more he realises radical action must be taken. His commitment to his career as a Judge only grows stronger, brighter—yet, as the days and weeks pass, his work seems ever more hollow and without purpose. As he talks to his colleagues in the Justice Department, he becomes more and more determined to take a new approach. Break his city out of the high-crime, low-order cycle it's become stuck in, do things differently, challenge the establishment consensus. Make real, tangible changes to people's lives. Clean things up. Rebuild the city's respect.

But how? How? That's the million-credit question. He's one man, overworked and time-short. Sometimes he looks around him and it's like he's got ten years to save the world, maybe—tops—before it all goes straight to hell, and he wants to yell with frustration because he can see it all going up in flames before him and he doesn't know what to do. It's like a maelstrom in his head that he can't silence.

Even if he did find an answer, he thinks at night, lying staring up into the dark, tired and sad and too worried to sleep; even if he did know what to do—would it help?

No one seems to care. No one's listening.

"It's really not that bad, honestly," people keep telling him. "You're burned out, only seeing the negatives, you need a break, that's all. Take a few days' holiday." And the worst of all: "Well, no, obviously it's not like it was when we were kids. And thank Grud." Might be worse, sometimes, he thinks, if he did find a way forward, and no one wanted to hear it. A thrill of horror: he sees himself on a street corner shouting to the wind, while people bustle past, ignoring him. So much noise, so much chaos in the world that no one can hear him.

They're all so stupid. So ignorant. Sheep, he thinks. Not people. Sheep. He wants to help them, tries, every day he tries, and they throw it back in his face. Don't listen. *Won't* listen. He turns up at crime scenes, does his best to help, and they... they... His sister doesn't call him as often as she used to (she got sacked from her job at the wedding salon, and for some reason she blames him). He's even beginning to suspect some of his colleagues are laughing at him. He goes home and lies in bed staring up into the dark, and his life stretches ahead of him to his death, and no one ever listens.

Let them laugh! he thinks. Shortly afterwards he arrests a young woman for littering and it's the bride from the wedding, the one with the mother in the ugly hat who sobbed her way through the whole damned thing 'because it was so beautiful.' The satisfaction he feels can't be put into words here. He knew! Didn't he predict this?! From happy newlywed sunshine Mrs Oh-So-Nice-and-Kind-and-Everyone's-Happy-For-Her to felon in three months! Dropped a crisp packet, and those can be very slippery, especially in the wet weather they've been having recently, someone could easily have slipped over on it, broken their leg or worse. A moment's thoughtlessness and there's a little girl with pigtails or a little old lady on the ground bleeding, crying, in pain: let's see you smiling *now,* wedding guests!

He gets suspended from duty for a week while the matter's looked into. Judge Muqtadir expresses some deeply inappropriate views in private, but ultimately clears him. Andersen promises to be more careful in future. As indeed he is. A valuable lesson, and he senses that an idea is stirring… he feels it in the back of his skull, but when he reaches out it flits away beyond his grasp. He tries to give it time. Like a maggot, it needs to grow fat before he can pick it up.

But it's so frustrating. How? How? How? He's so near, but so far from an answer to his questions.

Life's Last Stand: Third Battle

He watches the enemy coming towards him

HIS HANDS ITCH to touch them. *Hunger* to give them his blessing. The enemy is forming a square. Straight-line ranks. Like unbroken bones. Like unbroken skin.

His hands itch and itch and he is almost drooling. They are alive, and very soon—mere minutes, perhaps—he could count the individual seconds they have remaining until they die, very soon, so soon, they will be dead. The astonishment of that is dizzying. Wonderful, almost beyond his ability to fully comprehend. They are alive, then with a touch of his hand—they will be dead. It is a mystery and a wonder, he thinks, that indeed very few can ever comprehend. It thrills him still. That moment of time between living and being dead.

Voices:

"Oh, Grud, oh, Grud, oh, Grud, I see them."

"Hold."

"I *see* them."

Gun fire. Rattles. Sounds like… teeth rattling. A screaming skull in a box.

Gunfire overhead, wide, at nothing.

"Hold. Wait."

"Oh Grud, oh Grud, I see them."

"No shooting. Wait. Hold."

"Wait!"

"I see them!"

Flesh wall of corpses. Clean fresh red-blood living men.

They are singing, they are sighing, they are waiting, on his hands the enemy's blood is already thick and corrupt and red. And the enemy begins to scream because it knows what is coming. Clean order breaking up. Hands on faces on bodies, adult men reaching to hold each other for desperate comfort. Weeping.

He steps out with his brother Dark Judges beside him. *We are death we are killing. We give this blessing to you happily, joyfully, despite your insistence on remaining our enemies.* The enemy wails at the sight of them. Stink of piss and faeces. Revolting: life stink. He sees smooth faces, man faces, all clean, uncorrupted, cursed faces and they are frightened, they are sickened at the sight of his face. They choke bile, they are afraid, and they see—ah! They see what a blessing it is he will give them.

He shoots his gun and many of them go down. Thrashing. Lifeless. So easy, too easy! Even before he was remade in death, he and his companions were never so weak.

"Shoot! Kill them! Take them!" Crackle of gunfire. Wall of gunfire, coming at him. Voices. Shaking. Trying.

"You see? We can hold them."

"Oh, Grud, oh, Grud, oh, Grud."

"Shoot! Shoot!"

He raises his gun, shoots back, bright shimmering sparkle-rounds of bullets. Beautiful red flowers blossoming. But there's such tedium in this distant killing. He wants to let them *feel* and *taste* their deaths. The moment of blessing is precious. Not to be wasted. After all, it can only be experienced once. To touch, to watch the life corrode away from a still-living body, eyes seeing, mind feeling its own self collapse into decay. That is truly what it should be to die. Death by gunfire must be so... so *dull* to experience.

He leaps at the enemy, hands outstretched. Their gunfire rakes his face. He reaches, brushes an enemy, gently, tenderly, the merest ghost of his hand against another's skin. Soft as moths. As cobweb. Savour it. A wound opens in the man's face. Dry. And the rot coming. The man falls screaming until the decay is in his throat and there is no flesh to scream. He closes his eyes, gropes his hands out, memory of a childhood game he loved to play. His hands meet what might be skin, armour, the hot metal of a gun. More rot, more scar tissue, more flesh corrupted. The movements of his arms stir up a breeze that blows dust into his face. Human ruin scratches in his dead eyes. Crunches between his teeth.

LITTERGATE PASSES AND is forgotten. Another few months drag by like a child on broken legs. He takes down another meth-heads gang. Again, questions are asked. Again, truthfully, as best he can—given he's still struggling himself to resolve the details—he answers them.

"I cut them into tiny pieces, Judge Muqtadir, to make sure they were properly dead. They were meth-heads, real criminals! I couldn't risk some deluded bleeding-heart medic trying to heal them."

"The baby had witnessed multiple drug deals, Judge Isaacs. I have reason to believe dealing was taking place in its primary residence: it had made no attempts to report said illegal activities to the authorities as the law requires. The law does not, contrary to whatever nonsense Judge McLean is about to come out with, make an exception for preverbal infants."

"Oh, really? Show me where it says that, can you, then? Not 'obviously it doesn't mean'—where it *says* it, in black and white. No? Told you so. Complicity in criminal affairs is a serious offense, Judge McLean, and always warrants severe punishment."

"I appreciate you have strong views on this subject, Judge Verbrugge. But the cat was also resident at the property, and thus clearly and unarguably complicit in all offenses carried out therein."

"The same applied to the rats and cockroaches, Judge Aujila, yes."

"And the woodworm in the understairs cupboard, Judge Ortez, that's correct."

Another week's suspension. This time on half pay. For killing meth-heads. Fools, he thinks! Idiots! Sheep! And the answer to all his questions is so close now, he can feel it, but the absurd questions they keep asking him are crowding out the answer he seeks. He just needs… needs…

He comes back from suspension rested, eager, ardent. Furious. On his first day back a call comes in for all Judges to scramble, a major emergency going down—but Judge Muqtadir is clear that Andersen's staying at his desk.

"Arson means a lot of paperwork, Andersen. All those kids… I need a good man to handle the forms. Do you think you can handle the forms?"

He looks at his feet. Spares Muqtadir the humiliation of not being able to meet his eyes.

Turns out the call was a mistake anyway. Not arson at all. He tries to feel pleased when Muqtadir comes back rain-soaked. But it starts getting obvious that he's not being sent out on the interesting calls. Seems to get a lot of meth-head fights to break up and not much else.

"The man was in the vicinity, wearing a hat that was concealing his face. I had multiple reasons to order him to stop so I could do a file check. There is nothing to indicate that he 'failed to stop only because he was deaf.' That's pure supposition on your part, Judge Muqtadir, and in no way supported by the evidence."

"What do you mean, 'He probably ran because he was scared out of his wits'? Why would an innocent man be afraid of a Judge?"

"Yes, but I checked and you could see my Judge's badge clearly through the blood."

When he looks in the mirror sometimes he barely recognises the face looking back at him. Looks tired and worn, grey and heavy. Almost lifeless. The job, he begins to think, is slowly killing him.

Maybe he should have been a copy editor, he thinks. There must be more hope in it. But being a Judge isn't a job, it's a vocation. Once you're in, you serve for life.

Despair overwhelms him. Even a huge meth-heads bust does nothing to raise his spirits. He looks in the mirror one night and it's like there's a skull looking back. Sad worn eyes, like some rough beast.

Life's Last Stand: Third Battle

The blessed are winning

He rips one of the enemy open, sees the heart and the lungs and the white bones, the red meat. The heart is beating, fluttering, the lungs rise and fall, wheezing last breath. He shudders, chokes on pleasure as the heart and the lungs and the pretty pink and white body corrode beneath his fingers. Crumble away as dust.

The power he has. To touch, to feel what is still living fall away into ruin—to know that *he* has done this. Panic on the face of the dying, then the man shudders also, eyes roll, tongue lolls, withers, pleasure accepting its fate. They enjoy their corrosion. Embrace, at the end, the wonder of the body's decay. *You should have done this sooner. I should have received this sooner. I wish, I wish…* Their bodies say this, so filled with ardour, every time he gives his gift to them. I wanted to, he thinks each time. Such sorrow. I wanted, I tried, believe me, I did. You realised too late. Fought or fled. Always, you reject my gift until the very last. Only then, at the end, do you see.

The gunfire is bright in his eyes, star-like and burning. Dry, searing, corrupting heat. He slices with his killing hands, sucks in blood that tastes clean and blood that tastes rotten. Tramples on a mountain of thrashing bloated limbs, black-green-red tongues lolling out. He takes one slowly. Caresses it. Delaying the consummation of its full collapse into death. He wishes, envies, *longs* to experience again the sweet feel of dying like that. What it would be, to die again and again and again… Watch. See it. Feel it. The slow thrilled tremor as the heart is rotted. The weakening, corroding limbs… He squats to be closer to the flailing body. Rubs his hands over the death. Watch. Wait. Count it: the last endless sudden rupture, from something almost living to closer, closer, closer, by increments, still almost living, living, living, closer, and then the vast gulf so sudden it still makes him dizzy at the wonder—closer, closer, it's coming, fast now, close, close—living—dying—dead. Gone.

Gunfire strafes his body. What? He almost cannot remember where he is or was.

No! Distracting! He tramples the body of his victim beneath his feet. Punishment.

Drew his attention from the killing. And that is wrong and must be Judged and punished, and this creature distracted him from the only true task. Gunfire strafes his body, his own dead flesh puckers, wounded, eruptions of flesh scarred and growing: but they are beautiful things, he thinks. He has reached his hands around himself, his fingers twisting to curl over his wounds, new blessed ornaments of death-gifts. He croons with pleasure, hammers his killing hands into an enemy body, parts it in its weakness and it is dead. His comrades behind him loose, and the enemy stumbles. His brother Judges beside him cleave at life, their bodies sticky, heavy with bloody death.

Living voice:

"Steady! Steady!"

"Hold!"

"We can take them! We can take them!"

"Oh, Grud. Oh, Grud."

He breaks an enemy's body. It is good, after his moment of distracted weakness. The putrescence of a welcomed death.

Gunfire in sparkling shimmering circles, maggot white pus white death white. More of the enemy falls away. He presses against a young woman lying wounded, their wounds touching, the rot of their bodies entwines. An enemy voice gurgles. Lashes out with the butt of a gun. A cavity of flesh erupts as he strikes it away.

Pleasure licks at him. His heart is singing.

METH-HEADS. DESK WORK. Valiantly he does battle with the office filing cabinet. At night he paces his room, struggles to sleep. Why? Why? How? What can he do?

Then suddenly, out of nowhere, everything changes.

He's hanging around the cafeteria to avoid Judge Muqtadir when a Judge he's never met before comes up to him. Young, maybe around Andersen's own age, lean, handsome, sharply dressed (how the same uniform can be all killer tailoring on some Judges, and a sack on… others, is another question Andersen fears he'll never find the answer to; if the mere thought of betting wasn't a crime and punishable with extreme prejudice, he'd bet a lot this guy never gets food stains down his front or his trouser seam wedged in his butt crack). To be honest, he's initially suspicious the guy's come to laugh at him. "*Here's a new biro for you, Andersen. When you absolutely, positively got to fill in every file in the room.*" He grits his teeth, readies himself. The guy waves to a young woman Judge in passing, she simpers back, Andersen can see it all about to unfold, same as. Ignore him, ignore him, ignore him. Gets up hoping to slink back to his desk and today's three-mile pile of paperwork.

But to his astonishment, the guy hurries over, greets him.

"Judge Andersen? I'm really excited to meet you at last," the guy says.

His badge says his name's Judge Fire. Which Andersen will admit is a curious name.

"I've been hoping for an opportunity to talk to you. You're not busy, are you? Do you mind if I sit down? Your record…" Judge Fire says. "Wow! I'm very impressed."

Andersen's mind… *boggles* is the only word for it.

"That shoplifting bust you did. The one where you blew up the mall. Damn."

Judge Fire… The name's ringing bells in Andersen's head. Beautiful silver bells, as pretty as the bells at that couple's wedding. Grud, almost as pretty as that couple's funeral bells.

"Can I get you a cup of coffee, my friend?" Judge Fire says. "I'd be honoured."

His mind… *boggles* doesn't begin to cover it.

"Umm… yes? Yes." Sits up straighter in his chair. His uniform feels more comfortable than it has done for months. They talk, and for the first time in years Andersen feels that someone understands him. Can put into words the feelings he's been struggling to articulate.

Better, even—to his astonishment, amazement, bafflement, joy and actually deep down inside no surprise at all, because hasn't he always, *always* known he was right?—Judge Fire says the same things about him. "I feel like… a new clarity in my head, talking to you, Andersen," Judge Fire says.

"That… that horror, looking at people in the street knowing tomorrow they might break the Law or have the Law broken over them. It drives me mad, lying in bed at night—if I'd stayed out on the street a little longer, been slightly firmer when I reprimanded some kid for littering, I could have prevented one more crime, chased down one more perp, saved one more person… It burns in me, like my skin's burning, my whole body… I can't sleep, thinking I should be out there on patrol. Not wasting time sleeping, eating, having a slash…

"You put it exactly right, Andersen. I never understood it before. So many people in this world and any moment, any one of them could do something horrible or have something horrible done to them. It's so frustrating that we can't do more. Stop it happening before it happens. Since we know it will inevitably happen."

Then Judge Fire says, "The things people do to each other… The things we've both seen. The state of the gruddamn world… It's not just individual crimes that need Judging. It's chaos that needs to end."

Andersen nods. He can see that suddenly and clearly. "It is," he says, "chaos that must be ended. Cleansed…" He can see it. He can see it like the dawn breaking after the bitter night. "That's what I've been trying to say to myself these long years."

It's beautiful. It really is like the dawn breaking in his head. Like it must be that moment when the bomb explodes and the pilot sees it a moment, just a moment, like a thousand suns rising at once.

"Life… is chaos," he says. "Crime… chaos… is inevitable… where… there is life."

He finds he's trembling. A door seems to open before him. He can see… through the door… just needs to make one final step.

The words are in his mouth. The final truth he's been looking for.

It's been in his mouth, in his head, the whole time, he thinks.

A skull in the mirror, smiling back at him. What rough beast is this? Why, I think I know his face…

Judge Fire says, "I think it's time you met a friend of mine, Andersen. Let's do a diary check and line up some possible dates."

Confused, excited, Andersen nods.

* * *

WHAT MUST HE be and what must he do, when he is not killing? His comrades, his fellow Dark Judges, his beloved brothers in death… He tries to remember, when they are not killing, they must be and do… something. He hears them, the living, sometimes when they are laughing, they find pleasure in other things and he finds that an insult and a thing he cannot understand or conceive. He was living once, before he was blessed and chosen, he must have done… done… something. He thinks: We are to kill. That is the only purpose. All else is waste. His comrades flicker around him. They are only the pleasure of killing. They also cannot remember other things. We are the knife, we are the sword, we are the death, we are the pain, we are the only joy, we are the end. We are nothing, he thinks, dust, husks, nothing, when we are not killing. What a merciful thing.

The ones he is killing, the living, the unconsumed, the undecayed… They think they are more than killing, more than flesh that will and must die and thus is already dead. Thus they must be killed, he thinks, because they are fools unfit to live. Corruption calls in his hands, laughing, red blood runs down the bones of his fingers. We are the blade, we are nothing but killing. We will teach them, show them. Press the gift of bloody dying on them.

The wounds opening in their bodies rejoice. He feels them. What is life but a wound that oozes corruption? Black flies swarm around his enemy, their guns, come down to die in drifts at his feet and the enemy's feet.

Life's Last Stand: Third Battle

The blessed are winning

HE HEARS LIVING voices crying. Keening. "Retreat! Pull back! Too many of them!"

Grief that they are leaving unsoiled. Contempt that they are afraid and retreating. Sweet joy rises triumphant within him. He cannot, does not, *will* not retreat.

"Pull back!"

"Oh, Grud, Grud, Grud."

"Too late."

"Pull back."

"Too late!"

Their fear is a perfume. White panic eats into their unbroken skin. Lash them, break them. Open them. They cannot remain untouched and unclean. He goes forward with his comrades. The living are calling him. Begging him. A body at his feet, thrashing, moving, a hand reaches out, a voice whispers something. He places his hands upon it, carves it open, makes of it a gift of love. Its mouth moves, its hand moves, clutching at his feet. It rattles a breath and the flies crowd in. It thrashes, screams, dies thanking him.

He presses out his hands, kills another, leaves another opened and wounded. A voice screams hoarse for surrender. He silences it. Flesh oozing out black liquid from a shattered body, running into the dust, watering it. Water of death, not life.

Living voices. Fading.

"Retreat! Get out of here! Now!"

"Too late. Oh Grud, too late!"

His hands are red and they are singing to him. Running red with putrescence. Melting flesh pooling around his wrists. He is nothing. Rot maggots murder. Blessed. Made holy. He gives such joy. Death-Bringer. Life's Judgement.

He is nothing but the killing. It is good. It is sweet. Here, killing, he feels at peace. He thinks, sometimes, remembers: what did we do, what was I, before… before… There must have been… something? A face, dying… It died, and it was gone into rot, decaying, blooming, sweetness rising from it. It was made good. He is only death. They're coming to him and he will take them. Show them what his blessing can mean. He's king of this, king of all this dying. His enemies cry out in acclaim as he kills them. He is a lord of slaughter; they yearn to be as he is. Children as yet unborn—in the womb they reach towards him, claw their mother's bellies open, in their yearning to be as he is.

On the edge of life. Red. Killing killing killing.

Voice. So few. So weak. "Fall back! Fall back!"

"Grud!"

He comes onwards, killing.

Life's Last Stand: First Battle

The Dark Judges drove the enemy back, defeated them

Life's Last Stand: Second Battle

The enemy brought gunships, heavy weaponry. Broke the Dark Judges' lines. Drove even the Dark Judges back.

Life's Last Stand: Third Battle

The Dark Judges, the blessed, the dead, break the enemy and consume the enemy, and life on this world will swift be ended

THE BLESSED ARE winning. The living are torn and opened, consumed by death. He breaks them. Consumes them.

He wades through ruin, soaks himself in human filth. Stands on a mountain of corpses, and the corpses crumble beneath his feet. And he kills and he kills and—and—there's—

nothing.

Left to kill.

He lowers his hands. Looks around him. All is destroyed. Only Fire and Fear stand waiting.

As is fitting, Judge Death stands over the last dying vestige of a human life. Rips into its heart and tears out its life force, raises it slowly, lets it fall and flop dead and empty to the empty and dead earth.

Fear says in ponderous tones, hushed, awed—dare he think it: frightened? "Thus the last crime was Judged."

The world has swift been ended. The four Dark Judges are all that is left. Murderers, Slaughterers, Beasts, Killers, Triumphant. Kings and Gods and Lords of Death.

Salvation. Didn't even take as long as ten years.

His heart singing sweet. His mind at peace.

Blank page.

Red blood fades to empty white.

19.

"*Enjoying it?*"

In her head, Anderson vomits across the cafeteria table. In her plastic coffin, Anderson retches, beats down the bile rising in her throat.

"*Mortisss told me this ssstory after we'd cleansssed our world,*" Death says. "*Told me how grateful he wasss for the direction I'd given him. Getting more and more depressssed, he told me, ssstruggling with the need for sssomething more in his life, before he found me.*"

There must be something Anderson can say in reply. Something—some curse strong enough, damning enough. But if she lets open her mouth to speak, she's frightened of what will pour out. She can hear a faint whimpering sound, far away, like a child in another room crying to itself, not wanting to be heard, smothering its tears. After a long time, she realises she's the one crying. The only noise she can make.

"*The bessst of them,*" Judge Death says. "*The bessst of the three. He'll never believe that. Sssuch a modessst, unassssuming man. Corpssse.*" He frowns at Anderson. "*Please tell me you're enjoying his ssstory? I know he'd be mossst upssset if you weren't. Never had any confidence around the ladiesss, it would be a blow to him if I had to tell him you found his ssstory boring.*"

Shut up, she tries to say. Spit it out, vomit it up on the tabletop. Into his lap. Shut up. What comes out is a sound like a laugh.

"*Oh I'm sssso glad I'm entertaining you. I'll carry on then, ssshall I?*

"*I confessss I do enjoy this ssstory myssself. Touching. Sssuch a good feeling, isn't it, when a friend tells you you've given them a boossst? If it hadn't been for me, I don't think poor Mortisss would be half the fiend he isss.*"

20.

A story from the Deadworld, part II

The true story of the strange death and stranger resurrection of Judge Mortis, as told to Judge Anderson by Judge Death

[So there might be a bit of bias towards Judge Death's point of view.

Maybe.

On occasion.

Once or twice.]

GRUD, HE WISHES he was Death. What a guy! What a hero! That jammy bastard Death has all the luck.

THEY KIND OF… tiptoe around it. Fire, Fear and Mortis. The three of them are younger than Death, admire him, you could go so far as to say *idolise* him, and that's only proper and right. He's the leader, the guru, their mentor in matters of crime and judgement. Named them—and Mortis knows he'd never in a thousand years have come up with a name as cool as 'Judge Mortis.' [Toyed with 'Judge Corruption' for five seconds or so before the obvious occurred to him; didn't mention it to the others, Grud be thanked]. Death's the head honcho. Numero Uno. The Big Cheese. The name alone is a giveaway, really. At the end of all things is... Death. Fire, Fear and Mortis are his lieutenants, his chosen, his happy few, his band of brothers—and that in itself is an honour sans pareil. All the world, and Death chose three to follow in his footsteps and one of those three was Mortis! That in itself, that Death chose him, Mortis, makes his head reel, is dazzling, baffling, wondrous. But...

It's awkward saying it, they usually try not to say it, but...

Grud, get it over with, say it, confess it, Mortis you coward. If this was a comic book, we'd be almost out of panels by now. Get on with it.

It's awkward, but... deep breath [yes, he can still breathe, he's not dead yet, feels more alive than he has for years, in fact], deep breath... he does sometimes feel a bit... cheesed off with Judge Death.

Death is literally dead. Thanks to Death's two beautiful demonic nymphomaniac witchqueen twin-sister-girlfriends Phobia and Nausea, who killed Death slowly and agonisingly over... well, technically it was over four days, but Death says it felt like a thousand years. Then brought him back to unlife again in the withered corpse his spirit had abandoned, raised him up monstrous, invulnerable, blessedly free of the impediments of life. A superfiend! And they, Judge Fire, Judge Fear, Judge Mortis (check that name! check that cool-as-drokk name! thrills!), they knelt in worship. "Arise, Judge Death," Phobia said, her voice heavy with emotion, curls of hair hanging long and luscious over her naked, heaving breasts. Or maybe it was Nausea who said it, he's not great at faces, often gets the two embarrassingly confused. Anyway, they knelt, hailed Judge Death their Lord their King their Master. Mortis had to restrain himself from kissing Death's skeletal feet.

"Well done that man!" The three raised a non-alcoholic non-caffeinated, sugar-free toast.

And now... Well, they don't say it, but by Grud they're envious of the old chap. The beauty of his new body. His skull-like face, his shrivelled flesh, his gaunt limbs. The smell rolling off him. He flexes long fingers. Casts a smile at Phobia (Nausea?) and the lady sort of... melts: "Oooh, Sidney, dear. Too much." There's a mostly complete, mostly dead body lying around that the sisters have been playing with. Judge Death strolls over—wobbly for the first few steps as he works out how to get his dead legs moving—reaches, digs in new-made claws, rips the last dregs of its life out.

Something like an electric shock goes through Mortis.

Imagine. Imagine. Being able. To do. That.

Fear nudges him. The same hunger on Fear's face. The same quivering. Longing.

JUDGE FIRE, THE most confident of the three of them, is the one to finally crack. Steels himself, swallows hard, marches up to Nausea. Clears his throat.

"Nausea... Would you do the same for us?"

Mortis recoils. He'd *never* dare talk to the sisters like that. Presumptuous. And as for asking... requesting... thinking you might be good enough, *special* enough to ask... for death...

But Nausea seems almost surprised he's felt the need to ask at all. Gives Fire a smile that even Mortis would have to call *dirty*. "Of course, dear." (And on a side-note she might be a beautiful nubile young woman living naked as the day she was born in a cavern deep underground piled high with bones and decaying flesh, but by Grud the way she talks reminds Mortis of a school dinner lady at times.)

"Be delighted to help you nice boys," Phobia says. "Who's first up?"

Mortis, Fear and Fire's hands leap up.

"Oh, deary." Nausea pouts, hands on hips. "I do love how eager you boys are about everything, but how's a girl to choose? Sidney, my sweet, do you have a preference for who goes first? No? Well, only way to decide then." Phobia points at the three. "Form an orderly line, boys. Right. Ready? Eeny, meeny, miney, moe..."

When she finishes

she's pointing

at Mortis.

FINGER JABBING AT his heart.

GRUD, HE CAN feel his heart beat.

ALMOST, KIND OF, wants to say 'wait.'

HIS HAND LEAPT up, yes, but it's a bit... sudden? One, two, three and he's sitting cross-legged opposite Nausea (Phobia?), who's holding a cup of poison out to him.

"Here we are, deary. Drink it all up like a good boy."

He swallows hard. Looks at Death, who nods approvingly. Tries to think: soon, you'll be as beautiful as him.

"Bottoms up," Phobia says. Then she says less kindly, "Come on. We haven't got all day."

"Death waits for no man," Nausea says. "Isn't that right, Sidney?"

Oh, Grud.

Oh, Grud.

He does say it. "Wait," he says. Only his mouth is so dry and he's shaking so badly it doesn't really come out and no one hears him.

He's dreamed of this moment. Can't deny it: his heart has long desired this. In the dark, staring up, running through his kills. The noises a child makes as his shoots it. The perfume that bursts from a dying woman's bowels. The wonder, dazzling to his mind: one day you too will be as they are. One day you too will know death. A thought that's kept him going, given him hope through long bitter nights when the walls close him around him like a cage. The anticipation. Counting down the moments. Squatting to catch the very second life stops and death begins. And every time it's as mesmerising as it was the first time he was witness to it.

Oh, don't misunderstand him: he's eager and willing. Just doesn't want to rush things. Feels a bit like prize day at school, when he got an award for neatest handwriting. Looked forward to it for weeks, wishing the days away, then his big moment happened and was over in about two minutes and it was like, "It's over now? That's it?" It's like a cliff edge in his mind. His death. His actual longed-for, long-seemed-impossible-to-realise, you-mean-even-someone-like-me-can-achieve it, it's-like-winning-every-school-prize-at-once *death*. Is happening. Now. This minute.

He'd have liked a bit of time to get his head round it. Savour the anticipation. Tell his sister the good news.

Nausea makes a clicking sound with her tongue that he recognises from his mother. Death drums his beautiful new fingers on a severed head.

"To a better world!" Mortis says. Louder than he meant. He blushes at the tremor in his voice.

Downs the cup.

"To death!" he hears his voice croak. "To death!"

* * *

It's more beautiful than he dared imagine.

He vomits. Bent and crying. Pukes until he's emptied out. In the dark a voice croons to him. Keep going. Purge out his life. Spit. Bile.

Blood.

He vomits blood.

Sweats blood.

That's the last thing he remembers clearly about living. Sticky sense of his body—sweat, soil, blood oozing, and the *smell*. It is. Disgusting. He cannot wait for it to end. Life is…

minging, as one of the meth-head kids he's busted would say.

After that it's fragments. Uncertain whether the memories are real or dreams. A woman's voice, very distant: "Come on," she's whispering. Or shouting? "Come on, you can do it. I know you can do this." A screaming, that's so high pitched it can't be him but he thinks might be him. No words to it, just pain. Terrible pain.

A sound like wet cloth ripping, and a great terrible sense of… of change.

"I want to die," he shrieks. No one seems to hear him.

"I can't do it," he shrieks. He's being ripped apart. His body is very dry, his throat is so dry the words croak out silently. His eyes are too dry and he can't see. Distant thunder, which he thinks—thinks—is—his own heartbeat. Fast as running feet, pounding down onto a roadway, chasing, running, hammering, crashing. The sound is huge. Shatters him. Leaves him shaking. Tries to cover his ears. His eyes. The sound is too much. Like the sound alone will drown him, kill him. Can't move. Can't block it out.

A voice says, "Don't fight it." That's the last voice he hears as a living thing. "Don't—" He screams and his body throws itself into coils. All sound but the thunder of his heart is gone. He can feel the speed of his heart racing. Sweating his body out, pounding to drive the life out of him. Faster than anything can run. The pain is as loud and as fast as the noise. One thing, the pain and the noise together, nothing beyond them. Unstoppable, unendurable onrush. Barbed pain erupting from his body, new wounds opening in his groin and his anus. Wounds like mouths filled with sharp teeth. The pain a wave rising black over him, white foam like teeth at its crest. Crashes down leaving him broken by the weight. A face opening in the earth as the black waves batter it. Hands urge the waves higher. Pull the new black sea back to show the world rawly naked beneath. Hurl a wave down heavy as a building falling, so many hands pushing on him, pushing his life down, pushing his bones to break. A woman, almost, or the waves move and the hands move and it might be a child, or a man, or a beast. Arms flailing, not… sharp, not… killing; soft, like water, but they tear apart his bones and the absurd frailty of his flesh and skin. So soft, so cool and pleasant, and his life is choked out beneath. Rising, mounting, towering over him, can't quite see it, can't quite feel or taste. Just a whisper, like it's sounds killing him. Or not sounds, not loud, not anything he can hear. A whisper that he pretends he can hear, crooning to him of worlds, universes, eternities waiting for him. And it's so bright he closes his eyes at last but it's no different, it looks no different with his eyes closed. And it has nothing, no hands, no claws, no teeth, not like man, child or woman, not like beast, and it has no weapons because it has no hands no arms, and it cuts with strokes that bite so deep. The world explodes in green and silver. He can't hear it or see it or feel or taste. Mouthful of mud and gravel and gristle and blood and bone. Spit it out. Wipe it off his face. Blink because it's making his eyes sting. Doesn't taste as bad as he might think. There's a smell in the air, hot metal, and the air's thick with oily smoke. There are bits of his body there in that smoke. His innards run together soaked into the sundering of this world, he's holding out his arms to try to reach death like a man reaching for a drowned ship. All just ghosts now, tomorrow, yesterday, always, never—only ever death and ghosts. He can't see or hear or taste or smell or feel, but he… he almost understands it. A shadow. A whisper. His life and his death rushing, shouting, screaming, breaking.

And slowing, steady, slowing, slowing, slowing, slowing, slowing, slowing, slowing, silence, silence, silence.

Silence.

He feels

Nothing.

He is nowhere. He has no body, no mind, no self left.

And then, slowly, slowly, creeping back…

there is…

There is…

He was…

Is…

Is…

Grief. Awareness.

He groans.

* * *

He so enjoyed being dead.

The world—a world—comes slowly back into focus. Shadows, fragments, flashes of light and colour he can't make sense of, and he's falling through darkness and fire and into silver light. And it's good, and then it's more terrifying than he dared imagine, and then he cries out, begs it to end. He's falling, floating, rising, the silver light is washed away. The joy he felt—is mercifully washed away. The world flickers around him. Waves. Broken images. Memories. Slowly resolves into a pattern he gropes at in recognition. He can see…

Nausea and Phobia—dancing. Delighted. They… are not beautiful. He sees the reality they have just about hidden from him.

That's a lie, of course. He always knew. The reality of what they are is the core of their attraction.

He sees Judge Death waiting to receive him. Judges Fire and Fear, still *living*. Grud, their living bodies are ugly, he thinks. For the first time in his life [...wait...?] he feels superior in every possible way to them.

And there, crumpled on the cavern floor, he can see a thing that he slowly realises with fascination is his own corpse.

It looks awful. And not in a good way.

Fear is bent over looking at him with some interest; from the position Fear's standing in, he can see right up Mortis's nostrils. Black nostril hairs poking out. Fear looks at Mortis's body and Mortis looks at Fear looking at Mortis's body, and whatever image he had of himself in his head, it's honestly worse.

He had no idea his hair had already thinned that much at the back. Or how badly his Judge's uniform hung on him. To be fair, his last moments look to have been appalling, a lot worse even than they felt, his head's thrown back to show off that bit under his right jaw that's impossible to shave properly, his hands are clawing into the earth so he's broken every fingernail, there's blood and snot and some kind of greenish foam he doesn't ever want to see again all over his nose and mouth. The nostril hairs are poking through the foam.

Many have been the times he's sat alone in darkness, consoling himself, exploring himself, with the thought of his own death. When the shadows fall and all is cold and only bleakness without hope of ending, the image of his dead body is something he has clung to. A comfort to him. A bulwark against the pain. A torch against the night.

And yet…

Some things, he thinks, no man should see. His own dead nose hair is unarguably one of them.

It occurs to him that Death's death and resurrection were treated with rather greater solemnity by all concerned.

But he is so… free. A ghost, perhaps? It occurs to him also that he cannot be strictly speaking what he's always understood by 'dead.' He's a rational man, whatever 'death' might mean when he shoots a perp and blows their head open and watches the blood pool and pump and cease—it never struck him as quite… like this.

Great mystery. Is there no end to the wonders he can find in death? For a moment, absurdly, hanging in the air over his only friends[?] he imagines all the death he has ever inflicted, every perp he has ever Judged, down to the rats and the cockroaches in the walls, floating free in the air above him like this. Those cranks and their afterlife were right, he thinks.

Laughs.

And his friends hear it. Look up.

Laugh with him.

Fire… waves at him.

"Yoo-hoo. Can you hear us?"

If he was Judge Fire, he thinks, he'd have a witty one-liner to throw at them. He manages to stutter out: "I'm dead. I'm dead!"

"That was the general idea, Mortis, boy," Nausea says. "Don't know what else you thought we were trying to do?"

"Ah, you boys are as enthusiastic as puppies," says Phobia. She smiles at her sister. "So sad that one can never recapture those days of heady youthful excitement. I say again, it was so nice of dear Sidney to introduce you to us. Almost makes me feel young again, spending time with you boys."

Nausea nods. "Really brightens up the day."

"Oh, it does, it does. Always look forward to a visit from you boys."

Death coughs. "…Ladies? Perhaps… the job in hand?"

"Eh? Oh, deary me, so sorry, Mortis dear, yes. Where would we be without you to remind us, Sidney? Forget my own head next. Or his. Right, stay there a minute longer, will you, Mortis? Just a few moments now… Oh, no, wait… wait… whoops!"

"Don't worry, deary," Phobia says. "Just our little joke."

Nausea cackles. "This is the tricky bit."

"Here we go, lovely. Here we go… Count of three…"

Glorious pain rushes through Mortis. Blinding, searing, purifying pain. Spinning, and the world is but maelstrom. Chaos. Crash of noise. Roar of multi-coloured bright-as-rainbow static. Lives piled on lives, voices shouting laughing, panting breaths and groans and coughs and all the sickly drowning noises of human life. The need, the hunger, the desire, the lies… The confusion. The pointlessness of it. And pain tearing through him, and a hot dry wind in his mind, and the pain of his rebirth into unlife is worse even than the agonies of his dying. He can smell it, feel it, blood rots in his veins. Makes him shudder. His body is pain, is blood. His skin weeping. Eager. Rot-death-hope.

And it's perfect. He tries to hold the memory, this he will savour, this is beyond… beyond…

The purity of it. White and clean.

The silence.

In his body. In his head. He opens his dead eyes and he can see a world stripped clear. The reek of living bodies, skin and hair and breathing—gone. He can smell only decay, blood, bones. Free of the stench of life. He raises his left hand. Opens and closes his fingers, holds his hand out. He can't feel it. Fat fingers, stubby, heavy, fingers like worms…and he's free of the weight of his flesh. The revulsion of his own body lifted. Such disgust at his living self. His head is clean, empty. His thoughts stripped away. Bare bones and rawhide. Empty of feeling. He is pure as the driven snow.

Very slowly, carefully, he climbs to his feet. Heavy, like clay. Just lumps of dead flesh. Slowly, carefully, he touches his hands to his face.

There, too, he feels nothing. He pokes himself. Rips at his cheek. The skin opens. Blood on his hands, red that fades and dries fast to black. His blood is as dust. He shakes his hands and the blood falls away. He cannot feel the wound that he has made.

JUDGE FIRE AND Judge Fear cower in the shadows. They were not afraid of Judge Death's resurrection, saw that as… inevitable, perhaps. A gift that Death would glory in, but that they, mere acolytes, followers, jealous and envious, they who are but Death's faint shadows, they could long for, dream of, but never achieve. Only ever imagine it. Now here stands Mortis, who of these three was ever the weakest, the most uncertain, the most filled with self-doubt, Loser with a capital L—now here stands Mortis, and he too has received the blessing, he has died and returned even from death.

Never would he or they have dared think he could be so blessed!

He opens his mouth, slowly, carefully, shapes the words without needing breath. "I… I am… I will… You are alive," he says, and he can see the life in them, and it disgusts him. Like a little flame inside them, pink and wormy, wriggling.

"You are revolting," he says. "Life is revolting. Come. Let me end it for you. Cleanse you. Give you peace."

Judge Fear kneels at Mortis's feet. Bows his head. Such longing in Fear's eyes, in the trembling of his body, Mortis can hear the gasp of Fear's rough fast breathing, the pump of blood in Fear's chest. The sickness in Fear. A lump of flesh. A crude ill-made thing, a beast. And Mortis before him is as a god. Fear closes his eyes, for he dare not look upon Mortis. The gulf between Fear's pitiful life and Mortis's power is too vast, too high, too great.

Mortis reaches out, and his own dead hand is trembling. In his embrace Fear will crumble away to dust. No wet seeping rot-wounds for Fear, he realises. Fear's heart is already dry as dust. All will be gone, that old cliché, mere dust on the wind. All must come to it at last, stumble onwards searching, and Mortis is the light to guide the way. "Come to me, Fear, my friend," he whispers. "Come to me, let me hold you, let me set you free." Fear sways. Yearns towards Mortis. "Come to me." The first of a thousand. Ten thousand. A hundred thousand, a million, all who live, countless as the stars in the sky, all who live or will ever live, he will render down to decay and dust and nothing.

Fear rises to meet his touch.

Panic in Fear's eyes as he breaks away.

"I don't want to *die*-die," Fear shrieks. "When I said I wanted to be dead—"

"*That's enough, Judge Mortisss.*" Judge Death puts a hand on Mortis's arm. Restraining? Reassuring him? The touch of Death's hand: that Mortis can feel. Cold. Delicious.

"Fear, deary, there's no need to be frightened," Nausea says. "We'll just get Mortis here into his new uniform and we'll do you next, shall we? Get it over with. It really isn't as bad as it looks."

"It was… wonderful," Mortis says. If he had working tear ducts, he'd be crying with gratitude to the sisters. "Thank you," he says earnestly. "Thank you."

Phobia giggles. Kisses his cheek. "It was a pleasure, Mortis dear, really, you don't need to thank us. And I must say, being dead does suit you. You look positively distinguished. Really brought him out of himself, don't you agree, Nausea?"

"Ooh, it has," Nausea says.

If Mortis were not dead, he might blush at the way she's looking at him.

MORTIS IS ALLOWED to watch as Fear and Fire too receive the gift of death. Tries to record every glorious moment, tries not to sink too deep into envy that they are experiencing what he has had and will never receive again.

Even before he died, it has long haunted him: such a shame, he often thinks, that the blessing of death can only be experienced once. What it would be to experience death over and over! Slowly, quickly, knowing it was coming towards you by inches, caught astonished and defenceless. To die by violence, feel the shock of a wound opening, look into your murderer's eyes and know they meant to kill you and are glad… to die again of lingering sickness, sweating, wasting, to feel disease blossoming in your flesh… then by fire, the flames licking one's bones clean, meat and fat boiling, the body rendered down, purified, made clean… by drowning, and that is a thing which he has never experienced, unless you count drowning in dead flesh. Now, he realises with a pang of grief, he will never know how it feels to drown. When he kills a perp he finds himself so often so filled with anger. Red rage, even: he is working so very hard to kill but those he is killing have no respect. They run, fight, resist him, they die fighting against death: thus they miss the crucial moments. Die, some of them, barely registering the fact of their death. He thinks of his father complaining over the dining table, "Your mother spent hours slaving over the stove to cook that good meal for you. The least you can do in return is eat it slowly. Savour it." More and more he wants to shout the same to the people he's killing. "You can only receive it once and then it's over. Slow down. Savour it. Otherwise: what a waste." Now watching Fear and Fire die he feels it like a hand clenched around his throat. It should have lasted longer. I should have enjoyed it more. I hate them for being able to experience it while all I can do is remember.

Fear, in particular, he suspects is rushing it. Don't waste this time, Fear, he wants to say, you'll regret it so much afterwards, you know you will. When Fear rises up dark and faceless, soft as a cobweb and as beautiful as starlight, Mortis wants to shake him for his ingratitude. Fear hisses in wounded pride: he knows that Mortis knows. *I confess, I was afraid*. But then, Mortis thinks, those churning fears are what Judge Fear *is*. How dull Fear would be, he thinks, if he was not afraid of life and death and everything in between. Just another little man: he has no real love of death. When he arises into his unlife Fear is blurred at the edges, ragged, like he's not quite real. Cloaked in shadows, if Mortis can indulge himself in the poetic. A wraith. When Phobia [Nausea? You'd think after all they've done for him he'd be able to tell them apart, but alas…] when Phobia holds out a gruddamn full-face horned black iron helmet to Fear, Mortis's first thought is to spit blood at the fiend. He sees Fire (still alive) make a similar face—and Judge Death looks a bit peeved himself. They get judges' uniforms with a few bones stuck on them. Fear gets a cloak and a massive horned black iron helmet? Fear whisks around to applause from the sisters. But Mortis has got to admit, grudgingly, that it does suit him. Looks and sounds and gives off all the vibes of some kind of Dead Lord King.

Then Fear kneels to Death to do him homage, bends his head until the helmet is pressing in the dust. And the scene is so beautiful Mortis would weep if he had working tear ducts and Fire (still alive) *does* weep. When Fire is remade as a burned man with the flames licked around him, then too Mortis feels envious. Jealous. Hate. Looks at his dead hands, huge and ungainly and the flesh mottled, rotting; he is but a flaccid corpse a thing of meat and bones, dissolving; he is so clearly lesser beside them. But then Fire too kneels and the very flames lick in sweet purity to kiss Death's feet, Fire is splendid, too brilliant for Mortis's poor eyes to see, but Fire and Fear are Death's servants, Death's subjects, something in the way Death receives their protestations whispers to Mortis that he does not need these fancy outward trappings because he is more precious, closer to Death, than they. He is but a corpse, rotting. Death's image, lesser, weaker than Death himself, granted—but—thus—he is far closer than they to Death. And at last when all is completed they stand the three together before their leader, all together three as one they kneel to him and the sisters kneel, long dark hair falling to trace patterns like fingers in the blood and the dust. And it is a beauty that Mortis could never have imagined, it is fairer and finer than dust and ashes and rot and the scabs of a heart's shed blood.

And fine and fair all together three and one before them as a lodestar to guide their passage onwards—they step out into the bright day as welcoming to them as the world's first morning.

He kills Judge Muqtadir almost immediately. One of the first. Should have been the *first*, but sadly after such dizzying perfection will come the inevitable drop-off. Regression towards the mean of Judge Mortis's life. New-made, shining with new confidence and power, the four of them do not need even to speak now to know what they must do. Their first task on this day of their resurrection. The first and greatest task from which all else will flow. *Fons et origo*. The fountainhead. Thus they march, one before and three following, and no shadows fall in their wake. Dead eyes blink and shift to refocus. Resee the world as it is now and will now be forever to them. The wind blows warm as living breath over dead unfeeling skin. The blue of the sky is the blue of lips starved of air, gasping; the green grass and the green branches are as gangrenous limbs that sway in the breeze. His eyes open wide seeking out the first living creature he will set these new dead eyes upon, and that will be a gift indeed! A flock of birds spiral skywards, lacework, a living shadow, a hundred lives living as one; he turns his eyes upon them, sees them not as living but as corpses flying, a brief idiot moment of life's lies pointlessly circling. He itches like his dead flesh is insect-eaten, he itches to kill these birds so that they rain down dying. But he must yet be patient. Greater deaths first, he thinks.

And he thinks also of these pretty little birds circling down to feed on the flesh of dead men. Singing so pretty in the morning as they glut themselves on the flesh of dead men. And that is pleasing to him.

They stride through the city together, one before and three following; they cast no shadows but they cast some greater, stranger, darker light. The ground is despoiled where they trample upon it, their passing leaves a trail like a line of mould down a child's bedroom wall. The people in the streets scream, flee, freeze, kneel. A woman covers her eyes in terror, though it means her baby falls from her arms onto the hard pavement; her screams are so loud, her horror so all-consuming, she does not hear her infant scream in pain at her feet. Mortis almost laughs. This too is pleasing to him. He thinks of pretty birds pecking out the baby's eyes. There are so many places here to judge, to destroy.

As they pass a hospital, Fire and Mortis look at each other and Fire licks his lips. A vile place: Mortis has always hated hospitals and doctors: his mortal [ha!] enemies, they see a man dying and they try to… he wants to vomit at the very words… they try to… keep a dying man alive. Absurd! Hard to believe! Yet he himself has seen it, his vision washed red with rage, tried to shout to the doctors what insanity is it they think they are doing? Stopping someone—sometimes, even, stopping a perp, a *criminal*—stopping someone who could die from achieving death. Fire has the same thought, without need for speech they share the vision: the hospital walls running fire, fire billowing down corridors and wards. Human fat igniting. The pus of a wound boiling up in steam. The agony of sickness and of burning. The pain of fire a counterpoint to the pain of illness or wounds.

They almost turn together, Fire and Mortis, walk together to the hospital. A temple to life, thus most fitted as their first place of killing. Yes! But Judge Death sees, orders them to stop, to focus. Reluctant, they fall back in line behind him. There will be time later, Mortis thinks. He thinks then: what did I just say about Fire rushing it?

A hospital is an abomination. An obscenity. But the Justice Department is worse. That word, *Justice,* set in cheap plastic upon the very wall of the building, all those who enter here walk in beneath that word every day. Justice is defiled here—every day. The so-called Judges here—let some people live.

They go in up the steps through the grand double doors of the main entrance. The plastic letters above them seem to light up to welcome them in. Judge Death first, head held high, proud, a king come to claim his destined kingdom. The great double doors slam shut after them.

The usual scene. Chaos, muddle, noise, voices shouting. Some tedious desk judge types, a party of school kids on a tour, a woman come to report a missing puppy, a couple come to post bail for their son. He wades through them frankly irritated, thinking only of the task ahead. Out of the corner of his eye he notes Fire burn a cadet Judge down to a heap of white ash. Brief waft of scent that reminds him of childhood summer parties. Nostalgia grips him; again if he had tear ducts he would need to brush the tears away. Fear heads to the holding cells where a handful of perps await transfer to prison. "Gaze into the face of Fear," Mortis hears Fear whisper. Hears also the pause, the silence then the scream. Death claws his way into the Chief Judge's office. There he will draw the Chief Judge's life out of him like a sword drawn from a stone.

Mortis—of course—searches out Judge Muqtadir.

"He's... in... his office..." Hardly a difficult question, but the answer is hard to hear over the sound of the man soiling himself. Mortis knocks on the closed door. Is astonished as the plywood turns black and liquid where he's touched it. Over the nostalgia-scent of meat cooking, the stench of something very old and long long rotted. Worms, fungus, mould. For a moment he can taste it and he gags, wants to vomit, he feels as though he is being forced to eat food that's rotten and filled with insects. Maggots in his mouth. Maggots in his hair, writhing inside his clothes. He shakes his hand, wants to rush and wash it clean.

Muqtadir's voice comes through the ruins of the door. Grumpy, as always, *I've got a billion things to do, can't I get five minutes to get one thing finished, is that too much to ask?* "Who is it? You'll have to come back, I'm busy. Oh, argh, okay, hang on..." Footsteps towards the door. A sharp intake of breath. "What's happened here?" The door opens. "Okay, what's up—?"

A silence and a scream.

Mortis reaches out, traces his hand across Muqtadir's throat.

His hand now is huge and swollen. Necrotic fluid oozes from his fingertips. Not quite a human hand, as he has the sense his face is becoming no longer quite a human face. The touch to the door, the touch to Muqtadir's skin: it's... started something, changed something, in him. His skin is peeling open. His bones are pushing, erupting out of him. He dances his right hand over the hollow at the base of Muqtadir's throat. So gentle. Tender. Healer's hand, he thinks, thinking of the doctors he was cursing earlier this very day, offering the only true healing. A stupid man, Muqtadir, all caught up in snares of friends and family and woolly thinking. Poor Muqtadir who could never see clearly for the chaos of life in his head. So now Mortis will give him peace. Sad eyes widen. Green lines, like the veins of mould in a cheese, spiralling across Muqtadir's face. Like a cheese, Muqtadir's flesh is... ripening. Time slows, Mortis watches frozen, fascinated, as the man's body decays. Worse than the door rotting at his touch: the smell, the taste it brings, he can't tear his eyes away and it is, and he realises this should perhaps not be a surprise to him, it is far worse to look at than a door crumbling away in rot; the smell, the sound of a body still alive dissolving into slush, changing colour from skin to opening bloody meat to bloodlessness and greening, blackening, stinking pulp. Flesh slides away at Mortis' feet, bubbles rise and he realises Muqtadir is still half-alive, breathing, trying to speak, to beg for mercy like Mortis can make it stop, and the ooze looks at him with eyes that are sinking into a mire and a last bubble rises, it stinks of methane, Muqtadir's life departs in ripples and in a rolling mud-churned fart. A stain that laps itself at Mortis' astonished feet.

He steps back, bumps clumsily into the doorframe, puts out a hand to steady himself, the bulk of his heavy, clumsy body that is heavier and clumsier than ever now that he is dead and he feels ashamed at his heaviness—briefly, he had thought, hoped, that his death would release him. He puts out a hand unthinking to steady himself, presses against the doorframe and he groans because he feels the doorframe too crumble away. Revulsion at himself, great lummox clumsy thing breaking things. He holds out his hand, trembling, big like a paddle big and ugly and swollen. Dust, in his hands. Just dust, blowing away.

There's a scream behind him, a Judge running mad towards him with such fear in her eyes looking backwards that she doesn't see him until she's almost falling into him. "Help—There's—You've got to—Thank Grud—" She clutches at his uniform because she thinks he's a living Judge. Then she sees him and she screams three, four, five times as loudly as before. He almost wants to let her go, horror at the thought of another body rushing into decay at his touch, but he watches himself grasp at her, hold her as she is already holding him briefly thinking he is safety and a help to her, and he is a help to her, he thinks, as seams of rot twist across her body from his fingerprints that show red on the fat of her arm. He plucks her up and plucks her naked, plucks and peels like feathers her skin and her raw flesh. Breaks off one leg then the other then the right arm then the left. Holds her up still just about living. Just head and neck and torso and no skin and muscle just the bones showing—holds her up, then studies her in interest. His clumsy fingers probe her skinless, fleshless face. Neatly, with thumb and one finger, he flicks off her skinless head. Raises what's left (what's left? nothing, just bones and a heart just beating), raises what's left to stare at, squints and stares then sniffs at it. Picks it, plucks it, peels it open. Makes gentle these coarse hard lumps of bone. He notes with interest that she is drier in her rotting than Muqtadir. Her decay crumbles, like picking and crumbling a scab or worrying at a patch of dandruff on his scalp. At the end she, like the doorframe, is scattered at his feet.

He finds another Judge and her death is different again—*claggier*, somehow, that's the only word for it, her body's decay reminds him of a sticky bowel movement. Another, and he watches fascinated this time as the man's skull falls to dust under his hands even while the man's body is unharmed. Another, and she only sighs like the wind in the trees as she dissolves into black liquid.

Curious, he dips his fingers in the liquor, tastes it—and it's good.

There's a line of poetry somewhere he read: *the wine dark sea*.

"*Mortisss. Where are you?*" Judge Death, calling him. He finds Death and Fire in the Chief Judge's office, Fire supervising a living Judge who's screwing a new nameplate to the door. Fear comes in after him. Seems to have grown taller, square shoulders, beneath his helmet he's holding his head high. Fire's flames seem brighter, and Fire has a new jauntiness in his manner, a proud jut of his chin.

Chief Judge Death seats himself at his desk. Adjusts his helmet. Straightens a pad of paper and pen that must have got disordered in the fighting. And Mortis suddenly realises—he's, what, fourth in command of the Justice Department. Never have to fill in a form again.

He, Fear and Fire line up in front of Death's desk. Ready to begin. Really begin.

Death spreads a city map across his desk. "*Let'sss sssee now.*"

"*Can we take the hospital firssst?*" Fire asks, ardent, almost frankly panting despite not needing to breathe. The shock like electricity again rushing through Mortis.

"*Or the new ssschool?*" says Fear. "*Sssave the little children from a life of crime while they're ssstill young.*"

As planning meetings go, this one is up there.

All is good, Mortis thinks.

21.

THE PLAN THEY come up with: first we take the city, then we take the world.

ONLY FOUR OF them—for all their powers, it should be impossible to take even one block. But there are enough turncoats in the Justice Department who claim they've seen the light.

"I've always admired your attitude to crime fighting."

"I've always thought people who are alive are a bit suspect."

"I always thought your methods were both by-the-book and highly commendable, Judge Mortis," Judge McLean says. "No, honest… And anyway, if they weren't by the book, the book should be rewritten."

"*Oh, don't worry,*" Judge Death says to Judge McLean. "*It will be. In fact… I think you're the very man to help Judge Mortisss rewrite it. I believe you have sssome authorial ambitionsss, on the ssside of being a Judge?*"

"I… I'd be honoured, Chief Judge, sir," Judge McLean squeaks.

It takes a while, but they come up with the perfect phrasing. The new law brings tears to many Judges' eyes. The new recruits recite it proudly, the tremor in their voices is as music to Mortis. March out of the Justice Department heads held high, high stepping neat clinking feet.

It is, Mortis thinks, a shame the bulk of their forces are 1) using things as crude as weapons to kill and 2) still technically alive. But, he tells himself, you mustn't make the best the enemy of the good.

"*Don't worry yourssself about it, Mortisss my friend,*" Judge Death says. "*Every living Judge that followsss our ordersss: are they not guilty of murder? Aware of the crime they commit through the very act of living? More guilty than thossse ignorant beassstsss they kill?*"

Mortis nods. Yes. Exactly, Chief Judge. In a nutshell. You've nailed it as usual. That's kind of the whole massive unsolvable conceptual problem we're wrestling with.

"*Thusss, when they have completed their tasssk, their punissshmentsss mussst be... fitting.*"

Oh.

Death leans closer to Mortis.

"*Look forward to it, my friend.*"

Oooh.

They share a smile, Death and Mortis.

On that happy note, the judging begins.

THEY STRIDE OUT of the Justice Department now not four but legion. The four Dark Judges may cast no shadows but the army that goes before them, ah, they march at dawn into the west where the sky is dark and the light has not reached the city's sleeping eyes and now will never reach, and their army's shadow is thrown vast before them. It seems itself a clawed hand. A skull with gnashing teeth. The Judges hold their guns like spears. They will shoot, fire off incendiary rounds and heavy explosives; their bike engines roar and throb; the bikes' guns and laser cannons are primed and pumped. But each has already drawn their boot knife. Beautiful it is to destroy a building, mow down the crowd fleeing the ruins only to find themselves running towards the bullets, yea, it is as roses, as precious gems. Some say indeed that to fire upon a crowd fleeing in panic is all that is most fair, is all that is best upon this good Earth. But Judge Death and his lieutenants have seen much and deeply, looked, thought long, pondered, drawn up a milestone plan, gruddamnit, and they say in their wisdom: more beautiful than any bullet is a knife wound to the gut. Stab, cut, kill slowly. Look down through shuttered helmets to see the dying face looking up. The pain of a good gut wound only grows over the hours. Hands beating like birds' wings trying to hold on to the slick ribbons of one's own intestines. Noses wrinkled, begging for death to release one from the stench of one's own shit.

THEY STRIDE OUT, four gods and a legion before them willing, hungry. Terrified, cacking themselves to prove themselves to the new Chief Judge. 'Before': Judge Death is a wise, um, corpse when it comes to planning: the living Judges take the brunt of any resistance. Form a shield wall. The Judges scythe through the city [and, Grud, is Death proud of that wording in the planning docs]. Reap the city like a field of overripe wheat [Mortis's poetic touch there, please note]. In the main, resistance is not so much futile as non-existent, "Life is a crime," the Judges chant to the rhythm of falling bodies and the citizens can only agree with this stark truth. Yet a few form up to oppose the Judges, even dare take up arms themselves, and thus the living Judges are a shield wall for their masters the Dark Judges. There's some rough magic, Judge Mortis thinks, in trampling his followers' blood beneath his feet.

THEY STRIDE OUT, the four lords of the world and their army; the killing as funeral games for the Dark Judges' still so-recent, painful deaths; they rend the city as a widow might rend her garments. They raise the war-cry, the paean: "We are restoring

Law and order. Taking back our city from crime. You have been Judged." The fires they start are the fires of hope new-kindled, the city burns as a torch of hope. Piss and pus rains from the sky in torrents. Piss and pus, pus and piss. Then shit and spit and spunk and spit and shit. Then human hearts and human heads. (A relief, human hearts and heads and human entrails. Easier to duck). The Judges take all life out of the city. Annihilate it. Piss and shit and jizz all over it. Open septic wounds and spread fungal spores and mouth rot all over—over—over—over it. The light in dying eyes is wondrous and pleasing. The air about them is as musk and lilies. The city rings like crystal bells to the sound of Judgement being given.

Fire raises his trident and his flames turn whole streets into ash. A Goodyear-starred restaurant is vaporised before its clientele have had a chance to try the merest mouthful of this morning's meal. Mortis crumbles men and rocks down together into compost. Meat, bones, household items, all broken down into a nice, rich acidic loam. If Death touches a man, that man dies. Unless, sometimes, when he touches a man, that man… only wishes he were dead. Luckily for him, here's Fear to grant that request!

The CEO of the local hospital, blood in his beard, cut open in the guts, slowly dying, mould growing in his wound, maggots churning in his wound, his life clinging on encased in dead meat. All four of the Dark Judges stand over him. Could have cut his throat, taken his head off, ripped his life essence from his chest. So many ways to kill someone. Quick ways: stab, cut, hack, slice, shoot. Get it done, kill the man, kill someone else. Quick as a wink! The four Dark Judge smile down and the man lies on the pavement with a thousand bleeding holes in him turning green, knows from his medical training that without help he will be three, four, five days dying with his body rotting and his mind going mad with pain. And the Dark Judges laugh and laugh.

The headteacher of the local primary school, peeled open, skin stripped. Fire and Mortis grind her between them, joyful, playing together, throw and catch and toy and chase. Fire leaps up, white and blinding, hunts her down. Draws back teasing, hurls himself to clasp tight her pretty hair and her pretty dress. Mortis's rot laps cool to put the fire out in her clothing, he strokes her hair, soothes her, don't fear, don't run, see, you're safe now with me, the fire's gone. Fire watches, pretends horror. Mortis pulls his hands deep into the woman's throat. Her hair burns up and her body burns—even as decay dissolves her lungs. She drowns in her own death fluids, even as they extinguish the fire that kills her.

The head teacher of the local secondary school (newly appointed head of a shiny new school with all the mod-cons, and she can thank Fire for that, but did she thank Fire for that?). She's running away from the four Judges, fleeing in terror, Mortis might stab her in the back, yes. But, to be fair to him, she would never make it to safety. What with nobody in the city managing to make it, what with there being nowhere in the city that's safe. There's no word for 'safe' now. No word for 'city' either. Or 'body' as in 'whole intact torso,' come to that. She's a fast runner, starts up running away as soon as she sees them coming, the coward, and leaves her pupils behind her for dead (lit.). Leaps a corpse, turns a corner, skids to avoid a corpse, vaults a pile of corpses. Speeds up as she sprints down an alley. Breath coming really fast, heart pounding, throat gasping. Mortis catches her as she runs out into the next street. Her legs stop running. But he touches her, caresses her face that runs with sweat, soon enough the flesh is rotting off her cheekbones so her flesh and her blood are running. All the bits of her run until there aren't any visible bits left. Just a mush on the pavement, until it rains and even that runs away down the drain.

THEY STRIDE OUT the four and their acolytes, the Dark Judges and those who serve as their tools, to remake their city and then their world free from crime. They are as wounds opened. Teeth. Claws. Power. Killing. Blood flows in streams and rivers and tides and oceans, mountains rise that are nothing but torn flesh and broken bones and clotted blood. More blood than… than… more blood than any words can express in any language. More blood than is possible for the mind to comprehend. No poet, no singer of fine songs or teller of great tales—no one should be able to describe that much blood. Buildings shattered into rubble. Rubble shattered into dust. The city falls like sand crumbling. Decay rips through the city; blood drowns the city; fire burns the city; these gods of things the mind cannot conceive of, these new gods tear through the city in ways no human tongue can or will dare speak.

When the city has been taken, they set up the new book of the Law outside the Justice Department for all to see.

THE CRIME IS LIFE.
THE PUNISHMENT IS DEATH.
It will be carried out.

JUDGE MCLEAN WAS such an inspiration, Mortis thinks. Thank you, Judge McLean, for all your help. You can tell the old chap had a literary bent to him: his skin and blood were the perfect writing materials. And—Mortis allows himself a private moment of joy—such beautiful lettering. Those years at school sweating over his handwriting, certainly finally put to good use.

For the first time in years, when Mortis thinks of the future… he feels hope.

CASEY

22.

Meanwhile, back in the Big Meg…

Crawling. Like a worm. Down on her belly, crawling and the sky explodes overhead. Pushing forwards. On, on, on, on, on. Everything's all lit up with fire, she ducks her eyes down to keep from going blind. The world explodes, pain in her face, gruddamn hard. Gets a mouthful of mud and gravel and a friend's blood and bone. Spits it out. Wipes it off her face. Blinks her eyes because it's making them sting. Doesn't taste as bad as you'd think.

Dark sky, and the light from the ruin behind her, outlining her so she still looks really alive, and the ruins she's crawling through are lit up also, blazing fire, because the enemy knew they were coming as they always know, but it's good, she thinks, it's good to die in the light. And the fire comes down in sheets like a blade falling, and she's crawling beneath it, with pain dripping down on her; in the fire her face looks red and black.

A blast of white light. Gold sparks. A scream. White light again, and white heat, and her eyes hurt. Lying on the ground in the mud gasping for breath, the air ringing, that silence after a thunderclap that's louder than the noise itself. And this screaming starting. Shrieking. A man whose bones are being ripped out. There's a smell in the air, hot metal, and the air's thick with oily smoke. There's bits of people, there in that smoke. Her companions and her friends.

Everything goes very still. Keep going. Crawling. Her companions around her are dead but keep on, like *she's* dead but keep on. A crash, the white light dies, the screams trail off. Over the reek of burning she gags on a smell of rot. Crawls on. The ground is thick and churned, clings to her like hands. It stinks of death.

She forces herself up to her knees. The ground sucks at her, tries to pull her back down. She feels it grasping at her. Dead bodies in it, grasping at her. She is crawling through one vast wound. Dust swirls over her, stings her face. She's up on one knee, struggling, her back is hurting her, her arms are hurting her, her face feels hot.

To her left, to her amazement, gunfire crackles. She raises her head, watches a shell fly over her, up over her, above her, like the sun rising. She thinks: it's beautiful. She watches it and it seems a long time, hanging in the air, all her time is getting lost and wandering. It crashes down against the ruins of the target. A further, smaller, pointless joyful wound. She cannot see the shell hit, but she feels the crash through her whole body, the earth shakes. She thinks: we can still win. She gets up onto both knees, and onto her feet. All the voices screaming at once. "Get up! Drokking *get up!* Fight!"

Yes, yes, get up. Drokking get up, get moving. She drags herself to her feet and her head is spinning. She staggers like a sick man. Braces herself, body eaten over with pain, begins to run. The ground shakes.

Eruption in the earth beneath her. She is running from her death by fire towards her death by gangrenous rot. Pus bursts from the ground. She gasps, swallows pus down yellow and sticky and sweet. Sinks into dead-filled mud. The world is spinning. She hears from somewhere voices cheering, as loud and distant as thunder. Realises the voices are only her own pain. Bones click and rattle. Figures rising. She cannot see for pain. Her head swirls with colours. Black, white, red, green. She can hear the fires crackle, and the crash as walls fall, and the sound of men's deaths. She tries to push herself backwards, on her back through the pus like a swimmer, wrestling in the death-stink mud. Buries herself in the mud and the pus that was recently her last companions and friends. Begs.

Four figures. Moving towards her across a sea of old blood and new blood. The fear that gnaws the heart away, weakens bones until they're brittle and snap, crawls in the mind when the night drags long. The fire that burns away any hope or beauty, punishes all without regret. The decay of flesh, of thought, of worlds, all things falling in the end to dust.

To death.

She raises her head weakly. Blinks eyes sealed up with filth. No matter: she can see them with her eyes closed. The figures pause, bend, feel and sniff the mire she lies in. Walk on. One strides like a king, crowned head held proud. One swaggers loose-hipped. One is ponderous, awkward, a shambles. One tramples corpses with every thrusting step.

They walk on. Leave her.

Her companions are dead and she is nothing to them.

Much later she's walking. Found their tracks, burned, rotted, frozen. Walked the other way. Years later, or days, or brief minutes. The sky overhead the colour of her wounds, and as painful to look at, churning red clouds mounting over columns of black smoke. The ground she walks on, buckled, pock-marked, crests and eddies where the road surface has melted, run as liquid, pooled and lapped around the dead. Ancient faces stare up at her trapped there, eyes open, mouths open, screaming pain. Some, the wisest, had thrown themselves into the molten bitumen to escape the enemy's reach. To die so, drowned and choked and boiled alive, gagging on poison fumes—merciful, some brief unlooked-for kindness the enemy had all unwittingly granted them. So gentle, soft, soothing, in comparison to the death the enemy would bring. On the horizon to the south a few tower blocks are still burning. The flames silver and gold. To the far west a thick column of black smoke rises. She has to readjust her course, stop herself walking towards it. Her head bent on one side constantly towards it. That, also, she can see with her eyes closed.

She stumbles. Her foot caught in a human torso, tripping in the hole where his neck has been torn off. Moans in revulsion. For a brief terrible second she thinks that his body jerked beneath her feet because he is alive.

She shoots him and shoots him and howls in revulsion, even though she knows now that he is not alive. Her bullets make his arms thrash, dancing. No blood, just dry wound-holes. She croaks to herself that she mustn't waste ammo. Though the ammo is pointless and useless. She screams and kicks the torso and its intestines spill in yellowing ropes around her ankles. She sinks down beside it. Sobs into the barrel of her gun.

An eternity has passed when she raises her head from her crying, and no time at all has passed. Her head aches, her eyes ache. She hugs her gun close.

"Come on, Cass. You can do this. Get up."

She looks at the torso hunched beside her, its arms thrown up, trying to hold on to its life. Thinks: You know what? No, I can't do this. A gust of wind stirs the dust, blows grit into her face.

Bone fragments. Half the world is ground bones.

Presses her head against her gun until the wind stops blowing. Too horrible, wiping bone dust from your face. Or an excuse to stay sitting there. Her skin and her hair are sodden through with bones and blood and flesh. A noise makes her look up again finally, long after the wind has dropped away. Eyes dart, cat-like, searching: maybe this time at last they've come and she can give in?

A dog, gnawing at a body erupted from the tarmac. It growls at her, snarls then limps away. Wounds on its back, chem-burns, rad-burns, maggot-eaten; fungus sprouting from its eyes and its mouth. She should shoot it. Clean kill, bullet in its brain, quickly. Poor wretched thing. Her hands are shaking too badly to aim when she tries to raise the gun.

"It's alive," she says very loudly to the dead world around her. Challenging them, perhaps, to hear her, to come. Those words are a curse, the way people long ago could summon demons. Say 'life' three times, laugh, enjoy something for one moment, and they will surely know and come.

A noise. The dog starts too, pricks its ears, hackles raised. Ah, Grud, she thinks, they *have* heard, they have come. Feels her bowels churn. I didn't mean it, she thinks. Please.

The dog yelps as a child appears clambering over the rubble towards them. A boy, Anderson thinks.

To her astonishment, the dog wags its tail.

"Oscar! Good boy! What you got there?" Months, Anderson thinks, since she'd last heard a child's voice. It sounds sweet as clarinets.

"Have you found something to eat? Oh, good boy, Oscar. Good boy!"

The dead body? Anderson's stomach lurches. But the child goes past her, so focussed on the dog pawing at the tarmac he didn't notice her sitting there, scrabbles around where the dog is nosing, crows as he excavates a plastic bag from the rotten meat.

"A synthi-choc bar… Oh, Oscar, a packet of crisps!"

She ought to… speak to him? Do something. Get him to safety, at least. Anderson stands up in a chorus of creaking limb joints. "He—hello?"

Fast as thinking, boy and dog disappear into the rubble.

"No… don't run away…" She calls out, frightened at how loud her voice sounds, "I'm… I'm alive, like you, I'm not going to harm you."

Silence.

"I won't…" She tries to remember how an adult talked to a child. "I won't even ask you to share your crisps."

Silence. Finally a tousled head appears, very cautiously, peeping through a gap in the rubble.

"You promise?"

"I, um, I promise."

"They're smoky bacon," the boy says, as if that explains everything.

"Oh. Um. Good?"

Silence. Crunching sound.

"No, no more, Oscar. Crisps aren't good for dogs. Miss… are you really… alive?"

"Yes. I mean, I hope so."

Silence. "No, not the synthi-choc, Oscar. That's not good for dogs either."

Silence. "Miss… you can have a crisp if you like."

Anderson crawls over towards the boy's hiding place. Slowly, carefully, like she might approach a perp with a bomb. Ten times a thousand pleas for help in that last sentence, his mind is begging *help me help me help me* but he'd be off in panic if she made him acknowledge that.

"I'm just here, behind the… um… the wall here…" Thigh bones, shin bones, rib bones, toe bones, and the mortar mixed with tears and blood. "…this wall here, is it okay if I come round to you now?" She says after thinking a moment, "I would really love a crisp if you can spare one."

"Just one."

She comes round slowly, carefully, her skin hot like she is burning because for the last few steps she has to stand straight, walk straight, her visibility is like hot bright sunlight on her skin.

"I'm coming in now. Is that okay? I am alive, I promise."

He's burrowed his way down. Him and the dog. The entrance is almost too narrow, she has to squeeze headfirst, her body blocking the light so she is climbing falling down, into the dark and the rubbish pressed into her, and the smell this close is putrid. And then she thinks: What if he's dead?

She can hear his breathing, and the dog panting, and they sound so alive.

She crawls through into a nest in the rubble, just big enough for the boy and the dog and for her if she sits crouched up. Wriggles herself until the faint light through the entrance is enough to just see him. Huge eyes in a gaunt face that could be dead, except for the fear that shines in his eyes. How we know we're alive, she thinks—We feel fear.

Also the crisp crumbs round his mouth. That's enough to make her blink back tears then let the tears out.

"Miss?" He holds out the crisp packet very solemnly. The most important thing in the world. They are as disgusting as Anderson imagined.

"Thank you," she says when she can trust herself to speak. "And you, Oscar, for finding them."

"He's clever like that."

"So I see." From the state of its wounds, the dog will be dead in days. Should be weeks dead. It thumps its tail. From the state of its wounds, it should have killed the boy weeks ago.

"So… Oscar. Good to meet you. And I'm Cass Anderson." She gives the boy what she hopes is a kind and gentle smile. "So what's your name?"

The boy frowns. Anderson can see him groping in his memory. *Name… Name… That's that word people used to show they meant me, when there were people and we needed to tell each other apart. Name…*

"Casey."

"Casey? I mean… that's a lovely name."

"You can have another crisp if you like. Actually, I don't like them, you can have the rest." Ten times ten thousand pleas for help in that sentence, his pleas for help are burying her, and she has no idea whether the correct answer is to refuse or accept.

"I didn't know there were still people alive round here."

A shrug.

"How long have you been living round here, Casey?"

A shrug. "A while."

"Is Oscar your dog? From… from before, I mean." I mean, he looks like a dire wolf, Anderson thinks, but he might have been some exotic breed. Might be handsome, even, under the wounds and the rot.

Casey pats the dog's ears. Even in the dark, Anderson can see the way his face has closed up.

"I'm sorry, I didn't… didn't…" What can 'before' mean, she thinks, to a child his age?

Silence.

"If you don't want them crisps, Oscar'll have the crisps."

"Oscar looks like the kind of dog who deserves crisps." They watch it bolt down the last few scraps, stick its nose so far in the empty packet it gets briefly stuck, wearing it like a mask.

"How long have you been living round here then? We haven't seen you round here."

We? A rush of hope to the head, dizzying. Then realisation: He means him and the dog.

"I was part of the… the battle."

"Battle?"

"You didn't… see it?"

Blank face. Shake of the head. Well, Anderson thinks, he'd have died, probably, if he had been anywhere nearby.

She frowns. "There were… there were ten of us." She can sort of see them, a line of figures in outline, silhouettes against a sky that is all green fire.

The boy looks around in panic.

"I'm the last," Anderson says. She can sort of see them falling. Dying. Sort of see herself, as from a distance, crawling away.

Running away, Anderson, she thinks.

"We were fighting the—"

In the darkness, the boy's face goes white. "We don't say it. Never. Never. If we say anything, the… the things we can't talk about might come." A different voice, when he says it. An adult's voice, drumming it into him.

"They're not… I mean, they can't hear us. They're not—"

"Never. Never. Never. We don't say it." The adult voice, and the rhythm makes her think of a hand beating down to force it in. Then the child's voice, almost feeling proud of itself for knowing something she doesn't: "How stupid are you?"

Anderson looks down at herself. The sky all green with fire. Silhouettes falling dying, ripped up, torn up, burned up. Bone dust in her mouth choking her as she crawls away. "Pretty stupid, I suppose, Casey."

"So you're, like, some kind of soldier, then? If you were fighting?"

Anderson says in astonishment, "I'm a Psi-Judge."

Blank face.

"A Judge. From Psi-Di—"

The boy screams so loud Anderson feels it like he's hit her. They'll hear that, drokk, drokk, drokk. "A Judge?" Like he's trying to climb out of his own skin, digging at the rubble, and she is between him and the entrance. "No, no, no, no, you said, you said you was alive." Like he's trying to tear himself open and die before she kills him.

"No! Casey!" They'll hear that, too, she thinks. A human voice full of terror and then a human voice full of pain. "No. I'm not—

"I'm alive, Casey. I'm not going to hurt you. I promise.

"I promise."

"You don't, you mustn't, you mustn't say that, you mustn't say that word, you mustn't—musn't—you can't." The boy is shaking. His thoughts and feelings frozen. A noise in his throat that's a scream he is too frightened now to let out. "Mustn't say it, musn't, musn't say it."

Anderson holds out her hands. "Look, you see? Alive. I'm not going to hurt you."

Holding her hands out like—fingers reaching—She drops her hands, folds them close at her sides. Breathes in and out, in and out. Very loudly. But that word 'Judge' is like a knife stuck into the boy's chest.

"I'm alive," she says again. "I'm alive." Like the word is a charm to bring healing. "I'm alive. I'm alive." Like she herself might eventually believe it.

After a long time the boy dares to unfold himself just a little. Anderson keeps her breathing loud and steady. Thinks: if I could make my heart beat so loud he could hear it... Let him see the blood pumping in my veins.

"...Oscar isn't scared of you..."

"No."

"...You ate them crisps..."

"Yes."

"...And they were really stale and disgusting and everything..."

"Yes."

THE DOG WHINES. Pricks its ears. Its hackles rise and it isn't angry, it's frightened. Cowered down flat on its belly and Anderson thinks of a perp grovelling before she shoots them.

Casey, so clever and good at surviving, says, "Oscar? What is it, boy?" Because terror has its limits for a child.

Shoot him then shoot the dog, Anderson thinks.

"Oscar?"

Grud, shut up. The rubble above them shifts. Rhythmic: heavy, treading feet.

A shadow in the dark. Fumbling, groping sound from outside the entrance.

Anderson has to force herself not to wet herself. Just about manages to raise her finger to her lips to try to get the boy to be quiet. He's on the edge between silence and screaming.

A voice. Might be in Anderson's head, or real, or a tumour speaking deep inside her body, a disease, a long-ago-inflicted unhealed wound. It hurts like a wound, at least.

"*Ssssomeone's alive here. I know you're alive here.*"

Holds her hands over her mouth to stop herself screaming. The boy too frightened to scream.

Shoot him! Shoot him! But the coward voice in her head: it'll hear.

"*I can hear you. Come out here so I can sssee you.*"

She does wet herself.

A hiss from the entrance. "*Sssomeone's alive here. Come out, come out.*"

So close. Its stink makes Anderson gag even over the rubble stink and the boy's stink and her own urine and sweat. Even over the smell of the dog.

"*It'sss too late to hide.*"

Rustling at the entrance to their burrow. Bones being peeled carefully away.

"*Oh, I do like your hiding placcce.*"

Casey screams at last. Loud as the sky, so that Anderson jerks backwards with the impact, bone rubble jabbing into her shoulders. Burning hot red scream. The enemy thing in the entrance scrabbles, trying to get in faster, in the silence as the boy's scream falls away Anderson hears it moan. "*Oh, and I do like your ssscreaming. Even prettier than your hiding place, your niccce ssscream.*"

The darkness is total as it jams its way inside their shelter. Huge dark lump of killing, blocking out all light.

Take him first take him take him. She just manages to bite back the words. Unless she is simply herself unable to speak. Black clot of darkness pure evil shifting black against the dark and something is reaching out towards her cold and stinking and so terrible that she can see it in the dark.

Judge Mortis. And she has always thought that of the four Dark Judges Mortis is the worst. More horrible even than Death itself.

The dog Oscar whimpers.

Growls.

A rush of warmth, Grud, the beautiful feeling of a living body moving, as the dog Oscar leaps past Anderson, hurls itself at Judge Mortis. A howl—from the dog? from the monster?—and the sound of teeth crunching into bone. A howl that must be Judge Mortis. Rattle of dog claws on bones. Light, brilliant, pouring into the shelter. Fresh sweet air.

"Get out! Run!" Anderson drags at Casey. "Now! Run!"

"Oscar!"

"No! Run! Run!"

He shrieks, "We can't run from it!" But he is running with her, he pulls her arm to make her go faster as she pulls him. No, we can't run from it. But we can go two steps, three steps, we can be alive for those three more steps. Her heart pounding in her throat telling her that over and over. The crack of feet on bones telling her that.

Anderson dares to look/can't *not* look behind her. The dog is running with the awkwardness of a dying creature, pain almost visible like flashes of bright colour in every jerking limping limb. Its head is bent awkwardly, its muzzle dragging down.

It has Mortis's skull in its mouth.

"Run! Run! Run!"

Casey shrieks, "Oscar!"

"He's rescuing us, Casey. He's sacrificing himself for us. Run!"

"Oscar!"

The love in that cry.

On, on, on, on, on. Run, run, run, run, run. So quickly, the boy is gasping, stumbling, once he falls and Anderson pulls him up, so quickly, too quickly, he is slowing. Failing. His legs pound across the bone rubble, his legs are as thin and brittle as the bones. Grud knows, she thinks, when he last ate beyond those stale crisps. If we keep running, he'll collapse.

A better death than he'll get if we don't keep running, she thinks. On, on, on, on, on. Run, run, run, run, run. The dog will be dead by now, Mortis will be groping to put his skull back on.

Memory: Neirn's stupid badly-fitting helmet.

Memory: A kid running with his hand clamped over his cap to stop it falling off.

Running for her life and a child's life across a world of bones, Anderson hears herself laugh.

BUT THEY HAVE to stop, for she herself is wounded and the boy is shaking and crying now as he runs. His face has a blindness to it, he has run beyond the limits of his body but his fear drives him on. The sun is setting, the red wound-clouds changing to green and grey and purple, a bar of silver blazing on the western horizon before the smoke chokes it out. She cannot run further, he could run forever now but would lose his mind in the running, they cannot run on through the night. The ruins of a tower block scrape up out of the bone rubble, Anderson steers the boy towards it.

The remains of a sign read *SYLV__ P_A__ BL_C*.

Ha!

Casey gives Anderson a look. "Are you okay, miss? You blew a snot bubble," he says with all the sudden innocent righteousness of a boy of eleven. "That's gross, miss."

"Nothing. Just… funny how things go… I busted a couple of perps for illegal poetry distribution here once. Using psi to project sonnets straight into innocent peoples' heads. Particularly mopey bunch."

He shakes his head blankly. What's *psi*? What's *poetry*? What's *busted*? "Okay, miss. Whatever."

They clamber in easily enough through a long-broken window. Inside it's very dark and smells good, strong damp scent of old rockcrete. They grope their way through rooms and corridors, bumping against furniture and into walls, groping for door handles. Find a room where the door closes and the window looks onto an inner courtyard accessible only from the sky above. *If* you ignore the ranks of open windows, which Anderson tries to because the boy has to stop and she has to stop. She sets up a chair to hold the door closed… A child might be stopped for a good two minutes, she thinks, so there's that.

The place is almost pristine. Looted, obviously, but no sign of violence. Just frozen here, overturned chairs and tables, open cupboards, a rug mouldering away beside a double bed complete with mattress, both too heavy to carry off.

Casey sits down on the bed with a sigh that is obviously: *soft*. The sunset light falls on his face. Pale skin, pale hair, a scar on his right cheek. He turns to the window, realises he can be seen through it, comes to join Anderson sitting on the floor.

"It's not a good place here. Not lucky to use things from here."

"No?"

"Not lucky to shelter here."

"Bit late now," Anderson says.

"Doesn't matter now."

"Oscar saved your life, Casey."

Silence. Then: "It was... It looked really funny, what he did."

"It really did. And very brave."

"And he had them crisps. Loves crisps. The people who lived here lined up to be killed. Right back at the beginning. Queued up and let themselves be killed. Said it was right."

She'd heard about people who'd done that. Families. Whole communities. Hard to believe. She looks at his young face. "How do you know?"

He looks away a long time and then he looks straight at Anderson. "My mum's best friend lived here. My mum used to take me here. We had to remember, she said. Then she'd say..." Still looking clear and unflinching at Anderson. "Sometimes she'd say her friend was right."

He's what, eleven? His eyes say that he understands everything.

"How long ago did your mum die?"

Shrug. "Dunno. How should I know? No time left now, is there? Before I found Oscar. But me and Oscar, we manage.

"Never saw the—until you came along.

"I think Oscar was being thick," he says. "Not trying to save our lives. He just saw a nice new bone."

THERE IS NOTHING to say. They sit together as the night comes on, the wind blows through the open window down Anderson's neck. Absolute silence. Absolute dark. The fires choke the sky to hide the stars—I remember stars, I think, Anderson would tell herself, I think. The city skies has been lit day and night by streetlights, tower blocks and office blocks glowing neon silver, pink, green, red, day and night and the stars had been hidden, then the cities began to wither, the lights blinked out and the night sky... One brief moment of beauty, one thing you could say, "This is better, we should keep this, somehow, when we win…" and then the fires, the smoke, whole cities burning, bodies burning in piles a hundred, a thousand deep, and the stars again were hidden. And they knew by then, anyway, that they couldn't win. Even the fires are slowly fading out now. A limit to how long even a thousand piled corpses can burn. But the smoke remains.

Anderson's stomach rumbles.

"Oi, miss, stop making that racket."

Anderson thought the boy had fallen asleep.

"Sorry. I'm hungry."

"Hungry? You ate them crisps."

She says, trying to be dignified here at the ending of the world, "That was hours ago."

"Yeah. So you can't be hungry again that quick."

Cosseted Judge final-resistance lifestyle, Anderson thinks. Sleeping. Eating.

Casey says, "There's food here. I mean, it's like, years stale, like them crisps, but there's food in the cupboards."

"No!" She starts to get up. "Why didn't you say last night?"

Food! Actual food! Her stomach rumbles and her dry mouth is watering. Grot Pots, maybe! Munce!

Casey grabs her arm, pulls her back down.

"But you mustn't eat it," he says. "People do come here and take it, then they die. Like the man I got the crisps from. Cursed, like I said. I expect them crisps was from here." Shudders. Rocking. "That's why the—you know—why it came, and that's why Oscar's gone."

Howl of pain: "Cause I ate them crisps."

"That's not true, Casey."

"It is. I ate them crisps and you turned up and said the—the word and it—and Oscar's dead, all because I ate them crisps and they was horrid anyway and now it'll come and find me and kill me. All cause of me being greedy about them crisps.

"I'd never seen—

"Not till you turned up and said—"

"We was safe, me and Oscar, till I ate them crisps."

Finally, the boy is crying. Long, raw sobs so that his body shakes, his hands pressed over his face. Then whispered sobs. He rocks back and forth. Seems to be trying to bang his head against the wall without making a sound.

"You were safe, Casey, until I turned up," Anderson says.

23.

"So WHY ARE you here? You said you was a—a soldier. What you doing here?"

It isn't until dawn that the boy Casey finds enough kindness inside him to speak to Anderson. Faint light falls through the window, staining them both red. His head twitches, turns towards her, tries to look at her without weeping. Tearing at her with his little clenched fists.

"I am a—a soldier. At least, I was." Anderson, too, has begun to fear that word 'Judge' as cursed. Had used it unthinkingly for years. Her title: Psi-Judge… Repeated it in her mind in the night and it sounded strange in front of the boy. Psi-*Judge*. She had a badge, with that word proudly displayed. Pinned to her chest. Over her heart. Must have lost it in the fighting… She grips her chest where the badge should be, sudden relief that it's missing.

That word. Over her heart.

"We've been fighting since the beginning. Never gave in. Never gave up. We came here to destroy the Grand Hall of Justice. Take all four out at once."

Casey finds the kindness inside him not to laugh. "You came here to fight—*them?*"

Anderson's turn to stare around in panic as if the word would summon *them* up.

Now he does laugh. "That's more stupid than lining up to be killed."

Couldn't in all honesty argue with that. But because her comrades had died for it, she says as if it was something to be proud of, "I've been fighting *them* from the beginning, Casey. Since the first day."

So LONG AGO now. Years and years. So few of them left. The last true Judges holding out against the darkness. For indeed they came down upon our city like the night. We fought them, but we were defeated. The first of them, whose name is the King of Terrors, I fought him once hand-to-hand. Mind-to-mind, rather. A true battle of wits.

I lost.

It's all hazy in her mind now. Those long ago days when she believed she could stop Death. Or do something.

The message coming in: something big had gone down, and badly. Could hear the fear over the comms. Fear, and a lot of confusion. A Judge was dead; the perp was, um... no one could quite make sense of this bit; but Dredd was at the morgue with the perp's corpse, wanted a psi operative. They sent her. Judge Anderson. She stood before Death's corrupted body. Made contact. And Judge Death was there in her head. Took her and filled her mind. Showed her his plans. Made her a part of them.

She had a plan. Albeit a desperate one. A sealed room, her and Death and Death's body. Dredd bursting in, lantern-jawed never-have-I-been-so-happy-to-see-you hero. She'd been rude to him earlier that same day, she remembers. For some reason that memory, embarrassing, is clear in her head. Sweating, staring, she whispered to Dredd in despair and thankfulness: "Do it—the Boing® tin." And Dredd let rip like a true lawman. An explosion around her; Judge Death screaming in rage; she herself was filled with both joy and grief. More Judges piled into the room. “There was only one way,” she could hear Dredd saying. Slowly, solemnly, almost awed. “He’s trapped in Anderson’s head.”

No way out, creep! she remembers thinking. You gave me the idea yourself! You—

Her arms flying out, her legs flying out. Watching herself hack and kick with more than human strength at the Boing®.

Watching the Boing® shattering into fragments.

Watching the fragments pierce Dredd’s body. Shards of plastic sharp as knives slice into his shoulder, his face, his chest.

Watching Dredd fall, dying.

Watching Death claim Dredd’s dead body.

She screamed as Judge Death rose up before her stronger and more terrible than before. She fell tiny and helpless before him. But he didn’t even bother to pursue her. Thought her too weak to be concerned with. Walked out of the room in Dredd’s body while she crawled away spitting and gagging on plastic shards, defeated.

And that was the first day of Judge Death’s rule over Mega-City One.

The people… welcomed him.

They cheered him. A parade winding its way through MegCentral down the Superslab, floats and music blaring, marching bands and majorettes and carnival-hatted revellers throwing themselves beneath the oncoming vehicles.

“Hail! Welcome, Judge Death!”

“Isn’t he just the coolest?”

“Oh, I want to be like him.”

“Ooh, I’d like to *sleep* with him.”

“Oooh, I wonder if my cosmetic surgeon could make me *look* like him.”

“Get your very own replica Judge Death helmet!”

“Get them here! Judge Death posters only fifty credits!”

“Judge Death t-shirts, all sizes XS to XXXXL.”

"Judge Death cigarettes, available now in all good Smokatoriums."

"Get them here! Judge Death balloons!"

"Have you tried the new Judge Death cocktail? After a couple of these, you won't feel your pain. Or your legs. Or your head."

"Special exclusive Judge Death kiddy meal deals—a burger, small fries, a cyanide shake!"

"I knew one of the people he Judged in the Rabbit Hutch! Not one of the last ones to die, either. One of the first, in fact!"

"That's nothing: the very first person he Judged was a next-door neighbour of a friend of my dad's!"

"No? Get you, man! Get you!"

She thinks: some of us resisted. We tried to hold the line. We were forced back and back. We fled the Hall of Justice rather than see him enthroned as Chief Judge. The world was run mad, and *we* were the enemy, not *them*. We were opposed, betrayed, mocked, no one would help us. Not only City Blocks, but whole sectors lined up to die happy and eager, willing, keen—and they spat in the dust and the ashes that came down like snow where the pyres burned, they saw us coming begging them to resist and they spat in the dust at us. Called us traitors. We were the enemy, for wanting to live.

We took up arms, Lawgivers locked and loaded; we formed the battle lines.

We fled.

Regrouped. Held the line until the line broke.

Fled.

Fled again.

And again.

And again.

The sky was cracked open. The earth was torn apart. The world was a charnel house. We pretended we were fighting. We fled over and over until there were so few of us left. 'The last true Judges,' we called ourselves. 'The last heroes.'

'A diverting game,' I think Judge Death called us.

The image of her companions blurred, like trying to recognise a long-lost friend from their reflection in a puddle. There were ten of us... Once there were thirty of us... This morning—which draws red stripes across my skin as the sun weakly shines through smoke and ash-clouds—this morning there is only me.

Memory: A headless torso dragging at her feet, I knew him but I can't remember his name, his face. But she knows that if even she'd seen his dead eyes staring up at her only yesterday, this morning she would still be unable to remember his name or his face.

Memory: A tiny figure leaping from a building, falling, I knew her but I can't remember her name, I can't remember her face. But I know in my heart that she was smiling in relief as she fell.

"We've been fighting them since the beginning," she says again. "We... Maybe we scored a few victories against them."

We did, she thinks. We must have. One or two. Or at least... a few battles where more than half of us got out.

Casey says, "You been fighting them for years, how come I've never seen you or any soldiers before? Never seen any fighting around here."

"You didn't see the explosion? The Hall of Justice?" Grud, it had been beautiful and terrible. The home of Law itself. It should have been destroyed years ago on the first day of Judge Death's reign.

She thinks: *cleansed*.

Wrong word. She shudders.

"No?" Casey blinks at her. "No explosions. Just the usual fires. Flicker up, burn out. There's so much stuff down there under the bones. Fires deep down."

"Two... three days ago, we blew it up."

"No. Didn't see anything. We was probably hiding, Oscar and me. Don't really come above ground much. We was unlucky, like I said, being above ground to run into you."

"You must have heard it?"

Blankly: "No."

She thinks: There were ten of us that morning, and there were three of us that evening, and the sun rises today to cast its light on the only one of us that's left. It feels like a new wound, that this boy is the only living thing left now, and he didn't witness it. Didn't notice it. Just like that, an era of the world is passed and ended, and the world goes on as if nothing has happened.

I thought, we thought—destroying the Grand Hall of Justice might mean… something. To… someone.

Then the boy says, "What's a 'Hall of Justice,' anyway?"

"It's… That huge building? With the gold eagle on it?" Astonishment, then horror, then wonder, joy. "*Want a trip to the Hall of Justice?*" one could whisper and a battle-scarred veteran would break down weeping, soil themselves, "*Not that, don't speak of that place.*" This boy's innocence, his blank eyes… So afraid of words and cursed places, but the worst place of all, the most corrupted words of all, mean nothing.

"It was a bad place," Anderson says. "We blew it up. That's all."

He still looks doubtful. "Why?"

"To destroy *them*."

She can't look at him now. We all knew it would fail. Insanity. As we have been told over and over, you cannot kill that which does not live. But in the end, we thought… I thought…

She shuts her mind to it. Squeezes her mind closed, finds she had screwed up her fists, tensed her shoulders.

We all thought… And we were right. Memory: The faceless man and the faceless woman and Anderson and another seven who have no form at all in her mind beyond shadow-shapes as human, the last of the Mega-City One Judges, planning a glorious, futile death.

That's all we've done all these years, she thinks. Dream up increasingly desperate ways we can die fighting.

"I'm a… a soldier, Casey," she says. "It's my duty. Someone had to stand up for what's right. And I wanted to do it. I had to do it. Didn't have a choice but to fight."

The boy Casey gives her a look that says he has no idea what she's talking about. Anderson wonders then how long it has been since he last heard a human voice beside his own. What can words like 'fight,' 'duty,' 'right' mean to him?

She says, "I'm like Oscar if Oscar hadn't managed to rip Judge Mortis's skull off. So let's leave it there, shall we?

"Now, look, I know you said this place is cursed, and I—I do believe you, what happened here—

"But, look, I'm hungry and thirsty, and I need to eat. You need to eat. And there's maybe blankets, stuff we can take… It might be cursed, but it will keep us alive. We need to get moving, though. Get stuff together and go."

He is still sitting trying to understand anything she's said. "Go?"

"Yes, go."

"But I live around here. I'm not leaving. I've been safe here for, dunno, years."

"Safe here?" In the shadow of the Hall of Justice itself, so close to them? How had he survived? she asks herself. Then she thinks: he survived by hiding, being so small and insignificant Death himself has overlooked him.

"Casey, you don't understand. What Oscar did to Mortis… You think he'll forgive that? Ignore that? He'll be searching for us. He's been searching for me for years. After what happened yesterday, he'll be looking and he'll never stop. We have to get away before he finds us."

His eyes fill with tears again. Snot bubbles from his nose. Rocking, silently, silently banging his head. "Like I said before: I was safe until you came along."

Like I said before, she thinks, it's all my fault.

THE BOY FOLLOWS Anderson through the tower block, trailing behind her, watching but not helping her gather up supplies. The place is mouldy, filthy, and frighteningly untouched. Beds neatly made, clothes folded in drawers, a closet full of high-heeled shoes. Anderson thinks of the residents ensuring everything is tidy before they go out to die. Eating a final meal and doing the washing up and stacking plates back on the shelf, *"Ready to go, then, dear?" "Yes. No—wait, there's a glass there needs putting away." "Do hurry up, dear, we'll be late." "There'll be quite a queue, I should think, darling, I should think we've got time to wash a couple of glasses up."* No wonder this place is thought of as cursed.

There is indeed food in plenty. Tins of beanz. All the different Grot Pot varieties [flavours? no, totally the wrong word]. Her fingers linger over a jar of caff. Too dangerous to light a fire. No water to boil anyway. She opens it, takes several deep breaths. Rancid grease smell: real caff! One apartment has a false cupboard back, she hasn't busted a place for sugar and coffee for years, obviously, but it all comes back to her with the caff scent, she takes the boarding down and there are bags and bags of the white and a bag of Ismael dry-roast, and she wants to cry worse than she did when Casey talked about Oscar the dog.

"Right. Let's go."

The boy's eyes are fixed on the bag of supplies. "You sure...?"

She's found a jumper, too. Holds it out to Casey. "Clean. And warm. So let's say you're right and it's cursed... but I've got my gun."

He hesitates. Puts it on, takes her hand.

Grud knows where they are going. Where do you go, Anderson thinks, when you've failed to kill Death?

The world's dead, she thinks. There is literally nowhere to go. We could walk forever, and we'd never find another living soul. Best-case scenario is that we walk on alone until we die of old age.

She thinks: So that's what we'll do, I guess.

"We'll go east, Casey. You know what we'll find, if we go east?"

"No, miss?"

"First, we'll be walking into the sunrise. Which is a good thing to be walking into. We'll see the sun born in the mornings. We won't see the sun die at night. And if we go east, Casey, we'll come to the ocean. We can watch the sun rise over the ocean. I saw it before once. Always wanted to see it again. What do you think?"

"The sun's a big ball of fire the Earth goes round, miss. Sunrise is when the bit of the world we're on turns towards the sun, miss. Sunset is when the bit of the world we're on turns away. The sun's not born and it doesn't die." He shrugs. "That's what Mum told me, anyway. Maybe she was wrong."

24.

Going slowly, picking their way through the ruins of Mega-City One. Anderson feels dead eyes watching her. Her skin prickles. She thinks: Someone's walking over my grave. They're out there hunting me down. This huge empty world—they have nothing to do but search for me. Huddling in the shelter of broken walls, towers of rubble, bone heaps. Would provide cover, if they knew what direction the enemy was coming from. Look to the east, to the west, to the north, to the south. The enemy could be anywhere. Everywhere. The mighty army of… four. If you'd told me, once, Anderson thinks, that I'd be fleeing across the world from four perps, I'd have laughed until my tampon came loose. There were eight hundred million people living here once. All of whom were afraid of me. Empty sky above, empty land below. Dust and ash miles high, dust and ash and shattered rockcrete miles deep. Casey's breath, so gruddamn loud, Casey's footsteps, her own heartbeat. Then only silence. She tries to think if the Dark Judges make any noise as they move. They must, she thinks, make footsteps.

She imagines Judge Fear cursing because he's stepped on a twig.

A long time since she's last been here. Casts her mind back, reckoning the years, but Casey was right, no time passes in a dead world. She last walked the streets of downtown Mega-City One... before all her friends were dead. She's seen it burn, seen its rubble, gunned her Lawmaster through its shattered streets with the warm wind in her hair fleeing in wounded panic away. Long reconciled herself to its destruction—and she herself has so recently brought down its final terrible landmark, the Grand Hall of Justice. She fixes her eyes straight ahead, pretends she sees nothing beyond the rubble that makes up the world. Pretends she is pretending she can't recognise anything of Mega-City One.

And that's easy enough, because there is nothing she can recognise as Mega-City One.

So she is wallowing in self-pity. Maybe? Unfair? The sky overhead the colour of her wounds, and as painful to look at, churning red clouds mounting over columns of black smoke. The last few City Blocks still burning. And most of those are built of human bones. Hard indeed to trace out any memory of the wonder that had been that Bride of Cities, that fairest of the fair, Pearl of the Eastern Seaboard, that city golden-roaded and crowned with topless towers, that far-fallen long-lost world-renownéd marvel that had been Mega-City One. Her feet stumbling in the dust, the boy's feet dragging beside her, sometimes his head jerks up thinking the dog Oscar is running towards them, sometimes her head jerks up thinking a very different thing draws near. She can pretend she recognises this lump of rockcrete, tumbled with a human skull crushed beneath it; she can pretend she recognises this patch of cinders where a building has come down in blackened lumps. Once upon a time she could have walked this city blindfolded, knew it like a lover, its scents, its sounds, the current in the air around the high buildings, the patterns of rain and wind—ah, the shift in the cracks between the paving stones here means we've turned into Parallel Alley, the way the light feels on my face, dappled, flashing like a minnow, it can only be the morning light reflected in the windows of Stacey's

Department Store. All lost. Like her friends' faces, her friends' names, she can no longer remember enough to see it. Thus, yes, after these long years in exile, killing, hiding, hunted and hunter, after the failure of her hopes for a martyr's hero's death—she can be forgiven for her self-pity, her wallowing, her distraction. And the boy, too, has his drowning, soul-eating, forgivable grief for his dog that keeps his mind and his senses numbed.

THE BOY IS a child. He can be forgiven.

ANDERSON'S FOOT SLIPS, she skids, almost falls over. Grabs out at Casey. He pulls her steady. "What?" Distracted, dreaming. Her eyes sore with waterless tears. "What?"

She is standing on the edge of what looks like—wait, cast her mind back—an… an ice-rink. Smooth flat surface. Shiny. Like… water? Solid. Hard. Dark.

Glass.

A lake of… glass.

Casey says, "We have to go round, miss. Sorry, I should have realised, we shouldn't have come this way. It's miles and miles round. Sorry."

He's backing away, tugging Anderson with him. The ground beneath their feet is slippery as glass and as they step back it's oddly yielding and soft. Anderson says with sudden horror, "What is it?"

"Mum said it was virtri… virtrified… vitrified organs." He shrugs. "People what got turned into glass cause they burned so hot."

Both backing away. So like a cool, dark, deep lake that Anderson can see monsters rising up out of the depths.

"There used to be, like, hundreds of people living round here. That apartment block we was hiding in—there used to be lots of blocks like that. If you can believe that! And they piled them all together when they was dead, or some of them was dead, and the fire was so hot they turned into glass. That's what Mum said, anyway. It was like a really big puddle of liquid, Mum said, then it set like that." Casey's eyes are bulging. "Imagine! That many people alive, they could be as big as that when they was all up dead."

"A beautiful mirror. Reflecting the sssky. I like to tell myssself that it'sss ssstill liquid. Underneath the crussst. One could ssswim in it. Or I could. Being fireproof.

"Imagine it."

And she'd thought the burning smell was the usual smell of a world burning. And she'd thought the heat was... Scrub that, she hadn't smelled the flames or felt the heat. Self-pitiful. Wallowing. Disgusted.

Thus: distracted.

Almost, she can be forgiven for being distracted.

THE SPEAKER IS just a man. A man, and man-sized: except his trident is as huge as the huge night sky. A man, and man-sized: so Anderson herself must be a child again. His trident glows like the sun when it is dying. He is the size of the sky and the stars and bigger and taller and more terrible. He is the size of a man, not even a tall man, and he smiles at Anderson. A creature of golden fire, faceless, formless, toothed, clawed, all-devouring.

THERE ARE FOUR Dark Judges: Judge Death, Judge Fear, Judge Fire, Judge Mortis. And of these four, Judge Fire is in Anderson's eyes the most dangerous. Death and Fear and Mortis kill individually, with... Grud help her, she has been doing this so long now she almost thought 'with care.' Certainly, they, um, *tailor* their killing. One-on-one, a cold hand's caresses, a stolen glimpse beneath Fear's visor. Fire alone of the four Dark Judges can kill a battalion at once and from a distance. Pour out fire from his trident.

Grud, how many times she's seen it. Seen her friends, yes, *swimming* in fire.

The most dangerous, yes, but she thinks of him also as the least frightening of the Dark Judges, sometimes, in her more hopeful moments. The most... human. If that isn't too absurd. The *way* he kills, perhaps; the need for a weapon. His coat of flames that makes a barrier between him and those he kills. She has thought, sometimes, in her more hopeful moments, that he needs to be apart from those he kills, keep his distance from them, because the act of killing bothers him more than it bothers Death and Fear and Mortis. He... feels things that the others do not. She has thought in her most hopeful or most desperate moments that on occasion he would hesitate before he killed.

Guilt burns like a fire. Hot, like a fire, burns up in one's face and chest. And shame burns like that.

And he still has a human skull as his face.

So, she sometimes thinks...

He rears up before her vast, blackened bones and golden flames and the reek of his smoke, and in that moment he is the worst of them, for he is there to kill her and the boy and there is no escape. And she thinks: To die by fire... to die consumed by his guilt and shame, the flames of his self-hatred... that is the most terrible death.

Fire in her eyes. The boy Casey screams.

CRASHING, SURGING, RUSHING, breaking in endless rising waves. Burning and it's pain on her body and her mind is red and gold, pain and fire and the brilliance of her body lit, illuminated, raging, her body is become as the sun. Fire running everywhere all over. Running, running, burning, her whole body is fire and it hurts and it will make her clean. And she's burning and all is fire and burning everywhere, running everywhere, and she hurts and she is so beautiful dressed in fire, she shimmers like a queen in a silken gown, she is become like unto a god. She is blind and dumb and the fire is all her world that she has ever been, all she ever was and is and will be is burning. All she will ever be—is burning. Consumed by her own guilt and shame and self-hate.

She's falling a thousand miles.

She's floating on this sea of warm flames.

She's sinking into warm soft fire like sinking into a warm soft bed. It is sweet and good against her skin.

She's so very tired. She hasn't felt warm like this for a long time. Years and years since she had a warm bath or a warm soft bed. Felt the sun warm on her skin. Her eyes are closed and the light behind her eyes is golden. Beautiful colour. And the light is bright, she hasn't seen bright light for so long either, clear and gold not choked by filthy smoke. It's so good. Pleasant. She rolls deeper into this dying. It's not painful at all. Not terrible. In this warmth, this peace, she's cleansed. I have sinned by living. Now I am stripped bare to my dead bones. I too will be clear, clean glass, she thinks.

"Miss!"

The boy. Casey. Screams.

"*Ssshe's dead, boy. Burned to a… crisssp.*"

"Miss! Please! Fight him!"

Tries to get up. Thinks: I will not let anyone get away with a joke that feeble. A clunking noise, a grunt. The fire that holds her seems to lessen. The boy screams and Fire's voice comes triumphant: "*You will burn, boy. And yet: for what you did to Judge Mortisss… I don't know, boy, whether to punish you worssse or reward you with a quicker death.*"

Anderson staggers to her knees. Spews fire. Spits out her own cremated ashes. Blurred vision, afterglow images and mostly just red, red, red. Glittering. And a lot of motes floating before her—that's my ashes getting in my eyes, she thinks. The boy Casey is crouched, pulling himself into a ball, making himself small as small. Judge Fire stands over him, trident raised, his flames flickering from gold to white to red.

"He told me what you and your dog did, boy. He was... ssshaking with rage. He'd had to... had to... he had to grope around in the rubble to find his ssskull, boy. To put it back on. And the firssst time, he found the wrong ssskull. And the sssecond time, he had his own ssstupid sssheep's ssskull, but he put it on backwards."

A horrible coughing sound. Judge Fire is laughing.

"*He was ssstumbling around unable to ssseeee out. And your dog, boy... your dog...*" Judge Fire is laughing so hard he almost drops his trident. "*Your dog... has left... tooth marksss... in his ssskull.*"

The fire that had consumed Anderson had burned for... ten seconds?

Judge Fire has no interest in her, no idea she is the Last Judge.

"*I might take you back to sssee Mortisss, boy. He'd like to sssee you.*

"*I'd like to sssee him sssee you.*

"*Sssee hisss face. I'd almossst die laughing.*"

"Drokk you, monster." Anderson doesn't laugh when she shoots Fire in his face.

Bullets rip into Fire. She knows from bitter experience she can't harm him. He jerks, head and arms thrashing, holes opening in his charred torso. Cool air around Anderson as the cloak of flames Fire wears is half extinguished. She shoots again, heavy bullets she once used for riot control in those innocent golden halcyon days of her youth. Fire crumples backwards. Bends oddly and horribly back at the waist. She thinks of plastic burning, folding up into itself, shrivelling up.

The way a crisp packet burns.

She lets rip until she's afraid she'll be out of ammo. Makes his body dance. His flames guttering: reeks. Burned hair. Burned tyres. He squeals and it does sound like a man being burned alive. Like the pain of what was done to him is finally coming out.

So she shoots again and faster, pummels him with bullets. Wonders what would happen if she shot an incendiary round at him.

Fight fire with fire, right?

CASEY STAGGERS TO his feet. "Miss! Stop! Miss, we gotta run! Miss, you can't kill him!" Mumbling, lost in the crackle of gunshots. "Miss!"

"I've got him, Casey."

"Miss! We have to run!"

Judge Fire jolting like he's a maggot on a hook. Beautiful. She could keep shooting him up for hours, keep watching him thrash about.

"Miss!"

Casey breaks from her, runs, vanishes behind a mound of rubble. A hiss from Judge Fire. His flames burn up black. Billow out like wind-blown hair. Like he is reaching a thousand arms out.

Anderson's gun stutters to silence. Her finger frozen on the trigger. Mostly out of bullets.

Fire's burned skull face leers at her. Shattered from her gunshots. Eye holes bright with flames. Flames leaking from the cracks. Dribbling flames.

Smiles.

Reaches out.

"*Well, that was a bit of pointlesss fun. Are you quite finissshed?*"

Casey screams louder. Anderson begins to back away. Heat building on her face.

She throws herself sideways as a blast of flame turns her vision to a red void. Smell of her hair, her boots, her skin charred and grilled. Hot metal stink, her gun so hot in her hand she has to fight herself not to drop it. Rolls and crashes and rolls to shelter, coughing out hot air and her body's ash and smoke. Everything white. Fading to merely red.

Then—darkness.

Cool air.

Too cold.

Gasped in, grateful. Lungs, skin, vision soothed. She thinks, dimly: Grud, that's good.

Her skin seared like prime steak, covered in goosebumps. Her teeth chattering. She thinks: too cold. And a shadow in her mind and over her eyes. A veil of darkness, and in the darkness there are horrors moving. A shadow puppet play of Anderson dying and killing over and over again.

She blinks. Shakes her head. Fire-bright and shadow-dark resolves itself into seeing. Like a kaleidoscope set down and falling still. Judge Fire and Judge Fear stand side by side with Anderson at their feet where Fire's flames have cast her. Fire raising his trident. Fear raising his visor to show his face.

The boy Casey is nowhere, and she thinks, thank Grud for small last mercies.

SHE AND HER comrades fought Fire and Mortis in the rubble of the Grand Hall of Justice. She watched Fire rise out of the flames unharmed, perhaps delighted; watched Mortis pull his crumbling form into larger pieces, flail out at the ruins that covered him so that the rockcrete crumbled into dust. She ran then, as Fire loosed his trident and her companions fell into his embrace. The last thing she remembers of that battle is the smell and sound of roasting, rotted flesh. She fought the Dark Judges many times before—the purpose of her life now is only to fight them—but even so the shock of seeing the two Dark Judges up close again leaves her reeling; last time, one of her companions shot himself rather than face them in battle once more.

Judge Mortis makes her want to vomit in revulsion. Judge Fire is her secret horror of death by burning. Judge Fear is...

Well-named.

She has not seen Judge Fear up close for a long time. Years, if the word means anything. Since the last-before-the-last-desperate-last-stand resistance, *charge in, fall back, fall back, we can't hold them, fall back.* The memory is so terrible she still wakes sweating from the nightmare, weeping out, "Fear! He's coming! Help me!" She sees him in her mind so often. And the reality standing proud before her, gauntleted hand raising his helmet visor to show himself to her: that is worse than her memory's fear.

A black great helm, crowned with wings like those of a bat, and the bars of its visor seem to smile at Anderson. Mantraps hanging at his waist crusted with her lost comrades' blood. And he raises his visor to unveil himself, reveal himself, and Fire beside him is eager and keen to see her die in fear.

"*Gaze into the face of Fear.*" She can't close her eyes. She can't look away. Forces herself to stare at Judge Fire, but it's painful and her eyes flick back to Fear's helmet, she can't not look.

To see her worst fears… She has to look.

A thousand mouths, all screaming. A thousand eyes, watching Anderson with reproach.

Her fear, her horror, the deepest sickness in her heart… is that they're right. That the Dark Judges are right.

Life is so putrid and messy and hurtful. Life is too painful to endure. Life is a terrible, bad thing.

Death is—

A great weight crashes down on top of her. Knocking all the air out of her lungs. Dragging her life away. She feels herself falling. Sinking. The void opening beneath her, she is falling through the dark, with Fire and Fear tiny staring down above her. Falling away into the darkness even from them. Spinning away out of time. A roar in her ears that is her world ending. Darkness covering her eyes, choking even Fire's red flames away. She can't breathe, she can't hear, she can't see. Her mind is blank but for her death.

25.

And it's dark when Anderson opens her eyes. So utterly dark she thinks: That's it, I'm dead. It's all over.

Thank Grud.

Years and years of fighting, resisting, telling herself, telling others, that they can still somehow—in some impossible to understand way, through some increasingly absurd plan, with guns and sticks and in the end their bare hands—defeat Death. Go in in something vaguely resembling battle order, make an attempt at a fighting retreat, shooting to provide cover, then make a mad run leaving her gun abandoned and her companions abandoned. Regroup days later, counting the spaces where friends had been, not speaking a word. The usual routine, until there were kids in the resistance who thought that that was what 'battle' meant. We never give up and we never give in, because the alternative to dying in battle is… dying. While there are ten of us left alive on this ruined earth, we keep fighting, drokk it, until there's no one left. Because the alternative is… there being no one left, only slightly quicker.

Better to be killed by the Dark Judges than be killed by the Dark Judges, right?

That's unfair, she thinks. Death in battle would mean something. Grud only knows what, but *something*.

Shaking her fist at the idea that she'd die one day. Me? No! If I go on running about with a gun in my hand fighting, I'll live for ever, me.

And finally it's happened, and she can rest.

A great sense of peace sweeps over her. The dark is absolute, and for the first time in years she doesn't need to stare into it in case something monstrous might come creeping out. A silence she can enjoy.

She stretches out her legs. Luxuriates in her death as she had luxuriated in the flames she had hoped would kill her. A hero's death, she thinks, taken down by Fire and Fear. That's more than I could have hoped for. Always imagined she'd die of hunger in the end. The last best hope for humanity, a handful of ex-Judges drawing straws to decide who ate whom until there was one left alive to starve.

I'd have cut off my own legs and eaten them if I had to, she thinks. Kept myself alive a few weeks longer gnawing on my own finger bones, as some final *drokk you* to Death.

Grud, it's peaceful being dead.

"Miss? Are you alright? I thought you were crying. We need to run, miss."

Casey's voice.

She sits up. "What?"

Dead? Falling? Her hands touch warm soft rubble. Cosy comfortable, like a blanket.

No wonder she feels full of peace and rest.

Draws back with a whimper as she realises what it is.

She isn't dead, and Fire hasn't killed her, and neither has Fear killed her despite her eyes staring up willingly into his face.

She's fallen into a hole.

"Miss, we need to go really *quick*. They don't like scrabbling about digging and that, miss. Running and whatnot. Not proper for, like, undead superfiends, I guess. But they'll come for us. Dig and run."

She says distantly, "What happened?"

"It's like Judge Fire said, miss—the… the ground round here, in places it's still all burning and liquid underneath. If you're not careful, if you tread in the wrong place, you can sink."

"And I... trod in the wrong place?"

"You was lying in the right place, miss. Sort of. I could see that you was sinking a bit. And that... Judge Fire, he'd made it worse by making everything all hot. You was sinking too slowly, though. They was killing you. So I climbed up that lump of rubble I was hiding behind. Jumped off. Landed on top of you.

"Weight of me falling on you made us sink real quick, miss. Then the... the ground closed over us. I think that Fear was a bit... taken aback."

She says distantly, "I thought I was experiencing the bliss of eternal peace."

"Umm, no, miss, you was experiencing me belly slamming into your guts."

"That..." Anderson considers. "That is probably to be preferred."

"I thought so, miss. If you crawl along following me... It's a bit sticky, you have to push your way through..."

It's like crawling through wet rockcrete. Pushing it away, like really slow, strange swimming. Almost like fingers of it trying to force their way into Anderson's eyes and nose and mouth. A strong, strange memory flashback, the choking, terrified, triumphant moment so long ago when she'd held Death in her mind and a Judge—Judge Dredd, that was his name—Dredd had caught her and Death both in plastic, Boing®, liquid, spraying over her, fingers of it cupping her face, covering her mouth, her eyes, holding her like clasping clenching hands, and she had thought, and Dredd had thought, that the plastic would set and hold both her and Death trapped. Encased. The memory makes her gag, reflex horror of being suffocated alive; she still sits up gasping in panic every time she gets a blocked nose. Then the despair that followed, the memory of the Boing® holding for one, two, three seconds, perhaps, that had felt like eternities, before Death shattered it apart to release them both. In the warm wet heat of this rubble, the familiar rush of panic and regret.

For perhaps three seconds I thought I had him. I thought I'd saved the world from Judge Death.

The memory, choking, horrifying, painful, is so strong.

The relief that she had failed, her joy at escaping a living tomb—that, too, she feels in a rush again now. Even now. It makes her want to cry with shame. She is blind and dumb and trapped, human flesh setting around her. Encasing her. Entombed alive.

Breathe! she thinks. Breathe, crawl, get away. Her body isn't moving. She can't move her arms or legs. Can't turn her head. The boy has vanished, she is alone, trapped, buried.

Breathe! Breathe, Anderson! Come on.

"Miss. Keep going."

His voice, very far away.

Heavy as lead, she moves one arm forward. Taking all her mental and physical strength. Pushes through jellied flesh. There is no space to move, clawing through digging her own tunnel, and she thinks: this is... like being born, I suppose. And she wants to stop and laugh more than she has for years, at the thought of being born.

Setting flesh. Pushing harder. Ache in all her limbs. Exhausting. She isn't moving. Can't be. She has to rip soft flesh apart now to drag herself on. They are going *downwards*. Not up, towards the sun.

She has a sudden memory of a couple she had once known who had a baby. He'd be ... maybe the same age as Casey now, she thinks. She'd visited them soon after the birth. The boy's head had been weirdly soft, the crown of his head pulsing. "His skull bones aren't closed yet," the baby's father had said. "It's just sort of soft, down to his brain..." And she'd felt this desire to touch the baby's head there.

Fingers digging, clawing, through soft flesh. Down and down. This is how we survive. How humanity survives a few more hours and days.

Isn't there a story, she thinks, about the world being made of flesh and people being maggots breeding in it? How it begins and how it ends.

She says in panic, choking out into human ruin, "Where are we going?" Fingers digging, clawing through soft flesh. Down and down.

There's nowhere to go. All I've ever been—is crawling and digging through human ruin and human flesh. I don't exist beyond crawling onwards. Came from nowhere. Going nowhere. Just on down through burned flesh and rotting flesh.

Stop moving. Stop breathing. Give in.

"Miss." A voice. She can remember…? "Miss, there's an old tunnel. I've broken through. Follow me, come on."

Clawing. Ripping. Flesh in her mouth.

Then—still dark, warm, rot-scented—but she is in an open space. Anderson can sense air, emptiness, stretching away left and right.

"Old tunnels from when there was more people," Casey says. "We lived down here for a while. Me and Mum. Stretch yourself out a bit, miss." Then, seeming to feel her hesitation: "It's mostly just old bits of buildings round here, miss. Not… If we're where we might be, could be, there might be a way into another old apartment block. We can have a quick rest here, miss, if you like. I think it should be safe."

"How can you possibly know where we are, Casey?"

She hears him shrug in the dark. "Can't you feel it's different round here, miss?"

"No." She thinks: if this boy survives to adulthood, meets a woman, if they have children… A new species of humans, crawling around eyeless underground. Really like maggots.

Too horrible. Better it ends in a dead world than that.

Anderson digs around in the backpack, pulls out two tins. "Here." Grud knows what's in them. As they can't see anything or smell anything beyond rotting flesh, they'll never know. But thank Grud for the everlasting wonder that is modern processed food.

The boy takes the tin silently. A movement in the dark that's him staring at it.

"Look, Casey… You saved me from two of the Dark Judges. Eat!"

"Yeah, well, if you hadn't taken this stuff, we wouldn't have run into them, would we? Said I never saw them until you turned up."

"Casey..." Anderson pops a tin. Makes a vague attempt to wipe her hand on her legs. Gropes, digs her hand in, eats.

Yum yum.

Possible beanz?

She sits back and lets out a great sigh and the heat and the terror seems to peel away. And there are stars above her. Stars, shining bright.

Pinpricks of light from the surface, she realises. Filtering down through cracks in rock and bone.

"Casey... they were hunting me, it's true. If I hadn't stumbled across you, maybe you and Oscar would still be safe, it's true. But, Casey: They're hunting down every last living thing in the world. They'd have found you in the end."

"Yeah. In the end." Casey pops his beanz tin. Munching sound. "This is good. Better than them crisps."

A pause.

"I wish Oscar was here to eat this."

"I don't think beanz are good for dogs, Casey."

A pause.

"This *world's* not exactly good for dogs, miss."

"Well... no."

They eat beanz and Anderson pretends the chinks of light are stars. She thinks: Do you know what stars are, Casey? They're other suns far off in space. There are other planets round those stars. There's life, up there in space.

She says it, fierce and sudden: "There's still hope, Casey. The war can go on. The other planets, colonies, the prison on Titan—they can fight. If we stay here, safe, stay buried long enough, someone will come and liberate the Earth."

A long silence. Then: "That'd be nice to think, miss."

WHEN THEY'VE FINISHED the beanz, they crawl on through the tunnel. Anderson has to trust (pretend) that Casey knows the way. At times she can think they're crawling through something left from the city she knew. A few metres of undersked or subpass, a sewage pipe, a flyover buried so deep it's become a tunnel. At times the passage is so narrow, her shoulders scraping the walls and ceiling, dirt slithering down her neck.

"There's a place we can stop properly up ahead, miss." His breathing is laboured. There's little air down here.

Yes: rockcrete walls, bent at odd angles to form a sheltered open space like a tent. Maybe an alley or a collapsed pedway. In the faint light coming down that she is still pretending is starlight, Anderson traces graffiti tags and a spraypainted picture of a woman's face. *Frebz waz ere. Mela gives a good time girlies. Hot dogz!!!!! Drok the Drokkin' Judges, Drokkin' Drok the Drokkin' Law.* Bloodstains and water crust.

"We can have a rest here," Casey says. "Can I have another tin of them beanz?"

"I thought you didn't need to eat much?"

"Yeah, but them beanz is delicious."

"We should ration them."

Then she thinks: what's the point?

She sits listening to him eat.

"Yum."

Then: "Miss...?"

"Yes, Casey?"

Casey says, "There hasn't been fighting anywhere for years, miss. Years and years. I've never seen fighting. There's nobody left and there's been nobody for years, miss. I've not seen anyone alive since my mum died, until you came along."

Anderson puts down her tin of beanz. Thinks: stop, Casey. Don't say it.

"You keep talking about a war, miss. But... there wasn't a war, was there? I mean... there was a bit of trouble when the Dark Judges first took over, Mum said."

Stop it.

"But it was over really quick."

Stop. Please.

Don't say it.

"If that's what you mean by a 'war,' miss..."

Stop.

Stop.

"Your side lost years ago.

"After a few weeks."

WE BLEW UP the Grand Hall of Justice, like, four days ago, Casey. Ten of us—that's enough for an army fighting a war! Ten soldiers, warriors, *Judges*. We crawled on our bellies across the ruins of Mega-City One, faces pressed to the dirt. Crawled like maggots, she thinks. We knew they knew we were coming. We knew they knew we were coming to die there. Perhaps that's why they spared me, she thinks then: because it amused them to keep me alive when I finally wanted death. The Grand Hall of Justice, a beacon, shining—in all these years of war, it had never occurred to the surviving Judges to destroy it. Not quite a good place, even before: a beacon, shining, and thus it cast a long shadow across the Meg. "Want a trip to the Hall of Justice?" one could whisper and a battle-scarred veteran would break down weeping, soil themselves, "Not that, don't speak of that place." And that had been as true in the innocent days when the Judges were only Judges and the Law was only the Law as it was under the rule of Judge Death. But the Law, Justice, Judges, these words had, she had hoped, *meant* something. As she had said of the starlight that had blazed down for a few astonishing brief nights at the beginning of the war, "This is better, we should keep this, somehow, when we win," so, "When we win, we will recreate the law and justice and the way we judge crimes," she had said. The golden eagle of Justice, the towers rising, rising over the city, the windows that watched the city as a thousand unblinking eyes. A temple to Justice and the Law, something worth holding on to, a vision in the mind to cling to even after the reality had fallen into darkness and despair. Judge Death had seized it as his headquarters even before summoning

Fire, Fear and Mortis from the Deadworld to Mega-City One. Even before the city fell to the Dark Judges, it had become too terrible to look upon. But even after the world had fallen to the Dark Judges, it had seemed impossible to Anderson—to any of them—that it should—could—be destroyed. A symbol, like her badge, of the world they were fighting to reclaim. These fragments I have shored against my ruin. The war is not over, as long as these few things remain.

She puts her hand to where her badge should be proudly displayed.

Crawling towards it with the explosives strapped to her, heavy like carrying children. Crawling through worse things than merely dead and rotting flesh. Setting the charges. Counting down.

Like a sun going nova. The blast so powerful buildings half a mile away caught fire. Then, too, she had thought that she had died, not because she was plunged into darkness but because she was become only white light.

She holds her hand out in the dark that's too dark to see. Faint traces of false stars on her skin. Dancing, twinkling, like stars, because her hand is shaking. See—My hand—I hold it out—You see the scars, where the explosion burned me. If it was lighter, if we weren't buried alive, living like maggots, you could see.

It is so hard to hold her hand out. Such an effort it leaves her sweating. Has to grit her teeth.

The last battle. Life's last stand. Destroy the Grand Hall of Justice and finally admit defeat. We crawled on our bellies knowing we would die there, but we had our guns still—I have my gun still even now. If we saw one of *them*, we would shoot it, however pointless we rediscover it is to shoot them every single time. We would die fighting, and therefore it was a battle and therefore we were soldiers and therefore we were fighting a war.

She thinks: a war that ends on our terms.

* * *

"I SAID: I'M like Oscar jumping at Judge Mortis. Now, look, you said there was an apartment block we can get to round here."

"Well, I mean... probably."

"One that didn't give in as easily as Sylvia Plath Block?"

"As what?"

"One that isn't cursed."

Blow another snot bubble from laughing, Anderson, why don't you? she thinks.

THEY CRAWL ON through what is definitely a bit of old roadway. Crumbling asphalt and the remains of—Grud, of a median strip. Anderson is almost tempted to make a *broom-broom* noise as she crawls.

"We're currently guilty of jaywalking and being in the wrong lane. You're possibly misusing a Judge's Lane, Casey, I'm afraid. But I'll let you off this once."

A grunt from Casey. I'm only trying to lighten the mood, Anderson thinks. He pulls her off the road down a narrow tunnel dug through almost solid rockcrete. A hole at the end that Anderson has to wriggle up and through, twisting her body round until she feels like a disco dancer. Glass ripping at her clothes and her hands. She comes out headfirst, falling into empty space with her cut hands scrabbling against floor tiles. Sits up, strikes something cold and hard against her shoulder. Utter mystery what it is, she gropes at it in confusion until she finds a handle and realises it's a toilet.

Grud, that's something else she hasn't seen for years.

Casey pushes a door open. Light floods in. Luxury bathroom with shower, toilet, bidet, basin shaped like a shell. A corroded mirror over the basin. Anderson's face is reflected in the mirror. She'd have liked to have panicked, to have thought there was some vicious old woman in the bathroom beside her.

The place is really high-end. En-suite to the gutted remnants of a bedroom. Walk-in wardrobe. Floor-to-ceiling mirrors, thankfully long broken. Massive bed. Unlike the Sylvia Plath apartments, it has all been turned over, the wardrobe and cupboards gutted of clothing, the bed stripped. Flood marks and fire marks. The mattress is on the floor by the window. Looks like someone pushed it against the window to try to block it. The broken window and the rents in the mattress suggest it didn't work.

The skeleton at the back of the walk-in wardrobe also suggests it didn't work. Unless the inhabitant had blockaded herself in and then cut off her own head.

Another skeleton in the kitchen. Might have been hiding in the fridge.

"So… I'm guessing this block isn't cursed?"

Casey nods. "Yeah. I like it here. You can see, the people here"—he looks at Anderson, thinking suddenly—"they was like you, miss. Soldiers. Fought."

The guy had been hiding in the salad drawer. His arms and legs had been ripped off. Tooth marks on his leg bones.

"I'm not sure I'd call what happened here soldiers fighting, Casey."

Casey frowns. "They held out here until they got killed. What else would you call it, miss?"

26.

THEY MAKE CAMP in the apartment. The two skeletons are indeed oddly comforting to Anderson. The light that had blinded her when Casey threw open the bathroom door comes from half an inch of sky at the top of the bedroom window, where the rubble ends and the new ground level begins. Anderson would guess from the roadway, the fancy furniture and fittings, that they are at least seven or eight storeys up. The block has collapsed in on itself, its higher floors form the rubble that buries it. Must have been targeted, destroyed because the inhabitants had resisted. So, yes, a good, safe, fine place.

"We'll stay here and rest a bit."

The boy nods. He looks grey and tired, heavy shadows under his eyes. Anderson thinks of her first sight of him, his triumphant shout of 'crisps!'

"How have you survived, Casey? If I'm a soldier… you're the greatest soldier that ever lived, I think."

Big eyes. "Yeah?"

Sort of a smile. "I promised Mum I'd try to keep alive as long as I could."

From the food they have left in the pack, that will be… a few more weeks?

"Your mum sounds like a good person, Casey."

"She was."

His mind's begging her to ask the question. His mind's setting up a wall with barbed wire and gun turrets in case she asks.

Anderson summons all her courage. "What was your mum's name, Casey? Did you have any other family?"

He screws his face up like he's trying to remember. Her name and her face both. "Her name was Kat, miss. My dad… I can't remember his name. 'Dad.' I had a baby sister, but I can't… She was really small. Mum said it was… that she died not knowing what she'd lost."

The half inch of light from the bedroom window is changing, shifting, turning deeper bloodier red. Sunset.

"Sun's dying," Casey says. "Like you said."

"Yeah. Like I said, tomorrow we'll go east."

He's staring at the sky as the colours change there. Red, then green, then slowly choking black. "Funny, miss, I never thought of the sun as dying before. But… Yeah. Be nice if it died for real, miss. Then we wouldn't have to see no more."

A patch of dark against the dark that was once a tower block. Bone walls and bone mountains. Eruption of blue flame on the horizon.

"Yeah," Anderson says. She takes a Grot Pot and a last precious tin of beanz out of her pack. "Here. Which do you want?"

Casey's eyes light up joyful. "If I eat any more I'll be sick and stuffed, miss. No one needs to eat this much. This is, like, a month's worth of food I've had today already."

"I know. Which do you want?"

He gives a look like he almost understands. Then he says, "No, Miss. We need to save it. I shouldn't have ate all them beanz earlier, except I needed… Taste better," he says, "if we save it."

Anderson thinks: I'm trying to give him hope, and he's trying to give me hope.

* * *

SHE THOUGHT THEY might come that night in the dark. Fell asleep even so. Isn't sure if the boy slept. But of course they wouldn't come in the dark, she thinks next morning as they eat, Casey throwing her a triumphant, *You see? Told you* look. They'd want her to see them coming from a long way away.

They are not going back underground. Casey suggested it, half-hearted—"Years, I've lived down there, miss"—but Anderson is certain. And Casey can understand, she sees in his face. "We walk in the air into the sun," she says. The apartment opens into a corridor and stairs, two flights up the stairs end and the block ends raw and jagged and sudden into the sky. A stump, like an amputated leg. Walls sheared off clean.

"Good view from up here."

The sun is rising. Being born. Clean light, in the east where the ocean must still beat on the shore, and the ocean is dead and empty but it cannot burn, it cannot be rubble and blood and bone, and when the wind blows from the east the air there over the water must still be almost clean. Drizzle blowing in Anderson's face. Making jewels in Casey's hair, making jewels in his eyelashes. Anderson rubs her face with the pleasure of dampness on her skin. Sticks out her tongue to taste the rain.

Vile with chemicals. The droplets leave dark smudges on her hands that are human ashes, human dust coming down in the rain. She rubs her hands over her burned hair. Closes her eyes, raises her face, lets the water fall on her eyelids.

The rain grows heavier as they clamber down and begin to walk east. Puddles forming in the city's rubble. Oil-slicked with human fat. It makes rainbows on the dark water and it is beautiful. Then the rain stops and the wind blows harder and they both shiver, wet and cold. Yesterday, Anderson thinks, they would have found shelter, and indeed there are the ruins of tower blocks all around them and they could indeed crawl inside or crawl back underground. But today they simply walk on. Another lake of human glass. Smoke billowing from an underground fire. A great strange twist of flyover curled across the sky that makes Anderson think of Saturn's rings. A pyramid of skulls taller than the Statue of Judgement. A pyramid of children's teeth.

They walk on all day. The wind changes direction. Blows dust and cinders that scrape at Anderson's face. The sky is changing to green and purple and silver, red clouds race in from the west to chase them. They walk in the clouds' shadows and look ahead into heavy watery light. Then the sun is behind them, already falling, the day is half-over, reaching towards its end, their own shadows fall before them with the clouds' shadows, the sun is briefly warm on the back of Anderson's neck. The clouds reach in fingers rushing to choke the sky before them. Like dogs, the clouds, running to steal the light. The wall of a City Block thrusts up before them strangely unharmed amid the desolation, the sun flashes sudden in a gap in the cloud and their shadows on the block's wall are enormous. The clouds swallow the sun, stain the sunlight green and murky, they walk around the block's roots and cross another skedway where the dead are sealed and boiled in asphalt. Their feet trample down on human faces. Yesterday, Anderson thinks, she would have tried to avoid treading where the faces were. Casey doesn't seem to notice.

There are no other people anywhere left. They are the last two living things le—

A barking. Scrabbling. A howl of utter joy.

The last... *three* living things left?

The dog Oscar bursts from behind a bone pile. Just recognisable as Oscar—as a dog—as alive. Three legs. No ears. One eye.

Gangrene dripping liquid from his flanks.

"Oscar, Oscar, Oscar, Oscar, Oscar, Oscar!" Boy and dog embracing and the dog licking at Casey with half a tongue that is blackening and too swollen to fit within its broken half-a-mouth. Jawbone smashed until the marrow shows. A hole open in its chest where its lungs are visible, wheezing to breathe, wounded and crisped and almost the same pink-grey as its raw skin. Its sides gleam golden with pus. "Oscar, Oscar, Oscar, Oscar, Oscar, Oscar!" It throws back its head and howls. Its innards hang in glistening ribbons from its opened belly. Blood and brain stuff running from its opened skull.

"Give me them last beanz, miss. He's starving, see?"

Cut throat. Can't swallow. Yellow foam bubbling from the wound. Anderson sits down. Clears a flat area of ground for the dog to lie on. Casey carefully feeds it handfuls of beanz, helping it swallow, holding the skin of its neck closed, massaging its neck so the food goes down. "Who's a good boy? Who's the best, bestest boy?" Blood and pus and worse all over Casey. He doesn't notice. Kisses the horrible remains of the dog's face.

When it has eaten the last of the beanz and snuffled at Casey enough, Casey says, "You going to do it now, miss?"

Anderson holds out her hand and Oscar snuffles at her. She turns her face to the east where the dark is coming on faster. They won't get as far as seeing a trace on the horizon that might be the sea.

"He can still walk, Casey. He can walk with us a bit."

"That's kind, miss."

THEY LIMP ON into the gathering dark with the dog hopping on its three legs beside them and dear Grud it stinks, and the noise it makes, dripping its life's filth out behind it, but it goes on close to Casey and Casey walks with his hand resting on its shoulder, doesn't care his hand is sinking into its liquid flesh. And it's night now, they are the last three living things in the world perhaps, a woman a child a dying animal, and they walk all night in the dark. Gouts of fire in the distance. A pit up close to them where blue fire flickers over white bones. A chasm reaching down bottomless, blocking their path, just too wide to step over, they have to walk its length for what might have been hours or minutes, and it seems to Anderson that there might be something else alive down there. If it was light, she thinks, she could look down into the depths of the city, there would be buildings, shops, roadways, bins overflowing with rubbish, layers of city life down there, beautiful and beloved. She thinks, briefly, that they could hide down there. Go on living years and years in the sweet dark underbelly of her city, as Casey could have done before she ran into him as his doom. The chasm ends abruptly in a hump of rockcrete that might have been a collapsed Smokatorium. Fitting.

Anderson says, "What?"

"You was laughing again."

"Oh... I..." She pats Oscar's ruined head, careful to avoid the worse wounds. "I thought they might have left these standing. Seeing as the only purpose of a Smokatorium is to kill you.

"Didn't like the competition, I guess."

The boy looks blank again.

"Never mind, Casey." Some things from the before times, Anderson thinks, are rightly inexplicable.

THEY WALK ON into the east and perhaps, perhaps, they might reach the ocean, because she would like so much to see it again. Been crouched so many years now in the Cursed Earth Badlands where all was dust and dry cracked ruin long before the Dark Judges came. Bled out there, bled dry like a person dying slowly, years and years before Judge Death. Her skin abraded, stained dust-yellow; her clothes worn and stained. She remembers with almost a thrill the way Judge Fire's flames had licked around her somehow soft as warm water. The damp warm softness of layer upon layer of slowly setting liquid flesh. To put but one hand into real flowing water! To see the waves rise and break!

Water, she thinks, the ocean—that's almost like something alive. The waves rising and falling, the tides, the way water ebbs... She thinks of Oscar's lungs visible and heaving, Casey's chest rising and falling as he drew breath.

False hopeful, knowing it is false, she walks on holding Casey's hand and Casey with his hand in turn on Oscar's dying shoulders, they walk on, the three of them, all through the night and into the sun as it rises green and pink as bloody wounds. They crest a hill of ruin and corpses, Anderson sees a flash on the far horizon and points and lies to Casey with a cry, "The sea!" They slip down the hill stirring up dust surfing bones. The wind blows from the east and sends a rain of human blood and human fat on their upturned faces. They crest an ash heap. "We'll be there soon," Anderson lies. The ocean has gone and boiled away.

THEY WALK UNTIL the sun is high and bright enough through black clouds to cast faint dim shadows that fall long behind them, so that as they walk they cannot escape the darkness that follows them. Their shadows point into the west where the sun is dying in blood.

THEY WALK A little further across an ash-field. Clean and fine as a beach. Three sets of footprints. The last living footprints.

THEY WALK A little further, until they reach the end.

27.

MORTIS IS THE first. Naturally. He's raging. Or laughing: his sheep skull face shows no expression. Though he showed little enough expression in his life. Lumpen, dreary, sterile man. Death, Fire, Fear, one might imagine could have had lives, partners, children, friends and family, in some other world less cruel and less filled with violence. Mortis: not. His blank skull face meets them over the next bone hill. Juts between Anderson and the morning sun. His huge, clumsy, killing hands.

Oscar's tooth marks in his skull. The sunlight comes in pinpricks through them.

Like stars.

Oscar barks in delight. The funny nice bone man! Anderson and Casey stop, look down from the bone hill's crest. Mortis looks up at them. Shakes his head.

FIRE STEPS FROM behind a chunk of rockcrete. His flames are dim to mask him from their sight. His head turns from Anderson to Mortis. So much more expression in his burned human skull face. Crispy black like spare-ribs: slap some barbeque sauce on him! Plants his trident firmly in the ash-field. Sets off a trickle of cinder lumps that flow down and bury Mortis's feet. Mortis shifts his feet. Glares at Fire. Fire ignores him. Leers, like the handsome, over-cocky young man he had once been, might regret no longer being, at Anderson. Sends his flames out as dramatic as a cape swirling. Golden fire. Almost handsome.

FEAR RISES UP as if he has been waiting underground hidden like a spider. Grud knows, perhaps he has. A tiny patch of dark, a faint stain on a child's bedroom ceiling, and from that such nightmares come. His cloak swirls, stirring dust-devils. Would hardly let his glamour be eclipsed by Fire the sentient toast crust. Shifting movement beneath his helmet's visor. Flickers that might be his eyes darting, or his tongue as he licks dry lips. The mantraps hanging at his side clank together. The only sound from any of the three.

"THEY'RE A RIGHT ugly old lot, aren't they, miss?" Casey says. "Right bunch. Can't decide which looks the most stupid." He squeezes Anderson's hand, she squeezes back. Patter of urine as the boy wets himself. "Wouldn't give any of them a single crisp if they was begging me," Casey says.

"No, Casey. It's all right, Casey. It's all right."

She should have shot the boy and the dog both after she'd lied that they could see the sea, Anderson thinks.

MORTIS'S EMPTY EYEHOLES move to look behind Anderson. Fire's fire eyes move. A sense of movement behind Fear's helmet. Cold, foetid smell, worse than the dog. Anderson turns around. Casey turns around and she wants to say "Don't look."

Oscar whimpers. Howls.

They can try to laugh at Judge Fear and Judge Fire and Judge Mortis.

Impossible, for all his absurdity, to laugh at Judge Death.

* * *

He looks small, compared with the other three Dark Judges. A small, neat figure. From a distance he looks, indeed, far more human than his companions. The swing of hips as he strolls towards Anderson. His wide smile.

"*Well, then. Look who it isss. My old friend. My firssst guide to the sssights of thisss fine metropolis of Mega-City One. There at the very beginning. Here—at the very end.*" He sighs. "*Still wearing those absssurd high heels, I sssee. But: you look ssso worn out, Anderssson.*"

"Go to Hell, creep!"

Death spreads his hands expressively. "*Ummm...?*"

Even Casey seems to snigger. Anderson feels her face flush red. Hefts her Lawgiver, ready to pointlessly shoot.

"*The mind is its own place, and in itself can make a heaven of hell, a hell of heaven.*" Mortis's voice. Solemn. Dry. Heavy. Intoning.

Death shoots him a look of profound irritation. "*Yesss, yesss, thank you, I think we've all got the general idea, Judge Mortisss.*" Swings back round to Anderson. His smile now a gaping leer.

Thrust of his pelvis in his tight leathers. Long fingers curled and flexed. His mouth open, pouting, beckoning.

Sliding forwards towards Anderson like a cat. Arching his back. Stretching out.

The other three Dark Judges forming a line behind him. Holding a respectful distance.

Oscar growls and whimpers and howls. Mourning for Casey. Stretched out on Casey's grave.

"It's all right," Casey whispers. "It's all right, Oscar, boy. She's a soldier, remember?" His voice is blown away in a hiss of the wind.

Anderson lets rip with her Lawgiver. Old, jammed up, lovingly repaired. Useless and pointless. Bullets flying, showering, pummelling Judge Death.

As she knows he will, he stands and smiles as she shoots him. Pierces him and penetrates him. Over—over—over again, and he stands and smiles.

Dry holes. Red light shining through him. Like stars, Anderson thinks.

The bullets slamming into the three Judges behind him. Ricocheting off Fear's helmet. Melting in Fire's flames. Tracing patterns like cracks in a saucer across Mortis's skull.

She shouts, "Get down, Casey! Oscar!" in case the bullets rebound to strike the boy. That would be ironic, don't you think?

Her finger on the trigger pumping and the bullets spraying, hailstorm hammering the four Dark Judges. Closes her eyes, firing blind. Her mouth tastes sour. The stink growing worse. You cannot kill that which does not live. But you can shoot and shoot and beg and beg and you have to try. Pointlessly try. Squeezing the trigger so hard her hand hurts. Over—over—over again.

The Lawgiver judders.

Bullets out.

Anderson stands with her eyes closed. Void in her head. She drops the gun, hears it thud on the ash-field. Hears the patter of bone and ash thrown up and falling back.

Opens her eyes. The light is very bright.

Casey's voice whispers, "Miss?"

Judge Death stands before her, smiling his wide inviting grin. Riddled with holes in his face and body. Flakes of himself drifting on the wind. Mortis's skull traced out with cracks like a withered autumn leaf. Fire's flames low and pale. Fear's hand already waiting to raise his visor. Whatever she had seen last time, now it will be worse.

Death stretches and curls his hand out. Draws it out to brush her throat. His dead hand hovering over her heart.

"*Are you ready to die, Andersssson?*"

I've been ready to die for years, a part of her thinks.

"*Death isss very easssy. I don't know why you look ssso reluctant even now. Ssso afraid.*"

A twist of his hand. Flick of his wrist.

A conjuror making magic.

The dog Oscar howls and falls dead.

"*Sssee?*"

He stinks worse when he is preening after a kill. Like the pleasure of it runs through his body, even dead.

"*I've ssseen a lot of death, Anderssson. I think I can claim sssome expert knowledge when I sssay that you don't want to die. We've ssspared you ssso many timesss.*

"*But what do you want to live for, Anderssson?*

"*This world has been dead for yearsss.*"

Almost civilised. The villain giving his evil speech.

Then Anderson is on her knees crying. Death looming over. He is the destruction not of worlds but of whole universes. The all-devouring, the ruination of all hope. His smile is a wound in existence. No escaping. No escape. All that ever was and is and will be, will come in the end only to death. Life is futility. Death is king and lord.

And Death is… disgusting. Reek of decay. Drip of rotten fluids. Oozing. Dryness of old, leached bones making Anderson's skin crawl. His mouth opens and he is panting with need and urgency. A gaping hole sucking her life into it deep. She shrinks down, claustrophobia seizing her. Swallowed and lost.

"No… please…" She likes being alive. Clinging on: one more breath, then one more breath.

"*I could ssspare you again, Anderssson. If you wissssh.*"

Yes… She thinks in despair: I do wish. I just want… to live.

"*What would you give to ssstay alive? To be the last living thing on thisss earth?*

"*What would you give?*"

She'd give… anything.

She almost understands what he's offering…

"*But of coursse you're not quite the lassst.*" Death's long fingers stroking, toying with Casey's hair. "*You like ressscuing children, I think, Anderssson.*"

Casey sobs. Whimpers like the dog that lies dead at his feet.

If she hadn't stumbled across him…

"*I'll let you live. You, alone out of your world. All you have to do isss—*"

And the face of Death looking down on Anderson. And Anderson looking up at Death.

"*You know what you have to do, Anderssson.*"

She sobs. Whimpers like the dog at Casey's feet.

Reaches out her hands. The bridge, once, between this world and Judge Death.

It is harder than she'd thought, to break Casey's neck.

28.

THE DARK JUDGES are walking away. Fear, Fire, Mortis, Death himself… walking away. Leaving her. As they always do.

The fear that gnaws the heart away, weakens bones until they're brittle and snap, crawls in the mind when the night drags long. The fire that burns away any hope or beauty, punishes all without regret. The decay of flesh, of thought, of worlds, all things falling in the end to dust.

One striding as a king, crowned head held proud. One swaggering loose-hipped. One is ponderous, awkward, a shambles. One tramples corpses with every thrusting step. Small, thin figures against the vastness of a dead world. The sky changing from red to ebbing evening green. The sky itself rotting, fading, extinguished.

"Kill me, then," she shouts after Death. "I'm guilty! I deserve Judgement!"

Tiny figures. From this distance they are just four men.

"Kill me! Come on!"

Small as children now.

And gone.

Anderson is alone in a dead world. Human ash and human dust blowing in her face. A dead boy and a dead dog.

"Kill me!"

The sun sinking in the west behind her. Splendid. Such a beautiful sight, the sun's death. Her begging voice the last words. How it ends.

"Kill me! Come on! Please!"

Silence.

29.

AND THAT'S ALL folks.

HOW IT ENDS.

30.

NO, SERIOUSLY.

A LONE WOMAN dying in a dead world. A dead boy and a dead dog at her feet.

THE END.

PSI

DARK JUDGES

31.

"…No…"

Death hisses through his teeth. "*No?*"

"No…"

She's trying… to see…

A dead wasteland. Dust, and nothing more. The sky fading to dust now. The ocean fading. No difference between sea and sky and earth. The end of everything.

She's trying… to see…

Grey. Fading to white. Empty.

Boring.

Dead.

But… she's… trying… to see…

To see…

See…

THE GRAND HALL of Justice cafeteria. Anderson sits up very straight in her chair, staring straight ahead. A cup of caff cold and forgotten by her right hand. Her fingers curled. The shape of a hand squeezing tight around a child's throat.

Her voice comes out very faint. "No."

Sidney De'ath says, very reasonably, "It was painless, Anderson." He shrugs his thin shoulders. Dandruff sparkles on his shoulder pads under the neon cafeteria lights. "I don't know why you're making such a fuss."

"No!"

The table goes over in a storm of broken crockery. Caff and synth-milk spilling across the greasy floor. The people Anderson's populated the cafeteria with shift away. Frightened, at the corner of her vision. They don't have faces, but she can tell they're upset by her.

She kicks a cup across the room. Hears it smash. Curls her fingers around Sidney's throat.

"It wasn't like that! It. Wasn't. Like. That."

This close, she can smell him. Not the death stench that makes his victims cower—the smell of a mortal man with poor personal hygiene. Greasy stains on his shirt collar. Yellow crust on his left ear lobe. Dirty skin on his neck. And underneath that a faint sick tang of rot that isn't frightening but only rancid, like a cat's teeth.

He whimpers.

"This isn't—" She stares around the cafeteria. That's not real either. "You lost!" she screams. "None of that happened." She stares around her. "Did it?"

Sidney's choking. His stick-thin arms thrash, trying to tug her hands from his throat. Sweat stains under both armpits. Makes a grunting noise that might be him saying something.

Anderson closes her grip. Squeezes. Sidney's eyes bulge. She feels the bones in his neck crunch.

It's easier than killing Casey was.

Practised, she thinks.

Snot trickles out of Sidney's right nostril.

Blood trickles out of his left.

Foam appearing around his lips.

A stain at his crotch.

He goes limp. Anderson squeezes harder. Harder. Harder. The snot and blood trickle stops.

She gags in revulsion at the crusted scalp beneath Sidney's greasy hair. Drops his body. He crumples over. His head flops into the spilt caff.

Now it looks like he's vomited caff. Or had a very liquid shit.

She yells, her voice trembling, "It didn't happen. You lost. I won."

Sidney De'ath's body just lies there flaccid, caff lapping around his open mouth. Her fingerprints stand out vivid on his neck. Her hands feel disgusting from his unwashed skin.

She kicks his body. Harder. Harder. Hears his bones crack.

"It wasn't like that! It wasn't like that! It wasn't—Wasn't—"

He's dead. Dead-dead, not Death-dead. She kicks his head and his ribs and his crotch.

It feels amazing. Warm. Pleasant. Her foot meeting Sidney's groin is fair and fine. The sound of her boot grinding Sidney's groin hard is sweet music.

"Wasn't—Didn't—"

Her hands clench so tight her nails dig into her palms. Draw blood. She clenches her teeth. Bites her teeth together.

Grins.

As a child snaps his sister's favourite toy, so Sidney's body—snaps. Dead-dead, but jerking with every kick.

Dead-dead dead Death. Her heels grind. Mash his belly, liver kidney bowels pulped. Mash his ugly nothing gruddamn face.

A stain on the floor tiles. Human grouting. Wash it off later with soap like after a perp's vomited. Scrub it all clean. She kicks and stamps and stamps and kicks. When there's nothing left big enough to kick or stamp, she grinds mince and gristle under her absurd high-heeled boots.

He spreads across the floor tiles. Laps at the overturned tabletop. A spreading stinking pool called Sidney De'ath.

Bloody annihilation. Not even bones. Not even gruddamn ash. Wipe him away. That's what he deserves, gruddamn sick sack of shit. What do we do with spilled shit?

We cleanse it.

* * *

SHE COLLAPSES IN her chair. Exhausted. She's mired with him up to her waist. Droplets and lumps of Sidney in her hair, on her face. She wants to say to the meat-smear that was Sidney De'ath, "I didn't mean it. Are you all right?" Except she did mean it and she hopes he's not all right.

Droplets and lumps of Sidney on her face like… rain. Like…

She wipes them away with her sleeve. There. Done. Nothing happened. She just spilled something on the cafeteria floor. A service robot will come and clean up. Clean her boots. When her heart rate's dropped a bit, she's stopped panting and the sweat's dried on her upper lip, she strolls over to buy herself another cup of caff. Her feet slip a bit, greasy boot soles, the service bot's not done a great job. She gets a caff and a packet of crisps.

Wonders if Winstanley or Neirn or anyone will be in for a meal and a chat soon.

32.

THE CALL CAME over her comm literally as she was swallowing the last crisp. Good timing. She washed the crisps down with the caff dregs, hurried out. The lift pinged, the doors opened, she smiled at her reflection in the mirror-wall, adjusted her badge. Grabbed her Lawmaster, kicked it full throttle, gunned it down the street. The sun was shining. Rare joyful occurrence in Mega-City One. The sky was almost blue. Bunch of kids hanging on a pedway that stretched almost in the shape and colours of a rainbow over the Judges' Lane she'd taken. Chatting, dancing, flirting, boom-box music blasting out. A discarded synthi-choc wrapper sailed over Anderson's head. It was bright in the sunshine, fluttering in the breeze, looked pleasingly like a bird.

She said into her comm link: "Littering in progress on the pedway by Lizzo Block."

"Copy that, Anderson. Receiving. We'll send a squad."

Drove on fast, but kept an ear and a mind out. Pleasingly soon she felt yelling drifting from the way she'd come. The music clicked off mid-beat. So that was all good and sorted.

She parked the Lawmaster up next to two other Judges' bikes. Checked her Lawgiver. Fully loaded. The block entranceway was already open. One of the biggest blocks in the sector, a wall of rockcrete with no windows and few external doors. A homeless guy was sitting with his back to the wall next to the entrance. Strumming a tune on a guitar with three remaining strings. He was chewing sugar cubes openly, but Anderson ignored him.

She approached the entrance with caution. No lights on inside the corridor. She let her mind open for a wide scan of the area. Two Judges inside and the perp they were chasing. The Judges stood out as gold threads in the rich tapestry of the block.

Grud, there was a lot going down in this block.

A long corridor, stairs at the end going up. Anderson's heels clicked on rockcrete steps. Up, along, down, up, along. Place was a maze. She seemed to be in a service area, barely used: a sense drifting over her that this had once been a Lux-Block. Fancy apartments, private gardens. Real flowering plants. Stalactites were forming on the ceilings now where the aircon system leaked. Drops of dank water splashed down the back of Anderson's neck. A faint humming thrummed through the blotchy walls. The damp made her sneeze. Her feet splashed in a puddle of Grud-knew-what that leaked in through her boot seams. She decided she hated this place. The perp had better be worth catching. And she'd better be the one to catch him. If she turned up to find him already down and cuffed with a Lawgiver pressed to each temple, she'd not be entirely pleased.

The corridors ran on, stairs up, stairs down, stairs down. She suspected she was below ground level by now, heading into the cellars that had once been storage floors for the pampered citizens above. Typical, Anderson decided. Finally a sunny day in the Big Meg, and she was indoors underground heading deeper into the gloom. The few lights were cobwebbed, grimy. Service pipes creaked like they were straining not to burst. Water gleamed on the pipe seams. In one corridor, water was dripping from one of the ceiling lights. The neon flickered and made a popping noise in time with the drips.

Never mind the perp she was hunting. This block was guilty. Crying out to be condemned.

She could feel her fellow Judges up ahead. Close to her, but the endless stairs and passageways meant they could be *miles* away by foot. A corridor spread before high and narrow, rockcrete walls seamed with mildew. No lighting. Anderson flicked on her torch. She was navigating with her mind now anyway. Traces of the Judges. Traces of the perp. Leading her clearly on. She kept her feet in line with the torch beam. Balancing on it. She could feel her fellow Judges up ahead, she could hear their footsteps, but she turned a corner and the corridor went on empty and blank.

How big *was* this place?

That was when the voices began.

Crawling like fungus out of the walls.

A WOMAN, PLEADING for her life. Begging. A man who isn't interested in listening. Anderson heard the man's punch. Felt it in her own jaw. A drug deal gone bad, the standard double-triple-both-parties-too-wacked-to-remember-who's-betraying-whom-cross shoot-out. Annie pulls a gun on Ben, Ben misses Annie but hits Carl, Carl's dying but he's determined to take Dev out before he goes. Things go downhill at this point. A voice screaming, "Shoot! Shoot!" Blast of heavy weaponry. "Not me, you dolt!" Another blast, from a different weapon. Cuts out sudden. Like someone died and dropped their gun. A drug debauch gone bad. User's basically still a child. Can't take it. Crashes out.

ANDERSON CLUTCHED HER hands over her ears. Didn't make it stop. In her head. In the bowels of a City Block with thousands of people wallowing in crime all around. A woman sobbing because she'd got a parking ticket. A man embarrassed to tell his husband he'd been cautioned for jaywalking. They'd all lived here. Many had died here. The weight of them pushing onto Anderson. She staggered on down a staircase, along a corridor, up a staircase. Up and up.

* * *

A WINDOW. HIGH up in the stairwell wall. The light was faint and dirty and she had guessed correctly, she was underground. At the top of the next flight the staircase turned right and the window was above her. Nothing to see but a dead grey wall, leprous with damp and birdshit. Faint lacework of dried dirty rain. Tremor of reflected streetlights.

Anderson stopped. Looked out at the nothing view.

Couldn't feel the Judges. Lost them in the babble of past and present crimes. Little lights easily snuffed out.

Scrub that. Two of the myriad voices chuntering away about their guilt. As impossible to track down as two strands of hay in a haystack.

But—wait—

Someone was climbing the stairs behind her.

Footsteps.

Labouring, wheezing breath.

She turned.

Reached out.

A MAN'S HEAD flicked up, fear in the man's eyes, fear smell heavy in the air. The perp the Judges had been chasing. Repeat offender. Career criminal. Guilty. Guilty. Guilty. Judge him. Coward: his hands went up in surrender. A criminal without even the courage of his convictions.

Anderson reached out.

Reached *inside* him.

Cheap nylon t-shirt—sweat stains—material stretched over his gut. The cloth parted easily. The pallid skin beneath parted. Deeper. Nails. Fingertips. Sank her hand in. His heart there beating. Flabby as his belly. Arteries all gummed up. Rub it. Tickle it. Squeeze it.

Do it slowly. Savour it.

A long time, since she'd killed the boy Casey and the man Sidney. Hours, in the latter case. The delicious sound of a neck cracking—Judgement Day, they said, would come with a crack of doom. But after a long wait, it was, inevitably, over all too quickly. The man slumped back with a groan and it was done. She pulled out her hand. Sighed. Sucked her teeth.

Speaking of Judgement… the other Judges were following. Drawing near. She considered waiting to meet them. *Too slow, fellas. I got him first*. But then, she thought, there'd be questions, prying, paperwork. *So… how exactly did he die, Anderson? Looks scared to death.*

Anderson turned on her heel, strode away into the darkness. Left the perp for them to find, with the grey daylight striped across him. His mouth and his eyes open in death. The pale light dripping into him like he was drinking it.

She wandered the corridors and stairwells. A drokking maze, this place. Couldn't find the drokking exit. But yet, as she walked, sensing the crammed-in lives tantalisingly hidden out of reach behind rockcrete walls, she began to feel a certain admiration for the building's architect. Damp air, mould in the walls, too cold in winter; in summer, foetid and too hot. A perfect breeding ground for disease. If she listened, she could hear children, especially, sneeze and cough. Feel the pain wracking their hollowed-out chests. Fungal threads and fungal spores, basking in children's blackening lungs.

People's own homes, killing them. Some poetry in that. Went out to commit crimes (stayed at home to commit crimes: she felt again a man's blow to his wife's chin), came back to what they thought of as shelter, and their own homes Judged them.

When she finally found an exit, she stopped again, again stunned. The noise. The chaos. The sheer dizzying impossible amount of life. She had… forgotten? The city reeked of guilt. Chaos of sounds and scents, currents in the air where people were moving, speaking; every movement, every word, was of crime and sin and guilt. She staggered backwards, clawed at the air. For a brief, terrible moment she felt as if she herself was dying. Something so powerful it was breaking her open. Had to clutch at the walls to hold herself upright. She was standing in the lee of the City Block, a few cars parked nearby, a strip of pavement, then a backroad. Lamp posts. Graffitied walls. Rubbish and dogshit. Quiet, peaceful, nothing happening. Her entire life spent in places like this. But she felt suddenly that she was sick unto dying. Drowning in life.

She could see it. How filthy it all was. She… didn't know where to begin.

Her Lawmaster was parked up where she'd left it. Ignored it, walked fast down dirty streets. People spewed out around her, running, driving, strolling, crawling chaos. Under the brown fog of a Big Meg evening a crowd flowed over Angeltown Bridge, so many, she had not thought life had bred so many. Sighs, short and infrequent, were exhaled, and each perp fixed his eyes before his feet. Flowed up the pedway and down Chief Judge Goodman Street. Unreal. She didn't know where she was or where she was going. Stumbled on hoping she might find a face she recognised. There was no one.

A hundred thousand million faces, each one vapid, filled with crime and need. Venal, corrupt, violent, pig-shit thick. The stupidity was the worst. *"Why did you do it? You must know it's illegal?" "Yeah, but… it was funny, when I did it." "Yeah, course I know it's illegal, but I wanted it." "I dunno why I did it, Ms Lady Psi-Judge Ma'am." "I saw someone else doing it and it looked cool."* Gruddamnit, we work night and day to keep you people safe and it's like carrying water in a gruddamn sieve.

Look at them all! Vapid, listless, thoughtless in the most literal sense. She watched a citizen cram down a burger, drop the carton without noticing, walk over it smearing burger sauce across the pavement. He prodded his companion, a woman possibly even more bovine-looking than he was; they shared a snickering joke.

I mean, Anderson thought, in what possible way is Mr Citizen there not already dead? When you think of the muties out in the Cursed Earth scrabbling for resources, and Mr Honest Citizen there… would the world not be better off if he was already dead?

He walked off, chortling with his wifey. Burger sauce trail of footprints. Fart smell and belching.

Then she saw the nightclub.

And it did not seem dead.

A Judge does not go to such places. Stands outside, arrests their clientele. She went closer, the door opened as a couple stumbled out. Through the doorway the dancers made shapes like flags. Like kites flying in the wind. Tinny music. Bass notes of laughter. Hot salt smell, sweat and other fluids; condensation glistening from the walls. Glitter of hot faces, cheeks puffed out, lips flushed. Clothes marked every colour by the ever-changing lights. Mindless noise, mindless dizzy rush.

Life as fireworks. The antithesis of a dead place.

Flashback: the ash-fields, the bone-fields, the drying blood-crust seas. Fighting, pointless, hopeless, despairing, perhaps here in the rubble of this very building. It was packed with lives being wasted.

When she crossed the threshold, she was uncertain what she was doing.

As the door closed behind her, she knew.

She *knows.*

HOT, EAGER FACES, flushed, kissing, laughing, singing along. And the things she's seen, through Death's eyes and through her own. A world, dying. Butchery of children. Desperation. Toil to resist. It's pain to see these faces blithe and pointless wasting life's gift. "You fools," she shouts over the roar of the music, "you stupid lumps, can't you see how precious life is, how important it is?" Blank eyes turn towards her, puzzled and then dismissive. Some joker off her nut on pills. Futsie victim in a tizz. Dull. Get back to dancing and snogging.

"Cool Judge's costume, lady!" The button jock's seen her, points her out to the crowd. "Loving it! This next track's for Judge Blondie before she gets cubed. Let's see you all throw some hot Judge shapes!" His eyes like pinwheels. And the music, the dance moves: so inane.

She shouts louder. Clenches her fists until her nails dig into her palms. Spit comes out of her mouth when she shouts. "Look at you! If Death was to come here, you would give in to him. Let him kill you all. Many of you, I think—I know—would collaborate with him. You don't care about anything beyond yourselves," she screams. "You don't understand what death is! What life is!"

She sees her hands rip out, her nails, her fingers, stained with her own blood.

She tears the button jock's throat out.

SHE WADES IN, killing. Swimming in death. The place is crowded; as if in a fertile summer orchard, she only has to stretch out a hand to pluck another life out. As if in a summer orchard, she gorges herself. Tender flesh both ripe and sweet. But she is surprised—taken aback, even—by the fear her presence inspires. The panic. The screams. The vomiting and soiling themselves in terror while attempting to flee. Discourteous, she thinks. Surely the people of Mega-City One didn't used to be so rude? In her memory, now, the boy Casey held out his arms to welcome death. The perp in the stairwell had come to her eagerly, welcoming death.

A girl seems to hear the unspoken words. Stops, turns, walks back towards Anderson. Pale face, cloud of dark hair. A trusting, innocent look. So sweet, so pretty, difficult to think of her as rank with sin… indeed, the thought crosses Anderson's mind to make the girl's death easy. Gentle. Quick.

Shameless little hussy! Playing games like that with a Judge!

Give her what she deserves. For a moment, indeed, she wishes Judge Fear was here to show the girl the depths of her poisonous existence. She slicks out her hand, caresses the girl's heart, slowly, slowly squeezes out her life. Her bones feel soft and weak as Anderson's fingers creep over them. Her skull feels soft as Anderson's fingers probe it. When Anderson finally lets the girl die, she has begun to beg for death. Anderson treads down on the girl's crumpled body. Grinds her into fragments beneath her feet.

That, Anderson thinks—now *that* was a good death!

New mouths open in her body. Mouths filled with sharp teeth. Her new mouths shriek. Spew murder. Taste blood. Her claws rip flesh. Crush flesh. Wring bodies dry of blood. The rubble of the rubble of the city, gasping, choking, cramming it down her throat. Meat runs together, soaked into the sundering of their world, holding out their arms to reach for death like men reaching for a long-departed ship. The music beats on louder as each heartbeat fails. She flows into the music. Makes a pattern to her killing. Her body living-not-living becomes faded. Shapeless, molten need to kill. She is nothing, blunted, not like man, nor woman, nor child, not like beast, and she kills with wounds that bite so deep. Embraces the corpses and kisses them as they scatter. Gluts herself plump and sleek.

33.

"...No..."

Death says with a laugh, "*No?*"

"No. None of that happened. None of it."

"*Are you sssure?*" His voice is everywhere, soaked into her pores.

She's in the Grand Hall of Justice cafeteria. Someone pushes a chair out with a horrible tinny squeaking noise. Her chair is digging into the small of her back. The air smells of caff and beanz. Her mouth tastes of blood and crisps.

"You... you did that..." She hesitates. "Not me..."

Her worst fear: she can remember Judge Fear's visor lifting, and she saw beneath... in the visor's shadow she had seen... glimpsed... a Judge's face.

"*I could tell how much you were enjoying it, Anderssson. It wasss sssso easssy to ssshow you how much you enjoyed it. And I must admit, Anderssson, even I was impresssed by what you did to that girl. Ssssweet thing! She reminded me a little of my dear Nausssea and Phobia. Not as pretty, of coursse, but sssomething about her hair, her eyesss... I feared for a moment that you would let her go. But what you did to her, what you felt...*

"*Ssso... imaginative, the way you trampled her to sssshredsss.*"

"We're in my head." That's right, yes? Some of this is real and some of this is him playing with her and some of this is her own terrors—and Grud knows which is which. She risks a glance at Judge Death. He's a puddle on the floor splashed over her empty caff cup. A smear of pulp scraped from her boot heel, holding her breath in disgust like when she's trodden in dog shit. A cleaning bot is making ineffectual attempts to wash him off. She snaps her inner eyes closed. Sealed. Won't look. Won't look. Floating in dark, white nothing. Nothing else is real. But even here she can see the nightclub and the dead. Her dead.

I have to confessss, Anderssson, I'm not sssure I could have done better mysssself. It took you half the time it would have taken poor Judge Mortis." Eddies swirl in the slime puddle. She notices a plastic spork bobbing on the filth. "*Ssspeaking of Mortisss: you remind me a little of Judge Mortisss when I first met him. Yearning with all hisss heart to be good. Ssstill doesss, in hiss ssstrange way, I think. You could be like him, Anderssson. The enjoyment you took sssimply from ssseeing people die...*"

Anderson says slowly, firmly, as cold as Death himself, "What I saw wasn't real. Images—lies—that you put in my head."

"*Reasssuresss you, doesss it, to think that? You keep believing it, then.*"

"I beat you... I won..." She fights to remember. A locked room, Dredd bursting in with a spray can. Plastic in her face, her mouth, wet chill then dry and solid. Spitting, begging for it to hold. Anderson and Judge Death in their different ways both screaming as they realise—it will hold.

Nothing that happened after that was real. She didn't lose. She defeated Death. Oscar and Casey weren't real for her to have killed them. The Big Meg is still standing. Slouching. Slumped half-cut in an alley with its trousers round its ankles and its pockets picked.

Long, deep breath. In. Out. In. Out.

She wants to open her real eyes. Look up at what she thinks should be the Hall of Heroes ceiling, complete with cobwebs and damp patch and traces from passing headlights. The fear she'll see the dead world and herself alone is too terrible. She knows it's not true, but it's so *vivid*. Far more vivid than an off-white plaster ceiling can be.

Flexes her fingers. Meets the plastic that holds them fixed. She had forgotten, in the dreams, how closely she was trapped. She struggles, wants to thrash her body. Needs to. Her legs want to run, her arms want to reach out. She needs to move, she was moving, running, reaching. It's pain—agony, frustration, desperate claustrophobia; in her memories she is in a vast city with no limits.

She thinks: go back there! In that dead world where she was the last living soul, she could at least move her limbs.

She thinks: it felt so good, to move her body. When she was—

Killing.

Death laughs. Ripples in the bloody ooze. A bubble breaks the surface. Pop!

She says in a fury, "We're in my head. You don't have to look like squashed flies. You can literally pull yourself together, creep."

"*You trampled me into mince, Andersssson. Don't try to pretend you didn't.*" Death's voice smiles. Pouts. "*Top my remainsss with passstry and I could be one of my late mother's meat piesss. Although better tasssting, I'd like to think.*"

She says, "That didn't happen either. You put it in my mind."

"*What you did to me was your fantasssy, Andersssson, not mine.*" He sounds genuinely honest-to-Grud insulted. "*I may have enjoyed sssome perversssions in my youth, but masssochism wasss never one of them.*"

Trapped in plastic, her body is sweaty and sticky. Her mouth is dry and her teeth are fuzzy and so is her tongue. Her joints feel swollen. The soles of her feet feel dry and hot. Her bowels creak, desperate to empty themselves. Twitching like insects inside her legs.

Her worst fear. Judge Fear's visor lifting, and she saw beneath… in the visor's shadow she had seen… glimpsed…

...her own face.

Great sudden desire to churn up even the liquid filth of blood and shredded flesh. Splash it and kick it. Her legs screaming to move and kick. She says nothing. Stares at nothing. The cafeteria walls, her hands on her table. Sits in her mind perfectly still.

Her eyes are drawn back and back to the pool of filth that used to be Judge Death. More bubbles rise, pop sluggishly. Possibly what's left of him laughing. A bubble sets the spork moving. Tiny voyaging boat. Its tines are covered in Judge Death scum.

Slow ache in her legs. Needs to twitch them. Wiggle her feet. Puffy, heavy ache in hands and fingers. She was running, fighting. Doing things she's trained her life away to do. Real. Vivid. Tracing the banister as she climbed the stairs. The weariness in her thighs from climbing up and up. The music in the nightclub throbbing through her, swaying to the rhythm as she killed.

The vast space of the Meg's ruins. Sky going on forever. A million miles to run like a dog.

I just want... to live.

After the dreams, the revulsion of her body is too overwhelming. Anything, to escape it. Sink back into the lies Death's spinning her, go back to his Mega-City One necropolis where she's alone with her dead but she can move, stretch, piss, if she walks east she will come to sea. Go back to Mega-City One where she, not Death, is the Dark Judge, because she might be a monster in that world but she'll be free and clean.

The faces of the dancers she was killing. She wants to vomit—she already wants to vomit, as much from the sticky horror of her body as the horrors in her mind, the image of dancing faces merely pushes the bile a little closer to her lips and she gags as she swallows it—she wants to vomit in pain at the memory, and at her own sick hatred.

She killed the people in the nightclub, she thinks, because she... because she hated them, for being free and alive. She thinks: that wasn't me. But—it could, easily, have been me.

* * *

SHE OPENS HER eyes.

Her real eyes. Gritty and clotted with sleep. The Hall of Heroes ceiling, shabby white plaster, a damp stain in the corner, cobwebs, dust.

Grud, she's seen enough dust to last—Never mind.

If she strains her eyes to look as far to the left as possible, she can see a blur on the other side of the Hall of Heroes. If she squints and really strains her eyes, she can see it's a Judge. Comes up close, looks at Anderson's body, bows his head, walks off again.

No idea how long she's been here now, she could have spent days, weeks, *years* trapped in Death's visions—but people are still coming here to see her. Because of what she did.

She says it aloud. To Death, to herself: "I killed those people because I envied them." Her lips can just about move in the plastic as she mouths it. If anyone had been watching her closely, they might have seen.

She says, "It felt good to kill them. Of course it did."

THE RELEASE OF saying it! We're Judges, we're trained to kill from childhood, you don't think we have to enjoy it? We'd go mad, she thinks, if we didn't on *some* level enjoy it. We'd be as wretched as little Sidney De'ath and his pathetic handful of friends. Enjoy the thrill of the chase, the hunt, the kill. Imagine the pointlessness of our lives if we hated every moment of what we do. Back in the cafeteria it's nice and tidy, the mess she made killing Death has been swept away. Judge Death is sitting opposite her, back in his corpse form, his fingers steepled in front of his skull face. He's smiling his rictus dead grin, but his shoulders seem slumped.

She says, "You were easier on the eye as meat pie filling."

He growls.

"Ooh, hit a nerve, have I?"

"*I don't have nerves, Anderssson.*"

"So you won't feel it if I punch your gruddamn face to mush again now?"

He's really quite cross now. "*That's not the point.*"

"Talk about Mr Touchy."

The ache in her joints is fading. A little. Maybe. She flexes her shoulder blades as much as she can in the plastic—which isn't much, granted, but possibly eases things. The damp horror of her body, sticky thighs, sticky armpits, itchy puffy feet.

"You must miss farting and belching?" she says. "Surely?"

Death's face might be a skull under a closed helmet like the iron gate to a torture chamber, but good *Grud* it's a picture of shocked lower-middle-class outrage.

"Having a really good wee when you've had to hold it in for ages? Honestly?" Babbling, keeping talking, pushing the memories, the images of what she did away. "Come on. Everybody enjoys that."

"*The living body is nothing but sin and revulsion. Must be cleansed. As you yourself realise, lying here in your filth. I rejoice in being freed from such disgusting things.*"

"Prude." Inside, she's shaking. But she spits it out. It's so small, her voice is so small, she doesn't think he heard it.

Judge Death rises up before Anderson. Towers over her, huge, as she saw him in the dead world he had made of her Mega-City One. The neon light of the cafeteria casts shadows: Fire, Fear, Mortis, they creep and writhe across the walls. His maw opens to devour her. A maelstrom to tear her down. She can remember—vivid, true—Death ripping Judge Dredd apart, Death smashing apart the ranks of Judges, Death trampling the city beneath his skeletal feet. She can remember—true, vivid—her comrades dying and dying and dying and dying and dying, her own desperate pleas to die herself. The cafeteria is crawling, she sees it flicker and change. The floor tiles peel, exposing raw dead flesh beneath. Scabs picked off. Fungus erupts from the walls, its threads enveloping chairs and tables, eating the furniture away. Fruiting bodies blossom, spew out spores, liquify into black slime trails over grey flesh. The room she's sitting in is an overflowing pustule. A bubo ripening to burst. Yellow fluids pool at Anderson's feet. Judge Death flexes his fingers. His claws to lance the wound. Grud, life is disgusting. It's pain. She'll die like this.

She hears Casey's voice: "Poo and wee! Warts! Bottoms! Would you rather have a bath in snot or eat an earwax sandwich?"

She says, slowly, carefully, her mind quaking and weeping with fear, "I enjoyed killing you, too. I'd do it again. No regrets. I saw what you once were, and maybe even you could have been worth something once. Scrub that—I'm sure of it, you were a child no different from me or Casey, you had a life ahead of you that you could have lived. I would never have kicked you to pie mush when you were a boy called Sidney. Probably have given you a hug." That's the truth; she says it to hurt him as much as anything, but it's true. Doesn't quite know how she feels confessing it.

She says, forcing it, and this, too, is true: "But now, what you've become—I enjoyed killing you. A lot. I'd do it every day for a lifetime and never stop enjoying it. The best way to pass the time I can imagine. Killing you."

She says, "But the difference between you and me, creep, is that even knowing what you are, I still feel guilty about enjoying it."

"*Spare me the moralising lecture, Anderssson. What makes you different from me isss your ssself-doubt, blah, blah, blah.*"

The response to that is so obvious to both of them, Anderson doesn't bother speaking.

Coughs politely.

Death opens his mouth.

Closes his mouth.

She says after a silence, "You long to die, Judge Death. Yearn for it. Want someone to put you out of your misery. I can't imagine how it feels to go on looking at yourself knowing what you are, knowing you can't change anything. Can't escape what you've become."

In her mind: atomic clouds, churning fires, a hundred thousand million hands begging as the knife falls on them. Planets washed away in a sea of blood. Death's mouth gapes, a black hole sucking the universe away. She can see herself old and worn, her body broken, Death standing before her and his mouth opens and his teeth are gravestones and his teeth are swords and she is falling upwards, spiralling into his mouth, into darkness, and beyond darkness; there is nothing there, not even pain, not even guilt, not even despair. The void, extinction of all self, and his teeth are closing and all is at an end.

"*I am changeless. Eternal. I am Death, Destroyer of Worlds. The All-Devouring. The King of Terrors. The Graveyard of All Hope. I am all that remains when the light fails. I am the beginning and I am the end. I am Justice. I am Judgement. I cannot be escaped.*"

She takes a long breath. Meets his terrible eyes. Puts her trembling hands over his terrible claws. "So you keep saying."

She says, "A thing I learned early on at the Academy: when a perp insists on something, he's usually lying."

"*I mean it. I am Death.*" He does and he is.

"So do I," Anderson says.

34.

A Story from the Deadworld Part 3

Judge Mortis: This Time It's Personal

By Judge Cass Anderson / Judge Cas Andersen

THAT'S THE PROBLEM with using symbolism to impart a profound lesson about the potential for evil that festers within all of us. Once you've identified with the monster, you can see what the monster sees.

GRUD, HE WISHES he was Death. What a guy! What a hero! That jammy bastard Death has all the luck.

THEY KIND OF... tiptoe around it. Fire, Fear and Mortis. The three of them are younger than Death, admire him, idolise him, and that's only proper and right. He's the leader, the guru, their mentor in matters of crime and judgement. Death's the head honcho. Numero Uno. The Big Cheese. The name alone's a giveaway, really. At the end of all things is… Death. Fire, Fear and Mortis are his lieutenants, his chosen, his happy few, his band of brothers—and that in itself is an honour sans pareil. But…

But…

But…

He pushes the thought away. As he always does. Lumbers to his feet.

HE'S NEVER BEEN what you'd call athletic, has old Mortis. But being dead has made him more, not less, aware of his bulk. This strikes him as unfair. The beautiful skeletal limbs he's watched emerge from their fleshy prison, graceful, slender as willow trees. The liquid softness, like velvet, as a body decays. In purely measurable terms, setting aside the poetry, a cadaver takes up rather less space than a living person. And Judge Death and Judge Fire both have a certain virile elegance to their movements. Typically, predictably, however, Mortis has been rendered only more lumpen in his decayed state. His hands seem to be growing bigger. His feet flap like dead fish as he walks. His head is losing flesh as it once lost hair; in place of his bald patch he has holes down to the skull. Thus, admittedly, concealing his bald patch. But the bones that are digging themselves out through his face—he is becoming certain they are not human. He is changing into something ugly and wrong.

His head wobbles on his neck at times. If he runs too fast. Flashback to school sports day, that kid he and everyone else laughed at because his hands flapped when he ran. Death's most trusted lieutenant, and his hands and his head flap when he runs.

"*Honessstly, I'd never noticcced. Don't worry about it, Mortisss old chap.*" Thus Judge Fire. Whose tall, muscular, slender-waist-broad-shoulders-long-legs physique is only emphasised by his aura of golden flames. Fire's head has been burned to crispy bits, his visage is a charred human skull. He still looks dashing. Winks at the ladies before he barbeques them. The flames rise, the smoke of her own body chokes her and makes her eyes water, the lady bats her eyelashes back.

Worse, Mortis is beginning to suspect he's growing a tail. An odd lumpy thing in the small of his back. Makes sitting down awkward. He spends hours twisting himself up before a mirror, head craned over his shoulder. Definitely something there. Being dead, he can't feel anything, but it looks bony. More bones erupting. Ahem. And the way it's poking up under his trousers... Finally, he has to accept the reality. Cuts a tail-hole in his trouser seat.

Judge Fire gets straight to it: "*Going to hang from a tree, Judge Mortisss? King of the swingers, eh? Hey, wouldn't it be cool if you could use it as a weapon? Like, strangle someone with it? Use it as a whip?*"

Cold dignity in ignoring these witty japes. Fire's feeling the strain of their workload, he thinks charitably. Always the most unstable of the Dark Judges. As is evidenced by the guttering and exploding fires. Humour him.

Killing a person with his tail! he thinks. The indignity! Fire needs to wash his mouth out. The gift of death is so precious. The shared moment between Judge and sinner. His caring, healing hands that bring sweet peace. Death is beauty, beauty death. If his fingers have grown bigger, larger, positively flipper-like in some lights... they are like the fingers of a concert pianist or a skilled surgeon, beautiful and strong and skilled. To use his... tail... to grant death's kindness would be a travesty of all he believes.

Also, the tail stops growing not halfway down his thighs and is therefore nowhere near long enough to use. Hangs inert behind him. Bony yet flaccid. It makes a clinking noise when he runs. It reminds him of a saint's relic. If he concentrates, he can wiggle it.

He can no longer remember what he looked like before he died, but he has a strong sense it wasn't like this. A big, hulking, rotting body topped with a sheep's skull, flippers for hands, a skeletal tail hanging down his back.

* * *

He kills at Judge Death's command, willing and—well, not *smiling* now he has a sheep's skull for a head, and he didn't smile much before he had a sheep's skull for a head, a nervous frown was more his habitual expression, as his sister used to point out—willing and eager and not smiling but deeply down-to-the-bones happy, happier than he's been for years, him and Fire and Fear shoulder to shoulder beside Judge Death. Towns, cities, farmsteads: he flattens whatever Judge Death identifies as the target. In the great war they are waging he is a doughty fighter. Never hesitates or flinches, always he throws himself into the fighting where the battle rages thickest. Holds nothing back. And there is a great pleasure to be found in these struggles, a few lone heroes against the world. The enemy sends out waves of troops: men, women, children. Rabid fanatics, the red mist of murder clouds their minds and eyes, they will not see reason, they will not listen. In battle, they froth and foam at the mouth. They fight with limbs missing, bleeding wounds; if they have no weapons left they fight with their nails and their teeth. They disgust him. He and his fellow Judges can only put their shoulders to the wheel, keep on and on and on. Four against the barbarian hordes!

So yes, the battles are fulfilling. And he never has cause to question Judge Death's plans. And sometimes, exquisitely, Death will reserve a treat for him. A kindergarten. An old people's home. A hospital. A hospice. Rewards for his loyalty and his dedication in battle—and, yes, he will admit his dedication in battle is partly driven by the rewards Death grants him. And these are the best days of his unlife. Slower, more considered, more personal and elegant ways of death. There is firework beauty in mass slaughter, taking ten, twenty people from adrenal running-fighting life to death in one brilliant well-timed explosion. But the slow individual creeping death he can bring with his craftsman's hands… that is…

Choosing how and when a person will die, to the second.

Tailoring pain, relief, pain again, again brief relief. Weighing up exact degrees of suffering. Witnessing the moment before and the moment after death.

There are no words that he can find, for what that is.

WHEN HE HAS a good number of the living at his mercy, he likes to arrange the deaths. Like a pianist indeed. Creates different moods, variations in scale and tempo and feeling—a symphony, a concerto, a chamber piece. Textures and colour palates. A master perfumier blending the body's dying scents.

He takes thirty living, ties them firmly, paralysed from the neck down. Lines them up in six neat rows of five bodies. Wanders slowly among them, touching or not touching as the mood takes him. Conducting, composing their deaths. Faster, slower, faster, slow, slow. Rot blossoms on faces, limbs, torsos; bodies corrode, crumble, burst. Thunder rush of six at once quick dying. Lingering tremorous note as one alone dies slow and soft. Some blushing rosy as the dawn. Some spreading green like unfurling leaves. He returns to one body three or four times in succession, sets him fully into bloom almost to blousy overripeness, a rose tree in midsummer heat. Another he has the self-restraint to leave untouched, save for one trembling caress of her white hand, and she is filled with promise as yet unwoken, a tree in winter with the frost upon her, fair but frozen, waiting unfulfilled to bloom. Kills her quickly, tears would surely cloud his eyes if he could but weep, cuts her off before she has had her chance to flower. The promise of what might have been.

He finds identical twin boys. Is fascinated to find that one dies quicker than the other, despite identical experiences of death. Marvels at the different patterns of gangrene lacing their naked skin. In one it forms dancing lines like the veins in old marble, makes of the child's body a cathedral wall. In the other it is thicker and more mottled, like clouds racing across the sky. He can barely take his eyes off one to see how the other is progressing, changing, so beautiful it is.

The glories of nature and of human artistry, he realises, exist as a reminder of decay and death. The great works that artists have toiled a lifetime over, sacrificed health and happiness to create; the splendour of a waterfall, a forest, a sunset; these things are beautiful to the human mind because they are a blurred reflection of the greater, more splendid beauty of death.

He takes a woman and works his hardest to keep her alive while he opens her into wounds until her skin seems a murmuration of starlings, decay moving across her body so like the way the birds he dimly remembers would turn, billow, eddy, twist and narrow to a dark point, burst open to fill the horizon. Thus her rot ebbs and flows. Thus her cries, like his memory of the birds calling. When she dies, he is bereft. Truly moved. It is days before he can bestir himself to find another to kill. He keeps her bones in a special box. Time passes, alas, the memory fades. He knows her death was unique and beautiful, but he cannot remember quite how. At last the box too is forgotten; when he recalls her suddenly, the quality of the light on a single shard of white bone his gaze happens to fall upon, perhaps, bringing her suddenly again to mind, the box is of course long lost.

HE REFLECTS OFTEN on the wonders of his own death. Wishes he could better remember it. Perhaps, he thinks, the concerts, the ballets, the paintings in death he labours over, the poems he creates in death, perhaps they are attempts to recollect his own experience of dying. One day he will find a smell or a sound that brings the memories rushing back so vivid he can experience it all again just as it was. "*What do you remember about your death? Tell me,*" he begs his fellow Dark Judges. They humour him in much the same way he humours their foibles. "*I died,*" is really all they can say.

"*Can you... can you kill me again?*" he dares ask Nausea (Phobia?). Takes him three massacres—that's the best way to measure time now—to work up the courage.

"*I wish I could, deary,*" she says. Clucks sympathetically. "*But dead's dead.*" He had not expected any other answer. But still the disappointment is crushing.

A brilliant idea: could he… ask Judge Death to kill him? Those beautiful hands, far more skilled and far, far more beautiful than his own, sinking deep into his chest… He is very close to asking, a fine bright day, sunshine and blue skies and they've gutted a town street by picket-fenced street, yet at the last words fail him. "*Nothing*," he says. The gift Death gave him, the kindness Death showed in letting him, gauche-rookie-two-left-feet Judge Mortis, die and become a Dark Judge. Some things are so huge, so perfect, you can't touch them. Fragile as bubbles of blown glass. What if he asked and Death refused him? What if asked and Death agreed, and it wasn't as good as he'd hoped? You have the moon, Mortis, he thinks. Don't ask for the stars and the sun. Tread carefully, Mortis, he thinks, for you tread upon your dreams. They're frail things: don't damage them.

He is afraid, sometimes, when he is alone, that this must be but a dream. That he will—must—soon wake up. Clutch the threads of his dream memories, and they will slip through his fingers and fade. "*I dreamed I had… I dreamed I was…*"

He is afraid he will be cast out of this bright heaven. Be forced back to life as it was before his ascension into bliss. And by life he does mean *life*. If he was to wake, now, to find himself a man and living… He shudders, folds his hands together as if to hold on to his dead self; terror rises at the thought of it. The Deadworld as an idyll born of honeydew and lotus fruits, dreams piled upon dreams upon dreams… It horrifies and haunts him. How, he sometimes thinks, can something this wondrous be real? It seems to him he has no right to exist in a world as perfect as this. Someone or something will soon snatch it away.

He can no longer remember what he was called, before he was Judge Mortis. In his heart, he was always Mortis and he was always dead. If he loses that, he thinks with dread, what could he be? He used to think his sheep's skull head was ugly. Now, in panic, he clutches it. The horror—returning to a human face.

Stop! It's all right! It will be all right! he whispers to himself. With difficulty he calms himself, stops his trembling. Walks through his garden to soothe his mind. Bone trees and flesh flowers. Bone bells that so silvery ring. Heart's ease. Love lies bleeding. Dog roses. Lords and ladies. Black-eyed Susans. The light falls dappled and it is fair and fine and good.

If this is but a dream, it is a good dream, and he has not yet woken. If this is reality, then he is thankful and truly blessed.

But.

But.

But.

There's...

It's...

Judge Death. Just... something... about Judge Death.

35.

It's not a big thing.

Okay, it is a big thing, Mortis thinks.

Their battle is mostly at last won now. The Deadworld reaches now across most of the face of the earth, and upon the Empire of Death the sun almost never sets. Life clings on only in the hidden places. Caverns beneath far-off, snow-girt mountains. Barren patches of shelter in the desert wastes. Life, animal and vegetable, is fading away, bleached out of existence. A man cannot eat dust. A man cannot drink dust. Where there is water, that water is poisoned. Human shit, human blood. Rotting meat makes the soil rich, and at first the fields grew only greener and more fertile in Death's footsteps. Which was surprising. In some way poetically pleasing. Yet after enough killing, the earth was too choked with ruin to grow green. Too damp with human tears, saltier than sea water. Too crusted with human fat. Funeral pyres burn day and night and their smoke blocks out the sun. The plants die. The animals die. On the other side of the world from Judge Death's wars, the plants and animals and people die.

There were a lot of flies. Huge clouds of flies, and these also blocked out the light. People ate the flies. Now there are so few creatures left alive that the flies are themselves scarce. No carrion left for them to feed on.

A statue of Judge Death rises where the Justice Department where it all began once stood. Its foundations are sunk down to bedrock. At the crest of its helmet, the air is thin. Any taller and it would have erupted up into space. For fifty miles in every direction in a great circle around it, the bones of those who raised it lie piled a mile deep. It is made out of human teeth.

This is perhaps when Mortis's doubts first set in.

Judge Fire: to whom Mortis suspects the act of killing is more important than the death the killing brings. Judge Fire will never be sated in his killing.

Judge Fear: for whom, Mortis is certain, both the act of killing a person and the fact of their being dead is but a step towards a world where Fear has no one around him. Judge Fear craves not a dead world but an empty world.

Judge Mortis: he alone of the three feels the true commitment only to death. Killing is a pleasure, yet he could live without killing. Could simply sit idle and watch the world die. Indeed, to look to the far horizon and know that out there a child is dying: there is such joy and hope in that. A wonder, that out there unseen so many every moment are dying. Say that word 'death' and in that brief time a person has gone from life. The thought is dizzying. Soothes him: he will count, sometimes, beat it out from one to ten, and in that time someone somewhere who was alive is dead. That knowledge is enough for him. He treasures killing, but he remembers always that killing is but a means to the greater end. Death is the purpose. It matters not how the world dies, so long as it is dead.

He thinks on these things, assesses his companions, and thus the suspicion grows—the fear—that of the three he alone is pure.

As they once set in stone on the Department of Justice wall: *The crime is life. The sentence is death*. Those words are all that Judge Mortis needs. The sum and consummation of his faith. All his life he felt them, struggled to speak them aloud or to himself. He found Judge Death—or rather, better, Judge Death found him—lost and wandering. A lost sheep, he thinks, and if his sheep's skull allowed him to make the sound of laughing he would laugh. Judge Death looked deep into his heart and soul and understood him better than he had understood himself. As if a stone had been upon his tongue all those long years, and Judge Death so easily plucked it out to let the words run free. He swore to serve Judge Death forever.

He loved, he *loves,* Judge Death.

Far more than Fire and Fear, Death understands him and he—he thinks it no mere arrogance to say it, no empty braggart boast—of Death's three chosen lieutenants he, Mortis, best understands Judge Death.

But.

But.

But.

He has tried not to think it, pushed the words back, swallowed them.

But they keep wriggling back and he can't find a way to shut them from his mind. Despair eats into him, he has not felt so lost since before he met Judge Death.

The suspicion is mounting within him.

Growing, spreading, like… ha! like gangrene.

Judge Death—is something of an egomaniac with a depressingly superficial understanding of what death means.

36.

THEIR FIRST MEETING. Mortis overawed, shaking like a leaf. He feels like he's up before the school principal. He spent all last night rehearsing this. Got to the office an hour early. Somehow still ended up on the wrong floor, had to run up two sets of stairs to get here on time. His deodorant seems to have failed (maybe that's his imagination/paranoia working? maybe if he doesn't stand too close?). His uniform digs in at the waist. He adjusts his jacket until, if anything, it looks worse.

Judge Fire knocks on the door. A voice calls, "Come in." As the door opens, Mortis feels a fart building.

"Ah, Judge Fire. And this must be the young man you were telling me about? Good."

A hand held out for him to shake. Mortis walks forward, keeping his buttocks clenched.

"I… I'm honoured to meet you." Naturally, the nerves mean his first words come out in a weird croak.

"Oh, nonsense, we're all friends and fellow Judges here. Have a seat, my man."

The fart sneaks out as Mortis sits but he doesn't think the other two notice. Judge Fire gets them cups of water from the watercooler. Judge Death steeples his fingers, peers at Mortis.

So what does Mortis see?

Disappointment.

A THIN, WEEDY sort of a chap. Receding hairline. Tired eyes. Bad teeth. Sweat stains under his armpits. Piles of clutter all over his desk: gum wrappers, used tissues, a coffee mug that can't have been washed for weeks.

If a man can't keep his desk tidy...

WHAT ELSE DID you expect? Mortis asks himself. Knew from the moment Judge Fire told him about 'Judge Death' in awed tones that it'd be a crushing disappointment. A small guy in a damp office. Whiny, nasal, 'the-world-owes-me a living' voice that Mortis knows only too well.

"What do you think? Isn't he...?" He and Judge Fire go for a coffee afterwards. Judge Fire's so excited he's bouncing in his chair. Reminds Mortis of a labrador puppy he helped recently. "What he says, I mean, it's like... And you know what he did? His dad and that? He's like... And he wants to mentor us!" A wide, handsome grin. Except, up close, Judge Fire has bad breath. "He likes you. I could see he was impressed."

"He's..." As with the puppy, he can't let Judge Fire down. "I'm excited to work for him," Mortis says. "It's great you introduced me to him."

"I'M EXCITED TO work for him." Say it enough and it's true. Say it every night and every morning. "I'm. Excited. It's. Great. What else did you expect?" *You meet a man, who says he can, express your deepest thoughts. He's a natural leader, when you're but a dreamer, he knows what to do, far better than you, for a master plan, why, he's your man! Yes?* Say it! Sing it! Once more! Belt it out! You built it up in your mind that he'd be some colossus, handsome as the sun in splendour, wise as some ancient from an old book. You always do this. What else did you expect?

Not someone who's a bigger dweeb than I am, Mortis thinks.

THE FIRST IMPRESSION fades; meeting two, once expectations have been sufficiently lowered, feels more positive. This guy really gets it, Mortis thinks. By the third or fourth meeting, Mortis is honestly won over. The nasal voice and the little throat-burps Judge Death makes after drinking coffee remain irritating, but Mortis feels the passion of the words burn through. A few killings later and the blood they've shed has washed the memory of Mortis's disappointment away. He is delighted, honoured, humbled, by Judge Death's trust in him. Looks with awe at Judge Death. Will freely admit to looking with *love* at Judge Death. The man's busy masterminding a revolution. We can forgive him not being one hundred and ten percent focussed on his personal hygiene. He's preening, self-obsessed, his jokes are dad-level terrible, you know in your heart that he's as loyal to his followers as… um… a very unloyal thing, he'd stab you in the back, the front, the head, the goolies, as soon as look at you if he saw an advantage in it for him. Mortis knows all this, knew it from that first heart-sinking meeting.

"He's the leader," Judge Fire says. "He's got that… thing. Unlike you, Mortis. Drive. Charisma. Whatever you want to call it. A man of destiny. You can't deny it, Mortis, can you? I know you know."

"I know." There's a brilliant colourist at his sister's salon, she's a right pain in the backside to work with but that's the price you pay for being in the presence of genius, his sister would say.

"And he's got a great sense of humour. That punchline as he killed that perp—'Die laughing, joker!'— I thought I was going to wet myself."

Mortis, still alive and sans sheep skull, keeps his face composed. He's pretty sure it was 'Die of laughter, you joker,' but he doesn't say anything.

"You're just feeling a bit down cause he's spending more time with his mysterious lady friends. The plan is working itself out, you just need to leave him a bit of time and space. We'll be up and running soon. This is, like, the morning before the party or something. Pull yourself together and buck up! Yes?"

"Yes..."

Judge Fire is himself beginning to remind Mortis of his sister. Similar sparkle in the eyes. All lit up. Fired for life. Stoked.

Fire claps him on the back. "Good man! What you need is a good perp to kill. Coming? And you, Fear?"

The new recruit Judge Fear has sat silent at the far end of the table for the duration, picking a styrofoam coffee cup to pieces. He finally looks up, nods assent, grabs his jacket. They haven't been on patrol two minutes when they pull a perp over for jaywalking; he was looking at a shop on the other side of the road, screamingly obvious to all three he was about to jaywalk, besides there were some children around he might have set a very bad example to if he had stepped out into the road; they let Judge Fear have a go with him and it's shocking how many crimes the guy turns out to have committed.

Oh, yes, these doubts can be forgiven and forgotten fairly painlessly for Mortis. Death's death-and-resurrection-as-a-withered-corpse trick deals with the hygiene issues and the coffee burps. As they step the plan up a gear they spend less time together in the office, and thus Mortis has to endure fewer of Death's jokes. All doubts fade. The warm glow of happiness Mortis feels extends back into his memories of the past.

UNTIL, IN THE perfect beauty of the Deadworld, the doubts again begin to wake. Looking out upon the barren vistas of the Deadworld, marvelling yet again at what they have so miraculously, impossibly, wrought... and the memories of those early, living years flash back and the images of the living Judge Death are worse. A frail, pasty man clenching his chewed-up fists as he bangs the table, dislodging a pile of junk.

Mortis walks his garden in the cool of the evening to find some comfort, treads out the winding paths he's laid. His movements stir up wafts of sweet putrescence; he shakes a tree to scatter flakes that whirl and tumble as they fall. Bends his head back, pretends he feels them soft on his face. He has made himself a bower hung with bones as music; ofttimes the rhythm soothes and heartens him; but in the click and rustle of femur, humerus, phalange, he can hear only his doubts beating out ever louder as the wind rises. He sinks into a mire of pearlescent innards, wallows there; he inspects the sculptures he has carved from unborn babies' skulls. Nothing can comfort him.

It beats out, like blood pumping from a severed artery. Unlike blood from an artery, it does not stop.

37.

"PASSSTY? WEEDY?" A silence. Choking on the words. "*Coffee burpsss?*"

38.

THE GRAND HALL of Justice cafeteria. Anderson sips caff. Crunches a smoky bacon flavour crisp.

Babble of noise. Judges, tech boys, support staff, snatching a quick meal between shifts. The counter staff shovel beanz and sausage. The drinks machine buzzes, dribbles caff into styrofoam cups. "Get some more fries on, will ya?" "This synthastry should be a crime, Judge!" "You calling that a full serving of gravy?" A clatter and a round of applause as someone drops their full tray. A squelch as a portion of synthetti bolognese slops onto a plate. "Something smells good today, Brenda." "Mm-mmm, that's a gruddamn fine cup of caff."

Judge Death prowls the room. Being figments of Anderson's imagination, the Judges ignore him.

"You hear Judge Dalton took out a gang of umpty-baggers single-handed yesterday? The monsters offering the stuff free to kids to get 'em hooked." "I heard, Gibson. Took five Judges to tear the packet out of Dalton's hands, they said." "Yup. Guy's on sick leave, getting counselling." "Shame, shame. I thought Judge Dalton was better than that." "Be fair on the man, Barker. Could happen to any of us."

Judge Death leans over the table. Rips Judge Barker's heart out. Rips Judge Gibson's throat out.

Anderson sits back in her chair. Eats another crisp.

The room explodes into violence. Judges and Brenda the canteen lady screaming, yelling. Guns leap into action. Bullets spew in every direction, pulping food, chairs, cups, plates. Eruption of spilled beanz. Synthetti bolognese splatters the walls.

Death dances in the bullet rain. Doesn't attempt to avoid being hit—twists, swirls, lets the gunfire caress him. Opens arms and hands wide, his legs splayed out, making himself big. Tall and wide, an easy, perfect target. Bullets clatter on his helmet and his bone shoulder pads. Bounce off. He turns to meet an assailant face-to-face, takes the bullets, turns to another and beckons the gunfire on. A bullet pings off his grinning teeth.

His dead flesh is shredded. Points of light shine through his uniform. Like stars, Anderson thinks. His body is fragile as old dry leaves and the bullets tear through him without stopping, strike people behind him. He's thin as wire, so the bullets miss. Slam into people behind him. Judges, tech boys, Brenda the canteen lady, slump, full of lead. Crazy raining bullets, hailing, snowing *blizzards* of bullets, a Judge shooting left-handed because their right arm has been shot so many times it's hanging off, a Judge dropping their gun not shooting either-handed because they're dying and they're dead.

Judge Death wiggles his remaining fingers. Stumps, mostly, and cracked open like a dog's been gnawing them; old brittle thin bones, his fingers, easy to break. The *stumps* of Death's fingers, then, wiggle, stunted like... Even more obscene, somehow, than the long curling of his fingers towards Anderson. At his command, in time to Death's finger stubs jerking, the dead begin to rise.

Shooting each other. The dead shooting the living. The dead shooting the dead. Weapons at close quarters. As the guns fire, their muzzles burn hair and skin. Guns held in position, inserted into the wounds they've previously made. Fire, fire, fire, fire, fire full automatic. Heavy explosives, ricochet rounds, let off minus-point-blank.

Judges dripping wounds. A tech guy has no face. A Psi-Judge appears untouched from the front, but she spins round clumsy and she's missing the back of her head. Those are the more coherent ones. A Judge standing firing, his body stops neatly at the chin. His Adam's apple bobs up and down every time he pulls the trigger. A living Judge makes a noise that's beyond screaming. Shoots him, shoots him, shoots shoots shoots shoots shoots shoots. The headless Judge collapses. Explodes. The living Judge keeps shooting, shredding the remains. A bullet takes her out straight between the eyes. She jolts backward, sways, blood trickles from her nose. Goes cross-eyed as the life in her fades. Carries on shooting what's left of the headless Judge. Shredded meat torso flaps its arms, struggles to shoot. Blood roses blossom on the female Judge's chest.

Dead meat shoot-out. Dead hands on triggers until limbs are too floppy with wounds to shoot. The air sparkles with gun smoke. Spent cases crunch underfoot, deep as pebbles on a beach. Rich game smell—blood, offal, cordite.

This isn't real, Anderson. Take control of this. It can smell like real fresh-opened June roses if you want it to. Babies' hair and bubble bath and clean sheets. The guns can fire gruddamn confetti. The Judges could be having a food fight and that blood on the walls could be synthetti sauce. (Feet kick and slide on spilled food, the counter explodes under sustained gunfire, rubber rounds—all that's left now—bounce off serving trays and heat lamps, some of it already *is* synthetti sauce.) (Human blood and human meat and offal, gristle, bones, hair, toenails would taste far better than whatever they put in the Grand Hall of Justice cafeteria's synthetti bolognese sauce.)

But Anderson only sits and watches. She's so covered in gore she looks in a worse state than the dismembered corpses surrounding her. She's had to wipe her face clean several times already so she can see. Her blonde hair (again!) stained red. Blood laps around her ankles, leaks into her boots through the stitching. Blood has soaked through her clothes until it's oozing from her cuffs and collar. She wipes her hands on a napkin after she's finished the packet of crisps. Moves stiffly from the sheer weight of blood she's sodden with, and the movement makes her suit squelch.

The room finally falls still. The smoke dissipates. Silence apart from the drip-drip-drip of blood.

Judge Death looks himself over. Stumpy no-finger left hand, missing his right arm entirely, his left leg gone at the knee. He shakes himself and spent bullets pour off him.

She says mildly, "Remind me what you were trying to achieve there, Sssssidney?"

Judge Death only growls at her. Fidgets with a bullet that's lodged in his left clavicle.

"Just working your anger out?"

Anderson gets the impression the bullet's making Death itch. He gropes around inside his shoulder with his ruined hand until it falls out and bounces with a pinging noise off his foot.

"You ever considered hot yoga? Mindfulness colouring books? I know a good art therapist I could recommend... He usually works with children, but I can explain about your stunted-mental-development thing."

The cafeteria shivers. Like heat haze, like the place is a mirage in the desert of the Cursed Earth. The bodies pull themselves back together. Fragments of bone reforming; minced flesh congealing into lumps, fillets, muscles; skin smoothing out, unfolding itself. The flesh gift-wraps the bones, the skin gift-wraps the flesh. Judges, tech boys, Brenda, all slowly rise to their feet. Sit. Eat, drink. Form an orderly queue at the food counter. Brenda bangs her beanz ladle. Bolognese sauce burps under a heat lamp. The drinks machine dribbles caff. Everyone in the cafeteria looks almost like they did before the gunfight. Greyer, more crumpled. Greasier. Snot around their noses, pus crusted on their eyelids, sores in the corners of their mouths, uniforms that don't fit. If Anderson looks at one person straight on, they look ill but human. But the people in the background are wrong.

Everyone's queuing for food or sitting with a plate in front of them, but no one eats and no one speaks.

"*That'sss not how it wass with Mortisss. Not how it isss. He isss loyal to me beyond any of the othersss. Knowsss hisss place.*"

"Yes, I'm sure he does."

"*He wasss overawed when he first met me. It took him a week to sssummon up the courage to return.*"

Anderson smiles sweetly at that.

"*Thisss isss all liesss, Anderssson. Filthy, criminal liesss. You wonder how I came to ssssee the world asss only sssinful? Your liesss about me, about Mortisss—they themssselves ansswer that quessstion. You yourssself only demonssstrate yet again everything I know to be true.*"

Mould blooms over the people in the cafeteria. Maggots seep from eyes and mouths and nostrils. The food on the diners' plates is maggots, the liquid in their cups is pus. The room itself is carved or spun out of dried blood. People sit or stand in silence, acting out being alive, don't notice what they've become. Anderson feels herself crawling with decay. Feels maggots nuzzling at her lips. She fixes her eyes on Death to avoid looking at herself. Shrugs an imitation of Death's shrugs.

"It made a good story, though, didn't it?"

"*You're becoming boring, Anderssson. I warn you...*"

She smiles more sweetly still. "So kill me, then."

Broken hands reach out. Broken bloodied stumps; bone shattered into nests of jagged needling claws. Ruin upon ruin upon broken ruin. Gaping broken mouth. Closer. Reaching. Pawing at her suit top. Fumbling at her throat. His jaws open into a stinking mire. Closer. Closer. She can see, almost, what it is that hides beneath the closed helmet. His teeth are human skulls. His body is formed from human corpses. His skin writhes and crawls with human maggots. Human maggots that feast on each other and on themselves. Judge Death is himself the Deadworld. The remains of his hands sprout new bloody fingers, he touches Anderson's throat. Fingers with mouths, biting down, burrowing down into her, prising her skin from her flesh. His mouth opens wider, his mouth is a raw red hole sucking her in.

Anderson spits in his face.

Grips her hands around his neck. Squeezes.

Grud, the skin of his neck is disgusting. Flaky and leathery, rough as sandpaper. Creaks beneath Anderson's grasp. Through its dry folds she can feel his windpipe. Beneath the old chicken-leg skin it feels like… an actual pipe. Like for plumbing. She squeezes hard. Tears open in Death's neck skin. His seams popping. His windpipe's ridged and brittle but soft enough to crumple inwards. She's choking him.

His hands fall away from her. She holds him as a sack of old bones hanging from her closed fists.

"You can't kill me, creep. Not in here."

His neck gives way. The skin breaks, the windpipe breaks. His head lolls back in her hands. She can see inside, to the dry strands of muscle and the dried-up spinal cord just about holding his head attached to his neck.

Forget plumbing. His insides look like a dog treat.

You cannot kill that which does not live: somewhere between fascination and horror as the broken windpipe heaves, his voice comes out hissing on her face as a warm dry wind. "*You can't kill me either, Anderssson. In here or out there.*" His voice blows flakes of his neck skin onto Anderson's face.

She drops him. Sack of particularly articulated old bones. The uniform's the only thing keeping him together.

Always was, she thinks.

"These games you've been playing. Passed the time." She kicks his helmet-and-skull across the room. "But now let's really play, creep."

She sprints out of the cafeteria. Slams the door behind her but she can hear Judge Death hammering it open as she runs.

PSI

ANDERSON

39.

"GET DOWN!"

Anderson crashes into two cadet Judges, throws them sideways. "Get down, get out!" Children: even in her head, she won't let them get involved. They gape at her, then the training kicks in and they run before she needs to hit them with a psi-command. She's broadcasting anyway, blaring out the alarm around the building and across the Meg. *This is Psi-Judge Anderson calling all Psi-Judges. Critical situation at the Grand Hall of Justice. If you hear this message: get armed, get prepped, get here now!* Non-psis can't hear the message, but she pushes out waves of anger, fear, hope: *Disaster—Grand Hall—urgent. You feel the need to go there heavily armed.*

Death's voice howls behind her. "*You can't kill me, Anderssson. I do not live.*"

I can enjoy beating you to crap and back, though, creep, she thinks.

She hits the lift button. Hits it again. The light says it's on its way down, but it seems to be stopping at every drokking floor.

A desk Judge joins her in the lift lobby. "Pressing the button repeatedly doesn't help, ma'am. Confuses the lift, in fact, makes it go slower."

She hits the button again. The lights show the lift has descended all of two floors. "That's an urban myth."

"No, really. A good friend of mine is a lift engineer, it's a simple matter of the call-circuits versus the command circuits—"

"Whatever. Never mind." She runs for the stairs. It's ironic, she thinks fleetingly—given she's trapped immobile in plastic—how much time she's spent running up imaginary stairs.

"Ma'am, the lift's coming now."

A ping, the swoosh of the lift doors, a gargling wail. Scream from the people in the lift: "My Grud! Close the door—!"

Another gargling wail.

The fire doors in the stairway bang closed—open—closed—open in her wake. Like to think they caught Death in the face and the shrivelled-up privates. She takes the steps two at a time, using the banister to haul herself faster, harder, up and up. A Judge is coming down and unlike lift-button-ma'am guy she's caught Anderson's help-me broadcast. Helmet on, gun in one hand, daystick in the other. Badge says *Judge Kell.*

"What's up? I heard screams."

Anderson gestures behind her. Judge looks down the stairwell. "Drokkin' Grud on a drokkin' greeny! What's that?"

"Old bones," Anderson pants.

Judge Kell lets rip with her Lawgiver. "Eat lead, skull-face!"

"That's not going to stop him," Anderson shouts over the crack of bullets. "Come on."

Kell looses one more round. They run on up the stairs together. Feels good to have a fellow Judge at Anderson's side. Kell's gun clicks against her belt buckle. Two sets of boot heels click in tandem. Such music! Also the woman's choice of cuss words was magnificent. Dredged from the bottom of Anderson's subconscious, Grud only knows where from. She'll have to remember them for conscious future use.

They fly round a corner up to the next landing. Still three floors down from where Anderson's planning to go. She pulls Kell's hand to keep her going up.

The stair doors crash open. Kell makes a sound something between an infant mewling and an animal in a trap.

Judge Mortis.

From the depths of the stairwell, Judge Death hisses, "*Two can play at thisss game, Anderssson. If you can have back-up... ssso can I.*"

"Drok!" Kell gets herself together kind-of enough to fire. Or her brain's in shock and she's going into autopilot panic kill-every-mutherdrokker-in-the-building survival mode. Or as a figment of Anderson's imagination she's simply a self-targeting gun in Judges' boots. Bullet holes write words across Mortis's torso. He staggers backwards. One flailing hand brushes Kell's cheek.

Kell drops the gun. Clutches her face.

"Come on! Run! Run!"

Mortis reaches for Kell to finish her.

Below them—is Death.

Kell smashes her daystick into Mortis's sheep muzzle. The wood crumbles away as it touches him, but the impact is hard enough to knock him to one side. He falls against the stairwell doorframe. Anderson grabs Kell's gun. Drags her up another floor. They burst through the fire doors into a corridor. Three more Judges run towards them. Nearly run into them. Kell collapses, hand still clutched to her face. Anderson yells, "Help her!" She shoves the barrel of Kell's Lawgiver through the door handles. That'll hold for all of, ooh, ten seconds. The new Judges' confusion turns to horror as dark patches of rot sprout across the doors.

"Incendiary rounds," Anderson barks at her fellow Judges. "Now! Fire! Fire!" Might work. Should. If—

For a moment, she thinks the Judges are shooting in the wrong direction. So panicked they've lost control and are shooting behind them. Hands shaking so bad they're holding their guns the wrong way.

Because at her command fire explodes at the far end of the corridor they're crouched in.

One of the Judges seems to have the same thought: stares at his gun then at the flames then at his gun. "Wh—?"

A figure appears in the flames. Running towards them, slow and held by the fire, arms beating, rising, falling. Flowing against the fire's currents. Like seeing a swimmer underwater in a glass-walled pool. No telling whether it's male or female. The mouth opens. Tries to say something, call out to Anderson. Black, like a shape carved in charcoal. A child's toy crudely made of burned twigs. The flames pour into the open mouth. Like seeing a swimmer drown. Fire holding its body together. Ribbons, tendrils, sinews of running flame. Then a ripple in the fire, a change in pressure, and the figure crumbles away in black lumps. The fire sucks inwards. Inhales.

Exhales. Bells out. A gout of fire singes Anderson's face.

The doors crack open. Two Judges blast out with a hail of bullets. Too braindead with terror/panic/confusion for this to make sense. The third, quicker on the uptake, manages to reset her gun to incendiaries. Yells "Burn, baby, burn!" as she and Anderson let rip.

The firedoors are—fireproof.

Rotting away at Mortis's touch, but—fireproof. Best engineering in the Big Meg.

Incendiary fire beating backwards at the Judges. Of all the times the Justice Department didn't skimp on construction costs.

Then the incendiaries hit Kell's doubled-up-as-a-doorstop Lawgiver.

Which is already cracking with corrosion and metal stress.

It explodes. Lets out all its rounds like the most immense fireworks and finally freed from constipation relief.

Fire to the left of us. Flames to the right. Something Fearful in the shadows. Death and a white sheep mounting the stairs.

* * *

If I die, Anderson thinks, I'll just wake up in my head again. If I open my eyes, I'll see the Hall of Heroes ceiling.

These Judges aren't real. Their deaths won't be real.

(In the real Grand Hall of Justice, she thinks, I'll bet they cut all the corners when it came to fire doors.)

She flutters her eyelids, ready to open them.

Thinks: no.

This might not be real, but she's seen Judge Death win and win. This time she won't let Judge Death win.

One of the Judges collapses, vomiting blood. Black liquid is oozing from between Kell's fingers where she's clutching her cheek.

They're not real. They're not really hurting.

A red-hot bullet casing or a piece of shrapnel or Grud knows what catches Anderson's forehead, a bullet hits her shoulder pad hard enough to slam against her collarbone.

Dust and shards of rockcrete are coming down from above the ruined doorframe. The hall lights flicker. A ceiling panel rips off, crashes on top of the dying Judge. A bullet takes Incendiaries Judge in the thigh. She screams. Cracks open along the walls. Even in the red of the fires, Kell's face is turning green.

Heavy crunching footsteps at the far end of the corridor. The heat and light of killing fire smothered by something dread and fell and cold.

This isn't real. Their deaths or your pain. Just open your eyes, Anderson.

Admit…

…defeat.

"There's a door!" Incendiary Judge yells. "Go, go, go!" They wade, limp, *stagger* through fire, bullets slamming wounds in bodies, bouncing off boots, shoulder pads, helmets.

If this miracle door is locked. Or a broom cupboard. Anderson kicks it open, drags Kell inside. Incendiaries Judge and Too-Shocked-To-Fire-Incendiaries Judge follow. Leave a trail of blood. The lights flash on automatically as they enter. Anderson slams the door closed, turns the lock.

"Tables, chairs, anything to make a barrier!" Incendiaries Judge orders. It crosses with Anderson's "Make a barrier! Anything: chairs, tables!"

Too-Shocked-To-Fire-Incendiaries Judge makes a croaking noise. Kind of like the noise Judge Kell made on seeing Mortis.

This definitely isn't a broom cupboard. A room the size of a football pitch, glass windows at the far end showing a distant view over Mega-City One. Towers, flyovers, blue sky of a sunny day.

Dead bodies literally stretching to the horizon.

They're in the Justice Department central morgue.

40.

She can remember kicking a morgue tech through that window. She can remember gathering Death into her arms. She can remember joking around to wind Judge Dredd up over a perp who looked like the neighbours' garbage after a Sunday barbecue, and then the pain as Death entered her mind. She can remember feeling proud as she walked in here, that Judge Dredd had demanded the best Psi-Division could offer and they'd sent her. She'd made her boot heels click extra loud when she walked in.

"That lock isn't going to hold those things," Incendiaries Judge says. Her badge shows her name as *Judge Katz*. "Suggestions? Anyone?"

They wedge a gurney plus occupant against the door. A second gurney holding the first in place.

"Think that'll work?"

"Uuuuuhhhhh..."

"There's a freezer room," Too-Shocked-To-Fire-Incendiaries Judge says suddenly. They're standing looking at their useless handiwork, waiting for the first bloom of rot and lick of flames. His badge reads *Judge Arjuna*. "That might... I mean... that thing... the rot, I mean... and the flames... A freezer might... stop them?"

I mean, it might. Katz says, "Anyone got a better idea?" and Anderson shakes her head.

She's really starting to like Judge Katz. The woman's at least ten years older than Anderson, long pale hair spangled silver-grey at the roots. The kindest eyes Anderson's seen in a Judge, but something in those eyes says that by Grud you'll regret it if you let her down more than once. Doesn't need an art therapist to work out why and how Anderson's subconscious has conjured her up.

The freezer room has a door as thick as Anderson's waist. Takes Anderson and Arjuna to pull it closed. So there's hope Mortis will take a while to corrode his way through it. Inside there are more gurneys, more corpses. The unidentified dead of Mega-City One. Five organ-legger victims, four blitzers, three victims of illegal house plants, two illegal Boingers (don't cry, don't laugh, Anderson, ignore it, walk on), and one overambitious fatty in a batglide suit. Feels good, Anderson thinks, feels nostalgic, seeing people who died normal deaths.

Movement in the corner. Every guns whips up. How, how, how, *how* did one of the Dark Judges get in?

Fear, Anderson thinks. He'd like it in here. Bleak, cold place.

Arjuna shoots wild. A gurney overturns, spilling the batglider at Anderson's feet.

"Isurrenderdon'tkillmeGrud."

A morgue tech crawls out from beneath the gurney. "Don'tkillmewhatdoyouwant?"

And breathe. Four long puffs of white steam.

"Does this door lock?" Katz barks at the tech.

"There's a control panel on the wall. But—Wait! Don't!" The tech guy pulls his coat more tightly around himself. "Well… on the bright side, hypothermia can lead to paradoxical feelings of warmth and even overheating, as well as a sensation of euphoria and a delightful drowsy sensation like falling asleep in a feather bed. Or so I'm told."

Katz shrugs. "I'll take that over whatever those things can do to us."

"We might also feel an overwhelming desire to take our clothes off."

"We'll be either dead or out of here long before it comes to that," Anderson says. Hopes.

Brief chance to look over their wounds. Bullet wounds, burns—they're Judges, they can cope. But Judge Kell is huddled in the corner, hand still clutched to her face.

"I need to look at it, Susi," Judge Katz says. "Please."

"…Hurts…"

"I know it hurts."

"…Hurts…" Kell's hand comes away taking her skin and her cheekbone with it. She opens and closes her wet fingers. Croaks.

Her face, dripping through her fingers.

Katz turns to the tech guy. "You got any medi equipment in here?"

"This is a mortuary freezer, ma'am." He says, "Of course, outside that door you just sealed…"

Katz points her Lawgiver. "Take your coat off."

"I'll freeze!"

"I'll shoot you if you don't."

She wraps the coat around Judge Kell. Carefully wipes Kell's hands clean.

"The cold'll help," Anderson says. "Might slow the… the decay." We should shoot her now, she thinks.

Like I failed to do with Oscar and Casey, she thinks. She can feel the building, filled with death and murder. Red, rising tide of blood. Judges running mad with terror. Judges falling captive to Death's words. First they take the Justice Department. Then they take the world.

I already failed to stop Mega-City One failing in one dream, Anderson thinks. What makes me think it'll be different this time? Nothing can stop the Dark Judges. Why did I run?

It's getting really cold in the mortuary freezer. A sheen of ice is crusting over Kell's wounds. The blood the Judges are covered in is freezing solid. Anderson opens and closes her mouth to keep the blood on her face from icing her jaw shut. Flash-burn freezer burn. Kell whimpers. The morgue tech guy whimpers worse.

Judge Arjuna is inspecting his gun. "I'm basically out of ammo. Luckily, my fingers are too numb to shoot." He shakes his head, rubs his face wearily. Looks about as together as Kell and the morgue tech. "What do you reckon's happening out there?"

"People are dying," Anderson says. She can feel it, little individual sparks of pain and fear, and then, worse, a spark flickers out, gone. What had she said to Death once? *Death is nothing.* She can feel the Grand Hall of Justice full of lives, and she can feel it slowly emptying.

Stars going out, she thinks.

Judge Kell makes a louder noise. Gurgles. Kind of like a blocked drain. Kell's facial muscles are the stuff blocking the drain. Slumps forward in a shower of black ice.

"She's dead," Judge Katz says.

The morgue tech briefly brightens. "Can I have my coat back now?"

Katz's hand closes on her gun. A single tear runs down her face, freezes there. She looks at the guy, and if he meets her gaze he should die like Fear's victims do. But she says nothing as the guy scrapes Judge Kell's remains out of the coat and puts it back on. "Going to bill the Department for dry cleaning costs," he mutters. He snuggles deep. "That's better. By the way, it occurs to me: Did I mention this place is airtight? Race between whether we freeze to death or suffocate."

"My money's on freezing," Arjuna says. "Can't feel my fingers or my toes. Not meaning to be nosy, but what was the point of hiding in here? Why didn't you let that thing kill us straight off?"

"You suggested the freezer room, Judge Arjuna," Katz snaps.

"You went along with it, Judge Katz."

"We're still alive," Anderson says. "That's what counts." Her right foot jerks out, knocks what's left of Judge Kell. The cold making her muscles spasm. That's all.

"Oh, behold the mighty kingdom of life," Judge Arjuna says.

The freezer lights flicker. Off-on-off-on-off… thank Grud, on. The floor shakes hard enough to rattle the gurneys. A frozen arm flops down. Fingers combing through Anderson's hair. Her heart howls in pain as she feels multiple Judges die, badly, and close. Their screams—*something's* screams—are audible even through the freezer door.

Drokk. Drokk, drokk, drokk.

This isn't real, she thinks. Their deaths or my death. All I have to do is open my eyes. I'm in the Hall of Heroes in the undamaged Grand Hall of Justice, Judges Katz and Kell and Arjuna don't exist. Open my eyes. Feel righteous indignation they haven't dusted me for a while. This can stop.

The lights flicker off-on-off-on-off. Off.

A scream comes through the freezer door that can't be human but must be. No Judge should scream like that.

You don't have to let these Judges die, Anderson. Open your eyes and they vanish and they don't die.

This is a story in your head, Anderson.

Just open your eyes. Make it stop.

Admit…

…DEFEAT.

Anderssson.

Red emergency lights flash on. Anderson gets to her feet. She's hiding in here because she wants to stay alive. She loves being alive. She's got people here around her, she can talk and bicker and hear people's breath and smell their sweat and their farts and she could sit in this freezer with her imaginary acquaintances forever, if it meant Judge Death didn't catch her or them.

She's gruddamn terrified of her own death and other people's deaths.

I like telling myself stories where I'm alive, so I keep running from Death, she thinks. But everything dies in the end. Death's inside my head and I'll never beat him. I tell these stories or he tells these stories, and I always lose because that's how it has to end.

"Death!" Anderson shouts. Mighty war cry that rings around the freezer unit. "I'm here! I'm waiting! Fear! Fire! Mortis! Death!" She breaks off to snigger. Witch words summoning spell of Olde Earth. *By rock, I call you, by sea, I bring you, by my blood and my good right hand, I abjure you* or something, something, something, then I'm supposed to break a twig or blow out a candle. Kill a cat. Ride a dragon. Stand on one leg. "Death! I'm here waiting! Mortis! I'm waiting for you! Fire! Fear! I barely know you! Come on, then! If you think you're hard enough!"

The morgue tech tries to hide under his gurney. Anderson throws him her daystick. "Hit him with the fat end," she says. "Got it?"

Tiny voice: "No."

"Never mind. You can learn on the job. Let's lock and load, people. We've got Death to kill."

Tinier voice: "I never signed up for this, Judge, ma'am. I just work with dead bodies."

Anderson gives him a wide grin. "Cometh the hour, cometh the man."

She pounds the freezer door with her fist. Another summoning ritual: the door rings like a school bell. Katz joins her, smashing the butt of her weapon against the floor. After a moment, Arjuna joins in. Then, slowly, to the rhythm of his wee dripping out of his trousers, so does the morgue tech.

Four voices raised in triumph. "Come on, then! Death! Death!"

41.

SHE CAN HEAR them and feel them. Prowling like cats on the other side of the freezer door. She can feel Mortis in particular. Wave upon wave of joy. All. These. Dead. Bodies! So pleasing to mine eyes!

In her mind, in the story and out of it, Death whispers, "*You'll lossse yet again, Anderssson. I gave you the chance to retreat.*"

"Scared, are you?"

Judge Arjuna says, "A bit. A lot. Shedloads."

"Tough. You're a Judge."

She bangs on the door. "We're in here! Fire: I'm waiting for you! Mortis: focus on the job!"

Three Lawgivers take aim. One daystick is shaking.

"*Come out, come out*," Fear's voice hisses through the door.

"*Or we'll burn your houssse down*," Fire joins in.

"If you want us, you'll have to come and get us," Anderson shouts. "We're waiting. Unless you're too scared?"

Noises on the other side of the door. Then louder noises.

Then: "*Anderssson! What have you done to thisss door?*"

"Nothing?"

Judge Katz shouts, "Are you making excuses out there?"

Scuffling, a long silence, what could be a muttered conversation.

Rust patches begin to appear on the door.

"Supposed to be stainless steel," the morgue tech says.

Spreading. Thickening. Bubbles up like acne, bursts to release red-brown flakes. The door is peeling away in layers. Like… Anderson can't help herself… like a chemi-peel on a manky foot.

And when he's done with the door, he'll do that to your face, Anderson.

Open your eyes. Give up. You're dead as soon as this door opens. Give up now before you see your friends killed.

Anderssson.

It's hypnotic, watching the door corrode. A piece as long as a Lawgiver barrel collapses into rust. There's a fault line in the metal, must have been there since casting, it unfurls and cracks snake across the door. Watching the countdown to their deaths.

"You all right out there, Mortis?" Anderson shouts. "Taking you drokkin' ages."

"We're fine if you need to take a break or something, maybe have a rest," shouts Arjuna.

"Why are we waiting?" Katz sings.

"Should have called a locksmith," the morgue tech squeaks. Both sides ignore that one. Moving swiftly on.

The door collapses in a swirl of rust that looks and tastes far too much like dried blood. Warm air blasts Anderson's face. Familiar stink of smoke and rot.

She shoots. Incendiaries. Fire pouring in pent-up fury out of her gun. She feels, briefly, like Judge Fire himself. That the fire is a part of her. Cleansing fire to burn the filth away. Purge the world of sin.

Yeah, I get it, Death, she thinks. Profound. As always.

But—you *are* filth that needs purging. I'm going to embrace that.

Judge Katz fires. Judge Arjuna fires. Three streams of purifying flame. The Dark Judges are black and charred. Writhe. Cannot escape. Squeal. Anderson always imagined burning maggots would squeal like that.

Rather—three Dark Judges are black and charred and writhe and burn.

One Dark Judge is already on fire. Gloats in his bath of flame.

Katz's gun runs out of incendiary rounds.

Anderson's gun runs out of incendiary rounds.

Arjuna keeps firing incendiaries. His face has the rapture in it.

The morgue tech waves his stick.

Katz switches to normal bullets, which simply rattle through and off Judge Fire. Judge Fire steps forwards. Arjuna's hand drops from the trigger. Arjuna's Lawgiver stutters out. Katz's Lawgiver, too, stutters out.

And Judge Fire—

Judge Fire—

The morgue tech's stick explodes in flame. He drops it, screaming, crumples and runs. Judge Fire doesn't so much as glimpse at where he's gone.

Judge Fire raises his trident.

"Get DOWN!"

Arjuna's flying. In Anderson's face. Too close: hands, teeth, an earlobe. She falls sideways, flying herself, collapses into a gurney and a frozen body, both suddenly red-hot. A new and novel kind of pain. Katz comes down on top of her. They sink together into the dead batglider fatty, who's cooked flesh and raw flesh and a hard core of frozen flesh that jabs into the small of Anderson's back.

Arjuna stands between Anderson and the fire.

Arjuna burns.

HIS HELMET BURNS green. His Lawgiver burns blue. His suit sizzles and melts, liquid metal runs from his shoulder pads, droplets of plastic and metal burrow into his skin. As he burns, he is melded with his uniform. The golden eagle on his right shoulder holds, holds, shimmers, fights—proud symbol—to hold its shape. Pours away in a wash down his chest. He holds himself in the fire, his body fighting to keep alive long after he should and must be dead. His eyes are steaming, rise in mist from the ashes of his face. The pride in them. The gold metal eagle is beyond molten—the liquid metal itself burns with a heat like the sun.

He hurls his burning corpse as a weapon onto the burning ruin of Judge Death. Wraps arms of fire around Death's neck. Holds him closer than a man can hold a child or lover. Presses and melds with Death.

DRY DEAD SKIN and bones burn well, Anderson sees. Oily rankness of decay; putrid fat spattering, spitting; old, dirty, claggy grease that burns well—like a dirty chip pan burns and spits. Hiss and rush of bright, fast, living, dying, smokeless flame as the sinews and the dried parched patches of scalp hair and the parchment skin flare up furious and futile as straw burns fast and burns out. Sound and fury and quickly spent and cold again. Big floating petals of black and white ash. Cinder roses in first bud. Beneath, the bones are old and dry like boiled bones, burned bones, bones long butchered, rendered, defleshed and buried, long dug and prised from dry, dead earth. No marrow, no fat to blaze and spit and spark-rush. Not a tide of fire, a wave of fire, a cleansing burst, not fire like horses' manes flying, like horses galloping free and wild and fast. Yellow flames tremulous in their burning, timid, small as children, licking around the bones half-starved. White bones crack, blacken, the flames flicker and fade. No food on these dry bones to feed the fire. Stutters out. Dribbles out, like the last drops of pee.

Arjuna is dead and burned and gone to running fat and charcoal innards. Fine, good smell of well-cooked meat and the strange smell of molten gold. His remains are gilded. Dipped and held in gold. A golden skull.

Death is what he was when Anderson first saw him. The only way she's truly seen him with her real and living waking eyes. A charred mass of bones. The rubbish from a barbecue. The way he truly is?

* * *

And see Mortis: he, too, is burned. His sheep skull head is black and cracked. The incendiaries have done their work. He scrabbles on his back and his hands and feet are still burning, two hands of glory, ten birthday-cake-candle toes. His arms thrash at his sides, groping for corpse flakes. A weak, bleating triumph when he fumbles onto his lower jawbone. It crumbles into lumps at his touch.

And see Fear: doubled over, defeated, his cloak burned away, the bat wings on his helmet burned, the helmet glowing red and distorted by the heat. He looks better without the cloak and the bat wings on his helmet, Anderson thinks.

And see Fire: laughing at her, quite unharmed.

"*Any more? If you ssshoot me, Anderssson, the bullets will melt before they reach me. Asss they can't harm me anyway, it would be doubly pointlesss.*" He raises his trident. "*Who'sss next?*" Sprays fire. Again.

Seems… unfair. Beyond all and any consequence. Immortal, invulnerable, can kill from the next room. At least, Anderson thinks, the other three Dark Judges have to get *close* to their victims. Any hair she has left is gone in smoking curls. Her eyelashes, her eyebrows and her nostril hairs. Her lips pucker and smoke.

She's blinded, then, by white smoke.

White steam? White gas? It swallows up Judge Fire. Chokes all his fire out.

Beautiful, like mist rising from a stream as dawn breaks to warm the earth. But colder than ice. And Anderson coughs, can't breathe, and where the mist plays against her skin to make her some fair ghostly fairy maiden—her skin burns with cold.

And Judge Fire screams. As if he's looked Judge Fear in the face.

"Turn your face away! Try not to breathe!" The morgue tech, Anderson thinks dimly. Well trained, she follows his command, presses her hand over her mouth.

The white mist vanishes as quickly as it appeared. The floor is crusted with ice.

Judge Fire stands… frozen. Trident pointing at Anderson, mouth open in a bony shriek. He's just a skinny guy in a Judge's uniform, with a skull where his head should be. Like someone dressed up a skeleton in the morgue for a joke. Without his tendrils of fire, his eyes are blank holes.

"Freezer coolant uses liquid nitrogen," the morgue tech says. He's holding a cannister. Anderson notices his arms are shaking, his hands clutching the container too tight. "Any more of you creeps want a cold bath?"

Silence from the remaining Dark Judges. The morgue tech's sweating, gritting his teeth and screwing his eyes open and shut. He whimpers to the Judges, "One of you two… do it."

Judge Katz kicks Judge Fire. He falls forward. Rigid. A statue, not a man; he makes no attempt to stop himself or block his fall.

Shatters into a million pieces at Katz's feet.

Anderson has a sudden image of a child dropping a glass vase. Shock at the change in state. Shock it can't be fixed.

Judge Katz grinds her heel into the detritus, sends up a lovely sound like a frozen puddle crunching on the walk to school. Hefts and pumps her Lawgiver.

"Freeze, baby, yeah!"

Moment's impasse. Moment's thinking: we've won! Fire is ice shavings, Mortis and Fear are down, Judge Death is literally toast. Moment's wild joy. We—

Moment's over.

A plume of gas seeps out of Death's open mouth. Forms itself in Death's grinning face. "*You cannot kill the dead,*" it hisses.

Anderson could swear he *winks* at her through his ghost helmet visor. Floats towards her. Bobbing on thermals.

Katz says, "That's all it is? A bad smell?"

There's horror, then there's horror, then there's *horror.* Anderson can already taste Death forcing himself down her throat. Trying to swallow and keep her throat closed, trying to squeeze her throat muscles shut, trying not to breathe. Every muscle rigid.

Inssside your head... inside your head. Could we go on forever? Like a reflection of a reflection. You must have stood in a public toilet somewhere where the mirrors do that, go on and on, played around waving your hand at yourself?

You can ssstill end this, Anderssson. Jusst open your eyesss and admit I've won.

She's in too deep now. Grits her teeth and waits.

"*But there are far more interesssting bodies than yoursss here, Anderssson. Don't flatter yourssself.*"

Anderson shoots him. Pointless waste of a bullet, but she can't *not* shoot. A hole in the wall, a scatter of plaster dust. The gas cloud floats around the room. Contemplates the corpses lined up under crisp white sheets.

"*Let me sssee now... Choicesss, choicesss...*"

Hovers over a corpse. Moves on.

"*Does this one sssuit me, Anderssson? Or thisss one? Flattering on the hipsss? Brings out the colour of my eyesss?*"

The gas cloud sinks down. Anderson's body twitches. Muscle memory. Fighting off her possession. Katz whispers, "What's...? What...?"

The corpse rises. Throws off its white sheet.

Of all the places for a last drokking stand.

It's a Judge. A man. Young; big and muscular; not a Judge many perps would care to tangle with. A single bullet hole forms a perfect circle in its forehead.

It stamps its booted feet. Claps its hands. Dead eyes snap open.

Again, Anderson shoots. Can't help it, can't not shoot. Katz shoots too, for the same reason. Or more reason: Anderson has a sense that Katz knew, liked, this dead Judge. Bullets sink into the dead chest. Maybe it staggers. A little. Rocks on its heels maybe. Its mouth opens. "*Judge Death livesss,*" it says.

A second gas plume coagulates from the shattered remains of Judge Fire. It, too, hovers over the morgue corpses. Dives fast down into one. Eager to warm up.

An old woman rises from her gurney. Hair in curlers, towel round her shoulders, flushed cheeks. The tag on her right arm says she died in a freak hairdryer accident.

"*Judge Fire livesss*," she croaks.

Mortis heaves himself onto all fours. An animal, ragged backbone connected to half a skull, four stumps for legs and his tail dragging behind him. Corrosion spreads across the floor, a slug trail of black rot. He bleats.

Judge Fear staggers to his feet. Wreathed in smoke.

Four voices in chorus, absurd, horrifying, a croon, a banshee wail. "*You cannot kill that which does not live!*"

After everything Anderson's seen and done, this, also, seems…

…unfair.

"*NOW KILL THEM*." She senses Judge Death is bored now. Accepted that Anderson won't admit she's beaten, will insist on playing this out to the bitter end. Doesn't like that. She should be doing as she's told. Certainly shouldn't be hurting him. "*Judge them*."

Fear raises his visor, his hidden face fixed on Katz.

Mortis, blinded, only an animal, charges the morgue tech. Crashes into him, wraps his fire-maimed hands around the man's knees.

He's dying anyway. Anderson knows this. When he threw the liquid nitrogen, it slopped over his hands, froze them solid. The cannister crashes to the floor, spraying its contents up into the man's face. His hands are frozen to the cannister. Are torn off at the wrists. Wet decay, luscious, glistening, chases up his legs to meet the ice. The rot of fruit and flowers, almost warm.

Overripe peaches. Gamey meat. Death by ice and death by gangrene battle over the man's flesh. He chokes on nitrogen gas. Suffocates as his lungs freeze and rot.

Mortis sits back on his haunches. Frost patches dapple him beside his burns. His voice comes out slurring. "*…I feel… pain… Sssweet.*"

Fear's visor rises, and Katz sees.

Anderson almost sees it. Reflected in Katz's huge staring eyes. She finds herself craning towards Fear. Has to see. To know. How can she not? Something moving. Scrabbling, changing colour, all reflected in Katz's eyes. Her pupils grow big as the world. Katz *sees*.

Sees: and whatever her fear is, it's got death and guns and killing in it. Or at the least a closed fist. She squeezes her Lawgiver. Bullets cartwheel in every direction. Slam into Fear, into Death and Fire and Mortis, into Anderson.

"*Pain…*" Mortis croons. It ends in a bleat.

Katz slumps to the ground. Thrashes, caught in her deepest nightmare. But she's gripping the trigger of her Lawgiver. Her hand spasms: squeeze, squeeze, squeeze. Won't. Let. Go. The Lawgiver spasms with her, spewing bullets as hard as Fire spewed his flames. Judders on the floor. Sparks. It's alive. Bullets ricochet off the morgue gurneys, off the metal walls of the freezer room. Anderson throws herself down, rolls for hopeless cover. The Arjuna/Death doner kebab makes some kind of shield. Bullets score her body. Tearing the room to shreds. The floor is creaking, cracks opening, ice damage, fire damage, Mortis's rot. She wheezes on nitrogen fumes. Mortis crawls in circles. Laps bullet wounds up. Fear takes the brunt of the gunfire, his body all holes, bullets spangling his helmet. Fire's chosen body oozes dead blood and hair curlers. The great hulking Judge corpse Judge Death has chosen to inhabit jerks as bullets strike it, the arms and legs twitch. A bullet takes out Death's handsome new Roman nose.

Fear makes a strange noise then. A croak, a moan, a sound like, a feeling like—guilt.

"*My... comrades...*"

He dives. His body closes over the gun. The gun's muzzle cradled to his chest.

He lies there taking bullets until all the bullets are spent.

AND SO THERE'S another moment's pause. A moment's strange silence. Katz is dead, her gun is dead. Anderson is coated in crispy smoked meat. She thinks in a dim way: I taste... bacon.

The Dark Judges seem almost concerned. Perturbed that it's come to this. Fire stutters out: "*Not... fun.*" He's in the body of an old woman in a hand-knit cardigan, slippers and curlers/blue rinse. The left side of his face has been shot off. Half a jawbone and a few shreds of tongue mash up and down when he speaks. "*You're... ruining it... Andersssson.*" He lurches forward. Punches Anderson in the face. He's in the dead body of an old woman. Not in the best of health, even *before* her fluke hairdryer accident. A thin fist with knuckles like Grot Pot gristle connects with Anderson's jaw. Smells of lavender soap. It hurts. But it doesn't exactly *hurt*. She punches back, right in the chest—she is not touching the remains of that face—sends Fire ass over tit into a gurney. Hears the old woman's spine snap. The body flails. A beetle stuck on its back. Falls still.

The hope, again. How many times can it die?

42.

Fear rises as a gas-plume. Claims a new body. A child's body. Little girl with blonde hair, little sad dead version of Anderson.

It is difficult to comprehend still. That they will keep on going. Killing. No matter what she or anyone does. It is impossible to defeat them. Destroy them, grind their bodies to dust, scatter the dust on the wind to the furthest reaches of the earth… they'll come back killing and killing and endlessly killing.

There is nothing the living can do to stop them. Smash their bodies, they'll find something new. A Deadworld, and she'll be fighting them as beetles, earthworms, gas clouds, and they won't stop and they won't stop. A Deadworld down to one rat alive somewhere buried, and they'll be there in the spent bodies of insects to track it down. Dragging themselves to kill as shapeless lumps.

Anderson begins to run.

Out of the morgue. Down corridors soaked in murder. Through chambers that are like the chambers of a dead heart.

* * *

"*Are you running away again, Andersssson?*"

Bodies slumped and piled. Bodies burned. Bodies too rotted to have ever been human. She has to drag bleeding legs over them. Stumble, jump, stumble on. Blood trail behind her she could hope is blurring into her dead colleagues' blood. Unsteady so that she catches her shoulders, her hips, her arm, as she turns corners. Twice, she slips and falls, comes down hard, splashes to her feet. So slow. She passes the lift to the Chief Judge's quarters. Passes the entrance to the Hall of Heroes.

The doors to the Hall of Heroes are open. If she went in, she'd see…

As she runs past, she thinks for a moment there's something moving in there. Someone. A man. "Help me!" she wants to shout, but it seems unfair, if he's managed to hide, so she runs past and on.

But she shivers as she runs. The hair on the back of her neck stands up. That old crazy saying: A ghost walked over your grave.

The Dark Judges are scrabbling and squelching behind her. Drawing close. She pushes herself harder. The pain is too much. She slows, hand clutched holding her heart from leaking out of her chest. Limps on. Crawls on, on all fours and on her belly, like a worm, like what's left of Mortis.

She comes to a halt in the Grand Hall of Justice Central Hall.

A fine, wide, high chamber, marble floor with the eagle of the Justice Department laid out in gold, big enough to hold all the assembled Judges of Mega-City One. A statue of an eagle cast in solid gold glowers down the length of the hall, wings spread. So much blood has been shed in this building, but the hall and the golden eagle are untouched. Not, Anderson thinks, a room even the most ardent Judge would choose to die for or in. It's almost as cold as the morgue. Arguably less friendly. But it's the only place this can end.

The room's in darkness, like the rest of the building. Dim emergency lights blink on and off. Make it look as though the eagle is alive, ruffling its feathers. Her footsteps echo huge as she walks over to stand beneath it.

The eagle looks displeased. *All crime is committed by the living, thus the living are all guilty of crime.* She's long suspected that the eagle would agree with the sentiment behind these words at least. Its displeasure could as easily be for her as for the Dark Judges.

She shouts, "Come on, then! You want this to end?"

In a noise of sucking and squelching and sticking and the scrape of jagged splintered bone on marble, in the shambles of hope's end, the Dark Judges crawl and ooze into the Central Hall of the Grand Hall of Justice where the Judges of Mega-City One have long met together in grave judgement, and where the last living Judge in Mega-City One now waits.

THE LITTLE GIRL; Katz's handsome if now noseless Judge friend; the maggot remains of Judge Mortis; Judge Fear who's more holes than body with a dented lump of metal balanced on the shards of his head: all four Dark Judges throw themselves at Anderson. Take her down. Wrestle her. Smother her in dead flesh. Fear's face on top of her face, lips almost against her cheek. Mortis is a slime coating her skin.

Death grips manly hands around her throat. "*You... have been... Judged, Andersssson.*"

Four voices, barely able to form words, to speak, a howl and a shriek and a liquid gobbling: "*The punissshment isss death.*"

Press her Lawgiver. Hold it. Hold it. Can't breathe. Can't feel her legs. Fear's eyes on her eyes. She can *see*.

Reach for her trigger. Reach it.

Keep them close.

Suffocated by dead flesh. Mortis is grave fluid seeping into her lungs. She's decaying from the inside. She's liquifying from the feet upwards. What's left of her shakes with cold fear. Burning heat of her heart giving out.

She bites down on whatever it is that makes up Fear's face. Dried cartilage like a mummy? A hundred insect mandibles? Gouges at dead eyes. Her throat is eaten away, her teeth and jaw bones crumble. Her fingers are meat-jelly. No strength. Her nervous system failing. She's drowning in her own putrefied lungs.

Closer. Closer. Soaking into the bodies crushing her. She and the Dark Judges are one mass of filth.

She squeezes the trigger of her Lawgiver one last time.

It's possible the gun only goes off because her body fluids cause it to short-circuit.

But

It goes off.

One last round left. High explosive.

Range: zero. The dead hold the killing ground.

The golden eagle falls like a hammer. The Grand Hall explodes.

PURITY OF WORLD's exploding. Glory of falling tumbling gold. She's seen sunlight from space, pure radiant light without the dulling effect of the Earth's atmosphere, and her death as it comes down over her is more beautiful. Her last moments are perfect, annihilating, cleansing pain.

43.

Nothing.

44.

NOTHING.

45.

HURTS.

46.

Dear Grud, it hurts, hurts and hurts and hurts. Every cell of her body—scrub that, every atom in every cell and every subatomic particle within that—IT HURTS.

After a long time, it occurs to Anderson to be impressed she has cells left to hurt.

Cautiously, she opens her real eyes. Just darkness. Flashes of white and gold, too bright. The explosion in her head is making her real eyes blind and her real ears ring. She can't feel her real body for the pain. Like the opposite of phantom limbs. Just a mind adrift on a sea of pain. Just go with it. Float.

Cautiously, she says, "Are you there, creep?"

Cautiously, she waits. Waits.

Waits.

"Are you there, creep?" She can barely hear herself in her head over her ears ringing. Maybe she can't hear Judge Death's response.

"Speak, Death, you gruddamn creep."

The pain ebbs a little. Enough she can grit her teeth against the pain.

Her eyes might be improving. Flashes of red along with the white and gold. But it's possible she'll spend the rest of her life with the eagle of drokking justice singed into her retinas. Double vision of a beak and wings in gold fire.

"Are you there, creep? Say something."

The pain eases enough she can feel it in distinct places. Headache, neck ache, shoulders, back, chest, both arms, both legs, ankles, wrists, feet, hands, indeterminate number of toes and fingers. Oh, and tongue and nose and cheeks and internal organs. Gosh, I never knew where my pancreas was until today!

It's not real pain, she thinks. It's pain in my head. She has experienced another's pain telepathically more times than it's fair to remember, been deafened by telepathic screams. She knows, she's been taught since childhood, how to cope with this. Concentrates very hard on her shoulders. Feels the tension—that's real. Now, relax it, Anderson. Breathe out. Let go. Relax. Relaaaxxx.

The calming voice sounds too much like the Dark Judges. She swallows bile, her mouth is clogged with rot. Plunges back into the moment of the explosion, the Dark Judges squealing the way she imagines maggots should squeal. She's nothing. Rendered fat and broken bones choking on a fellow corpse. Embracing annihilation.

Shrieks herself in shock.

Breathe. Calm. You can see... okay, you *can't* see, but that paler blur behind the explosion, that's possibly the Hall of Heroes ceiling. Concentrate on that. Your feet, your ankles, puffy and hot and vile in your boots—feel that. The pain in your skull like a nail—that's real pain, feel that.

She wiggles her left big toe a fraction. That gooood feeling of a cracking toe joint.

The ringing in her ears has faded. And the paler blur, yes, that's the Hall of Heroes ceiling.

"Creep?" Summons up the courage: "Sidney? Judge Death?"

But her head is empty. No trace of him. It.

Suddenly she feels very light and clean. Her real body feels better. Sweaty, clammy, itchy, bloated, soaked in pee—but Grud, she feels better without Judge Death's muckheap.

She laughs. Light and long and loud. Her whole body full of laughter. Makes her belly shake. They are remorseless. All-consuming. Destroy them, grind their bodies to dust, scatter the dust on the wind to the furthest reaches of the earth, and they'll come back killing and killing and endlessly killing. It is impossible to defeat them. No one can stand against death.

But she, Anderson, she has defeated Death.

She shouts at the silence: "I knew I could do it, Death you dried-up old dog turd you. I won. Beat you." I mean… Grud only knows how. The purifying fire, she thinks. The gold eagle of true Justice crushing Judge Death's perversions. Or something equally absurd and manifestly untrue.

Sheer force of life and willpower. She thinks then: everything dies, but the desire for life is far stronger than death.

AH. WAIT. ALL this talk of life reminds her…

SHE'LL DIE NOW without Death to keep her alive inside the Boing®. She can already feel the difference. Hunger, thirst, muscle weakness, all that jazz. Everyday common-or-garden killing things. Her great victory prize is death with a lowercase d.

Old memories come back to her, some real memories of real people, some stories that could have happened if she wasn't lying here. Her death is a price worth paying, she tells herself. Yes.

Yes. It is.

Ah, Grud. Images flood her mind of herself in the Mega-City One Deadworld, running, eating crisps, chatting with the boy Casey, standing shoulder to shoulder with Judge Katz.

Sitting in an imaginary cafeteria drinking imaginary execrable synth-caff and trading insults with a corpse. "You want to debate moral issues with me, creep?" "*We have eternity, Andersssson. What elssse isss there for usss to do*?" Ah, Grud, Grud, Grud, Grud.

She's going to drown in her tears. Her heart will actually honest-to-Grud break. Thrashes, fights the plastic encasing her, hurls her body at it, every muscle every sinew straining, bites it as she bit into the Dark Judges, pounds it and hammers it and rips at it with her clawed fingers as she pounded and ripped open the Dark Judges' flesh. Foaming at the mouth. Squealing like the Dark Judges did.

She manages to rock her feet a little inside her boots. Possibly flex her right shoulder. Bite the inside of her lip.

THE LIGHT ON the ceiling changes. Suddenly she's staring right into a citizen's face. Pink and glossy and plump, a horror of double chins and nostril hair from this angle. Vanishes as suddenly as he appears, to be replaced by an old woman and a little girl. Anderson has a few seconds of panic it's Judge Fire and Judge Fear in their borrowed corpses. Then the girl picks her nose, inspects what she finds there, wipes it on Anderson's coffin. The old woman notices, clouts her granddaughter round the head. Gets out a hanky, spits on it, rubs the snot off the coffin. Does that nobody-saw-nothing look-around-her thing.

Panic turns to relief turns to amusement turns to disgust.

A young man barges his way past the child, stares down at Anderson intently. His lips move. He looks worried.

I'm alive! I'm awake! I'm free! Judge Death is dead! Let me out! She blinks and rolls her eyes frantically. *I'm awake! Get me out!*

The old woman and the girl leave, bickering. Can we go to the gift shop? Please, oh, please, oh, please, Gran. The man lingers. Puts one hand on the plastic coffin. Runs his other hand through his hair.

He's seen her eyes rolling! He has! He can tell she's alive! They're staring straight at each other. Right into each other's eyes.

The man turns his head, seems to be listening to something. Then he's gone and they're all gone.

At least, Anderson tries to tell herself, the gawping faces were free of blood. The fat faces of living, well-fed people with little to fear in their lives and a healthy respect for the Law. Rejoice! Anderson tries to tell herself. You made the ultimate sacrifice precisely so that children could grow up feeling free to wipe greenies on your coffin.

TIME PASSES. SEEMS like longer than everything that's gone before. Days running across the Cursed Earth as the last of the Judges resisting Death—she can remember, the time lasted forever; that final crawl away from the Hall of Justice when it blew had lasted a lifetime in her mind—but this lying alone and dying for a few hours, it goes on longer and longer than lifetimes. *I'm here. I'm alive. Death's gone.* Her mouth is dry, her throat feels dry like she's swallowing broken glass. She begins to suspect she's dying. Where's a cheery tech guy to spell out the end stages of dehydration when you need one?

The lights in the Hall of Heroes flicker off. Evening coming. Headlight beams trace across the plasterwork. A figure seems to be approaching her coffin, but it's hard to see in the dark now and she can't focus properly and she can't summon the energy to blink. Or care.

Shuts her eyes. Tries to go back into her head. Tell herself a good story. *The perp fled into the tower block, and the Psi-Judge followed him. Then she... did... something. Helped... someone. Judged... someone. One of them... was a perp... and one of them... was the perp's victim. Victim. Victim.* Tries to go back to the cafeteria. Table, chair, plate, cup. *A bad thing happened, then a good thing.* No: table, plate, cup, fork. *And a bad thing then a good thing.*

She was running, fighting, exchanging banter with Judge Death. Her legs cramp up. Her tongue feels like a scouring sponge. Memory failure and failure to hold together a coherent sentence in her head, with her thoughts getting muddled and tangled, slowing down, a jumbled sort of mess of thoughts, kind of heavy thinking them, lack of focus, slowly is kind of beginning, suspecting symptoms of not thinking straight, of dying. She saved… saved… *The perp fled into the block tower, and the Psi-Judge… the Psi-Judge… then she… did… a cup, a plate, a spork… fork… One of them… and one of them… and the… the Psi-Judge… and then…*

And then

And then

And then

Man, she thinks, dying is a bitch.

And then

Then

HER EYES SNAP open as the lights in the Hall of Heroes snap back on. A flurry of movement round her coffin. Tech guys. Judges. Two figures are manoeuvring a machine over her. The coffin starts to shake.

They're cutting her out. The plastic unfolds. Fresh air pours over Anderson's face. The smell makes her gag even as she gulps it in. Panic: the babble of voices is deafening, a chaos of sound she can't decode. Her skin's raw and the feeling of air moving on it rubs, hurts. Being breathed on rubs and hurts and the breath stinks. She still can't move. She can't remember how to make herself work. Shapes bend over her. Her skin wails. Knives and slime and burning: Mortis! Fire! She thrashes to make her real throat make sounds. Move her tongue. Her arms and legs all jolt suddenly, spasm upwards. Did she do that? Instead of talking? The pain of movement is hot blades thrust in.

"Easy... easy, Anderson."

That's Death! Saying her name! She gurgles what might be "No." Her hand jerks. Punch it. Hit it.

Her coffin swings open like double doors. The psi-blast of thoughts and feelings hits her. Whirlpool of voices in her head. All afraid and angry. Too much. Too much. She can't see for shapes crowded over her and she can't see for thoughts and feelings. It's worse than being in the plastic. Pressing against her skull until her head will implode.

"Easy. Easy. It's okay."

From far away and very close, a voice says, "She's alive." Its thoughts are mostly anger. But there's a little sparkle of relief that's good and calming. She knows the voice and the thoughts.

Her hand touches her forehead. She can feel her face. I'm alive? she thinks.

I'm alive. I think. The feeling on her skin is hands holding her, lifting her up. She struggles against the pain of contact. Forces herself to accept being sat up. Fractal chaos in the background, vague figures buzzing about. Noise. Judges, Anderson thinks... and the figure standing over her seems familiar. She recognises its sense and its thoughts.

"Neirn?Isthatyou?"

She tries again. "Nei—Neirn? Is. That. You?"

Warm good voice: "It's me, Anderson." Patterns of light and shade. Eagle's beak and wings.

"...Water..."

A hand presses a cup to her mouth. She drinks. Grud! Sweet! Finally she can think and focus. She screws her eyes up, blinks heavily. The light resolves itself into the ghost of Judge Neirn's face.

He looks older.

He *is* older, she thinks. She's been in the plastic a long time. Long as it felt.

She stands up, falls over, with Judge Neirn's help she's sitting on her plinth clutching her aching head. More water. Food. Grud—a bath. A change of clothes. She says weakly to Neirn, "I stink."

"Nah. Not too bad. Considering we thought you were probably dead for a year and a half now." A pause. "Judge Winstanley nicknamed you Schrödinger's Judge."

"A year and a half?" She rubs her eyes. "What… what's been happening? Is the Meg safe?"

She realises the Judges who were milling around in a state of panic have all disappeared.

Neirn says, "Ummm… I guess that depends on how you define 'safe.'"

47.

Two days later. She's sitting in the Grand Hall of Justice cafeteria. A cup of caff in front of her. A big plate of chips and beanz. Sunlight streams in through the windows. If she cranes her neck she can see City Blocks choppy to the horizon, flyovers with the traffic flowing freely, vapour trails, flashes where the sun is catching fliers reaching toward the edge of space. Grud, the Statue of Judgement! Gaze fixed far off, looking out over the city as guardian and guard. The square jaw—hard, dense muscle of a living man. The strong living, human muscles of its chest, its arms, its legs. She can see streets churning with people, too far off to make out individuals but the crowd is a riot of colour, the changes in its tempo are visible in shifting patterns of light and dark. Something of interest in a shop window drawing in the punters; a Block War going full throttle, the line between the two sides shifting back and forth. Oh, and what she'd estimate from up here to be a three-vehicle crash. Lawmasters heading for the fight and the crash. Again, she's too far off to see they're Lawmasters, but she can recognise them from the way they're driving. Now she can see tiny figures she knows are Judges wading into the fight. Almost hear the crack of daysticks on heads.

She turns her attention back to her meal. Her elbow sticks to the table when she goes to take a drink of caff; she has to peel her sleeve off the tabletop. She eats and savours the taste. Savours the sound of her cutlery scraping against the chipped plate.

It took her a while to get up the courage to walk in here. Stood in the corridor outside three times, unable to go in. Spent a year and a half in her head here, you'd think she'd never want to drink the gruddamn caff again. And there's a chair she'll never sit in. And, okay, she checked the menu very carefully to be sure they weren't serving synthetti bolognese.

At some point, she'll have to face the Grand Hall's grand hall. Not today.

At some point, she'll have to face the morgue. Not today/this week/month/year/decade.

Because today, she feels so good she could dance and sing around the cafeteria. Hug the Judges who are staring at her. Most unJudgely behaviour there, Anderson. She restrains herself to flashing them both a smile.

One Judge taps his helmet: "These Psi-Judges are crazy."

"Certainly, uh, highly strung," the other Judge says.

You have no idea, boys… She could waltz over and kiss them both. Until one of them recognises her, panics, his thoughts shout in her ears: *It's the woman who came back from the dead.*

She'll be back at work tomorrow. Can't wait. Chief Judge Griffin insisted she take a few days off to 'get some rest.'

"I've been resting for nearly two drokking years, Chief Judge."

"You've been hovering somewhere between dead and alive for nearly two years, Anderson. That's not quite the same thing."

It would be nice, Anderson thinks, if people stopped saying that word. 'Dead.' 'Death.' It's like they see her and can't not find a way to spurt it out. So scared of saying it they can't help saying it. She's walking in a cloud of people's thoughts all shrieking 'death.' Follows her around like Fire's flames or Death's stink.

"You've been through one heck of a lot, Anderson. Just… settle yourself first. Walk around. Catch up on what's happened the last two years. A lot has happened you need to catch up on over the last eighteen months." He looks at her. "You heard about the monkey business with Professor Fribb? Or the Sump Ugly craze? Been a mad couple of years, I can tell you. Almost as mad as the couple of years before that."

"Yeah..." The whole city looks different. It always looks different, but at the moment it looks... different-different. And what's been happening out there? To be honest, she really doesn't want to know.

"Catch up on the new gangs and crazes. Check what's been made illegal."

She thinks: can we also stop banging on about the time I've missed, please? It's not that long in the grand scheme of the world, I mean, the law says two years in an isocube is a fit punishment for reading comix. She makes a non-committal noise at Chief Judge Griffin. Eighteen months' worth of penal code updates. The thrills! Maybe I would rather hear about 'Professor Fribb.'

"Or..." Griffin's a Judge. He grins at her. His one eye can only be said to twinkle. "Or you could go for a fast ride on your bike."

So THE EVENING light is falling on Judge Anderson, and she's riding along through Mega-City One with the warm wind in her hair. The tower blocks are neon lit and sunlight lit and the evening sun pours on them gilded, as golden as her hair. She's laughing all the way. She kicks her bike to go faster harder, corners and turns down a Judges' Lane; another Lawmaster slides beside her to race. The air is sweet with bike fumes. The engines purr. She wins.

At this speed and distance the city's burble in her mind is just a quiet blur. It's soothing, after the silence of her plastic coffin, a white noise like the bike engine's growl, a sense of reassurance that she's not alone. Grud, she feels so good, so peaceful. The road rises high in a loop swirling over a tower; on the crest, before the spiralling plunge down into the city's shadows, she can catch a glimpse of the eastern horizon dark and filled with flickering lights and the line of cloud or distant sea. Anderson slows, sucks it into her. Fills her lungs that still ache with the memory of—No. She pushes the memory away. Fills her lungs with traffic fumes and breathes deep for no reason other than because. Puts her foot to the pedal, the road twists and spirals down and she races plunging into the city's embrace. Blocks burn bright lush with life overflowing; closing time in the stores that spew out sale-sated shoppers; new fashions, new haircuts, new tunes, new music, new clothes, and the sidewalks sing like rare birds.

Stops to help break up a petty riot in a parkarama. Petty violence. Perps and Judges both all leave with bare bruises, all limbs and digits intact. Warm lazy day given way to warm lazy evening, even the gangs seem content to bask. So Anderson puts her foot to the pedal, her bike rushes on riding through the Big Meg laughing, filled with joy and warmth. Riding through a city that exhales soft psi-waves of calm.

She swoops and wheels, kite-like, bird-like, bright-light, down a wide curved skedway that skirts a long green park. Plastic trees and plastic flowers. Children playing a ball game. Juvies hanging out. A kid running with his dog. She should stop to bust the children's ballgame and the juvies for being juvies and the dog for cocking a leg. She's off duty. There are dappled shadows falling on the juvies' faces. She'll let some other Judge handle it.

The dog barks loudly. Grud, it's an ugly old brute. Big and lean. Runs beautifully, though, and there's a joy in its running, its own sheer pleasure in its muscles pumping it on. She can sense it: look at me! I'm running! Running! The juvies, even, break off whatever depravity they're engaged in to watch it run. It loops behind a plastic rose bush taking the corner tight as a Lawmaster. Anderson sighs with satisfaction. Fine thing to watch.

A bark and an angry shout from behind the rose bush. Then the owner is running rather less gracefully. "Oscar, no! Those aren't your crisps! Oscar! I said stop!"

Wait.

What?

Anderson freezes. A brief wonderful rising rush of joy. Very much like the dog. Oscar! Casey! Alive and well! Anderson finds she's running herself towards them. Shakey legged, still. Not at all like the dog.

"Casey! Oscar! It's me! Ander—"

Son.

She stops running. Half trips over her own feet. The boy emerges from the bushes. "I said leave them crisps, Oscar. Crisps aren't good for dogs. How many times?" He looks a lot better than he did when she last saw him, unsurprisingly. Clean and cleanly dressed, hair brushed.

He recognises her. Jogs over, pulling Oscar with him. The dog recognises Anderson too, lets out a bark.

"Miss! Haven't seen you for a while! How are you?"

"...Well..."

I'm not a figment of my imagination based on a combination of myself, young Sidney De'ath and whatever the himself largely metaphorical and symbolic 'Judge Cas Andersen'/Mortis was like as a boy, dreamed up for narrative purposes by Judge Death as a way of adding emotional heft to my struggle in the Mega-City One Deadworld and ultimately only present in the story to teach me a profound lesson about the darkness and capacity for murder that lurks within us all, Casey. So... I guess I'm doing good compared to you?

Although you and Oscar look pretty good, considering.

Casey frowns. Oscar yaps. Anderson casts her eyes over the plastic trees, the plastic grass, the happy juvies, the clean evening light. Should have known it was all too good to be true. Since when did she or any Judge get one peaceful day in the Meg?

Casey says, "Oooops."

The earth shakes. The juvies and the children playing ball and the parents watching—they all fall down dead. The sky explodes, everything's all lit up with fire, churning red clouds mounting over columns of black smoke. The ground Anderson stands on is buckled, pock-marked, crests and eddies where the earth has melted, has run as liquid, pooled and lapped around the dead. Ancient faces stare up at her trapped there, eyes open mouths open screaming pain. On the horizon to the south a few tower blocks are still burning. To the far west, a thick column of black smoke.

Anderson draws her Lawgiver. Shoots Casey in the chest.

"Is that supposed to hurt?" Casey says. He's changing. The world is changed. She's not in any place, real or imagined, Death's Deadworld or her own. Empty void-space. Not black, not white. Casey's briefly a teenage boy with a mop of fair hair who could be a male Cass Anderson and then he's briefly the scowling wretched young Sidney De'ath and then the sad-eyed young Judge Mortis. And then he's dissolving from his humanity and his pink boy's flesh peels off him.

"*You poor innocent fool, Anderssson. 'The desssire for life isss far ssstronger than death'? How very romantic that ssssounds as a perssspective on the universsse. Might even have brought poor young Judge Mortisss sssome hope.*

"*But you cannot kill that which doesss not live, Anderssson.*"

The void is not dark and it is not light. Crushing her away.

Eyes opening. Thrashing her hands and feet. Look with her real eyes and there above her will be the Hall of Heroes ceiling. Feel with her real skin and she's wrapped in plastic and cannot move. Her eyes open and her eyes beyond that open and her eyes beyond that but it's dark and void and a nothingness falling beyond dark through every set of eyes. Her skin can connect with nothing.

She has annihilated only herself. She is a fragment that Death is allowing to be Judge Cassandra Anderson. Death's mind is trapped inside her body. She is trapped inside Death's mind.

Her arm comes up, her gun fires and fires. The bullets—of course—tear holes in Death's chest but do not harm him.

She smashes the gun barrel into his face. Uses the gun like a hammer. Pounds skin and bone. She screams it: "The Deadworld will never happen here! Never! Never!"

Casey blinks at her, disappointed. Looks hurt like she's accused him of stealing her best pencil case. "You hurt me, miss. That's not nice." Marks on his neck where she held him the last time she killed him. Cut lip. Bruises spreading across his face.

A child with bruises across their face...

Death smiles his terrible smile. Bares his terrible claws.

"*A fine new world to kill.*" A smile. "*Indeed, I believe Judge Mortisss... hasss already killed.*

"*The crime is life, Anderson. The sentence is death. It will be carried out.*"

And silence. Only and forever—dead silence.

48.

Lights overhead. Shaking.
Sound.

The plastic unfolds like doors.

Fresh air pours over her face. They're cutting her out. Hands reach, lift her. A voice she thinks she knows says, 'She's alive,' as if that's a wonderful thing. The babble of voices is deafening, a chaos of sound. Her skin's raw and the feeling of air moving on it rubs, hurts. Being breathed on rubs and hurts and the breath stinks.

A brief moment of wonder. To feel. To hear. To smell real things.

Thunder bursts in her ears. So loud she has to close her eyes. Just… someone speaking softly in her face. She opens her eyes again, stares at pores and stubble a huge nose that slowly makes sense as a man's face. "Easy. Easy, Anderson," the man says.

She's weak and shaking and she needs to drink and pee and wash and she bends forward and she needs to vomit and by

Grud she needs to put on some deodorant and change her pants. Seriously, this is what being born must feel like.

Call me Sleeping Beauty the Second, she thinks.

She sits up with a scream. "Death! He's here! They're all here!"

"It's okay, Anderson," the voice says.

"Death..." She frowns. She can remember... She was running, killing, and there was no end and... no hope. "It's not... not..."

Warm hands holding her. Rough skin, the calluses you get from years and years and years of squeezing a Lawgiver's trigger...

She thinks: how could there be no hope?

She draws deep, frightened breaths, her body shakes, she can't remember the dreams but the idea of *no hope*...

She can see... she can remember... floating, fading, over this good kind hard face... a skull with a portcullis visor, leering... a dead man with a tail but no head... a winged helmet... a fiery flaming trident... There was a statue as tall as the Statue of Judgement, except it was all made of teeth. I killed Death.

What? A friend tells you a nightmare the next morning: "*It was... dear Grud... I can't tell you... this sock puppet, and it was, like, really big and small at once, and it... Grud, it could turn its head round ninety degrees... The indescribable eldritch horror! I woke up sweating and screaming! Got to stop eating synthi-cheese before bed.*"

She shakes her head. She can see Judge Neirn's shiny boy's face glowing at her, and behind him... what? You tell a friend a nightmare the next morning: "*It was... dear Grud... I don't remember a thing but it terrifies me still...*"

Fading.

Faded.

Too much life rushing back.

"There was a perp I was scanning?" Her voice comes out in a croak. Then suddenly everything's blurred and chaos and movement again, because half the Judges around her are moving, running, she has a terrible fear they're running from her because she is- because she will- she smells blood and fire, and then they're gone out of the room in a great wonderful clatter of boots and comm links and barked orders, and it's so good to be back home.

"There was a perp you were scanning, yeah," someone—Judge—Judge—Collins, she thinks triumphantly—Judge Collins says.

She says, "He had this stupid name. He was called 'Death'. I stopped him."

"You stopped him," Judge Collins says.

She frowns. She can remember—vile little shrivelled up *thing* she fought and trapped. She looks down at the Boing®. Plastic prison.

"He's escaped," she says.

An awkward silence, like they don't want to bother her with the bad stuff in her weakened state.

Collins starts to say something, then Judge Neirn says over the top, "He's escaped, Anderson. That's why you're free, remember?"

She says, "He's killing again."

Judge Neirn says simply, starkly, "Yes."

Then he says, "But you're free, Anderson."

She says, not knowing how she knows but certain she's right, "He has companions with him. Monsters, like him." She shivers, in her dream she was so afraid of them, these monsters, and she'd hoped, in her dreams, that she might be rid of them when she woke—which is absurd, she thinks, because Judge Cass Anderson isn't afraid of anything.

"Dredd's on it, Anderson, relax," Judge Collins says.

She snorts. "Judge Dredd needed my help to catch just one of the creeps." She gets up. Almost falls down. Stays up, albeit hanging on to a bust of Psi-Judge Feyy. The bust rocks alarmingly. She realises Judge Feyy's nose is pressed up to her—hurriedly lets go. Stands weakly. Then stands strong.

"I need my Lawbgiver, my Lawmaster, a cup of caff, and some deodorant."

"Are you sure about this?" Judge Collins says.

"Now, gruddamnit!" No, she's honest-to-Grud really not sure, maybe, somewhere, deep in her heart.

I remember... horrors.

But.

Neirn smiles. Claps her on the shoulder. "Get the little creep, Anderson."

HER LAWMASTER'S WAITING on the kerb outside the Grand Hall of Justice. All sparkling clean. A Judge holds out her Lawgiver like it's the most precious thing he's ever been trusted with, and she takes it like it's the most precious thing she's ever received. Mounts up, and, yeah, okay, maybe she has to fidget about a bit and remember how it feels to sit on this thing after so much time spent lying around, but when her hands close around the handlebars it's... it's...

Good. No fancy words. Just *good* and *right* and *real* and *yes*!

When no one's looking, she does a quick check of her armpits. Yeah, well, there's no law against busting a perp while having epic BO.

Unless they've changed the law in the last eighteen months?

Perfume of life, she thinks then. Poetic justice, maybe, or something.

Although—wait, no one ever brought her that cup of caff.

She revs the bike engine. Kicks the pedal hard as all hell. A warm wind in her hair. A City Block ahead of her where the perp has fled. East and west and north and south the sky's on fire. Shadows in the corners crouching, they writhe with dripping teeth, they stink of rotted blood. Ten times a thousand voices screaming. Distant thunder of the world's end.

As per usual. [Yawns] Just another average ol' day in the Big Meg. You think you've seen things we wouldn't believe, Anderson? While you were sleeping, a giant toad ate Judge Dredd.

She can feel Death's fear of her. She knows, he knows: Judge Anderson can and Judge Anderson will defeat Judge Death.

No, wait, that's all wrong there. Cross it out and rewrite.

She's the last word. The ending. Not him. Everything dies, but life staggers on.

Judge Death can and will be defeated by Judge Cassandra Anderson.

Acknowledgements

For this one, the thanks go of course to the geniuses behind *2000 AD* in its eighties glory, whose work left a permanent mark on me. Not so much a fangirl thing, more an 'essential part of my childhood and therefore the person I am today' thing.

Thanks also to Luke Youngman, who drew pictures of JD all over his schoolbooks and sparked something in me years before I first read the comic (or indeed could even read).

And thank you thank you thank you DEAR GRUD, THANK YOU!!! to David Thomas Moore and Rebellion Publishing for giving me this chance to live a childhood dream.

ABOUT THE AUTHOR

Anna Smith Spark is the author of the *Empires of Dust* grimdark epic fantasy series *The Court of Broken Knives*, *The Tower of Living and Dying* and *The House of Sacrifice*; the standalone *A Woman of the Sword*; and the folk horror high fantasy *The Making of This World Ruined* series *A Sword of Bronze and Ashes* and *A Sword of Gold and Ruin*; and is co-author of the grimdark fantasy horror *In The Shadow Of Their Dying*.

Her work has been described as 'a masterwork' and 'awe-inspiring' and compared to Tolkien, Moorcock and Le Guin. She's dyslexic, dyspraxic, ASD, PhD; previous jobs include English teacher, fetish model and petty bureaucrat. You may know her by the heels of her shoes.

@annasmithspark.bsky.social
@annasmithspark
courtofbrokenknives.net

"Exactly what you'd want: smart, fast-moving sci-fi that's filled with pulpy thrill power."
Wait, What? Podcast
JUDGE ANDERSON
YEAR ONE
ALEC WORLEY

PSI
JUDGE ANDERSON
YEAR TWO
"An exhilarating ride!"
Dark Musings
on Year One
DANIE WARE
LAUREL SILLS
ZINA HUTTON

"I'll come and out and say it –
it's even better than Dredd 3D!"
Pop Culture Bandit
JUDGE
DREDD
YEAR
ONE
AL
EWING
MATT
SMITH
MICHAEL
CARROLL

THE GENESIS OF THE WORLD OF JUDGE DREDD®
JUDGES
VOLUME ONE
THE AVALANCHE • LONE WOLF
WHEN THE LIGHT LAY STILL
MICHAEL CARROLL • CHARLES J ESKEW • GEORGE MANN
EDITED BY MICHAEL CARROLL